FALLEN SUN

Fallen Sun
by Harule Stokes

ISBN 978-0-9882211-2-3

ACKNOWLEDGEMENTS

Panya, you're totally amazing! Without your fantastic skills, I don't think I could have completed this novel.

TeresaAnn Wilkinson, I can't believe you actually read the first draft. Hardcore. You'll never know just how much that helped me. Thank you so much for honoring me with your time.

Tamara Blain, you're an amazing editor. Thank you for cleaning up this mess.

Darkness cannot drive out darkness; only light can do that. Hate cannot drive out hate; only love can do that. - Martin Luther King Jr.

CHAPTER 1

CASUALTIES OF WAR

Ophelia stands atop a pile of rubble covered in tall grass above the once-chaotic battlefield. Below her rests the remains of the mangled dead and shattered machines. There would be a nice breeze today if it were not for the billowing, acrid black smoke of war that occasionally blots out the warm spring sun.

I know she hears my approach. She's just as aware of my footsteps as I am of her breath and calm, steady heartbeat. Her uniform, torn in the back, exposes where she took direct hits from gunfire and a black-worm seed infestation. The bleeding may have stopped hours ago, the wounds completely healed, but her skin still shows remnants of black-worm's barbs and the rapid-growing roots that tore into her flesh. The scars are reminiscent of the mountain ranges on those old, plastic topographical maps my students loved to touch.

The remaining inflamed welts on Ophelia's back are slowly disappearing. It's a reminder that some scars don't fade so easily, like the haunting memory of her screams that linger in my mind. It's tough to get black-worm roots out once fully implanted. It's even harder to get them out of a Finger of God.

I reach her, giving her a hip bump as I stand by her side. Slowly, I scan the field replete with dead bodies, burning vehicles, and debris.

What draws my attention aren't the corpses and scorched earth, but the patches of vibrant green foliage, dotted with blue, red, and orange wild flowers. The growing patches of life punctuate the battlefield. The infinitely invasive Keynosian plants seems to grow anywhere and under any condition. Every Alliance territory taken by the Keynosians bears these beautiful green scars.

This city, Steel Harbor, was at the heart of our nation's war machine, its occupants armed to the teeth with weapons of death. The Harbor's citizens pushed aggressively for war early on, convinced that the primitive Keynosian forces would be no match for our advanced Alliance technology.

Steel Harbor was taken within a few days. Now all that's left of the city's magnificent factories are a few towering smokestacks blanketed in the gentle pastel colors of Keynosian occupation.

"I want to be with Chad, Jos," Ophelia says, breaking my train of morose thoughts. She smiles, although tears stream down her face. I can smell her tears, even with the scent of death, thick and foul, wafting through the air. Her tears smell like the chemical cocktail she is forced to take daily, nothing like the distant sea as they should.

"You'll get to be with him soon, Oa. The war's drawing to a close, I'm sure of it."

I turn into her intense gaze. Her lips move slightly as she silently addresses her fiancé. He's the only person she talks to outside of Patricia and me. The problem is, Chad died four years ago.

"He's always saying how much he misses me," she says.

"Does he now?"

"Yeah." She grins sorrowfully, wiping away the tears. "He never likes it when we're separated. We... we used to talk all the time, back home I mean. Now, we only talk when I'm outside of stasis. It's... just not enough time." A slow sigh escapes her lips.

She's talking crazy again. "How about we enjoy the victory and not think too much about that?"

She reaches down and plucks a blue-and-orange flower from the mid-calf-high grass. "Victory. We won, again. Right?" she asks, twirling the flower between her fingertips.

Unsure, I look out over the green-blanketed ruins. While I mourn the loss of the great city, I have to admit, it was never this beautiful. The Keynosian plants bring color and life to the many shades of gray that previously dominated the cityscape.

If only this war with Keynosa left the same imprint on our soldiers that it does upon our lands.

I look at my friend muttering to herself. How haggard Ophelia's become over these past few years. How haggard we've all become.

"Yeah, we won this battle, Ophelia," I say, nodding. "We've finally reached Keynosa's borders. We've gained the upper hand."

How much loss can we take and still consider ourselves victorious?

"We have the upper hand," she repeats as if in a trance, nodding her head as well.

"Jos," she says, dropping her eyes to the foliage at our feet. "They only release me from stasis when it's time for fighting nowadays. The rest of the time, while in stasis... Jos, I dream of terrible things. Terrible things," Ophelia says, staring out over the city.

"You dream in there?" I ask, looking behind us. Although I can't see it yet, I can hear the military truck carrying her stasis chamber approaching, hidden by the huge misshapen mounds of green blanketed rubble that surround us. We still have some time before the truck reaches us... and before she completely breaks from reality. "What do you dream about?"

"I dream Chad died. It's a nightmare I have all the time in stasis. But, I just don't know if I could live without him, Jos. I don't think I know how." She looks ahead blankly, her lips again moving in silence. Her hands start to flutter, punctuating the movement of her mouth.

He *is* dead, Ophelia, is what I want to say. "If you hear him, he's not dead, right? And, you do hear him?"

"Oh yes, I do. So, he's not dead, right?"

I smile. "No, of course not, Oa." I move closer and take her hand.

"I gotta say, Steel Harbor looks so different now. It's kind of nice actually," I say, changing the subject.

She whispers something that I can't quite make out before shaking her head and laughing. "Oh my God, you're so right, Jos! I remember coming here as a kid and thinking it was so chaotic. Cars, zip-buses, and mega-trucks going everywhere," she says with a sigh. "Just too much of everything."

"Really? I used to love it here, probably because I usually spent the summer here with my dad. He moved to Steel Harbor after my parents divorced. Ahhh, he so loved the Harbor. He loved being here, working here. He always smiled when he talked about this city, swelling with pride at the sight of its massive vehicles. They were his handiwork, he'd say, because they were made with *his* composite steel."

She tilts her head down and towards her right shoulder, finally noticing the approaching truck. She doesn't turn to look. "Jos, I really do want to be with Chad," she says, tightening her hand around mine. "I don't want to wait. I don't want to spend another day with my nightmares." She pulls me towards her slightly, urging me to face her.

But, I keep my eyes locked to the ground. I know what she wants. "Please don't ask me to do what I think you're asking. Not again, Oa."

She shrugs. "I'm sorry, Jos. I know it's a lot to ask and I know that the war is nearly over, but I... I just don't want to wait any longer. Just... when it's my time, I want you to do it. Okay?"

We've fought to reclaim Steel Harbor for nearly thirty-six hours straight. That's well past Ophelia's limit. There can't be much time left before she completely fractures. Sure, the conversations with her dead fiancé have been going on for a while, but now she's talking about me taking her life, again. "It's just a little bit further, Oa. We just have to run this race for a few more miles and it'll all be over," I say, ignoring the request. "Can you wait just a bit longer? Can you do that for me?"

She lifts her head to the sky, her eyes scanning the distant clouds beyond the smoke. Is she responding to the silent call of her imagination again, or trying to find the paradise she believes in?

"Ha... yeah, I guess," is all she says, swiping clumped strands of dirty hair from her face. Looking at her, you'd never know that she was a cherry blond under all of the muck. Her once-shiny long locks now hang limp and dull. But what saddens me most is the dullness in her eyes, which once shone so bright.

Ophelia began her steady mental decline three years ago, a full year after we emerged from our metal cocoons in the Sacrifice Chamber. The chamber was just a fancy name for a warehouse filled with stasis units designed to deliver the gene therapy that turned us into Fingers of God.

The Alliance leadership loved to invoke images of God during their political and military campaigns. The truth is, we were created to be weapons, plain and simple. There was no God in that chamber, and there's no God here and now.

I hear her mutter, but I'm not sure if she's talking to me or more phantasms. She giggles suddenly. "You're a good friend, Jos," she says, lifting my hand and pressing her lips to the back of it.

Her mood is starting to shift too fast to keep up. The final descent has begun. We don't have much time left.

The truck hauling her prison is on us. Such is her punishment for unwavering patriotism. "Oa, how about we just enjoy the new and improved Steel Harbor for a while?" I say, plucking a flower from the earth and gently placing it behind her ear. "It's not like we'll have this chance again anytime soon." I pull the shreds of her damaged uniform back over her shoulder.

She lifts her head and nods. "Sounds like a good idea."

"Private Rogers, please return to the stasis unit ASAP. We have orders to move you to a safe, stable environment before transport," a technician announces, his eyes fixed cautiously on Ophelia's bare back. His request is presented as an order. I find both his tone and attitude offensive. She's a hero, not some dog you can order into a cage.

Ophelia tenses. Her lips begin moving quickly, like a person trying to get the last few words into a phone conversation before it ends.

"I'm ah... just looking at the landscape. I want to look at the landscape for a bit longer," she mutters, her voice shaky.

She needs more time. She deserves more time. "Excuse me," I call to the approaching techs. "I'll watch over her for a few more minutes and see to it she enters the egg."

Such an innocuous term we've developed for a physical and chemical prison. The ominous ovoid sits on the back of a flatbed, the bottom of its silver skin reflecting the painted black of the metal it rests on, while the top periodically shines bright with the blinding, pure white of the sun.

"We have orders —"

"We've just taken one of the last strongholds of the Keynosian army. We're *taking* a few minutes," I say, loud enough to inform them I'm not asking for permission.

I can feel their stares and hear their heartbeats increase in tempo. I don't want them to feel threatened, but Ophelia wants more time. She's earned this patch of green.

One of the techs, his face hidden behind a thin surgical mask, takes a cautious step in our direction. "Listen, Martinez, I'm just trying to do —"

"I didn't ask you. I'm telling you, we need a break. She needs a break." I feel her warm hand tighten around mine. "We're just going to stand here a little longer and enjoy the silence. You can wait with us or in the truck. Your choice."

With a click, one of the techs presses the call button on the comm band wrapped around his neck. The jerk is probably going to report me to command.

I hear the sound of boots approach from beyond the parked truck. "You ladies starting trouble again?" I know that voice, and it brings a smile to my face. It's Patricia — Sergeant Patel to the other soldiers — and she waves the techs away. "You two take a break. I've got these troublemakers," she says to the masked duo, lifting her ARC-27 rifle over her shoulder, its barrel pointing to the sky. She always sounds as though she's speaking in a loud, forced whisper, her voice gruff and strained. She never fully recovered from the acid-seed attack, and she never will. It only took a few spores entering her throat to damage her voice permanently. She's not a Finger of God like Ophelia and I, so completely recovering from the injury was not possible. It's a miracle she can even speak. It's a gift from God that she's alive.

The rest of the seed attack burned the skin off of her left arm. Even after countless rapid-grafts and drug treatments, her arm, while functional, looks mangled. The skin graft appears thin and fragile, barely thick enough to contain the rippling sinew and muscle beneath its surface. Unfazed, she wears her sleeves rolled up to the elbow, proudly bearing her scars like a badge of honor. They remind me, and all who know her, of just how strong she is.

With a nod, the techs move back, but not too far. They decide to sit in the grass and wait. Good idea.

"So what are you ladies up to?" she says, leaning in to give me and Ophelia a peck on the cheek. Normally my adopted sisters and I only show such affection in private, but today we're throwing formality to the wind.

Ophelia turns, as if interrupted, to look at Patricia. "Umm, just... you know, looking at the... umm, landscape." She's now visibly struggling to stay present, to stay with us.

Patricia gives me a sideways glance. "Makes sense," she says. She faces the field littered with Keynosian plant life before taking a deep breath. "Well, this is definitely the best Steel Harbor has ever looked."

I laugh. "Oa and I just finished saying that."

"Umm, we... where are you coming from?" Ophelia asks, her voice going more hesitant.

Laying her weapon and specialized ammo case close, Patricia drops into the grass and sits next to me. Gently, she pulls down on my forearm, urging me to join her. I do, squatting on the long, thin blades of grass that find their way between my legs.

Ophelia grins and joins us.

"Since you asked, Oa, I just came from the command station," Patricia answers. "And it looks like what remains of our teams on both coasts will be merging. So, that means we're going to be shipped to the southwestern front, where we're probably going to start our final push.

"The Southies can't hold on without maintaining a huge stronghold near the mountains down there," she continues. "So, if we break the stronghold, we break them... for good."

The merge is unavoidable, even though I'd prefer we didn't have to go through with it. We've lost so many FOGs here. I can't imagine running another campaign farther into Southie lands. But luckily, the majority of the Keynosians on this coast have fled or surrendered. Command does not need us to collect refugees that'll be shipped to the prison camps on the northwestern shore.

"I assumed something like this would happen. There aren't many more strongholds the Keynosians have to fall back on," I say.

Ophelia shudders. "But why a-a mer-merger? Can't they just... let go? Let us go?"

Strange question, Ophelia. I doubt the government will allow any FOG to go free, war or no war. Although I pray I'm wrong.

Glancing at Patricia, I see concern fill her face as her eyes slowly drift from Ophelia, to me, to the egg behind us, finally landing on the tense technicians, who check their watches and hurry us up with their huffs and sighs. They're right to be concerned. It's becoming more and more obvious that Ophelia's time is up.

"Well they can't let us go yet — the war isn't over, Oa. And in regards to the merger, we're really down to our last FOGs. They need every heavy-hitter they can get. Just think, Valentino's lost both his legs, which no one has been able to find. At this point, after so much time has passed, they're most likely no longer viable for reattachment anyway. He's done his duty and is probably on his way home as we speak. Phillips, you guys remember Phillips, right?"

Ophelia and I nod.

"Well, he's blind now. Both eyes, gone." Patricia points at her eyes and swipes her hand away. "Poor guy got into a one-on-one fight with a Guardsmen. By the time reinforcements arrived and that bitch was put down, she'd already gouged out both of his eyes and mangled his arm and leg pretty bad.

"The limbs will heal somewhat, but the eyes…" She shakes her head. "Even a FOG can't recover completely lost body parts."

To be forever blind, how terrible. I can't imagine what he's going through. "My God."

"Then finally, there's Sun. Let's just say they've finally agreed with us that he's not fit for duty anywhere, ever."

Patricia leaves one thing out that she and I are well aware of. Many other FOGs, friends of ours, have completely lost their minds. Even after months in stasis, their brain chemistry is now permanently off-kilter. Ophelia is extremely lucky to have held on as long as she has.

How will they address these lost souls once this war has ended? How will they address Sun's crimes? Will he even stand trial? Should he even be allowed to be in a courtroom, considering what he's capable of? For the rest, the brass can't simply turn them over to their parents or partners, releasing them back into normal society. Just one powerful FOG can level a city.

Pulling a blade of grass from between her legs, Patricia shrugs. "Damn, we've lost so many FOGs, too many. I even heard about some officials at the capital openly talking about doing a third Sacrifice. How crazy is th —"

"What? No! No more people… time out, they need a time out!" Ophelia snaps. Her face twists in disgust and rage.

"Whoa… calm down, Oa. They're just talking —"

"I am calm!" she explodes, standing and frantically looking to and fro. "They've already taken an entire generation. It's enough. Enough! Enough!" Her hands shake violently, knuckles turning stark white against the pressure of tight fists.

She's going to be uncontrollable soon if we don't get her into stasis. Did I wait too long?

The techs behind us rise quickly, giving me a harsh glare as they stab at buttons on their wrist pads, setting up the egg for its occupant.

I better calm her down before this gets ugly. "You're right, Ophelia," I say, placing my hands, palms up, in front of myself. "I'm sure they won't do such a thing again." Slowly, I lower them, trying to relax her. For a tense moment, I'm not sure if she'll attack me. Then, as suddenly as her explosion began, it recedes. Like a snake following the sway of a charmer's pipe, she becomes peaceful again, lowering her head as I drop my hands. She looks down at the tall grass as my palms touch my thighs, and a slow smile slides across her lips. Without another word, her silent chatter with her ghosts begins anew.

"Are those stasis pods comfortable? I bet they are," Patricia says, her head turned towards the techs and the shiny silver container a few yards behind us. "I'm gonna try yours!"

Rising to her feet, Patricia dashes over to the container, smiling and glancing playfully back at Ophelia.

"Umm, that won't be for you, comfortable... for you, Pat! It's mine! That one's made... not for everyone else!" Ophelia calls to the fleeing, laughing Patricia.

"Well if you don't wanna get in it, I will! I'm getting tired of staring at all that boring grass," she calls back, turning her nose up.

Ophelia takes the bait and stands up, swaying from side to side. Her thin lips move, faster and faster as she sputters. "Don't let her claim mine! It's mine! Stop playin', Pat. No, you don't, go!"

Patricia hops up onto the flatbed in a smooth leap. For a normal person, she's incredibly fit.

"You may want to get in there before she screws up your settings. Remember what happened last time she messed with your stasis pod?" I add, knowing Patricia did nothing of the sort.

Before Patricia's outstretched hand can touch the egg, Ophelia appears in front of her with a rush of wind that whips Patricia's short-cropped hair and ruffles the long white coats of the nearby techs.

"Awww, come on, Oa! Let me try it!" Pat whines facetiously. Her voice would sound more childlike if it wasn't so scratchy and gruff.

"No... no. It has to be set right, right, right, right. Right for me, get it? My pod. I can't just let anyone —"

"Oh, all right," Patricia says, gently grasping Ophelia's hand, guiding her into the pod as it opens with a hiss of white smoke.

A smile, broken and awkward, is etched over Ophelia face.

This scene has played itself out in one capacity or another dozens of times before. With Ophelia's cognitive ability fading fast, Patricia coerces her into that prison – where she will stay until the Alliance needs to use her again, to kill.

The scene is humorous, but in the end, it breaks my heart to see her this way. Like so many other FOG soldiers who have this sickness, she has to be placed in the stasis chamber often. Once she's secured, two steady streams of drugs are pumped into her body. The first slows down her metabolism enough for the second drug, an antipsychotic, to take hold.

A wave of loneliness washes over my heart as the techs get to work, closing the egg around her... around my friend, my sister. She is my fraternal twin, just like hundreds of others that survived the Sacrifice. We were all born at the same time in a cold, smoky government building as thousands of others, going through the same procedure, died all around us. Those that perished were unable to integrate the virus that carried the FOG genetic coding into their own DNA and slipped silently into an eternal sleep.

As much as I love Patricia, she'll never understand what Ophelia and I have gone and still go through. We are weapons... living, reusable bombs. I can't imagine that our government would easily relinquish its hold on us, despite its promise of restitution and freedom for all FOGs.

Ultimately, I may have to take, not ask for, my freedom when this is all over.

Slowly, Patricia releases Ophelia's hand as the curved lid of the stasis pod draws down. She blows her a kiss as the egg hisses shut, then turns and walks to the edge of the flatbed. Immediately, the techs punch codes into a hidden keypad at the rear of the white metal structure to start the stasis process. "How long was she talking to Chad this time?" Patricia asks, dropping down and walking towards me.

"Only seven hours this time," I reply, my eyes still locked on the pod behind her.

The techs buzz about like giant white mosquitoes, each holding a proboscis that will deliver cryogenic chemicals.

They're stealing her life away, moment by moment.

"At least she's not getting worse. That's a plus." Pat looks out over the horizon, over the vast patches of green ground behind me, and frowns.

I look in the opposite direction. What could I have done to help Ophelia?

"Are you there, Jocelyn?"

"Huh? Oh, yeah. I'm here, Pat, just thinking again. You know me," I say, feeling the need to push up a smile.

Returning to her already flattened space in the grass, she sighs. "Exactly. You need to stop thinking sometimes and just be happy Oa is still here with us. And most of all, be happy you're not losing it with her."

"Should she be? With us, I mean."

"What the hell does that mean?" she says, eying me with suspicion.

I sigh. "She did it again. She asked me to help her... help her take her own life, Pat. I swear, it's like she knows she'll never be free of this madness." I tug at a large clump of grass beneath me. "So, is this the plan our government has for her? To run her into the ground? Push her to death like a workhorse?"

"Come on, Jos, you can't let her psychosis get to you. She doesn't really know what she's saying. You know that. After she's been in the egg for a while, she'll be right back to her normal self. So, come on, don't take that shit in."

As the truck rumbles to life, its cargo strapped down and safely locked away, I only question if Ophelia's plea was not wisdom wearing a mask of madness. "I know I wouldn't want to spend my life in stasis, waiting for the next target or my own death. Would you?"

Looking down at her withered hand, Pat grimaces. "I know I'd rather be alive and have the chance to change my path than to have it end on a single, sad note."

Patricia stands, reaches around Ophelia's egg, and slams her hand down on the metal roof of the truck's cab. "Hey! Watch the damn potholes!" Patricia's attempt at a yell comes out as a deep, loud growl. In a huff she falls into her seat, her brow furrowed. "You know, I think they may be doing that on purpose," she says sarcastically.

I can hear their giggling under the engine's roar. They've lightened up considerably since securing Ophelia in her egg and have been taking great pleasure in tormenting Patricia and me by aggressively driving over every pothole that litters the six-lane highway beneath us.

On either side of the highway, once-ornate buildings stand desolate, their long driveways now cracked by Keynosian weeds. The occupants that used to inhabit these expensive residences have long been evacuated. But, life has not ceased here, despite current appearances. I can hear movement everywhere. Birds flutter around, busy searching for sustenance to feed their squawking young who cry in hidden nests. Small animals skitter about along the broken sidewalks and rubble, which are partially covered in thick green moss. It's as if the city itself waged a war against the natural world... and lost badly.

Another bump and rough landing. Out of reflex, I steady the egg. I hope it's providing Ophelia with a comfortable, silent rest.

"We're almost there," Patricia croaks, peeking over the truck's cabin and towards the bleak Northern Alliance base in the distance.

Like a line drawn in the sand, there's a hard edge where the city-forest stops and the gray dirt of the base begins. There's a dead zone around the camp, a mile long in all directions. The destruction was made possible by RX, one of our most valuable weapons and our only defense against Keynosa's invasive plant life.

I find it hard to celebrate returning to base like I used to. Now, with so many of my FOG comrades dead, it is merely a place to store my things, eat an actual meal, and sleep just enough to feel human again. Ophelia won't even get these minor comforts. She'll be stored in cryo-sleep. While she's under, the techs will monitor and test her blood and vitals in an attempt to discover a way to stabilize her and all of the other FOGs who are slowly deteriorating.

She'll likely be subjected to an endless litany of drug therapies for the remainder of her life. Sometimes, it feels as if she's become nothing more than a guinea pig for drug manufacturers. At least the FOGs who are conscious can resist, but those that lie locked in that chemical prison, within a silvery physical one... they are utterly powerless.

It's strange to describe us FOGs, cursed with great physical strength and accelerated healing, as powerless. But, none of us can guard against the insidious nature of a disease that slowly strips us of our sanity. It's undetectable at first, but like a slow drip from a cracked vase, reason begins to slip away from the afflicted over time. Eventually, the sufferer starts to experience visual and auditory hallucinations, paranoia, obsessive compulsive behavior, and sometimes, homicidal and suicidal tendencies. Sadly, this is the fate of all FOGs.

How long before it happens to me? How long before I ask Patricia to grant me the gift of final escape, the pleasure of final freedom?

No, I won't burden her with that task. I'll kill myself first.

We enter the grounds, rolling past tall chain-link fences topped with barbed wire — a useless deterrent against our Keynosian foes. We move at the pace of a slow crawl, greeting returning comrades in platoons that are a fraction of their former sizes. Thousands of us left, and a few hundred return. The battered, but unbroken, survivors salute each other — hands raised, hands dropped to brow, hands over hearts — faces awash with a mixture of pride, relief, and sadness.

Cheers, jeers, and laughter echo throughout the thin green tents that line the area, as the conquering heroes of the Alliance return. The smell of alcohol, beer, and sweet burning meat permeates the air. Everyone's busy celebrating our biggest win.

Yes, this is worth celebrating. We survived.

"Martinez! Glad you're back!" I hear from the undulating wave of humanity as the truck jostles to an abrupt stop behind another vehicle with two eggs strapped in.

Patricia chuckles. "Your groupie is here to greet you, Jos," she sighs.

I see Clarence's dark-brown arm raised high over the oncoming traffic. He quickly makes his way to us as we drop off of the truck and a wave of white-clad techs swarm around us. They're here for the eggs and completely ignore our passing. The healthy are of no interest to them.

"Over here, Martinez!" Clarence beckons again.

I look at him in his stark white tank top. The war has devoured years off of his young life it seems.

"FYI, they're gonna have a huge party tonight to celebrate our victory, and I gotta get that first dance with you!"

I'm just not up for his advances right now.

"Umm, I'm here too, you know?" Patricia injects as he reaches us.

"Aww, of course I see you, Sergeant Patel. Glad you're back," he says, offering a smile.

Patricia turns to me, rolling her eyes. "Jos, I'm going to get cleaned up. See you back at the barracks."

"Okay, Pat." With her rifle dangling on her shoulder and ammo rattling gently in its container, she hurries off. "Aren't we supposed to be heading to the western front soon?" I ask Patricia, too late. She's already a good distance away. She can't hear me over the din.

"You in a hurry to get back to the fight? Geez, be happy they're giving us a day to rest and celebrate the retaking of Steel Harbor."

I nod, smile halfheartedly, and begin planning my escape.

"Soooo," he says, swaying his hips seductively, "you are going to the party, right?"

Those bedroom eyes have wooed more than a few FOG ladies during our time at this base. But I'm just too old for his nonsense. I shake my head, let out a weary sigh, and start my walk back to the barracks.

I need to get out of this noise, away from the swirling dust and ocean of people.

He follows, of course.

"I'm not sure if I'm up to it, Clarence. I just got back. I'm dirty, I'm tired, and I'm in dire need of a shower and some rest."

"Come on, Jos. When are you going to let me get some of that? Huh?"

Excuse me? I turn abruptly to face him. "How'd we go from talking about the party to you asking that stupid question?"

He shrugs. "Who else are you going to get with, if not me? All of the other FOGs are basket cases."

What the hell. Has he lost his mind? Who the hell does he think he's talking to like that! "How many ways do I have to tell you I'm not interested? Am I not making myself clear? I'm *not* interested!"

"Yes, there is a way to get me to leave you alone. That word is *yes*. Or even better, 'Yes, you can have me, young man. I've been keeping it at the ready for you all this time, you big strong buck you.'"

I turn away and continue my walk to the barracks. "No, Clarence, same answer as before. No. Guess what? It'll be the same answer in the future. No!" And the more you push, the more you'll push me away.

"Oh, come on. You'll enjoy —"

16

"Good bye, Clarence."

"So, are you at least coming to the par —"

"Good bye, Clarence," I repeat more forcefully, picking up my pace. Asshole.

"I'm breaking down, Jos."

With those four words, my defenses shatter. The words are spoken in a near whisper, but they hit me like a blow. Suddenly, it feels as if thousands of pounds of grief are pressing down on me.

I turn to meet his eyes. He's serious. I can tell by the steady pace of his heart, the smell of fear emanating from his glands, and the glistening tears welling in his large hazel eyes.

"Every time I look at myself, all I see is filth. I'm... I'm so dirty," he says, his voice straining. "It doesn't... I mean, I can't seem to get clean." His eyes drift down to the back of his outstretched hands. He sees something there I don't.

"Are you serious?" I ask, already knowing the answer. He's given me all of the information I need by letting his guard down, allowing me to use my enhanced senses to monitor his vitals. "How long have you known?"

He closes his hands tight. "For months now. Medics confirmed it after we took over Twin Lakes. I didn't believe it at first. Couldn't imagine that it'd happen to me, ya know?" He's smiling, but his lips are tight and straining against the weight of his confession.

How long before his inevitable crash? Months, if he's lucky. But at this point, it's a given that he will go mad sooner rather than later. It's only a question of when and how much of a danger he'll become. Most don't pass into madness easily.

In a burst of speed, I'm in front of him, just inches away. The throng of techs nearby nearly jump out of their skins at the sight of my outburst. His forced smile doesn't change as I glare at him. "Are you fucking with me?" I whisper, leaning in close to his ear, my eyes passing over his full lips, his cheekbones, the width of his nose, and the edges of his long, wet eyelashes.

"No. I'm not fuckin' with you, Jos. I'm being straight up," he answers, looking down past me and into the dry, dusty earth.

Pulling back, I stare into his face. He's so young. He, like so many soldiers, was recruited in high school. He can't be more than twenty-one years old now.

His eyes shift, and suddenly, he looks down at me. His beautiful eyes beg for something more. Then I understand in an instant. It isn't sex he seeks, despite what he himself may believe. It's a sense of closeness, a feeling of connection to another person. He doesn't want to face this, any of it, alone.

Damn it. "I'm so sorry, Clarence," I say, tossing my arms around him, hugging him close. For the first time, I'm actually considering spending the night with him.

He returns the hug, his chin resting on my shoulder.

"Clarence... are you grabbing my ass?"

I feel his huge frame take in a long breath. "Yeah... it's nice."

I can't help but laugh. I place my fingers in the hollow of his cheeks, squeeze and kiss him there. "The answer is still no," I say with a light, playful slap to his face.

If he asks me to bed again, I swear I'm going to sock him in the mouth!

"I know. But, at least I'll have the fond memory of a handful of your butt-cheek to enjoy while I'm stuck in stasis-sleep."

"You are a fool!"

We laugh together as the busy, bustling crowd sweeps past us and into their future. A future that won't be secured and enriched by young, talented men like Clarence. We've failed him. We've failed all of the young people who have died or been broken by this terrible conflict. And in failing them, we've failed ourselves.

This room feels strange to me with its buzzing lights, electronic devises, and rows of eggs.

18

I remember waking up in a room similar to this one, facing white-masked techs prodding me endlessly. The moment I was able to lift myself up from the interior of my stasis chamber, I was greeted by the sight of thousands working away, checking newborn FOGs... and disposing of the stillborn. Despite the vast number of dead, the room felt alive with buzzing machinery, whispered voices, and the weary complaints of patients popping up from their eggs. Each of us strained to look down the rows, checking to see who survived. We each probably breathed a sigh of relief that we were one of the lucky ones that made it.

But today, there is only eerie silence in this holding area. Rows and rows of bodies encased in silver stasis chambers lie side by side on the gray rubber flooring. Above each egg, a monitor pings the vitals of its prisoner, glowing bright in the dim lights.

I step towards Ophelia's stasis pod and look into a small double-paned, super-dense square of glass within the silver casing. It's frosted with an opaque white haze, and I can barely see her, although I can faintly see my own reflection. God, I look terrible. She seems peaceful, though, resting in her deathlike sleep. That's good.

Strands of her hair that once shone bright, now lie dull and weathered across her sleeping face. I lean on the egg and touch the glass, desiring nothing more than to whisk the hair from her eyes. How desperately I want to fix this mess for her. But some messes, some decisions, can't be undone, only managed.

Why did we choose this?

I love my country. My presence here and now is proof of that love. But, God help me, I'd never make this choice again.

"Oa," I say, fogging the thick glass with my breath. "Soon, we'll be headed to the western front. I think we're even going to fly there, and not in helio-rovers either, but in actual planes. They say the antiaircraft spores the Keynosians released have mostly faded from Alliance territories. Great thing because it'll take us half the time to get there by plane."

19

I keep expecting her to open her eyes.

"They're having a party tonight," I say, with a rap on her window. "Supposedly it's to thank us for retaking the Harbor and securing the eastern half of the country. But how can they thank us with you and the others cooped up in here?"

I feel an uncomfortable stirring in my midsection as tears threaten to fall. Look at her, she's only twenty-two, just a baby.

She was such a beautiful girl. When I first saw her, I felt a twinge of jealousy. Everything was perfect on her, nothing sagged or jiggled. Flawless, she turned to me, smiling, asking about my necklace. It was my most cherished possession, given to me by my students.

I lost that thing on a battlefield. I can't even remember which one now. It was a valuable reminder of my old life as a teacher. Now, it's just something else I lost on one of many battlefields.

"Oa, do you remember when we first met?" I ask, chuckling to the glass between us. "Oh god, I found you so annoying. So perky and outgoing — and you had no filter whatsoever. You know, I actually wanted to smack you when you dared to invade my space and touch my necklace.

"Do you remember that necklace?" I ask. No response of course, but in my mind's eye, her playful expression brightens the room.

I wipe the fog of my breath from the glass and stand straight, eying the flickering light of the screen above her prison. "Now that I know you, I can see you did it because you were nervous." I return my eyes to the receding condensation. "We both were. It's just, I didn't want to talk... certainly not to someone so sickeningly cute."

The egg beeps in response.

"I still laugh when I think back to the inoculation incident. It was finally your turn, and the long steel pole came down and injected you. That's when we first met Patricia." I laugh. "You jumped and let out that weird high-pitched yelp that terrified everyone in line behind us."

"I do remember that." I hear from behind me. It's Patricia. I'd know her voice anywhere. I'm surprised I didn't sense her entrance. The room must be shielded. Must save techs the trouble of calming the revived FOG soldiers when they wake them. "What are you doing in here, Jos?" Patricia asks as if she doesn't know.

"Keeping Oa company, of course," I say, turning to face her. The sight of Patricia stops my thoughts in their tracks. She looks gorgeous! "Oh my God, Pat, look at you!"

Her lopsided smirk quickly becomes a full smile. "What? I told you I was going to the party."

"I know that, but I didn't expect to see... this," I say, waving my hand up and down in her direction.

She grins widely, brushing her hands down her dress. "It's nice, right? I got it made weeks ago, had it shipped to the camp. I promised myself I'd wear it if we ever won back Steel Harbor."

"No, sweetie, it's not just the dress, it's the woman wearing it. You are rockin' that dress, girl!" I exclaim.

The dress hugs her petite, yet muscular frame like a second skin. The deep-crimson gown covers one arm, her burned side, hiding the horrible scar. The thin, flexible fabric rises up and around her neck, wrapping into a collar. But on the other side, the red disappears and exposes her bare, flawless, caramel-toned back and shoulder. On her uncovered wrist, she wears a thick golden bangle dotted with the same crimson of the gown. It's the perfect complement to the stunning outfit. For a moment, I feel a twinge of jealousy. She's so beautiful.

The woman now standing bashfully before me. This is hardly what I would expect from the hardened Sergeant Patel. This is the same person who stared down five Keynosian Guardsmen, fighting ferociously even though her body was burning. After receiving treatment for the burns, the very next day she led eight FOG soldiers, including Ophelia and myself, into combat. She led us to victory.

"Rockin' it, really?" Her hand flutters over her collarbone. "You think so? It's not too much, is it?"

"Pffft, please," I say, waving away her concerns. "You've got to model it for me, Pat." I twirl my finger, encouraging her to relax her arms and show off her beauty.

"Model it? What are you talking about?" her scratchy voice asks innocently.

"Oh stop it! I know you know what I'm talking about," I tease, raising my hands to my face as if I'm holding a small camera. "Let me see your best catwalk stroll."

Despite the eye-roll, she complies. Walking up and down the room lined with eggs, she moves like a child unsure of herself in a new Easter Sunday dress.

"Oh come on! You've got to do better than that, girl. Show me how you plan to get a man-slave to peel that off of you!"

"Oh please! I'll be lucky to get a dance tonight. Most of those clowns are too scared to even talk to me."

"Are you insane? Did you get hit in the head with shrapnel or something? Girl, you look incredible. They're going to be falling over themselves to get next to you. Now, show me how you work it!"

For a moment, we forget we are soldiers.

The deafening noise from these air-carriers always gives me a headache. Well, not really, although I continue the charade by rubbing my temples. How strange my behavior has become over the last few years. Even now, after so much time has passed, I continue to act as if I am experiencing discomfort even though I am completely immune to normal human afflictions like colds and headaches. It's like a phantom limb, a vestige of my human frailty before the transformation.

I wonder, is it the phantom remembrance of my lost humanity?

As the air-carrier lifts off, rising up from the compact earth beneath my feet, I look around our new base of operations. It's huge. This is by far the largest base I've ever seen. Larger than the Midwest base by a factor of three, at least. Many trucks and jeeps move out, tossing up the RX contaminated dust used to keep the Keynosian plant life at bay. The trucks spew gray exhaust into the air, giving it an iridescent hazy-brown appearance as it reflects the sunlight.

Strips of mud and dirt run down the tent walls. It reminds me of this morning's shower and how much I enjoyed removing the grime from my skin. There's no escaping the filth — dust covers everything at every base I've ever been to.

The west coast base rests close to the Northern Alliance's shoreline that borders the largest body of water on the planet, the Pantonic Ocean. It is, or was, the oldest and most contested base in this war. Even after its brief occupations, it still stands as a testament to Alliance determination. We took great pains to ensure it stayed in our hands, even if that meant poisoning the ground and rendering it useless for agriculture for centuries to come.

I look westward and catch the scent of the sea. It's surprising to me how clean it smells considering the city of Bordoro, a major industrial giant, second only to Steel Harbor, is located there. That city was only recently recaptured by us after years of Keynosian control. I'm positive this clean scent is a result of the enemy's prior ownership.

Bordoro. That place really takes me back. My mom used to take me to the beach and boardwalk there. It was fun just being there with her, even though we dared not go into the polluted waters.

As much as I want to end Keynosian opposition, I often find myself impressed with their treatment of the Earth. The Alliance's treatment of our own ecology leaves much to be desired.

"Jos, this way," Patricia says, her voice nearly drowned out by the sounds of human and machine chatter. I follow her lead, and we head to the airstrip's border.

She really should be a higher rank than she is. Patricia's the only non-FOG sergeant who's been able to coordinate, recognize, and utilize FOG soldiers effectively in the field. She understands and recognizes our needs and capabilities so well. The fact that she hasn't been promoted is a dark stain on the military.

"Can you smell the ocean air?" I ask, threading my arm into hers as we wade into the flowing sea of people.

Looking around, she sniffs the air. "All I smell is funky-ass soldiers."

I laugh. "Generally, that smells better than the ocean."

"That depends on which ocean you're talking about." She chuckles.

"True, but this is Bordoro we're talking about, so it's kind of surprising to me that it actually smells clean... crisp."

"Southies do have a way of keeping their side of the border clean. We could learn something from them if we weren't trying to kill each other."

"Jocelyn Martinez?" a voice calls to me. I stop, turn, and find myself pleasantly surprised to see a handsome young man. Holding up his hand in my direction, he waves. He's a FOG. I spot the bright red star on his sleeve. It's the one thing that identifies us from the others. His jet-black uniform struggles to hide the bulge of muscles. His sandy-brown hair is cut short and spiky, reminding me of just how well cared for we FOGs are despite being overworked. Yet, it's the long scar that streaks down his face, stopping abruptly at his chin, that reminds me of why we get this treatment.

He's a gunnery sergeant. He looks young for that rank. Very young.

"I am she," I respond, snapping to attention with a quick salute.

"Hello," he replies in kind. "I'm Gunnery Sergeant Jacob Powell," he says, nodding as he looks me up and down. "At ease, Martinez. FOG soldiers under my command aren't held to the same rigid structure as non-FOGs. One of the perks we've earned." He glances over to Patricia, giving her the same once-over, and smiles. "Sergeant Patel?" he asks.

"Patel. Yes, sir!" she replies, stepping forward with a hard, but muted stamp of her boot.

"As with Martinez, at ease, Patel. It's very good to have you on my team. You may not be a FOG, but your reputation for strength and leadership precedes you. Although it's not customary for my people to be led by a norm, if there's one tough enough to do it, it's you," he

24

says with a grin and nod.

Cute he may be, but there's a deadness to his eyes, an emptiness that appears to linger like an icy breeze. But ,that's something we all share, I guess. Maybe it's just because I don't know him well enough yet to draw a proper bead on him.

"Thank you, sir," Patricia says. "Can I make a request?"

For a moment he stares at her, his eyes squinting, his brow furrowing for a second or two before relaxing again. "Is this about Ms. Rogers?"

"Ophelia, yes," she answers.

"You don't need to worry about her. We have an excellent medical area for those... suffering," he says, understanding in his voice. "We have the best recovery center for FOGs here, not to mention a fully staffed research lab nearby." He points towards a distant, tall white tent. "This camp is the main staging point for the entire western coast, so we're given the best. I'm sure it's an improvement over the Midwestern camp you ladies came in from."

"Staging area? I assumed we were at the actual front," Patricia questions.

"No, Patricia. May I call you Patricia?"

She gives a sideways nod. "Ummm, sure."

Only the three of us call one another by our first names. Powell calling her Patricia feels intrusive.

"We're currently miles away from the actual front. Some norms, no offense, and a FOG are currently at the forward camp. They're holding the area, keeping an Alliance presence there and making sure the auto-mortars and launching turrets remain active. They're not to actually attack, only defend to make sure the site doesn't fall back into Southie hands."

"Why's the front so far away?" I ask.

"Far away for whom? Honestly, it wouldn't take us FOGs very long to reach the front." His eyes slide towards Patricia. "But I'd be happy to carry you there... if you like."

Her eyes go wide, as do my own.

Immediately he laughs. "Don't worry, Patricia, we have other norms that are carried into battle with us sometimes. You won't be the first."

"Don't listen to Gunny outside of official business, ladies. He's just trying to get a rise out of you," another voice calls from a few yards behind Sergeant Powell. In an instant he's by Powell's side, a smile on his lips as he nods to me. "I'm Santos. David Santos."

"Santos, don't spoil my fun," Powell says. He points his thumb in Patricia's direction. "I had Patel here speechless," the sergeant says, pushing Santos with an elbow.

"You ladies are a part of the new mergers going on, I assume?" Santos says, his dark eyes fixed on my own.

If I didn't see his rank of sergeant, I'd think he was in charge. Santos is older, around my age. Cute. His rugged face speaks to his maturity. It's filled with a confidence only a self-assured man can contain.

For a FOG soldier, he doesn't appear as damaged as so many others. "Your assumption would be correct, Santos," I respond.

"I gave my name, but I didn't catch yours."

"Martinez." I nod.

He nods in response. "Good afternoon, Martinez."

There's a moment of silence as we stand amidst the cacophony of war preparation, looking at one another.

"Patel," Patricia says, her hand reaching for Santos', breaking the not-so-awkward silence.

He enthusiastically takes it. "Nice to meet you, Patel. Welcome to the western front."

"For a FOG, you look unscathed. Are you a tech or something?" Patricia asks, her eyes passing between Santos and Powell.

"A tech, me?" Santos asks.

"Yes, you," her voice, humorless, scratches out.

Stepping forward, Powell leans in and gets closer to Patricia. "David here went in for the second wave. So he had the pleasure of missing most of the first year."

A distant explosion to the south draws all of our attention. The sound is loud enough for even Patricia to hear and the flash close enough to cause concern. Maybe it's a sun mine going off? That wouldn't account for the sound, though. Keynosian sun mines are nearly silent.

David's face tightens. "The explosion came from a nearby town. But why are they attacking there?"

"Are they attacking our base?" Patricia asks.

"The base would be beyond that point, so no. Bottom line, they know we're coming. Not to worry though, that base is a massive tree home. It'll hold up."

"Do they have range on us here?" I ask.

"Too far. Reports say they're mostly using tanglevines and spiketails anyway, all of which are relatively short ranged," David replies.

"They've been trying to recover some ground, and at times it's gone back and forth between us and them. I believe we launched RX attacks a few days ago, wiping the slate clean of all plant life. It didn't last long. It's a lot harder that far south. The ground there is too fertile, or so our intel advises," Jacob says, grinning towards Patricia. "Speaking of attacks, how did you survive an acid-seed attack and retain your good looks?"

"You survived an acid attack? Wow," Santos, looking at Patricia's hand and forearm. "I assumed the scars were from a sun mine. Most folks don't... well, it's tough for norms to survive acid-seed. The speed of the spore's growth, the damage, that's a lot for a body to handle."

Patricia touches my arm. "I had help," she says. "It only hit my fingers, but Martinez here ran me to the medic station some five miles away. Got me there just in time to neutralize the fungus before it spread over my entire body."

"Wow, that's pretty fast," Jacob says, his lips jutting out as he nods. "It'll be good to have a ranger as fast as you on the team."

"You didn't get burned, Martinez?" David asks.

"Oh no, I did. As soon as I touched her, the spores jumped to me. Burned like hell. But luckily, it wasn't long enough to leave a scar. There just happened to be some quick acting medics around when I got to the station. I just wish... I wish I had paid more attention," I say, glancing at Patricia. I almost lost you.

A knowing look, seemingly carried by the breeze, brushes across Santos' and Powell's faces. They understand. They both know the sinking feeling of loss. I can tear a car to pieces with my bare hands, yet do absolutely nothing to restart a bullet-ridden heart.

"You can't take that in, Martinez," Santos says, his eyes sorrowful.

"He's right, Jos, you can't save everyone... but I am happy you saved my ass." Patricia chuckles.

"I'm happy I did as well." My sister.

"With the addition of the Midwest and East forces, norm and FOG alike, we'll have the manpower needed to break the Southie's last stronghold south of our position," Jacob says to the large contingent of FOG soldiers under his command. Many are scarred as badly as or worse than Patricia. Only a few norms are in the audience.

Why they would call the non-FOG soldiers norms is beyond me. Wouldn't that imply that we, the Fingers of God, are not normal? Well... that wouldn't be far from the truth.

"How are you feeling, Oa?" Patricia whispers.

"Fine, just a tiny headache is all."

"Is it bad?" I ask.

"Oh, no, it's not bad, just... different this time around. Kinda weird. Whatever they gave me makes me feel more aware, sharper. It's like there's too much stuff going on around me. I feel pressure right behind my eyes, especially when I look into the lights.

"Anyway, it's not a big deal, nothing I can't handle," she says with a grin.

"I actually heard through the grapevine that they've added a new drug to assist the stasis recovery, maybe that's the cause of the headaches —"

"Uhh-hrm!"

Like children caught talking in class, we freeze and look up to see Jacob half-smiling at Patricia. Of course, he can hear us despite our whispering. He's a FOG.

Patricia stiffens in her seat immediately. "I'm sorry —"

"Don't. It's fine. But you do bring up something we need to touch on. So, I guess I should be thanking you, Sergeant Patel," he says with a nod. "As Patel's grapevine aptly stated, those of you that arrived in stasis were given an additive in the air-mix. It's a newly developed drug, meant to target the brain pathways specific to your condition. The drug should aid in your ability to maintain fighting capability for a much longer time period. The eggheads claim this new serum will enable you to remain outside of stasis for more than two weeks, at the very least."

My eyes drift to Clarence, seated in the distance behind us. He nods appreciatively at Jacob. Many here do.

"Look, I know it's hard to believe sometimes, but I'm doing all I can to look after everyone. I'm just as concerned for your well-being as I am my own, because it could be me right next to any of you in a month." His eyes widen with carefully crafted concern.

Something about him is definitely off, and I don't trust him because of it. Everything he says seems scripted.

"Now, if Santos can come up and address you all in regards to the discussion he had with the special FOG medic team?" He extends his hand to David, who's seated in the front row. For a moment, he doesn't rise. From my seat, three rows back, I hear him exhale softly.

Santos gives Powell a look. Annoyance? Reluctance? I can't tell which. Maybe both.

"I'm not a medic or trained in anything even remotely related to medicine. I'm just a concerned soldier interested in the safety of my troop-mates, Jefferson and Rawlings." Santos looks out into the crowd, his brown eyes searching the inside of the tent. They settle and he nods, allowing a faint smile to cross his lips. "We've all suffered the loss of a teammate, and not always from combat. The last five medications they've tried on them... let's just say they haven't had the best results.

"So, I began questioning the med-staff. As always, they gave me the runaround." We all chuckle along with him, having experienced the same nonsense. "But they did say that the new therapy has been tested thoroughly and they're really confident about its efficacy. So confident, in fact, that they're turning it into tablet form. With it, many of you won't have to be concerned about going into stasis any longer."

Cheers erupt.

Powell steps forward and places his hand on Santos' shoulder. "Okay, okay, calm down everyone. There's no guarantee, so keep your eyes open for problems and report them immediately. But still, I'm making sure that everyone who wants the tablets will have them as soon as the recon-team returns. I want these things in our hands before we get anywhere near the front."

"Recon-team?" a lone voice says, speaking our collective thought.

Looking in the direction of the voice, Powell nods. "Yes, I'm arranging for a few of our numbers to scout ahead, check on the front base if possible, gather intel, and return so we can start planning our push into Southie territory."

Powell smiles like a politician. If it were not for the scar, he would look like a fresh-faced civilian youth.

"The scout team will consist of Santos, Martinez, Jackson, Marshall, and Petersen. And on that note, I'm going to need you soldiers to stick around for additional briefing."

After just bringing Patricia, Ophelia, and I together under the same unit, he's now splitting us up?

"Anyway, once we hear back from the scout team, we'll move out.

So, get some R&R while you can. We've all received additional pay this week, and for those that don't know, there's a big town north of here. So, enjoy spending your well-earned credits. Dismissed." With a quick cheer in unison, the gathering rises and quickly disappears through the flaps of green canvas at either end of the tent.

"I guess we'll check you later, Jos," Patricia says as she and Ophelia wave to me before making their way out of the tent.

I look up to see who's left behind. Wait, he's sticking me in a team of all men?

No, I don't like this. I don't like this at all. Not after what happened in Verington.

I will never team up with a group of men again.

CHAPTER 2

STATE OF WAR

Martinez, I'm well aware of the Verington incident," Jacob says. "But I need you on this mission," he repeats, this time pointing at me, then the ground. "There are only two rangers remaining, you and Rawlings. Normally, I'd use Rawlings, but she hasn't been cleared yet, so that leaves you. So while the medics are evaluating her body's acceptance of the new drugs, you're the team's new main ranger."

"I don't think you're listening to me. I won't be in another group where I'm the only female —"

"Here, take this," David interjects, thrusting a micro-mine trigger resting in the palm of his hand in my direction.

What the hell is he doing that for? "What? I don't want that."

He moves closer. "Just take it please," he insists.

"For what? I don't want it."

He smiles. "Consider it a sign of trust."

A sign of trust? I glance around at Jackson, Petersen, Marshall, and Powell. They look just as confused as I feel. I look down at the trigger, then back to meet his brown eyes. "Take a micro trigger? Why? What does this... okay wait, before I take it, tell me exactly what mine this trigger is for."

He must be some nutjob, or worse, maybe another FOG currently losing his mind. Either way, I'll find out what's really going on with these guys and be done with this ridiculous assignment.

He retracts his hand a few inches and nods. "Okay, fair enough. The trigger, this trigger, is tuned to a mine I have in my pocket," he says, patting his pants pocket. "You see, the mine in my pocket was actually a gift of sorts. I got it from a friend, a FOG who I refused to... help out. You see, that refusal was my initial reaction. How could I do something like that, I thought. Denying his request was the first thing I thought to do. That was until I realized the extent of his injuries. You see, the guy that gave me the mine, he was definitely going to die. There was no doubt about it. He and I both knew he wasn't going to survive his injuries. So, he placed this mine I have in my pocket on his forehead and begged me to detonate it. I don't know if it was because he didn't believe in suicide or because he didn't have the will to off himself. I didn't go through with it. I kind of froze trying to come up with something meaningful to say, comfort him in some way. Anything but the obvious. Yet, while I was frozen with indecision, he was suffering. The guy was tough though. He never yelled out, never cried, didn't even whimper through the horror he must've been experiencing. He just asked me to kill him. At some point, I got up the nerve... but he'd already passed.

"So as a reminder of what's really out there, what we are really facing — not just the Keynosians by the way — I pulled the mine from his head and kept the trigger, just in case."

"Just in case, what?"

A thoughtful look comes over his face. "Just in case it's me who's dying slowly, painfully. Just in case someone else I care about is experiencing the same. No one should have to suffer like that. No one."

"Alright, that's a sad story and I sympathize, I really do. But what does that have to do with me? Is that supposed to be my insurance or something? Are you planning on giving me the trigger while you keep the mine in your pocket?"

He chuckles. "That's exactly what I was going for."

It feels like a standoff, David and I staring at one another, waiting for the other to act.

He makes the first move and nods. Once again, David stretches out his hand, the trigger resting in his palm. It's no bigger than a book of matches.

He's ballsy, I'll give him that. Cautiously, I pluck the trigger from his hand, my eyes never leaving his. "So what, now I'm supposed to trust you?"

Again, he smiles. "If you're on my team, I'll *need* you to trust me. I'll need you to trust all of us. Our lives could depend on it. But you especially, with that trigger, have my life in your hands. That's literal, by the way.

"So now tell me, does that put you at ease or do I need to promise you my firstborn too?" he asks.

I glance around at the others again. This is insane. Does he do this kind of thing often?

"Don't look at me," Clarence says with a huffing chuckle. "I like you, but not enough to get my nuts blown off."

There has to be something wrong with Santos. Maybe this is some kind of sick joke these Westcoasters play on new arrivals? "Look, I don't know what this is about or what kind of game you're trying to play here, but trust me, I am just crazy enough to detonate this thing." I bluff, trying to sell it with my glare.

I look down at the tiny device and find all of this rather hard to believe. All I'd need to do is move my finger over this tiny button. "You know, I'm tempted to do it now just in —"

"No!" he yelps, his hand flashing up to the device. "Let's, umm, not experiment to see what'll happen, if you don't mind?"

Oh my God, he's serious. He's actually serious. Does he not know the dangers of a micro mine? I've used them many times to great effect. The malleable mines are no bigger than a credit card, but the explosion is powerful enough to rip a melon-sized hole in an armored tank. And here, this nut has put one in his pocket and handed me the trigger.

35

With just a press of a button, he'd lose a lot more than his reproductive organs. The blast would rip through his hips, removing his lower half entirely. For a FOG, that's a slow and very painful death.

"This is insane," I say, looking at Gunny Powell for help.

Instead, he stares at Santos incredulously.

"Yep, that it is. But, I'll ask again, is this enough for you to trust me with *your* life?" Santos asks.

"This is too much. I don't need this."

"And why not? Why is it too much?" he asks. "Look, I *need* you to have it. I need you to believe me when I tell you that I will do everything I can to keep you safe out there. You're *our ranger*. Not some addition from a different camp that no one gives a damn about. No, you're one of us when you're on *my* team. And while you're on my team, I promise to do everything I can to take care of your safety in every way possible.

"You know as well as I do that it's the rangers that've kept the Keynosians from wiping us out. In a fight, your hit-and-run tactics can keep entire teams of Southie forces on the defensive and unable to rush us, forcing the fight into a hand-to-hand combat situation. And, unlike striker FOGs like myself, if you're in trouble, you can completely outrun a Guardsmen. And finally, it's the rangers who've been able to sense a team's surroundings with enough accuracy to keep groups from being ambushed over and over again. I'd be lying if I didn't say we *need* you more than you need us."

I don't know what else to say in protest. In fact, there's no protest left in me. "Okay," I say, removing my thumb and carefully closing the small metallic flap that protects the button from accidental activation. I close my hand tight around it. I better keep this thing safe. "Fine, whatever... I *trust* you, even if you're a nut."

Who is this man, Santos? What has he been through that would make him put so much at risk to garner my trust? I look him up and down hoping to see some kind of clue to how he works, checking in the hope that I'll find it pasted somewhere upon his form.

36

"Just know this, I am going to hold on to the trigger, just in case. Maybe, at some point, you can earn it back, Santos."

He laughs. "I plan to, Martinez."

Powell steps up, holding a small screen with a digital map of the southern lands. "Well, okay then," he says with a half grin. "Santos and Martinez now trust each other. Great." Turning the screen towards the group, he pulls the edges of the device, expanding it. "From this morning's report — the first we've received in weeks — either the forward camp has been taken over or it's in serious danger. A passing sky-eye captured these images before it was devoured by those Southie spores. As you can see, the area's been overrun with fauna, and there's been no word from the team... not even signs that they're still alive in there.

"So bottom line, we need a team to scout it out if possible, which means avoid fighting and just get info. That's even if they're in trouble. Get me?"

"No fighting?" David asks. "None at all?"

"Shut it, Santos."

Pointing at the map in Powell's hands, David touches the screen, illuminating the area on the soft flickering material. "What's this, a village?"

"That it is, Santos. And it's your first target."

Patricia shakes her head and drops her fork on the metal tray holding what the military keeps describing as "lunch" and "food." "Girl, I would have blown his nuts off just because he was being a nut," Patricia says. Drawing her lips down, she scrapes her bottom teeth with a fingernail.

Ophelia's nose turns up at the sight. "You know there are these things called toothpicks, right?" she scolds, slapping Patricia's hand from her mouth.

Patricia turns to Ophelia, expressing mock shock. "I can't believe you just did that," she croaks.

Ophelia laughs, her hand covering her mouth. "I can't believe you'd stick your finger in your mouth like that. In public no less." She sweeps her hand across the room, alerting Patricia to the many troops who're partaking in this noon's meal.

"Ladies, can we please focus here?"

"I gave my answer. Boom. Off with the nut's nuts." Patricia sticks one hand under the fold-out table, pretending to grab male genitalia, and spreads the fingers out on her other hand to symbolize an explosion.

We all laugh, but I'd love to know what they really think about Santos. Can I trust his gesture? Is he just gaming me? Is this some kind of strange pickup strategy? Even Clarence never went this far.

Ophelia tugs Patricia's arm from her crotch and shakes her head in disbelief. She slides another large sandwich wrapped in heavy brown paper in my direction. She knows I'll need fuel. "Contrary to Pat's apocalyptic vision of testicular homicide, I say you should trust him."

"Wow, now that's a mouthful. Testicular homicide, Oa? Really?" I ask.

"That was good, right?"

"Creative, yes."

She chuckles. "Okay, let me finish." Ophelia grins, placing her hand on mine. "One: he's cute. Two: he's literally putting his life in your hands. Literally. Three: Patricia is crazy. Why would you or anyone listen to her?"

"Oh come on," Patricia interjects. "Ya'll know I'm only joking. But seriously, there's no way to know for sure, right? Other than pushing the button." She points to my pocket from across the table. "If he's honest, that'll be the cost for his stupidity."

"See," Ophelia says with a sigh, "you'd maim someone for trying to get you to trust him and for him trusting you to do the right thing. Jos, I think Santos is being genuine. I mean, think about it. The guy put his 'stuff' on the line. That's serious! Especially to a man."

"I get it, Oa. But it's just so over-the-top."

"The fact that you're acting all confused is frustrating to me, Jos," Patricia says, jabbing her fork at me. "Isn't it obvious? Santos has got a thing for you. Any man that'll put the safety of his pee-pee in your hands is obviously hinting at actually putting his pee-pee in your hands."

We erupt in laughter.

If he is, that's a strange way to show it. Gutsy sure, but definitely strange. Regaining my composure, I sigh. "Sweet on me? I think that's taking it too far. Him and Gunny Powell are both into overly dramatic declarations."

"Ohh, now Powell, that's a guy whose nuts I'd never blow up," Patricia says, her eyebrows bouncing.

"No, you'd do a different kind of blowing," Ophelia says in a near whisper, a shy, almost embarrassed look on her face.

"Oa, oh no you didn't." I guffaw, leaning back and slapping the table.

So often we giggle when we're together, like high school girls during lunch period.

When all of this is said and done, I desperately want to keep in contact with them. I couldn't ask for better friends.

"So what are you going to do?" Ophelia asks, tapping the back of my hand.

I could go over Gunny Powell's head on this. Probably log a complaint straight to First Sergeant Gordon. I'm certain to get what I want with so few rangers available as a case can easily be made for not sending a dwindling asset into a potentially dangerous area. But Santos did make a huge effort to garner my trust. I've rarely seen a man extend himself to me in that way. My ex-husband certainly didn't during our entire five years of marriage. "What am I going to do? I'll go on the mission, I guess. I mean, the guy has put a lot on the line to get me to join the mission."

"Maybe it's a lot... maybe it's not. You'll never know unless you get his pants off."

"Oh my God, Patricia!" Ophelia yells.

Petersen, Jackson, Santos, and I check our meager gear as we stand outside the base's exit. I turn to see the dull-gray solid-steel plates rising seven feet up the fifteen feet of heavy chain-link fence that slowly closes behind us. Thunking along on gnarled, corroded black wheels, the barrier shuts behind us.

"Are we running to the objective?" Petersen asks, awkwardly tightening the straps on his large backpack. Generally, tanks wear a thick charged-harness that holds their dragon rifles. It must be odd for him to travel without that massive weapon.

As powerful as tanks are, they could never survive a one-on-one encounter with any Guardsmen. They're simply too slow. Their weapons, the insanely powerful dragon rifles, are all that keep Guardsmen from ripping them asunder. Without his, I wonder if Petersen's just a bit on edge?

"Wouldn't make sense if we didn't," I answer, making sure to pull my boot buckles tight.

Looking annoyed, Petersen sends a harsh glance at me before turning to Santos. "Are we running or not?"

Well... to hell with you too! I was only joking, somewhat.

David doesn't look at him, his eyes fixed on the distant border as he rolls up his sleeves. "Martinez gave you your answer, Petersen. This is a scouting mission. A vehicle would be too noisy." David turns and glances at the team, then back towards the closed gates of the base. "Where's Marshall?"

As if on cue, Marshall lands with a thud in front of the closed gray metal. He jogs to us, his black shirt flapping in the brisk breeze, exposing a bright-white tank top underneath. Once in our midst, he drops his backpack and begins to button up his shirt. "Sorry about that, Sarge. I lost track of time."

Santos sighs. "Martinez, I'm going to need you on point. Keep within a klick of us, at least. I don't want you getting too far away from your backup." Removing his collar comm, David manipulates its dials, turning the small buttons, probably tuning the comm for his leadership role on this expedition. "Alright, I've been given a new channel for this trip. So everyone, tune your receivers to 7-6-7-9."

"Gotcha," Marshall says, still tidying up his uniform by tucking his shirt into his trousers. He's up to his antics again. There are lots of new women here for Clarence to exploit.

"Are we keeping the main channel as one of our three preprogrammed links?" I ask. I need to know which one I can ignore so I can keep the channel Ophelia, Patricia, and I use active. The comms can only hold three channels at a time in its memory.

"Yes. But please turn that channel off. I need you all to be focused on the here and now, not listening to the pointless updates they give us."

With a grin, we all comply, removing our comms and tuning them appropriately.

"Marshall and Jackson will have our rear. Petersen, you're with me. We'll keep our eyes and ears open for Martinez's signals."

"Yes, sir. No problem keeping an eye on Martinez from the back," Petersen says, with a chuckle. This is going to be a long mission with him here. He's shown himself to be little more than a petty jerk so far.

"And I'll have no problem watching *your* back, Sarge," Jackson chimes in, grinning wide.

We all stifle a giggle.

"Good, at least I know you'll be attentive, Jackson. Everyone ready?"

Nods all around.

"Alright, let's move out."

41

I've never been this far into Keynosa. Despite our offensive strikes, and dropping tons of RX, the vast majority of the country is still covered in thick, nearly impassable greenery. Trees are as tall as skyscrapers, and flowers larger than a human torso dominate the landscape. The list of amazing sights we pass are endless. I can't help but wonder what this place would look like without the freshly made brown pockmarks of dead and dying plant life — poisoned by our deadly toxins — carved into large swaths of Keynosian land.

I stop a mile from the abandoned village and quickly climb the tallest tree. Tucking myself behind its large branches, I carve a window out of the thick, dark leaves so I can see the target clearly. From here, I start pushing my sight and hearing and begin my threat assessment of the village.

The entire area is darkened by a canopy of Keynosian home trees arranged in concentric circles. In the center is a massive fountain. At first glance, I assumed it was a lake or some huge slab of mirrored material. If it were not for the small stone border spanning the entire diameter and the occasional ripple brushed into movement by the gentle breeze of the late afternoon, I would still think that. Despite not actually being a mirror, the lake reflects the sights above with crystal clarity, transforming it into a ring of green surrounding a bright blue sky in the center. The sight of it all is utterly breathtaking.

Tree homes, hollow tree trunks that the Keynosians inhabit, fill vast swaths of the area. Each standing five to six stories tall, they're topped with what appears to be fruit bearing branches. Like swollen bunches of leaves, the immature green fruit adorn the branches in thick bundles. Each treetop seems to have a different variation of fruit. The harvest here must be phenomenal.

I drop from my perch and move closer, dashing from tree to tree.

What's this? Directly ahead, like dark sentinels, black trees covered with thick glittery bark stand before me in a row. They're foreboding. I catch a whiff of a sickening scent. Pungent and foul, the chemical odor seems to envelop the trees. It hovers around them like a cloak. I spot what looks like layers of bark littering the ground around each tree. The bark is piled up like winter clothing removed one layer at a time and dumped at the village's doorstep.

The scent is familiar in a way, reminding me of RX.

Is that how this place has kept the RX contamination at bay — using these trees to filter and shed the toxins through the bark?

Enough theorizing, back to the assessment.

I don't see, hear, or smell anything human ahead. I guess the village is safe for now. "Clear," I say softly over the receiver. The noisy silence of nature is broken in an instant. I hear my team approaching behind me, moving quickly to my location.

What is that bark? Is there actually RX locked inside of it? Curiosity takes hold, and I dash to the black trees. Grabbing a fist-sized piece of bark, I check it closely. It feels gritty. It's flecked with what appears to be dark crystals of blue set against the even darker wood. The bark has the same chemical smell of the antipsychotics so many FOGs have to employ for sanity's sake. Yet, despite the rough appearance, it's not rock hard. Like dried cakes of mud, the bark crumbles easily under the slightest pressure. Ughh, it also stains, like charcoal. I wipe my gloved hand down my pants, leaving a gray streak along the side of my uniform leg.

From the black trees, I continue establishing a visual on the village. Winding walkways, which look like layers of moss, carpet the ground. They remind me of streets, but they're nothing more than layers of wide dark-green leaves. Strange. I wonder if these moss sidewalks are as spongy and soft as they look or if the streets of leaves are as durable as it appears.

I'll find out soon enough.

Doing another sweep with my senses, I hone in on the home trees. Outside, there's nothing besides the usual sound of wildlife going about the business of living. Inside, all of the telltale signs of human activity are completely nonexistent. No breathing, no talking, not even the sound of water moving within.

It's clear that people were here at some point, made obvious by the signs of old human activity that sit underneath each home tree. Trash, that smells weeks old, lies rotting in fabric bags and large woven containers. This place was once alive. Now, it just reminds me of a graveyard, where all that remains are the skeletons of humanity.

"Goddamn birds keep shitting on me!"

"Keep your voice down, Petersen. We don't know if they're monitoring the village from a distance," Santos warns as he comes to a stop behind me.

"You should be happy, Petersen. Birds taking a crap on you is considered good luck," Marshall adds, handing Petersen a large leaf he snatched from a nearby tree. It's as big as his forearm.

"Luck my ass."

The milky-white feces slides down his shoulders and onto his chest. Wow, that must have been a really large bird. "I'd say you're lucky." I shrug. "At the very least, it wasn't one of those weird cat-looking creatures." I gesture towards the branches atop a tree ahead of us. Perfectly camouflaged, the animal is the picture of quiet and tense stillness as it stalks a bird, waiting for the most advantageous moment before striking. They're not a threat to us, but clearly they're a powerful predator here.

"Fuck you, Martinez. You could have brought us to a better spot than this." Using the leaf like toilet paper, Petersen frowns and tries to wipe the mess from his uniform.

This is the second time he's snapped at me, and I refuse to take abuse from him or anyone. "What's your problem, Petersen?"

"My problem is I just got shat on," he snarls, shaking his head. "You fuckin' rangers man."

He has a problem with rangers, is that it? I knew it couldn't be about me personally — I've done nothing to the man. Hell, I haven't given so much as a nod in his direction since we've set off on this mission.

"Give it a rest, Petersen. Martinez didn't do a thing wrong. In fact, it looks to me that she's done a stellar job so far," Jackson interjects, running his fingers through his shiny, thick mane of shoulder- length black hair, whipping it behind his broad shoulders.

Sliding off his backpack, Santos steps forward and places it a foot away from my left leg. "Strategically this location is perfect. There's enough noise to keep us hidden from the enemy's ability to detect us," he says, looking intently at the treetops. "But not enough to keep Martinez from hearing them if they're close."

"So, Martinez, what's the status of the area? Anything interesting?" Santos crouches in front of his backpack, his eyes fixed along the dark green road ahead of us.

I turn back to the village. "Nothing so far, but that's just a general scan."

"Alright then, let's get a deep read before we move in. Do your thing, Martinez. Everyone else, you know what to do."

They all go silent, slowing their heart rate and breathing. They know their chatter would make it more difficult for me to get a good sense of the area. Not by much, but every little bit helps. So, with my eyes closed, I begin pushing my senses outward.

Animals are moving above and below. Leaves rustle above our heads. I pick up the scent of the fecal matter on Petersen's shoulder, as well as the abrasive cologne Marshall wears too often. Hmm, Clarence slept with someone last night. Her scent is thick on him.

Further.

The sound of everything nearby increases — the wind scrapes against me while the worms beneath our feet cause vibrations in the ground as they burrow through the soil. My companions might have suppressed their heartbeats and breathing, but they still thunder in my ears. I pick up the putrid smell of a long dead animal, small, probably a rat on my six. There's food waste not disposed of properly in many of the homes. The people must have left in a hurry. Many children lived here. I can smell them.

Further.

45

Like the mind-numbing sound of a construction site, the din of the forest becomes utterly deafening as I push to the edges of my sensory reach. Still, I find nothing human beyond this group. This place is a ghost town. Even if there are Keynosians watching us, they're clearly nowhere close.

"Sorry to disappoint, but still nothing. No hostiles I'm aware of."

"Good, let's start getting things set up." Pulling a floating sky-eye out of his pack, Santos flips a switch on its side and lifts the now beeping, fist-sized device in Jefferson's direction. "Highest spot, since we can't afford to let it fly. There are probably still spores floating up there above the tree line."

Jefferson ties his hair back tight with a bright-blue ribbon. "Done." That's all he says before gingerly lifting the sky-eye out of Santos' hand and taking off in a burst of speed towards a gigantic tree southwest of us.

"Marshall, mark the area please."

"On it," Clarence says, pulling an armful of relay beacons strung together like festive lights from his pack. He also runs off, in the opposite direction that Jefferson took. The relay beacons will make it easier for us to keep communications open without the use of a sky-eye. The secondary benefit is this will make the sky-eye much more powerful in both range and data retrieval since it won't have to store captured sound and images within its internal memory module.

As always, there's something about these villages that the Keynosians have built. Maybe it's in the trees or the ground or who knows, but each village appears to be capable of blocking all of our transmissions. Since it's easier to plant relay beacons than to tear or burn down these very solid home trees, all teams who venture into Keynosa systematically plant these devices in the villages they stumble across. In fact, Steel Harbor was under Keynosian control for so long, it was necessary to do the same there as we re-captured each and every ten-block span.

"Petersen, Martinez, you're both with me. We're on the hunt for the previous sky-eye that was supposed to be somewhere... in there," David says, pointing to a cluster of home trees.

"You think the Southies got to it?" I ask.

"Gotta assume so." Santos glances down at Petersen's empty hands. "Petersen, you got the tracker, right?"

"Aww shit, the tracker," he says, rolling his eyes. "Right..." He yanks off his pack and flicks back the flap that seals it. "Whew, thought I forgot it." Quickly he produces a gray box the size of a pack of playing cards. "Now where's the on switch? Oh... okay, got it," he mumbles to himself. With a click, a circular screen rises and unfolds from the top of the box, extending as large as a dinner plate. "Ready."

"Alright, are you picking up the signal from the old sky-eye?" Santos asks. "It should be this way."

"Nothing yet... oh wait, yep, I got it," he confirms, lifting his head. "Yeah, it's this way."

I pull my blade out. "To the west we go."

"Looks like it," Santos says, giving my blade a concerned look. "You expecting a fight?"

"I'm always expecting a fight, and so should you."

The stark blue of Petersen's eyes appears almost green as they reflect the color of the tracking device he holds. Eyes wide and intense, he slows down as we near a deep brown, almost black in some spots, home tree. It looks partially burned. Wait a second, the wood itself is totally undamaged. In fact, the tree itself smells of... nothing.

A mound of various metal parts — very familiar parts — sits at the tree's base. Standing about as tall as myself, the mound is made up of spent and unspent Northern artillery, from RX containers to hornet missiles. Did the Keynosians gather all of this from two years ago when we were still able to fly bombing sorties into Keynosian space?

Other, smaller piles are nearby. Those appear to be made up of guns and rifle parts, mine parts, and the spying devices we launched into Keynosian space years ago. There's even a busted tracking device, an older model of the one currently held by Petersen.

It looks as if the Southies have gathered all of the tools we've used against them, disassembled them, and ultimately, tossed them here. No, not just tossed them here. These parts aren't placed haphazardly, nor are the mounds random. It's all sorted and stacked with some reasoning involved.

Could they've been studying our technology?

"Martinez, give me a check," Santos asks, his voice hinting at some unspoken concern. He's been on what seems like high alert from the moment I drew my blade. Seeing the mound appears to have made that worry grow.

"Checking." I walk forward and press my hand on the side of the tree. Again, I reach out with my senses. Nothing. Hmm, what's wrong with this tree? Is it dead? I look up and see small, bright green leaves covering the branches. Yet, despite the apparent health of the tree, nothing seems to be living on or inside of it. No vibrations from the movement of animals or insects above in the branches or below.

"It's... umm, clear."

"Umm clear?" Santos says, his tone questioning. "That doesn't sound good to me." He glances around the area for a moment. "What's the 'umm' about?"

"It's just quiet. Eerily so. I don't even sense the slightest bit of life in or around this tree." I point to the leaves above. "But, clearly, it's alive."

"Who gives a fuck how a tree sounds? Let's get the damn sky-eye and hit the road," Petersen bellows in his deep baritone. "The forward camp is waiting."

Tilting his head to the side, Santos takes a step closer to me. "I'm not understanding. What does that mean, exactly?"

"Well, it means exactly what I said. There's nothing. No birds, no bugs... nothing. Not an ounce of activity that one would consider normal for a tree of this size. It reads abnormally."

"Abnormal? Are you serious? What about Southies isn't abnormal?" Petersen says, his back to me, holding the tracker high towards the dark tree in front of us. "Look, the sky-eye is close. Maybe on the second floor? Close enough for me to retrieve in a few seconds, max."

Santos doesn't respond. He stands at the dark entrance, looking. I can almost see the wheels turning in his mind.

In a huff, Petersen turns. "We need to get the sky-eye —"

Santos lifts his hand in front of Petersen, silencing him. "I know, but just... just wait a moment, Petersen. Let me think."

What's going on in his mind? "Share please. Otherwise, we're just standing here waiting," I add, trying to solicit some response, some indication of what he's ruminating on.

He only shakes his head. "No. No, it's not right."

With a loud obnoxious sigh, Petersen smacks himself on the forehead. "Oh God, not you too. What's wrong now?"

"All of it. This entire situation isn't right. This tree is the only one in the area that has zero signs of life. The sky-eye was obviously taken, but not completely disabled, allowing us to find it easily. They clearly disassembled all the other machines, why not this one sky-eye? And look around, man. The area's littered with Northern tech, some of it recent, but not a single sign of patrols anywhere. Why?"

He's sharp. "Smells like a trap?"

"Reeks of it. Either this is a trap, or the Southies are getting lazy." He turns to face us. "I've yet to meet a lazy Southie, how about ya'll?"

Clearly frustrated, Petersen glares at the screen, then at the dark entrance in front of Santos. "We have direct orders to get the sky-eye, Santos," Petersen says, stepping closer. "Then we have to head to the front and make sure they're okay."

"I also have direct orders to keep this scouting team alive. That includes you, Petersen."

"I agree with Santos. It could be booby-trapped in there. Still, I doubt if we'll find anything useful. It's not worth it to hope they left something we can use on that sky-eye."

"You're assuming they've taken it apart and/or wiped the memory?" Santos asks, taking another step towards the tree's open doorway, stopping inches from the threshold. He cranes his neck, looking around the darkness from a safe distance. "If so, I'm inclined to agree."

"It's the most logical thing to do. We'd do it."

Santos nods. "Very true."

"What the hell? Now we're listening to the ranger about tactics?"

In a flash, Santos turns and dashes in front of Petersen. "What the hell, man, you got a problem with Martinez being a ranger?"

"I have a problem with all rangers! Her included," he says, with a nod in my direction. "Bottom line is, none of you civilian FOGs are my *real* team... my real team was lost years ago. They were soldiers, real ones, every one of them. Jacob and me, we're the only ones left alive. The rest are dead because we followed brain-dead rangers into fights. This? This is just another situation where the ranger doesn't know shit, but everyone still takes their advice anyway. If they actually knew what to do, they wouldn't be getting their asses blown off so often."

"Then be my guest, Petersen, head inside and get the sky-eye," I reply, sweeping my hand towards the entryway. "Go ahead and get yourself blown to shit." At this point, I couldn't care less.

A tense silence falls between the three of us.

The hard thumping sound of Petersen's heart drums out of his chest, and he prepares to run inside.

"Stop!" Santos yells. "What the hell is wrong with you, Petersen? We don't need to lose another FOG because he took on some idiotic dare."

"You heard what she said, Santos!"

"What are you, twelve?! Get your shit together, Petersen." Santos turns to me and frowns. "And you? You should know better. We need to succeed here, and success includes all of us returning, intact." Taking a deep breath, David looks up into the green canopy about us. "We *all* need to survive this little scouting mission."

"So what now? We stand here looking at one another and hope for the eye to come down on its own?" Petersen asks.

Facing the door frame, Santos pulls his black gloves tight and throws a sharp right cross into the dark wood. With a thunk, the punch is stopped dead. "Interesting. Nothing. Not even a scratch."

Donning his knuckle-dusters, Petersen sighs. "Really? Maybe it's because you're just a striker. Here, let a tank have a go." Handing the scanner to me, Petersen struts up alongside Santos. He rolls his shoulders and unleashes a thundering punch. The force of the blow causes the entire tree to shudder and sends shock-waves through the ground beneath us. "There ya go," he says, grinning at the massive fracture his punch created in the door frame.

A thick layer of bark begins to slips down, groaning with each inch it moves as it splits from the top of the makeshift door jam, threatening to fall. "There's a lesson for you. Don't let a striker do what only a tank can."

Too much noise for such a small slab of wood. "Petersen, step back," I order.

"What?"

Like metal scraping against metal, the chunk falls with a screech. "Step back now!" I yell as it dislodges and speeds to the ground.

To our surprise, the bark slab creates a crater far deeper than any one of us would have imagined.

"What the fuck! That little bit of wood hit the ground like it was made of pure compressed carbon steel alloy," Petersen says, not getting any closer, but straining his head forward to see. "What the hell kind of shit is this?"

"It's dense... far more so than any wood I've ever seen before." I step forward to pick at the slightly concave mass. Digging my finger into the jagged edges of the thick slab, I see the familiar crystalline specks. "The edges of it sparkle like there are crystals embedded within. Just like the tree bark at the village border."

"You knew it was going to be that heavy?" Santos asks.

"No, but I do know that wood scraping against wood doesn't sound like the noise we heard. But, in regards to the crystalline flecks, I saw the same or similar appearance in the bark of those black trees bordering this village." I inspect the tip of my finger, holding it close to my face. "It looks like impurities trapped in the wood. Still, it's not like the bark from those trees — this is far heavier."

51

I move towards what I previously thought was a scorched portion of the tree. "I thought this was burnt when I initially saw this mark. Possibly the result of something burning in these piles. Now... I'm starting to think my initial assumption was completely wrong. This is like nothing I've ever encountered before."

Coming close to the mark, David scratches the blackened bark on the tree. "What do you think it is?"

"No idea. But whatever it is, nothing alive wants to be around it. It's like the tree is infected."

In a rush of air, Jackson arrives. "We headed out now?" he asks, stopping inches from my side.

He's quickly followed by Clarence. "Looks like the gang's all here. We ready to move on to the forward camp?"

Slamming his fist into the bark lying in its self-made indentation, David creates a crack on the surface. "Amazing." He takes out a small blade and digs into the black wood.

His face bewildered, Marshall looks at each of us in turn as Santos picks at it.

"We're getting a sample I assume?" I ask.

"Exactly. Hand me the master radio, Marshall."

Clarence raises an eyebrow at me with a bewildered look on his face as he hands Santos a small headset from his backpack.

David inserts the small receiver in his ear. "Command, this is Jackrabbit. Patch me through to Powell." His brown eyes flow around the tree and between our team as he waits. "We have a situation with the package," he says, then pauses. "No, no casualties, but the package cannot be retrieved... no, it's not destroyed, it's just not within reach."

As good of an excuse as any.

With a flick of his thumb, he moves the call button into mute. "Martinez, please grab my scanner and a small sample container." He turns his back to me slightly.

"In your pack?"

"Yes, rear-left compartment."

With the pack still on his back, I search it exactly where he requested. Nothing but maps. I check the other side... ah, here it is. "Got them," I say, handing the items to him over his shoulder.

Facing me, he takes the container from my hand. "Scan it for me please."

Suddenly, I hear the thud of a heartbeat, the rush of breath, and the subtle clicks and clack of metal.

Rifle!

"Move!" I yell, tossing Santos over and behind one of the massive piles. "Sniper!"

I hear the buzz of the bullet pass the back of my head as David and I tumble into cover.

In a flash, everyone else moves behind mounds of metal as well. Instinctively, I push my senses even further outward, searching for more information on our assailant.

"Where's it coming from?" David says as we untangle ourselves.

"Our two! The sniper is firing from our two!"

"Command, we're taking fire. I repeat, we are taking fire," Santos barks into the mic. Even with the tumbling and fumbling, he manages to hold onto both the sample and the container, snapping the blue plastic lid closed over the black bark inside.

"Command, we're taking fire. I repeat, we are taking fire. Number of hostiles currently unknown. Martinez, give me a report."

He's so calm now.

"Only picking up one person, but... he's on the move. No longer at our two."

"Give us a direction, Ranger!" Petersen yells, his shoulders hunched up to his ears as he lies on his side behind the smallest metal pile. It does a poor job of covering him.

"Don't know anymore! As I said, he's moving!"

Another shot! With my senses open, I feel the pressure of the air as the bullet slices through it.

"Agghh!" Petersen yells out.

53

I didn't have the luxury of the shooter's physical cues on that shot. But, I can tell the enemy is close. "Shooter has moved closer. About five hundred yards..." What was that? Sounds like a cough. Got him! "He's at our four!" I announce.

"I got this mutherfucker!" Petersen barks, exploding up from his prone position and through the pile of parts that didn't hide him much. He races towards our assailant. He's slow and clumsy — maybe the wounded leg is a hindrance.

"Damn it, Petersen, stop! Fuck," Santos yells. "Martinez, go with him."

And I do, taking off in a burst. I enhance my vision, enabling my mind to react to the rapid influx of data racing towards me as I follow behind. The world blurs at the edges of my vision, leaving only what's directly ahead in total focus.

One of the benefits of being a tank is toughness, and Petersen makes full use of that trait as he storms through, never around, everything in his path. His black blood still leaks from the shot he took to his calf. The blood marks his path.

"Got your ass!" Petersen yells, wielding the most current iteration of the popular knuckle-dusters that tanks use in hand-to-hand combat. Painted black, the charged steel looks as if it grew from his gloves, its plates molded to fit his massive fists.

But, even with all of the inhuman speed FOGs can attain, the Guardsmen, with his eyes closed, easily sidesteps Petersen's explosive attack and prepares to blow his brains out with that odd rifle he's holding.

I push hard. Slowly the barrel rises closer and closer to Petersen's temple. I'll beat him to the punch for certain.

It's as if the Guardsmen knows exactly where attacks will land, and evades accordingly. Petersen would have been better served using one of the nearby trees to hit the Guardsmen with instead of actually trying to punch him. Even a Guardsmen cannot avoid attacks that cover a large area. If I were not here, he'd only succeed in getting himself killed.

I reach the Guardsmen and prepare to attack. Pushing all of the muscles in my arm and shoulder, I propel the hardened alloy blade I carry through the air as fast as possible. Even if he knows the path of my attacks, there's nothing the Guardsmen can do to avoid them all. They are varied, coming at many different angles, and as usual, at least one will land. As the blade speeds towards him, I can already see the first two slashes will miss completely as he's already moving out of their path. In truth, I never expected to hit with those anyway. It's the ones coming afterward that will find blood.

The third strike grazes his chest, splitting the skin of his right pectoral muscle. It's not deep enough to stop him. The fourth penetrates. I feel it cleave through the hardened bone and muscles of his calf, removing the lower half. The fifth strike, aimed at cleaving through his arm at the bicep, only succeeds in removing his left hand at the wrist.

No weapon, unable to retreat due to his lost foot, and outnumbered four to one... We now have ourselves a prisoner.

He's no longer a danger to me, so I allow my body to relax, and almost instantly I begin to ache from the exertion. Santos and the others arrive to the sound of my blade sliding into its sheath and the thud of the Guardsmen's body and limbs falling to the ground, separately. He squirts a stream of blood as dark as my own, yet already, the flow of blood is ceasing.

The similarities between FOGs and Guardsmen is clear as the process used to create Fingers of God is based on the biology of the latter. So, their blood and our blood is far more alike than different. In many ways, we are them.

"Where's the weapon?" Santos barks to the now disabled sniper.

He doesn't react. He doesn't need to. I spot the rifle he tossed at the first slash a few yards away in the underbrush. But why dump the rifle at all? It's not much of a weapon. "It's over there," I say, pointing to the beautiful purple-flowering bush. The bush was unable to hide the matte black of the rifle butt.

Moving where I instructed, Clarence picks it up. "I got it, Sarge." He gives the weapon a confused look. "Short magazine, really short," he says, appearing next to Santos with the weapon in hand.

Taking it, Santos looks to Petersen. "How's the leg?" he asks, yanking out the cartridge and handing the impotent rifle to Jackson. He flicks the remaining three bullets into his hand from the magazine.

Rubbing his calf, Petersen watches as blood leaks down his boot. "It'll heal," he mutters.

"Good," Santos says, kneeling in front of the wounded Guardsmen, who is attempting to quietly maneuver the lower half of his calf back into place. It does not go unnoticed. With a glance at the severed portion of the leg, then at the Guardsmen's eyes, Santos smacks the partial limb out of reach.

Given time, he could have simply held the sections together and the two would eventually fuse. They're tough bastards.

"Now tell us, Southie, why the hell would you bring a crappy rifle and only have... what, five bullets in total? Not to mention those bullets are some weird, glittery black bullets. What are these, some kind of poisonous ammo?" David says, holding one of the bullets up to the Keynosian before passing it to Petersen.

The Keynosian calmly inspects the already sealed stump that once held his left hand.

Drawing his hand down his face, David sighs. "Nothing about this is right. Not a goddamn thing." Getting closer to the Keynosian, David grits his teeth. "How about this, you give us information, I give you back your leg. Is that a fair deal? It's just us out here — no one will know about the deal but us. We want to go back home, and I'm sure you'd rather have the ability to walk again. So, maybe we can help each other out here? You tell me what I want to know, I give your ability to walk back, and we can call it even, okay?"

The Guardsmen's eyes quickly inspect each of us in turn, before settling on me. "You, you're a tracker, yes?" he asks, his voice as gruff as Petersen's.

Tracker? "Is that what you call us?" I ask.

"Not 'us,'" he replies, waving his remaining hand dismissively to the others, "*You.*" A faint grin crosses his lips. "We thought there were no more left. An error that was not accounted for."

Snapping his fingers a few times close to the Guardsmen's face, Santos frowns. "Hey! I asked you a question. What are these black bullets made of? Why are you —"

"I don't know," he snaps back, his chin slightly raised. Something about the way he expresses himself yells a level of self-importance. To be in this situation, crippled and surrounded, yet he still glares hard into Santos' eyes. It doesn't last long before he turns his attention towards me again. "Are there more of your specific kind remaining?"

"What the fuck... Do you not know how this works? This is *our* opportunity to interrogate *you*," Santos says loudly. "We can kill you right here, right now. Torture you for hours before you eventually give us the information we want."

"I do not fear death. I do not fear pain. Mother Earth will keep my spirit" — he coughs — "through all adversity."

"What the fuck makes you think you'll die anytime soon?" Petersen adds, his leg still oozing blood. He clutches it tight, gritting his teeth. Is he in pain? A single bullet wound shouldn't be much of a problem for such a high-level FOG. "I can make sure it lasts... days even."

He should have healed by now, like the Guardsmen, whose injuries are far greater.

"Yes, there are more of my kind. Many more," I lie. "They are turning us out on an assembly line as we speak."

He laughs, then releases a brutal hacking cough that makes Clarence clutch his chest in empathy. After wiping a smear of black blood from his lips, he composes himself and smiles. "I do not believe you. If that were so, you would have overrun us by now. Since you have not, I think it is safe to say that those like you, the ones that move with great speed and can sense the world as well as we, your numbers are finally dwindling. Finally." The wound on his chest is already gone, leaving

57

only the faint hint of a scar. If Santos didn't stop him from putting his leg back in place, he would be ready to make a run for it.

Those aren't moles on his neck. What is that? Portions of the Guardsmen's brown skin look hardened, dotted with strange protrusions that resemble plugs of bark. A large one sits just under the fading scar of where I cut him. His curly brown hair is well groomed and cut short, but on his head there are more of those strange protrusions. He sits up and places his stumped arm on his lap. There's a strange scent in his blood. It reminds me of mold. Never smelled that before either.

"Have you sensed it already, tracker?" he says.

Yes, I have. It's all over him. "You're sick... dying, right?"

He nods.

"Goddamn it!" Santos exclaims, thrusting his fist hard into his other hand, standing, and turning abruptly. He paces away, then back.

"What? What's wrong?" Petersen asks, confusion filling his features as he watches Santos. He doesn't get it.

Extending his hand towards the Guardsmen, Santos shakes his head. "He's a fuckin' dead end. That's why he's here by himself."

The Guardsmen only grins.

"It'll be a waste of time to interrogate this guy. Torture? That'll probably only lead to his death, and I highly doubt he's concerned about dying now."

"We can start now!" Petersen rushes over to the Guardsmen, grabs his collar, and stares in his face with a sadistic grin.

I clutch his wrist. "Petersen, I think we need to get that bullet out," I say, pointing down to his leg.

"What are you talkin' about?"

Concern on his face, Santos bends down to get a closer look at Petersen's leg. "She's right. You're still bleeding, a lot in fact." Turning to the Guardsmen, Santos holds a black bullet close to the Keynosian's face. "What did you shoot him with? What are these bullets made out of?"

The Guardsmen's lungs rattle as he chuckles. Whatever he has, it's killing him quickly. He does not have long.

"They are made of death," he coughs out. "And they are made for you, the Undying."

"Undying? Is that what you call us?" I ask.

The Keynosian nods, his dark eyes appearing darker still, despite the light of a glowing heat lamp, a device we all carry in our backpacks. No more than two inches tall, the lamps expand like putty into a column of bright orange, molten composite. He's yet to take his eyes from it.

"My name is Takdeer."

Interesting. "Takdeer." I nod. As long as there has been a Northern Alliance, there has been a Keynosa. Yet, at forty plus years, I've never had a conversation with my nation's only neighbor. I wonder if that extends to the vast majority of Northerners?

"It is a shame we have met under such unfortunate circumstances..." He leans forward a bit, coaxing me to offer him my name with a tilt of his head.

I oblige him. "Jocelyn." It couldn't hurt.

He nods, giving a tight-lipped smile.

"So, Takdeer, will the leg be salvageable? It looks fine, but I have very little knowledge of how Guardsmen heal."

"Doubtful. It does not matter though. I'm bound for Mother's embrace soon. Still, I must thank you for not allowing me to be tortured."

"Don't thank me, thank Sergeant Santos."

"Why? Would you have allowed me to be tortured?"

"Well, I don't really have a say."

His face changes. A look of sorrow fills his face. "No, sister, you always have a say. No one can take that from you."

"Southie, if I were you, I'd shut up about torture," David says, tightening the straps of his backpack as it lies on the moss-carpeted sidewalk. "Each time I look at Petersen here, my aversion to the idea of intense interrogation shrinks."

Petersen is still bleeding, but only barely. Even after retrieving the bullet, which took all of our combined strength and skill, the reluctance of the wound to completely seal is bizarre. Dressed and bandaged, it still shows a dribble of blood seepage, darkening the bandage at the site of penetration.

Still, it's only a gunshot wound! I've taken so many such injuries and recovered, I have to wonder if those bullets are indeed made of death. But, whatever those bullets are actually made out of, their chief ability seems to be the suppression of our ability to heal. That alone is indeed death for FOGs.

"Clearly the black bullet you fired into his leg hampers his healing. Is there anything beyond that?" I ask, kindness in my voice. Fear does not move him to speak, so I'll try sweet-water instead of vinegar.

"Does it have to do anything else, Jocelyn?" Takdeer answers. "Just cutting an Undying's healing to half would give us a huge advantage."

He's right of course. It doesn't matter what else it does. If it takes away our biggest asset, it needn't do much else.

"How the hell is Petersen sleeping? Shit, I hate sleeping outside. Too open," Clarence says, standing by the entrance to an empty home. "Why couldn't we just sleep in here?"

"And have us all in a confined space with only one exit? Not the best idea, Marshall," Santos says. "We have the charged-sheets up, so we're safe enough."

Santos walks to where I'm seated, places a hand on my shoulder, and turns to face our prisoner. "Takdeer was it?" he asks.

"Yes, Takdeer."

"You didn't answer the lady's question. Is that all the bullets do?"

For a moment, Takdeer appears to weigh the situation in his mind, breathing deep as he stares into a clump of grass bordering the moss sidewalk. "As far as I know, yes. If an Undying is hit, it will cause great injury. The bullets are a special ammunition."

"Where are they working on it?" I ask. "And we call ourselves FOGs, or Fingers of God."

"If you say so... but I don't have an answer to your last question, such information I didn't care to ask," Takdeer answers, turning around to face the heating element. Maybe he's hungry? Wisps of smoke slowly rise from within the pot standing on the element. We've decided to combine the insta-meals instead of eating them alone.

"Good planning. You certainly don't want a Guardsmen to be captured, tortured, and have that information cut out of him," Jackson says. He stands to check on our dinner that's beginning to boil. "It also helps that you're dying."

"So, is there a way to reverse the effects of the bullet?" Santos asks.

"I am sorry, David. I am only a soldier, not a scientist. All that I am aware of, is the fact that the bullets are not our usual ordnance. I was just sent to test it before I rejoin."

"Rejoin? Oh, right, you mean die. You have to know that even with these new bullets, your side can't win."

Takdeer nods and releases a reluctant grin. "We will still fight if there is even the slightest opportunity for victory. That ordnance, it gives us an opportunity," he says, motioning with his stump towards Petersen's wounded leg.

Santos grits his teeth and rubs his face hard before giving it a shake. "More people will die the longer your people keep this war going."

"I agree."

"So help us stop this."

"I would ask the same of you and your people."

And here we are, neither side willing to relent. Both sides are guaranteed to lose more lives as we continue our collective refusal to give in to the other. But, what choice do any of us have in war? To surrender would be tantamount to turning our backs on our families, on our friends, and on our country. No, neither Keynosian nor

Northern Alliance will give up unless completely cowed. So, more death is assured as this war will certainly continue. The death, the fighting, the dying... all over nothing more than strips of land floating atop vast oceans.

Yet, Takdeer tells me I always have a choice.

Santos walks to the pot and peeks in. "Takdeer, it'll be a while before we can ship you off to a military prison, so sit tight." Santos turns to me and shrugs. "There's nothing left for us to do here, and going on to the forward camp wouldn't make much sense knowing that Guardsmen have this new ordnance. We have to report this and have it examined as soon as possible. This is now priority."

"You're right about that. There's nothing left for us here," I reply, even though the comment was probably rhetorical.

I glance at Takdeer. "We'll have to keep you restrained. I'm sure you understand."

Even as the words leave my mouth, Clarence has moved behind the Guardsmen, a coma collar opened and ready to be placed around the man's neck.

He nods, regarding me with another tight grin.

Then, with a click, the collar locks in place. A barb stabs our prisoner at the base of his neck and injects a tranquilizing cocktail. He only winces slightly as his body slumps down. And so, Takdeer tumbles into a deep sleep. The complete oblivion of those drugs is probably no different than the stasis sleep our own FOG soldiers have to endure.

I wonder if he's dreaming?

"Okay, everyone, food's done," Jackson says, slowly stirring the pot with a small spoon placed so deep into the mixture his fingertips are barely able to hold the utensil.

With a slap, Santos wakes the snoring Petersen. In an instant, he's up and ready for a fight. We all chuckle.

"Come on, man. Calm down and get some grub."

Clarence has already ladled spoonfuls of the hearty soup into his small collapsible bowl.

Santos watches me from over the glowing light of our heat lamp, a worried look on his face.

This place is so beautiful. The fountain, the trees, all of it is like a fairytale. But soon, our Northern war machine will pass through here and destroy it all, laying waste to this man-made Eden. Until that end comes at the sound of sputtering exhaust and the hiss of poison spewing about, I'm content to enjoy the fleeting peace and beauty of both my surroundings and the joyous faces of men eating what could be their last meal.

CHAPTER 3

FRIEND OF MY FRIEND

A nd here we are," Santos says as he slices open the dead Guardsmen's face from chin to earlobe to remove a small device hidden under the skin.

"How long did you know he had a transmitter on him?" Jackson says, shaking his head slightly as he rakes his fingers though his hair. He casually whisks a lock behind his ear as his hand passes through.

With a jerk, Santos snaps the paper-thin cord tethering the transmitter to a receiver, then lets the parts slip from his hands. The device is so light it nearly floats to the moss sidewalk Takdeer's dead body lies on. "I had an inkling as soon as he mentioned he was testing the bullets. He needed a way to report back to his team without their usual whistle codes, but I doubt they were close enough anyway. Wouldn't want to risk unnecessary casualties."

Jackson squats next to Santos and brushes his finger along the still-bloody transmitter. "What if they all have these little comm devices? You think that's how they're able to evade our attacks so well? I mean, if they're in constant communication with one another it could be like seeing everything at once."

"That still wouldn't account for the times they move even before getting attacked," Clarence says, keeping an eye on our surroundings, his pistol in hand. "And it wouldn't make sense to also do those weird whistles if they could just talk."

Is he thinking what I'm thinking? There are more Keynosians out there... watching us, waiting for an opening to strike. I follow suit, placing my hand on my blade.

"Should've let me torture his ass," Petersen complains as he touches the black-stained gauze covering his wound. Incredible. Even now, he's *still* not completely healed. I can smell fresh blood oozing from the wound.

Getting up from his crouched position, Petersen stands over the corpse of the Guardsmen and frowns.

He died quietly. Good for him. I can't imagine him, or anyone, living their remaining days in that wasteland we call a military prison. I'm no bleeding heart. I enlisted willingly, and will fight for my homeland to the end, but it's shameful the way captured Keynosians are rounded up and placed into conditions that are far worse than any slum of a third-world country. Those camps are nothing more than massive, compacted landfills that we decided to put tents on top of. For a people used to this beautiful landscape, that must seem like pure hell.

"So what do we do with the body? We taking it back?" Petersen groans. "I'm not carrying it."

"Leave him," Clarence answers. "It's just another dead body."

Another nameless soldier's corpse littering the ground? Is that all you see nowadays, Clarence? But this one... he had a name. Takdeer.

"I'll bury him," I offer.

"I'll help," Santos says immediately, trench-shovel already in his hand. Was he already planning to bury the man? "It'll be a few minutes before the sun's fully up, and since I won't be sending any of you into this potentially booby-trapped building, there's not much else for this group to do but return to the base and report everything we've found."

"So, we're really not going to the forward camp?" Clarence asks.

"Not without a larger force, no. Remember, this is only a scouting mission. Information first, and the info I'm getting here is the forward camp is either badly compromised or already lost," Santos says with the shovel on his shoulder. "We also have the massive problem of these bullets. That has to take full priority over everything else, forward camp included. Then, there's that strange, heavy wood over the doorway. I'm positive there's a connection between the two."

Standing, Jackson wipes his hand on his black pants. "Powell's not going to be happy about the sky-eye."

"Well, he's not here, and I don't see the point. If the Keynosians are screwing around with our tech, I think it's safe to assume whatever we find on the sky-eye is going to be bullshit, and that's if we find anything other than a bomb or something inside. Command will probably just send a few norm sweepers in to retrieve it when we pass through here on the way to the camp. We're not equipped to deal with Keynosian mines and traps, nor are we going to be able to handle an all-out assault if they mount one.

"We've scouted and found some extraordinary information. Time to head back and have the techs figure it all out before moving forward."

Santos' eyes sweep over Takdeer's body, stopping at his chest. He squats over the corpse and raises his hand to me. "Hand me your blade, please," he says, not looking up from the body.

I do as requested. "What are you going to do now?" I ask.

Don't get my weapon all bloody, please.

Blade in hand, Santos carefully cuts the dead Guardsmen's thick forest-green uniform top open to reveal his bare chest, which is dotted with the same woody protrusions he had on his neck and under the hair on his head. Many are far larger, covering most of the exposed skin.

There's one in particular that stands out. It's white, not brown like the others. Reminds me of a giant pimple ready to burst.

"Just so ya'll know, what I'm doing is checking his Final Gift."

"His what?" Jackson and I say in unison.

"All Keynosian soldiers carry a seed close to their chest, just under the skin. They call it their Final Gift," Santos says, tapping the white growth with the tip of my blade. "From my understanding, the seed is tiny at first, about the size of a poppy seed. But, after death, it feeds on the decomposing body and starts to grow in size. It's something specific to Guardsmen — they allow their bodies to become food for a new tree. They say the seed will grow into a thirty-foot tree in little over a month.

"Apparently they make great mulch."

"They do that to themselves? Sounds sick," Clarence says.

"As sick as cutting the body open, taking out the organs, then pumping formaldehyde to the remains for preservation? No, it's just a different normal. After all, the Keynosians believe in cycles. Born of the Earth, and at death, returning to it. Nothing is new or old, it's all recycled material to them. 'From death springs life and all life must die for the sake of the new.'

"If someone has that kind of world view, it isn't crazy to use their corpse to grow new trees. In fact, placing the seed near the heart is a sign of respect for not only the planet, but for their offspring. What do we give our children other than bills to pay when we die? Southies, they grow food from their corpses," he says, squinting slightly.

"Yep, it's definitely some kind of fruit tree. See here, see the dark specks just underneath the seed's skin? That's usually a sign of the kind of tree it'll become." He hands me back my blade. Slowly, he slides his hands under the corpse.

"Okay, you've got some explaining to do. How do you know all of this, Santos?" I ask. I'm more curious about the man now than ever before.

He smiles. "I was a teacher," he says, standing to lift the corpse. "And as the war drew closer, my students began asking questions about Keynosa. Of course, I didn't want to sound stupid — can't do that in front of your students — so I started doing some research on their culture."

"I've seen you and Gunny fight before," Petersen says with a grin. "I woulda never thought teacher. Special Forces, sure, but teacher, never."

Santos turns towards the tree line, his cargo in his arms. "Gunny's the military man. I'm just a pansy-ass teacher who took a few boxing lessons," he responds with a chuckle.

"You see something?" Clarence questions, turning in the direction Santos is now fixed on.

"No, just looking for a good place to plant him that's far enough away from the village. In a few days this village is going to be dusted with RX, just like everything else Keynosian north and south of here. So, Mr. Takdeer will need to be planted no less than a mile away for his Final Gift to have a chance to survive and grow."

"No one else thinks this is stupid?" Petersen asks, his expression confused as he opens his arms wide, prepared to embrace all others willing to dissent.

"How about over there, past those trees?" Jackson recommends.

"Wouldn't further south be better?" Marshall adds. "Like over there in that brush."

"Not bad, but I was thinking about that hill over there. It looks like a great spot," Santos says, pointing his chin towards a distant, tree-bare mound.

"It'll fill in the landscape, get plenty of sun... a perfect location to plant a tree," I add.

Jackson nods, turning as he does so. "It's a shame we're going to kill all of this beautiful foliage."

"Hopefully, they'll just stick to potentially dangerous areas and not drop that shit on everything," I say.

Not likely, but there's always hope.

"Okay, we're burning daylight, folks. Petersen, please pack up the gear. We're heading back as soon as all of the loose strings are tied. Marshall, do me a favor and verify the repeaters are still up. I want to know for certain that, at the very least, our comms with the forward camp are functional. If they're damaged, tampered with, or removed, get back here as soon as possible." With a jab of his elbow into Jackson's back, Santos points with his head towards the massive tree he placed the new sky-eye in. "Verify and return ASAP. I don't want any missing equipment when we leave."

"On it." Jackson sighs.

"Martinez, you're with me?"

"Yes, sir."

Shaking his head in disbelief, Petersen gets started with the packing, limping about as Jackson and Marshall take off in a flash. I follow Santos westward.

Was this on purpose? Is he trying to get me alone with him? I feel a quiet smile rising. As much as I try to suppress it, a feeling of elation stirs in the pit of my stomach. I like him.

A shallow grave. Something about making a shallow grave feels disconcerting. Maybe it's the idea that the body could be mutilated by some animal, despite David's assurance to the opposite. We quietly look down at the mound of dirt we've created to cover the corpse of a person we barely knew.

I wonder if David wants to say something?

"You want to say anything, Martinez?" Santos asks, beating me to the punch.

I don't like funerals. All of the crying, all of the false words of adoration and concern. But yet, something should be said... but what? He was my enemy. I'm sure many Alliance soldiers died at his hand, just as I've taken the lives of many Keynosians. My country tells me I should hate him. But these thoughts, these beliefs about hate and patriotism, don't move my tongue.

He told me I always have a choice.

"I wish I knew more about you, Takdeer. Strange for me to wish that for my enemy, but I do." My eyes meet David's for a moment. "I don't hate you," I say, and shift my gaze back to the loose dirt covering the mound. "So I can't wish pain upon you. Instead, I wish you a good journey. Let your life be renewed and your sins washed clean. Enjoy the ride, Takdeer."

David's once stoic face breaks into a smile. "I was just going to say something weak like 'good luck, Southie,' but you took it *there*. Once again I find myself impressed by you, Martinez."

I chuckle. "I'm more impressed that you know so much about Keynosians."

"Considering the fact that I grew up a few minutes from Keynosa's beach city SeaSun, it shouldn't be that much of a surprise."

"Oh, you're from South Beacon?"

"No, Jefferson County."

Ugh. He seems like such a clean-cut guy, but growing up in Jefferson? To come from there must have been rough. I find my sense of respect for the man growing more and more. "Really? Jefferson's not the easiest place to grow up in."

With a shrug, David waves his hand past himself, guiding me back towards our vanishing camp. "So they say."

We walk slowly together, and for a moment, I think he's going to hold my hand. Silly image. Two hardened soldiers holding hands. Still, the image brings a smile to my face.

"So what did you teach, Sergeant Santos?"

He turns to me and smiles. "High school math."

"Wait, you taught math to kids, in Jefferson?" I ask, my eyes wide in mock shock.

He laughs and takes a big breath as he nods. "There were days I asked the same question... and with the same look of shock."

As I laugh, looking into his bright brown eyes, enjoying his gentle smile, I find myself wanting to make a deeper connection with this man. A more personal connection. If we were out in the world, I'd be tempted to ask him on a date.

But we are not in the world. We are here. We are at war, and I can only smile at the thought.

"What?" he asks.

"I just find it funny. I was a teacher as well."

He mirrors my earlier expression of false surprise.

I nod and chuckle. "Yes, me, a teacher. I taught primary school. Early development."

"Wow, not an easy task. But, if that smile is any indication, you really loved the work," David says.

"Yes, I did. Yet, here I am," I say, waving my hand across the soon-to-be-destroyed landscape.

"So, did you do it for the kids?" he asks. "The Sacrifice, join the war, all of this. Was it for them?"

Did I do it for the kids, the future of my nation? Yes, in a way. I looked into the eyes of my former students and imagined the horror all of the news clips showed, but instead of it happening over there in some far away land, it was happening here on our territory, to our people. It was happening to kids just like the kids in my classroom. I couldn't allow that to happen. I couldn't live with myself if I did. "Yeah, kinda."

He shrugs. "And so, here we both are: teachers fighting for our students. Trying to save an entire nation."

"I tell myself that tale every day." We're not this far into Keynosa solely for the purpose of self-protection. We are here to utterly destroy a foe that nearly wiped our country off of the map. There was a time when I could look in the mirror and see the reflection of a woman fighting for what she thought was the right thing to do. Now, I see only a weapon, made for murder, created by a nation driven by fear.

I truly miss seeing the reflection of a teacher, though. I miss the joy she carried in her expression. I miss myself every day.

I love spending time with Ophelia. Somehow she manages to hang on to her innocence even in the midst of war. Despite being in the recovery unit all morning, getting another pointless checkup, her humor and good cheer holds fast.

I wish Patricia was here as well, but she has to work out. Unlike Ophelia and I, she must keep her body fit if she wants to be of any assistance to us on the battlefield. Weights and her usual run around the compound eats up her free time in the morning.

"I assume you left his man-parts in their proper place?" Ophelia asks, leaning heavily over the counter, one leg off the ground of the dimly lit armory.

Her hair has already grown into a nice, thick carpet of gold. Even in this poor illumination, she shines.

"Not only did I *not* blow them to bits, the thought of explosive castration never crossed my mind," I answer, handing my blade to the older gentleman in charge of the weapons dispensary. "Could you sharpen it for me please?" I ask of him.

He takes it and inspects it for a moment, turning it over in his hands, checking the blade's edge with a small device he pulls from under the counter. "You know we have a new model of cutlass? A few in fact. Charged tech, super strong alloy and everything, never needs sharpening and can fold down to half the size. Why in the world are you still using this older model?" he asks, holding the hilt close to his face. "Oh yeah, the new one's definitely more aerodynamic. It even slides out of the sheath faster. It can also self-charge —"

"I understand, sir. But I'd rather keep the one I have if that's fine with you?" That's my first blade. I trust it. I neither want nor need a newer model. She's perfect the way she is.

He looks at Ophelia, who shrugs. Then, he does the same. "Your choice." On that note, he heads to the back of the armory.

From behind the counter, I can see the sharpening machine in the distance, past the long line of rifles and shelf after shelf of other equipment. It rests there, dusty and unused, in front of a rack full of black armored vests.

"Thank you, sir," I call after him. He doesn't turn as he waves in response.

"I thought he was very attractive when we were at that meeting," Ophelia says.

"Who are you talking about now?"

"Sergeant Santos! The guy who gave you power over his privates?"

The machine buzzes on with a click, filling the room with the steady hum of an old, but still functional, machine.

"Ahh, right. Didn't know we were still talking about him," I lie.

"I mean, he's no Chad, but yeah, he's cute."

As the blade is inserted, the screech of metal grinding metal pours out.

I roll my eyes. Here we go with the Chad talk again. Even with her sanity intact, she brings his name up too often. "So you really think David is attractive?"

"Definitely. Oh wait, hold the phone. You guys are already on a first-name basis?"

"Oh, don't look at me like that. I call you and Patricia by your first names."

"Denial is the first stage of romantic entanglement," she says, punctuating the words with light pokes to my arm. "That's like how *every* romance movie starts, so don't be a cliché, okay? Plus, you know darn well that no one here calls anyone else by their first names unless they're good friends... or lovers," she says with a sly wink.

"It's good to know that I'm on the road to becoming a standard movie cliché. But right now, I'm not interested in any soldiers, thank you very much."

"I get. But I don't think you should ever rule out love. It can happen anywhere at any time. You just got to be open to it."

"Well, thanks. That's good to know."

For a moment she just looks at me. Slowly, a grin starts to form.

"What? Why are you smiling like that?"

"Nothing... you know... just thinking and stuff."

"Must have been a really nice thought for you to smile like that."

She shrugs and her smile widens. "What?" she asks as I continue to look at her suspiciously.

"You tell me." I laugh. There's something brewing in her head.

Ophelia checks to see if the older man in charge here is paying attention. In the same manner, she turns to the entrance, peering to and fro, as if someone other than me is waiting to hear what she has to say. Finally, she moves in close. "So, Jos," she says, barely audible over the buzzing of the sharpening device, "did anything happen out there? Anything... interesting?"

"Like what?" I ask, with a look of incredulity on my face.

"You know, stuff... happening... stuff that happens between two adults. Stuff like that," she says, her voice rising.

She's so silly. "No. I don't know." I'm unable to repress a giggle. "I have no idea what you're talking about, Oa."

She leans in closer, her head bowed slightly, but her eyes remaining fixed on mine. "Did you and Santos have... sex?"

I can't hold back the laughter. "Seriously?"

She laughs, but it's obvious her curiosity isn't quenched. She leans in and gives me a push with her arm against mine. "Well, did you?"

I bump her back. "No one had sex during our *scouting* mission, Oa. If I did do something like that, I'm sure you wouldn't approve, Mother Highsoul," I say mockingly.

The grinding screech ends. The machine stops its whining and my blade is sharp once again.

"Oh, stop it. I'm not judging you or anything. You're not a God-Soul believer, and you haven't taken the Oath of Purity or anything. You can do whatever you like, Jos. And that includes doing stuff with men."

Ophelia quickly returns to an upright position as the attendant, with my blade in hand, makes his way back to us.

"Thank you so much, sir," I say as he hands me my favorite weapon.

I've never understood why so many runners exclusively use guns. They give away your position in a fight. But this, my LR-25 cutlass, made from the hardest metal we've created... she would never do such a thing.

I thank the attendant and head back into the crowd and noisy base. "Hey, Martinez!" I hear over the din. It's Jackson from the sound of it. I turn to see his head bobbing over the crowds of people milling about.

I wave him over. "Hi, Jackson. How are you doing?"

"Oh I'm good, girl," he says from a distance. He quickens his pace, weaving in and out of the foot traffic, and reaches us in a few strides. Immediately he flashes a toothy, warm grin. "A bunch of us are getting ready to head into town. We're going to have a party tonight, unwind a bit. Why don't you join us?"

As I take in all of the man with my eyes, my breath catches in my throat momentarily. My God, he is beautiful. His shoulder-length hair silhouettes a flawless complexion, unusual for a man, even more so for a FOG who has seen his share of battle. He's draped in a well-fitted blue blazer over a tight gray low-cut shirt. The entire ensemble hugs his chiseled torso in all the right places.

Is he wearing makeup? Well yeah, he is. It's so well done, I barely notice. The man just seemed to glow.

He turns to Ophelia and tosses her a smile that could light up Etchton City. "Oh my, where are my manners? I'm Junior Jackson," he says, giving a sideways nod to Ophelia.

"Rogers. Nice to meet you, Junior."

"It's nice to meet you too," Jackson says, broadening his smile.

His lips are glistening with what appears to be sparkling lip gloss. What brand is that?

He extends his hand to Ophelia, who gives it a firm shake.

"Since it's a party with a bunch of straight guys, I figure we can use a few more girls to keep them company." He chuckles. "It's going to be at Sparks, a local club. And since I know the owner, we'll have special seating. Come, it'll be fun."

I let out a slow breath and look around into the darkening sky. It's already getting late. "No, I don't think we'll be able to make it," I answer. "I mean, we'd have to go get dressed, do our makeup..." I scrub my fingers through my hair.

"Santos and Powell will be there as well," Jackson says, raising his eyebrows.

Despite myself, my heart skips a beat.

Ophelia taps me with her elbow. "Sparks you say?" she asks. "Since

76

I missed the last party, I'd love to go to this one."

Suddenly, butterflies appear in the pit of my stomach. "Okay then, I guess we'll be there."

The cool canvas floor offers little protection from the dirt and rock beneath. I stroll through the barracks, between metal-reinforced green beds positioned so close together that only a single person can stand or pass. A small hand-dryer in hand, I walk to my cot. Hopefully my thick mat of hair will be dry soon.

I'm greeted by Patricia standing in front of her bunk. Sparsely covered by a threadbare towel she grips with one hand, she rummages through her footlocker with the other.

"Should I wear this dress again?" Patricia asks Ophelia, lifting a red dress from the gray metal container. As I pass them, my eyes linger on her scarred left side. For a moment, I consider telling her to cover up the injury, but that would be me attempting to dump my shame on her. In truth, I wish I was so bold and confident with my body as she is with her wounded one.

"You should definitely wear it," Ophelia answers, looking up from a small hand mirror, eye shadow in hand. She grins. "You are planning to put panties on, right?"

An abrupt sigh escapes Patricia's lips. "What? It's not like you haven't seen my goodies, Oa."

"Who cares if I see *your* goodies? I'm not interested in seeing you parade your stuff around a club. You're better than that."

"And what would make you think I'd run around a club with my ass out?" Patricia questions. I can feel her getting upset.

Ophelia's expression turns apologetic. She knows she's offended Patricia. "Someone as bold as you? There's no telling what you'd do."

"No telling huh? What's wrong, Oa, you want some of this? Huh?"

"Uh no... I am not gay."

"Really... are you sure?" Patricia dances towards Ophelia, pumping her hands, thrusting her groin forward. "How'd you know if you've never tried?"

"Eww, what are you doing?" Oa groans.

Patricia ignores her and continues to advance towards her bunk.

"Oh my God, Pat, get away!" she says, her face angry, but all the while giggling.

The closer Patricia gets, the further Ophelia retreats, her pillow raised, threatening to bat Patricia away.

"Ladies, please. Have some decorum," a voice scolds. Our collective eyes instantly turn in the direction of an older FOG. She must be in her late forties, possibly early fifties, judging by the bundle of wrinkles at the corners of both her almond eyes and small mouth, as well as the completely silver hair cut short and tight against her skull.

Patricia stops and grabs her towel, covering herself more, her face frozen with shock. The comment has clearly pissed her off.

I'm not happy about it either, actually. Who does this old woman think she is? I want to tell her to shut up, but think better of it. Still, I ought to say something before Patricia does. "Sorry. We'll keep it down, *ma'am*. You must be tired."

The older soldier instantly draws her head back and frowns. "Ma'am? Please, let's not go there." She chuckles bitterly.

I hear Patricia behind me exhale sharply. I agree with her assessment. This woman is pushing all the wrong buttons for me as well.

In a flash, she's in front of us. "Rawlings," she announces. "Ma'am is for women much older than me."

Then it hits me. She smells like medicine. It's the smell of a FOG who frequently uses drugs to stay tethered to reality. "Fine, Rawlings," I say, with a nod. Before I can respond, she flashes again and now her hand rests on Patricia's red gown. She's a ranger. Must be the other one Powell spoke about.

"Are you ladies going to town tonight?" Rawlings asks.

Patricia pulls her dress from Rawlings' fingertips.

"Yes, we are," Ophelia answers for us. "I figure we could stand to have some fun. Enjoy civilization for a while before we head to the front."

Hands on her hips, Rawlings nods at the fabric and smiles. "That red dress is very beautiful." Not taking the earlier hint, Rawlings reaches out and touches the dress' sleeve. "Where'd you have it made?"

Instinctively, Patricia cringes at the intrusion. "Thank you. Had it made for me back East."

She rubs the fabric between her fingers. "And the one sleeve covers your scars?"

No one mentions the scars. What gives this woman the right to do so? Ophelia looks at me, her eyes wide.

"Yeah," Patricia replies.

"Very nice, you must have spent a fortune," Rawlings says, turning to face me.

Rawlings keeps her back to Patricia and looks at Ophelia. I silently mouth, "what the fuck" in slow motion to Patricia. She can only shrug her answer.

"And what are you wearing, young lady?" she asks, her eyes fixed on my comfortable jeans lying on my bunk besides me.

"Jocelyn is one of those relaxed types," Ophelia answers, to my dismay. She's too nice sometimes.

And what does, 'relaxed type' mean, exactly?

"I don't think I've ever seen you dressed up, Jos."

"I dress up," I snap back immediately. "I... I just haven't had either the opportunity, nor desire to do so yet."

Rawlings chuckles. "If that's what you're going to wear, plan on being a wallflower. No one can see how pretty you are in that club if you're wearing that. It's dark, light flashing, and just an all-out assault on your senses. With jeans and I assume that little black sweater on, you'll looks like you're going to a baseball game or something." She turns to the now partially dressed Patricia and the one eye mascaraed Ophelia. "Now they look like they're going to a club."

"She's kinda right. Your outfit is a little bland, Jos," the person I thought was my friend, Ophelia, says.

"What exactly do you mean by that?" I ask. I know exactly what she means. I don't want to hear the answer of course. I rest my hand on the faded blue jeans I've had for nearly a decade. I love these jeans. They're a perfect fit. "You guys don't like my jeans?"

Patricia makes a face that says it all. A one-sided smirk is the answer she gives.

Are they really that bad?

"It's not that, Jos," Ophelia says, standing. "It's just that I... I mean, Pat and I thought you'd wear something more interesting tonight. Something that can really showcase your attributes."

"Thanks for throwing me under the bus," I say.

I thought my jeans did that. "Is that true?" I ask.

She shrugs. "Well, because David's going to be there and all... and we figured you needed to cut loose and have some fun for once. With a man, though... not just us," Patricia adds.

Rawlings' eyes light up. "Oh my god, you know David?" she asks, her hand on my upper arm gently turning me towards her.

This woman is far too touchy-feely for my taste. "I do, yes. Well, sort of. I was on the scouting mission with him yesterday. We just returned," I reply, pulling my arm from her grasp ever so lightly.

A wide smile grows across her face. "Oh, it all makes sense now. You're Martinez!"

Her excitement and the fact that she knows my name takes me aback. "Yeah..."

"I'm the other ranger! Oh, thank God you're here. These Southies have taken out every other runner we have. I'm sure *you* understand the strain that puts on me."

"We had the same problem in the Mid-South, but we only had a few runners to begin with, so I wasn't shocked when they... when we lost them all," Patricia says. "It's not easy being the first people out in front of a firefight."

"I heard the Keynosians have been targeting runners specifically," Ophelia says. "I guess it's been totally confirmed now."

"That's absolutely true, and let's say I heard it from a very valid source recently." Also known as Takdeer.

"I hate that none of the brass say anything with certainty. It's pretty much been confirmed in the field here on the western front. To go from the most rangers to just me, that couldn't have been an accident or just random happenstance," Rawlings says.

Her lips pressed tight and her makeup still half done, Ophelia gives Rawlings a tight grin. "So sorry to hear that."

Her chest shudders as she inhales deeply, forcing a smile now. "Thank you." Rawlings nods. "I'm just so happy you ladies are here. All of you." Rawlings' eyes linger on Patricia, tears threatening to fall. Lifting her head, Rawlings waves away her grief. "Listen, you girls shouldn't dwell on that. Certainly not before going to a party, right?"

The four of us nod in unison.

"With that said, on to you, Ms. Martinez. I have an idea how I can be of assistance, because I'd feel terrible if I stood idly by while a fellow ranger, and a lovely one at that, went to Sparks looking so plain. We have a reputation to uphold."

She smiles, walking away and waving me to follow. I comply. Although I still find her to be an odd woman, it's obvious she means well. So, I probably shouldn't hold the prior boldness against her.

"I think I have something you'll fit into nicely."

Stopping at a bunk a few beds down, Rawlings opens a double-sized foot-chest and begins to rummage through it. Seconds later she withdraws what looks like a long, white satin pillowcase. "Here it is."

"What is it?"

"A dress of course. Try it on. I think it's prefect for you."

"Simple enough, no?" Rawlings asks, standing next to Ophelia and Patricia a few yards in front of me.

"You look good, Jos." Ophelia nods. "Really good."

Patricia steps forward, holding up my pair of black strappy heels, the same ones I intended to wear with my jeans. "I agree. The dress shows all of the good stuff." She hands me my shoes with a huge smile.

"On to the accessories!" Rawlings calls out, flashing back to her footlocker. Ophelia and Patricia do the same, all three now intent on finding something suitable for me to wear along with this revealing dress. It's very form-fitting, one would even call it tight, much to my dismay. It rises just above my knees and cuts low in the front, exposing my sternum and a lot of cleavage. The thin shoulder straps expose too much of my arms it feels. I have nothing for my fingers to fiddle. The exposure leaves me uneasy. So, I sit, my hands around my waist, feeling vulnerable. How bizarre that even with the perfect body, chiseled from the finest drugs in the world, I still find myself feeling insecure.

"I have some earrings that'll match," Ophelia calls out.

Letting the lid of her chest fall with a bang, Patricia stands. "Bangles here."

Rawlings glances up to see what the others are holding. She drops a bundle of white pearls back into her trunk and continues to search. "I have something that'll go perfectly."

How much stuff did she bring with her?

With Ophelia at my side, fiddling with my earlobes, Patricia slides on the bangles.

Finally, all things in place, I turn towards the mirror and smile. They're right. I do look good. "I like it."

"Like it? Are you nuts, you look great!" Patricia exclaims. She grasps my arms tight from behind, her chin on my bare shoulder, and gives me a squeeze.

"And here they are," Rawlings calls. She now holds a long string of simple black pearls.

Pressing her fingers on her eyes, Ophelia stands slowly. "So, up or down?" she asks, blinking hard and fast.

"Up or down what?" I ask as Rawlings pulls the string of pearls around my neck. It fits close like a comm collar.

"Your hair, Jos. You want it up or down?"

"Much more classy up," Rawlings suggests. I feel her fingers fiddling with the clasp against my bare neck.

"No, no, definitely down. Classy is nice, but down frames her face better," Patricia recommends, running her fingers through my hair from behind, bringing it in front of my shoulders. She seems more excited than I am about tonight.

"I agree, definitely down," Ophelia says.

"Why not a ponytail?" I ask.

Silence.

What's wrong with a ponytail? "Seriously? I can put it in a ponytail and fluff it out. My hair's curly enough."

Flipping my hair from the back, Rawlings places a hand on my shoulder. "Maybe we can blow-dry it straight?"

"Definitely not. Her hair is way too pretty for that. I say just let it out," Patricia says, giving a sassy head shake.

"Yes please," Ophelia adds. "I wish you'd let your hair out more. It's so gorgeous. I wish my hair had half the body yours has."

Rawlings, with her hand on her chin, looks up and into my still-drying hair. "We have a consensus, and out it is, but what about the gray?"

"Oh, leave it," Ophelia says, waving away the suggestion. "It gives her something more. Something..."

"Something strong," Patricia says, shaking her fist into the mirror from behind me. Ophelia, with a wide-eyed smile, nods in agreement.

I haven't seen myself like this is a very long while. There was a time when I used to dress up, a time I went to parties. That life was shattered when I divorced Timothy. As much as I loved him, we simply could not make it work. Specifically, I couldn't make it work, according to him. Even though I moved to his town and basically shaped myself into whatever he wanted me to be. It was never enough. The false Jocelyn he wanted was never enough.

I lost everything after the divorce. My friends were his, our home was on his family's estate. So, in one pen stroke, I was instantly estranged from the life I'd known for six years.

Now, with a heart patched together by personal discovery, friendship, and blood spilled, I can't help but question if I could love again. Even now my heart is still mending. It feels as if I'm eternally in the process of being stitched back together, and I loathe the idea of reopening those old wounds again.

"I can't tell you how long it's been since I've been to an actual club," Ophelia says, running her hand through her short spiky blond hair. After all of the pushing to get me to wear a dress, she's the one in pants. Tight blue slacks, of course, but pants nevertheless.

As we cross the roadway, Patricia thrusts her red-gloved hand up and a car screeches to a halt. "The way Rawlings kept talking about the fun we'd have, I assumed she would be coming with us. Crazy old bird went right to bed."

Nervously, Ophelia follows behind us. "We should be crossing at the crosswalk. It's dangerous to cross in the middle of the street."

As payment for stopping, Patricia blows a kiss to the driver. "Well, we didn't... and what do you care? You can take a car to the head and survive just fine."

With a huff, Ophelia moves past me and sidles up next to Patricia. "I care because if a car were to hit *you*, I'd have to do something rather unseemly to the vehicle, and the driver."

As a tank, there's very little, man or machine, that can stand up to her. "You don't want to go and make Oa wreak havoc on some unsuspecting driver, now do you?" I ask Patricia.

Taking Ophelia's hand into hers, Patricia leans into her friend. "Of course not, my angels." Suddenly pointing ahead, Patricia smiles. "By the way, here we are!"

This club called Sparks is draped in a rainbow of blinking and flashing neon signs. Life-sized photos of scantily clad women are pasted behind thick glass. Sparkling clean, dark-tinted windows show glimpses of flashing lights behind more bright glowing signs that promise instant joy and guaranteed fun. None of it entices me, contrary to the club's grossly obvious attempts to do so.

Sparks' mostly black glass walls are bookended on either side by thick concrete. Music hammers from behind the partially open, tall wooden doors of the club. Now that I hear the music, feel the bass, I'm enticed to enter. By the look of the long line of young partygoers, mostly men, who stand impatiently behind long red velvet ropes anchored by neatly spaced gold-painted poles, I'm not alone.

I feel tired just looking at the children waiting to enter.

"We better hurry up and get on line, guys. People are piling on still," Ophelia says, heading towards the rear of the winding line held in check by a tall, heavily built man dressed in all black.

"Where you going, Oa?" Patricia asks, heading towards the doors.

Her face twists. "Umm, to the back of the line of course."

"Oh no, only ugly girls and men stand in line." Walking straight to the door security guard, Patricia leans forward and whispers into his ear.

Moving closer to me, Ophelia leans near. "What's Pat doing?" she asks.

"Probably getting us in." Like Ophelia and I, some of the people standing in line look on with rapt curiosity. Others look on with complete annoyance.

"Ahead of everyone else?"

"Would you prefer to wait?"

"No... but it doesn't seem fair."

The guard nods. "You three, let's go," the guard grunts as he unhooks the rope from a gold-painted stand.

Patricia turns and winks.

"Let's head to the bar!" Patricia yells, leading us into the mass of gyrating bodies. She weaves through the people, holding my hand as I hold Ophelia's.

"Why are we going to the bar?" I ask.

"This is Jackson's party! The bartender probably can tell us where he is!"

"Up here, you grunts!" The yell comes from above.

Past a rainbow of colors strobing in my eyes, I see Jackson. He's swaying to the music, drink in hand, on the level above the bar, overlooking the masses. His lips almost glow in the club lights, appearing much larger than they truly are. Another very handsome man dances close behind him, oblivious to everyone and everything but Jackson.

"Come on up, girls!" He points towards a stairwell hidden by a long black curtain and smiles. He turns to the obvious suitor and slaps his hand on his bare chest. I can see both the pain and the excitement on the suitor's face, whose hand has drifted to Jackson's hip and grasps it tight.

"Oa, Pat, over here!" I doubt Patricia can hear me, so I tug on her arm and point with my chin.

She gives the okay sign with her fingers, and we quickly move to the black curtain.

Pulling back the drapes, Patricia reveals a soldier kissing and groping a buxom woman. She stinks of cheap perfume and the scent of more than a few men on her. Does he know she's most likely a prostitute? Does he care if she is?

We pass the couple and head up the stairwell. At the top, it opens up into a large platform bordered by thick metal railings. Good idea, you don't want people getting drunk and falling off and into the main bar below. A second bar, much smaller, rests in the rear corner, flanked by two massive semicircular sofas. On the distant one sits David.

"There's Santos," Ophelia says, her voice sing-songy.

"Hey! There's Powell and Santos!" Patricia yells, clearly unable to hear Ophelia over the music. She yanks my hand, pulling me towards the crowd of soldiers.

"I can walk, Pat," I say, but offer minimal resistance to her pulling.

Patricia bounces forward in her red dress and heels, headed directly to Powell, who quickly embraces her with a big hug. Hmm, they act like they know one another. Taken aback, Ophelia and I share a glance before following Patricia. Unlike her, we stop at the edge of the gathering. I don't know most of the people here.

David's eyes find mine and he grins. Quickly, but casually, he stands and excuses his way to me. "I'm surprised to see you here, Martinez."

"You shouldn't be. I'm obviously a fun and interesting person."

"Now that, I'd never doubt."

I find myself uncomfortable under his gaze. Why does he keep staring so deeply into my eyes?

He turns and nods at Ophelia. "It's nice to see you as well, Rogers."

I already feel the nerves in my chest tickling and dancing in the pit of my stomach like I'm some goofy schoolgirl.

"You can call me Ophelia, since we're not in uniform," Ophelia notes, before turning to wave at another gentleman. He's been trying very hard to get her attention since we entered this space.

"Ophelia it is then," he replies. "So, Martinez, may I call you Jocelyn? I mean, we're not in the field at the moment, but that doesn't mean I should assume I have that privilege."

"Well, that depends."

He chuckles. "On what?"

"Depends on what you do tonight," I answer, returning his chuckle. Flirting is fun, especially with someone like David.

"Hey Martinez," Powell says, pointing with a drink as he calls to me.

Why drink at all if you're a FOG? It has no effect on us.

"David mentioned your work yesterday, noting how impressive you were," Jacob says.

Patricia is leaning against him, and his arm is wrapped around her waist. Okay, now that's definitely a high degree of familiarity.

"Just doing my job," I respond.

I give Patricia the eye. He may be attractive, but there's something about him that rubs me the wrong way. She should be careful with him.

Placing his drink on a small glass table positioned directly in the center of the sofa semicircle, Jacob motions with his free hand for all nearby to come closer. "I'm glad you're all here tonight," he announces over the din.

"You're not going to talk shop tonight, are you?" David asks as he leans near my left shoulder.

I stop myself from leaning back into him.

"Come on, David, stop worrying. It'll only take a minute." He waves again, signaling for us to get closer still. "Because we have only two rangers left, I'm going to put together two main teams, each with one."

Patricia smiles and nods knowingly as she looks at me.

"I assume you know who's going to be on whose team?" I ask.

"Well, Jocelyn, since you're the first to open your mouth, I'm putting you on my team."

"What? Why?"

"Why not?" He shrugs. "It'll be you, Santos, Patel, Rogers, and myself. We'll be the strike team. The others will be our main defensive force and also act as major support. That'll be Marshall, Petersen, Jackson, Rawlings, and our lucky charm over there, Dougie."

A cheer erupts from the group as a stocky young man nods and raises his hand like a pageant contestant. He laughs bashfully.

"Okay, that was it," he says, smiling at David. "That's all the shop I'll be discussing tonight, okay by you, David?"

"Yes sir, it is."

As soon as the words leave his lips, the group disperses and we mingle amongst one another and the civilians who've apparently earned enough favor to celebrate with us.

Giving a nod to Jacob, David extends his hand to me. "Now that work is out of the way, care to dance?"

I hesitate. I can't be involved with David, not now, despite the attraction I feel towards him. Sure, it was fine to imagine, to dream of a possibility, but for the fantasy to become reality takes a lot more than I feel willing to give at the moment. I glance back at Patricia, curled up next to Jacob, and Ophelia seated on a glass table chatting with the young man who worked so hard to catch her eye. I feel completely left out.

"You need to ask their permission to dance with me?" David inquires, taking a step in my direction.

He has no idea how much I want to dance with him, but I'd rather not complicate things by mixing business with pleasure.

To hell with it. "Sure," I say, taking a deep breath and his hand. We walk towards the small dance floor at the center of the private ledge we're on.

"Tear it up out there, Jos!" Patricia cheers, a large glass of something pink in her hand.

She seems so comfortable ignoring the stickiness of these kinds of situations.

As the music hammers out of the massive speakers around the building interior, I succumb, allowing him to hold me close.

He's a better dancer than I expected. His movements are well-timed, smooth, enticing even. His smile, wide and bright, expresses his joy as well as his movements do. I'm finding it hard to stay in neutral and keep my distance and find myself melting into his embrace.

What could it hurt? It's just dancing. Right? It's just one night. Tomorrow we are back in the meat grinder of war, marching to the next engagement. But tonight, I think I can allow myself this simple pleasure.

Anyway... I still have the trigger.

CHAPTER 4

HUMAN CAPITAL

I watch as Patricia awakens with a start to the harsh sound of the barracks' morning alarm. "Oh, fuck..." she groans, her hand immediately covering her eyes. "Can someone hand me my rifle so I can shoot that bell down?" Slowly, painfully, she drags her feet from under the thin green blanket I covered her with this morning. She's still wearing her red, now terribly wrinkled, gown. Her feet swing out from under the blanket and off of her bunk, landing on the cold, canvas-covered floor with a slap. For a second she does nothing, just sits there, her head between her open legs, her eyes closed and her dress twisted underneath her.

Only the sober norms and FOGs laugh, the rest moan weakly in commiseration.

"You want some water, sweetheart?" someone calls out.

"I know the perfect remedy for hangovers," another voice calls to her.

"Oh my God, shush!" Patricia grumbles at the offers of assistance.

I strap on my blade, reach under my bunk, and toss a warm bottle of water next to her. It bounces quietly, coming to rest against her exposed thigh.

She looks up at me, her eyes red and squinting. "Don't say it, Jos."

"Say what?"

"I told you so. Don't say I told you so, okay?" Her head falls back down between her thighs.

I feel sorry for her. I remember those days.

I stand and walk to her bunk. Gingerly, I move her dress aside and take a seat. "Wouldn't think of it, Pat. At least not yet," I say, rubbing the back of her neck and gently scratching the hair at the base of her skull. "I'd rather wait until after you've recovered before scolding you. Maybe it'll stick then."

She raises her head, looks up and around, then plants her head back into the red fabric of her dress. "Oa's at the med-tent?"

"Yeah, she's been having headaches again. It was so bad last night, she woke up and immediately rushed to the infirmary."

She sits up straight and grimaces. "Damn, hope she's alright."

"It was probably the alcohol. She was fine until she starting sipping on that cheap wine they had at the bar."

"Ouch." With one hand on her head and the other on her stomach, Patricia falls backward across the bed. "You know, after you guys left, Jacob mentioned the possibility of drug interactions. Apparently Rawlings did want to come, but he suggested she stay in the barracks and rest. He was suspicious of mixing the drugs with alcohol."

Someone moans at the far end of the room.

"I should have said something to her the moment he mentioned it."

"Oa having headaches has nothing to do with you, Pat."

"I know, I know. I just... maybe it would have been helpful? I dunno..."

"Well, don't worry about it. Oa's a grown woman, and there's only so much we can do to look out for her. Although I'm surprised Powell didn't let all of us know about the potential side effects of the new pills." More evidence that he's not to be trusted.

"Well, it was only a theory he said. Probably wasn't something to worry folks with. They've got enough things on their minds."

I'm not keen on that "greater good" defense. It always begs the question, "greater good for whom?" Now is not the time for such a debate, though. "So, 'Jacob' mentioned it, huh?" I grin, hoping to lighten the mood. "You guys are certainly chatty. Something going on there?"

"Ugh... I dunno... maybe a little something, something? He seems interesting, but then gets all weird and stuff, so whatever. Who knows what really goes on in a man's head."

"Doesn't matter what's going on in their heads. The question is, what's going on in your head?"

Propping herself up on her elbow, she takes a breath. "Hmm, well I think he's really interesting. I also think he has a strong presence. I like that. Like a man's man. Reminds me of the guys in my family a little. Plus, everyone really respects him up and down the ladder.

"But, I just... I dunno. I think maybe I was coming on too strong last night? Maybe coming off as..."

"As what?" I ask.

She shrugs her shoulders. "A little slutty maybe?" she says, running her hand along the red fabric of her dress, untwisting it more and more each pass.

"Oh please. You are never... *never* slutty. Being aggressive and sure of yourself is far from behaving like a slut. And since when do you care what anyone thinks?"

"I just... I don't want him thinking of me as a tour-toy, ya know?"

"Oh my god," I say, my face full of shock. "I know what this is... you really like him, don't you?"

Her brown skin reddens. "Well, sorta, kinda. Oh shut up!" We laugh as she sits up and grabs the pillow, placing it over herself. "Stop laughing! I'm still not sure if he even *likes me*, likes me. You know what I mean?" She looks around for the words. "I don't want to be that girl some dude meets, has fun with, and then drops as soon as we get home."

"I know, Pat, I know... but you have nothing to worry about. He had eyes for you the moment we got here."

"He *was* flirting with me, wasn't he? I didn't make that up in my head, right?"

"Absolutely not. He was flirting like crazy with you! Plus, he straight-up called you Patricia like he knew you for years."

"Yeah, that was strange."

"Plus, no man who just wants a tour-toy would make you the center of his attention in a sea of single, hungry women. Powell made it a point to wait on you hand and foot, he got all of your drinks, sat with you, and danced only with you all night. That means something in the male code book."

"Yeah, I guess that's true," she says, grinning. Suddenly swinging the pillow, she hits me on my belly. "And what about you? What happened between you and David? You both looked pretty cozy last night... dancing and talking the night away."

We did spend a lot of time together chatting about our triumphs and travails as teachers. Mostly the travails. "I had a lot of fun, but now that we're on the same squad, I think it's better to squash that right away."

I see her hand rise. Calmly, she draws it back and swings. I hear the light slap in my ear, and I feel the blow against my cheek. "Did you... did you just slap me?" I sputter out.

She laughs. "Jos, you need to be slapped for saying that! If I, your freakin' sister, don't check you, then who will?"

Struck dumb by the blow, I look at her, shocked. "I can't believe you slapped me."

"Look, the man gave you a trigger to blow up his balls, danced all night with you, chatted about all of the things you guys have in common, which is a lot I might add, and all you can think about are the possible pitfalls of a relationship? Are you sick or something? That man's a good catch. You better get on that before some hoe tries to steal him away."

I quickly sit up on my elbow, facing her, my other hand on my cheek. It's not uncommon for FOGs to be allowed relationships in the service. A norm could be court marshaled for fraternization, but for a FOG, it is overlooked. A small concession for those who carry the front line I figure. Truth be told, most of us are more civilian than military anyway. Taken off the street, given vast power, and barely trained to use it before being sent to the front lines does not make a disciplined fighter. Not to mention the measly three weeks of training we *do* receive is woefully insufficient. Only half of us survived the first year of the war just because of folk making simple mistakes like improperly using their dragon rifles.

And yes, David is a good man. But... I don't want to be... I just don't... "I'm scared," I say, realizing the truth of my words as they slip past my lips. I don't want to be hurt. I don't want to be wrapped up in another man like I was with my ex-husband. I don't want to fail at another relationship.

"Sis, David ain't your ex."

Her words erupt a volcano of pent-up emotion. I feel the pressure of tears pushing tight behind my eyes. "I'm being stupid," I say as my vision begins to blur. I feel them, warm and wet, slide across the bridge of my nose down onto Patricia's blanket. "I'm too old to be acting like this. Like a stupid little girl crying over the past."

"I can't imagine what you went through back then. But, I do know that you have every right to be cautious," Patricia says, her rough fingers brushing my tears away. "Today, you're one of the world's most dangerous weapons and you don't need to hide behind fear ever again. You don't need to be concerned that you'll be hurt again by some asshole, because you can chop 'im up in like what... two seconds?"

We laugh. "Oh come on."

"Seriously, though, you got us as well, sis. I love you and I'd never let some jerk hurt you. And Oa, she'd rip anyone in half who dares to cause you harm, or die trying.

"Anyway, David is definitely one of the good ones. You should hear how Jacob and everyone else talks about him. They think he's one of the most honorable people they've ever met."

Why am I so emotional right now? How much of these feelings, these fears, have I been smothering? How long have I been keeping them bottled up?

"Hell, if David even tries to act up, just give me a call. I'll put a hole in his ass so fast even you would be impressed."

We both chuckle and I nod. "I'll hold you to that."

"You better. No one hurts my sister from another mister and gets away with it."

The dull roar of war machines, metallic and organic, wafts through the camp like a fog. There's also a far more destructive fog that permeates the air. It's the pernicious fog of ignorance, generated and maintained by the brass, that bothers me. This false information about the Alliance's exceptionalism and the Keynosians' savagery, as well as the suppression of their developing strategies... it's causing and has caused many deaths... too many deaths in fact. Will they continue to keep so many in the dark? Will they even release David's report about the village we got ambushed in — the disassembled weapons and those black bullets — all of it? So far, I haven't heard a word about what we found. Instead, there's only talk of the status of our forward camp, information they were probably unable to hide. Without the ability to communicate with the camp, most are assuming it's been blown off the map and all they have on their minds is revenge. Judging by the results, I'm sure that's a rumor they're sure to never dispute.

There's a grittiness to those gathered here, a coarseness of spirit born of impending combat. It darkens the mood of every soldier. FOG or non-FOG, we know the awful truth... the happiness of the days past is just that, in the past. We cannot stop the pain of loss that's soon to come in war. The pain will only stop when this war ends.

Ophelia, Patricia, and I head past lines of people who wait to board old, battle-worn transports. As usual, the non-FOGs boarding these vehicles have equipment that's being held together with rope and tape, carry threadbare knapsacks, and wear uniforms that fight to stay on their bodies.

All of my equipment is completely new. All except my blade.

"Looks like we're over there," Ophelia says, picking up her pace. She heads towards the line of FOGs boarding their sleek, well-maintained transports. I keep my eyes fixed straight ahead to avoid making eye contact with the norm soldiers. Why should they get less than us? They're dying for their country, sacrificing just as much as any FOG, why should they have to suffer in old dilapidated transports? Why should they wear threadbare uniforms? Those that surrendered themselves to the Sacrifice gave their lives for the nation and not so we can have a larger portion of the pie. The military is supposed to be a family, not an extension of our society's belief that power equals superiority.

Maybe it's not that simple. Maybe these perks, these small graces, are the last meal of those FOGS condemned to death or lifelong servitude. If so, I wonder if those at the top truly believe that these new uniforms and equipment are compensation for the lives we surrendered willingly for our country.

Suddenly, they no longer feel like much of a benefit.

"Good to see you, ladies," Clarence says, waving us over. "I thought I was in the wrong spot at first, since there's no one else from the Midwest crew here. Plus, all of their signs are different."

"Where did all these FOGs come from?" Patricia asks, scanning the human landscape.

Clarence glances back along the lines of FOGs and turns up his nose. "Pfft, most of them are low-level FOGs I think, probably from the second Sacrifice. So many of those dudes are weaker than those that survived the first run. I'm guessing most aren't much of a threat to the average Guardsmen and are used for supporting the norms."

"Cut them some slack, Clarence," I say. "Everyone can't be you." Who isn't much of a threat either.

"They don't have to be me, they just have to be useful when shit hits the fan."

"Every soldier is useful, Marshall," Powell's voice calls out.

Followed closely by David, Rawlings, Jackson, Petersen, and Dougie, Powell makes his way to the transport we're assigned. They're clearly the elites of this base, made evident by the way every other soldier, FOG and non-FOG alike, makes way for them, gawking as they pass. But even more than that, the very way they carry themselves tells of a state of mind, a sense of self-importance. Chests out, chins tilted just enough to tell the world how they see themselves. Only David appears to looks grimly into the sea of young faces that nod towards them.

"Good morning, ladies, Marshall," David says from the rear, his hand waving just above Jackson's head.

Rawlings walks forward, hands extended towards me. I think she wants me to hold them. I do, and she immediately leans in and kisses me on the cheek. "So good to see some other ladies here! I'm so tired of being the only woman amongst these brutes."

Welcomes and introductions are made between all.

"Enough chatter, folks," Powell says, his finger on the receiver in his ear. "They're calling for us to move out, so let's get this show on the road."

With a nod, we all make our way, single file, into the heavy, black-armored vehicle that flashes an approving beep into my receiver as I walk up the metal ramp and pass into its bowels.

Dougie, the young man that Powell coins as the group's lucky charm, stands to the side of the vehicle, fiddling with the shoulder comm unit attached to his uniform. "I still can't get a signal from the forward camp, Gunny."

"It won't be the last time, Dougie my man," he responds, slapping each of his followers' backs as they pass him and line up to enter our highly armored mode of transportation.

Despite the dismissive comment from Powell, the anxious look on Dougie's face remains. He is not reassured, none of us are. Not even the techs have any idea how the Keynosians are blocking long-range radio contact. The current theory is that the Southies have found a way to embed the trees with advanced jamming technology, because when we destroy the trees and foliage, our comms come back online. The problem is, the Keynosians can regrow the trees in a month's time, and the sheer number of trees currently out there is far too vast to consider RX'ing, and to top it off, the spores would stop any long-range bombing campaign. Relay points are the best way to keep communications up and running. Apparently, someone took down our relays near the forward camp.

RX is the safest method, but we'd have to cover the entirety of Keynosa to accomplish that feat. And now, they have those black trees. If they can neutralize RX, we're in a lot of trouble.

As I board, I'm taken aback by the sheer amount of technological amenities they've filled this transport with. The inside of the vehicle is aglow with screens and consoles, all designed to monitor and protect its occupants.

"How do you like the new transport?" David asks, sidling up next to me. "We've been calling it 'The Turtle.'" He's holding the new 16mm rifle. These are the normal issue for strikers like David. Soldiers whose strength and speed make them uniquely suited for the weapon. Far too heavy for any normal person to carry, they were previously affixed to armored jeeps that could move in quickly, laying down heavy fire. Now they are far more dangerous in the hands of a dexterous FOG than they were when bolted down.

"Not bad, not bad at all," I say, headed towards the rear. I cautiously take one of the rearmost seats.

With a thud, David drops the weapon and locks it into an angled depression topped with a smooth metal bump on the transport's bed. Metal clamps whirl shut around a matching depression on the butt of the rifle and pull the weapon inward, towards the sidewall of the vehicle. In seconds, his large 16mm weapon, dubbed the panther, is hidden away in the vehicle's wall.

From his side, David pulls out a mace and places it on a long metal sheet above our seats. With another clack, it sticks to the transport's side. Magnetized, I assume.

"A mace huh?" I ask. This model looks like a small baseball bat, extending about two and a half feet in length, with about three inches across of solid condensed-composite metal at the striking end.

"A necessary equipment addition, much like your blade. A proper soldier must have a means of being functional even after his ammo is exhausted, right?"

"Touche. But you didn't bring it on the scouting mission."

"No. It's hard to be quiet with a long metal rod clunking around, bumping into things."

"Makes sense."

"So, you don't want to put your blade up?" he says, pointing at my weapon.

"No. I don't."

"Hey, I like these new transports!" Ophelia announces, lugging her 22mm dragon rifle behind her. Turning off the power to the charge that keeps the harness rigid, Ophelia unlocks her weapon as she walks inside, taking the seat directly across from me. She begins to look around. I assume she's trying to find out where she should put her weapon. Like Ophelia, I'm wondering where her massive weapon will be tucked away in such tight quarters.

"The side compartment is only for panthers and scorpions," David says, standing hunched over to avoid bumping his head on the light strip above. He moves to assist her as she swivels and detaches the rifle from the harness and positions it between them. "Your dragon rifle is supposed to be stowed up here." He lifts the weapon from her hands and into a slot just behind Ophelia's seat and above the magnetized metal strip. Deftly, he slides the rifle in with a snap.

"What about the harness? Can I put this up there?" Ophelia asks as she begins to unhook her harness.

"No, that you keep on. The seats are designed to adjust when you press this lever down on the arm rest." David presses it, and the seat begins to adjusts. An outline of Ophelia's once charged, but now soft fabric backpack that links to the harness slowly sinks into the fabric. "Okay, you can lay back now."

As she does, tiny motors come to life and the fabric begins to wrap around the hard gray metal of the harness. "Oh! Now this is comfortable. Awesome. Thank you, David."

Hrm. "Well, you're certainly very helpful, David," I say, a twinge of jealousy in my voice.

I don't need to feel jealous. David's not my boyfriend. What the hell is wrong with me... and what's with these stupid seat belts? Where the hell does this strap go? And this one? And why are there all of these buckles?

"There's even a place for knuckle-dusters, blades, and maces, in case you don't want to carry them on your waist or leg for the entire ride."

I look up and his eyes are already on me. He grins. "Here, let me help you with your seat belts."

"No, I'm good. You can maybe help Petersen, stow his rifle as well."

"Could you, David? I'd love that," Petersen says, laughing.

"I'm confident Petersen can do that by himself. I'd rather help you with your seat belts." David looks around me, probably trying to figure out what the hell I'm doing.

"Are you sure? Maybe there's someone else that you can help?"

"Good lord woman, let the man help you with the seat belt!" Jackson belts out and laughs.

I sigh as he maneuvers around me, grabbing the dangling, black canvas straps of varying lengths that seem to be everywhere. "It won't take long," he says as the others look on and shake their heads.

"This locks into this one to the right... your right, sorry." He pulls the strap around and down across my chest, between my breasts, and cinches it tight. "You okay or is that too tight?" he asks, his lips far too close as he leans forward, reaching over my shoulder.

It's a simple question, but his tone and the look on his face tell me the words hold a greater meaning. "Yes, thank you." The smile I provide him with is cautious, reluctant. I inhale deeply and am overcome by the desire to turn into his scent, a musky mix of sweat and those circular striped mints he's clicking around in his mouth. I haven't had one of those in a long time. I love the way they taste.

"Okay, David, I think I can do it from here," I say, cautioning him back as I fumble around with the straps. Too much, too soon.

He chuckles. "Are you sure?"

"Ahh, yes. I'm not a child. I think I can buckle my own seat belt. Thank you." I look at his handiwork and find myself utterly befuddled. How did he fit that strap into this slot? What's this strap here for?

I look up to see Patricia assisting Ophelia. I watch her hands, deftly going from strap to lock, cinching as she goes. Where's that lock at? I look down, checking everywhere for it. How could I miss a lock with five points on it? I look up again to see both Ophelia and Patricia shaking their heads at me.

I guess I should have accepted his help. Oh well, too late now. Anyway, we need to keep our distance. I don't want either of us getting hurt. We're not in a situation where a romance can bloom. We're at war.

"Umm, Jos? I think that goes —"

"I got it, Ophelia..."

"Yeah, but maybe if —"

"Oa, I got it."

"Hey!" Jackson says, in my direction. He's strapped in perfectly, of course. "I thought rangers had to carry panthers too? You are not seriously going into battle without one, are you?"

"They do, but Martinez has already proven her effectiveness without one," Jacob responds from the sunbaked rear of the vehicle, peering from behind Petersen's bulky frame. "And save that seat next to you, Patricia. That's for me."

"No problem," she responds with a nod.

"Get ready for Jake's speech," David says softly, leaning close to my ear. He hands me the square metal locking mechanism.

Where did he get that from?

"He makes a speech?"

"Every time. It's kind of his thing."

"Blood of my country!" Jacob yells, his eyes suddenly fierce, his fist pounding on the transport's padded ceiling.

"Bones of my nation, flesh of our union!" the truck's occupants, myself included, reply, our right hands on our chests. The career military folks, like Patricia and Petersen, do it with such fluidity. Are they even aware of how robotic it appears from a distance?

Slapping the side of the transport, he steps further inside into the belly of the machine and flashes a big, almost maniacal smile. He is energized by our show of patriotism and our unwavering commitment to each other and our mission. I hope he doesn't take our commitment to each other and our country as a commitment to him. That would be foolish.

Strange, he has a pair of knuckle-dusters, like a tank.

"Some new faces here, right? First time we'll all be going out as an entire team," he says, his eyes passing over Ophelia, Patricia, Clarence, and me. "For you newcomers, although I am the National commander of the FOG unit, this group here... this is my family." He points around the small, dim space. "I want you to think of the people in this truck as your brothers and sisters, metaphorically of course. In the field, we ten are the hands of God himself.

"Now, I chose this ten as the vanguard — the point of the spear — because you are all the best the Alliance has to offer. The very top of every chart and in every aspect."

For a moment, chests swell and backs straighten. I find myself following along.

"Our cousins will be out there as well, angels of the most high, but it will be us... we are the lightning, the very power of God's hand." He punctuates his praise with a hard slap on Petersen's shoulder and continues his stroll deeper into the transport.

Reaching his seat but not taking it, Powell glances at David and widens his smile before spinning to face those at the other end. "Be ready, brothers and sisters!" he shouts, crouching down. "I will ask of you all just as much as I ask of myself. Serve this great and glorious country of ours with honor! I ask of you today, with God as my witness, to give me your blood, your power, your bravery as I give you mine!"

I cannot help but smile as a tidal wave of emotion and cheers sweep through the vehicle's glowing interior. "I am willing to give my blood to this country," he yells, his voice reaching a fever pitch. "Are you?"

An even greater explosion of agreement.

"I'm willing to give my bones to strengthen this country. Are you?"

Another explosion. Only David is as reserved as Ophelia and I.

"I'll give my very flesh to this union. Will you?"

I see why his fellow soldiers follow him. I can see why Patricia is so interested in him. He speaks a language they understand. He speaks the very voice of nationalism. They both chose to serve their country before the war. I don't know about Jacob, but I know for a fact that Patricia was and is more than willing to give her life in service of the Alliance. Jacob, although inspiring, still strikes me as a manipulative man. He knows what to say and knows how to move people to action. Sure, I love my country and will certainly defend her with my life, but I will never blindly follow any man again. That mistake wasted years of my life.

Crouched down, Powell moves towards me. When he reaches the back wall, he stands right in front of me, smiles, and bangs on the wall separating us from the driver's cab. "Now let's get this show on the road... and can someone get Martinez strapped in correctly? She obviously doesn't know what the hell she's doing."

Affixing his comm collar, David turns to me. "So what did you think of the speech?" he asks, breaking the silence that fell over the group after we left the main base. His voice is barely audible over the rumbling engine of the speeding transport.

"I'm actually surprised it was as good as it was," I say, leaning towards him, my eyes scanning as I watch the others on the transport.

A ten-man FOG team seems huge. Back in the Midwest, our teams never reached more than three FOGs, and even those were bolstered by a massive contingent of norms. A ten man team stacked with FOGs this powerful seems like overkill.

"And that wasn't even his best work," he says, shaking his head. "I've heard him *really* rouse a crowd when we had to retake Silver Arch."

"Really?"

"Oh yeah. It was right after a particularly difficult battle — we took huge losses and gained minimum ground. He stood in plain sight, right out in the open, screaming to all within earshot that our victory was a certainty. Of course I'm paraphrasing, but it really struck home to those assembled. As plastic as he appears sometimes, he really knows how to motivate battle-worn soldiers, and on that day, it's my opinion that the turning point was his speech, 'cause most were ready to walk away and let the Southies have that city."

"You don't sound like it moved you as much as it did the others."

He sighs softly, looking around our dim, tight confines before focusing on me again. "I understand the need for it. I mean it makes perfect sense. It's just that he peppers his words with so many derogatory statements against the Keynosians. That kind of talk... well, pisses me off. I even approached him on it a few times, and I totally understand why he does it, but I just want him to dial back the bigotry. It's unnecessary in my opinion. But in war, it's sometimes a requirement to dehumanize your opposition," he says, leaning forward and looking down the transport cabin again. "Just look around. Most of us are normal people, well, aside from Petersen, but most led pretty normal lives before the war. No one here is a sociopath, always ready and willing to murder their fellow man."

I agree. How can I not? He's correct. "What, are you some sorta hippy?" I chuckle, looking to lighten the mood.

"Me?" he asks, pondering the thought. "Well yeah, I guess. Peace, love, and all that jazz."

BOOM!

The transport screeches to a halt, jerking everyone into high alert. Hands slam down on buttons on the armrests, and it takes only a second or two for most of us to disembark and prepare our weapons and minds for combat. Faces and hearts harden, ready to do what's necessary. Patricia jumps out last and hoists herself to the top of the transport, her finger resting above the trigger of Suzy-Q.

"One of the norm transports is on fire!" Marshall shouts.

The rest of the convoy spills from their vehicles, FOG and non-FOG alike, weapons at the ready and ducking behind their vehicles for cover.

There's little movement from the vehicle engulfed in flames. I silently pray that its occupants escaped the blue fire raging from the driver's cabin and rear hatch.

"Rawlings, Martinez, top of the transport! We need eyes!" Powell yells. Rawlings and I move. "Patel, top of the gear transport over there. It's a better vantage point." He points behind us, towards the top of the massive truck hauling thick metal containers. The metal lip that sits above its compartment is perfect for cover if we're taking fire. "Don't shoot until I give the order, even if you have eyes on a target! Marshall, Santos, you're with me! The rest, get ready to lay hard lead downstream on Martinez's and Rawlings' order!" With that, Powell, David, and Clarence are gone.

Patricia leaps from the top of our transport and lands deftly on Ophelia's outstretched arm. With little more than a shrug, Patel is tossed gently to the top of the gear transport, her rifle ready again in an instant. How they never officially teamed us up before is beyond reason. It's like we were born to work together.

Vanguard. Powell is right, we are that indeed. It's obvious Jacob knows what this team is capable of. Ophelia, Patricia and I have fought together too many times to count. I'm sure the others have as well. With the decisions he's made, Powell has certainly earned my respect so far.

"Nothing this way," Rawlings says, her finger pressed against her comm collar's silver button as she scans the area behind me. "What about you?" she asks, releasing the button to tap the outside of my upper thigh from behind.

I focus hard, scanning the 180 degrees I'm assigned to by default. The once-mighty forest has been decimated by repeated RX bombs, and the air is filled with their sickeningly sweet aroma.

We're not far from the forward camp, only ten or twenty miles south of the now decimated village we scouted just days prior. I focus harder, beyond the gray, ruined earth and into the tree-lined distance beyond the reach of our RX attacks... still nothing. It's all as dead as it appears.

I press the comm button. "Nothing here," I say to the team.

"Keep your eyes peeled, Jos. They're out there somewhere," Rawlings warns, again using my nickname. I feel myself smirk. She barely knows me and still she feels comfortable using my nickname after hearing others use it. Her instincts are right, though, someone is out there, and they are watching. I can feel it more than sense it, just can't pinpoint them yet. Those Keynosians are testing us, trying to see just how large of a force we're moving with, just how many FOGs are in the fold. I truly hope the sheer size of this force scares them. I pray even more that it scares them into surrender.

"Sunrise mine I bet from the looks of it," Petersen says. "Probably some dumb-ass wasn't paying attention and got those dudes toasted," he says, his hand over his receiver.

No one can see a sunrise mine just driving along. You're the dumb-ass, Petersen.

My receiver crackles. "Confirming it was a mine, sunrise mine, of course," David says, his voice slightly muffled. I look at him in the distance standing next to the scorched trunk, the muzzle of his mouth pressing into his forearm and bicep. "Damn thing burned right through to the gas tank. No one escaped the transport as far as I can tell."

Petersen laughs. "Sunrise mine, told ya."

Asshole.

107

"Keep the comments to a minimum. We're holding here until we secure the area. Rawlings, Martinez, Patel, stay on alert. Anything moves, I want to know about it ASAP," Powell commands.

"Question. Can someone explain why we have a norm as a part of a FOG team?" Petersen interrupts.

Seconds tick by as tense silence builds over the receiver.

"Are you questioning my judgment, soldier?" Powell asks, his voice not in the least bit friendly.

"No, sir. I'd like to know why we have someone who cannot do what even the weakest FOG can. Sinclair's a good soldier, shouldn't she be in this team? It doesn't make any sense, sir."

"Patel is probably the best shot our military has ever seen, Petersen. The simple fact that she's been able to hit Guardsmen — consistently — that has earned her this spot.

"And by the way, Petersen, the next time you forget your place and question me on the group frequency and not my personal line, you'll find yourself on permanent shit duty, understand?"

"Yes, sir." His line clicks off and I watch him breathe deep. With his lips pressed tight, he draws his pinched thumb and forefinger across his mouth.

Good. Keep it that way.

"Santos, I need you and Marshall to work on putting that fire out while Jackson aids any wounded that may have gotten caught up in the blaze. Rogers, push the other trucks back onto the road — a few of them have fallen into craters trying to avoid running into each other."

"Yes sir," Ophelia chirps, removing her heavy weapon, harness, and backpack filled with ammo.

"Sir! Possible movement on our six!" Rawlings yells over the group channel. Everyone stiffens and turns as one singular creature. "Going to check it out." She stands, her eyes fixed on the distant trees.

"No! Stand down, Rawlings."

Her body screeches to a halt. She just barely stops herself from leaping off the transport. "But, sir —"

"I'll contact the norm commanders. They can send out a platoon to do that work. If confirmed, I'll dispatch Jackson and Marshall, not one of our only two rangers. I don't want either you or Martinez to go all cowboy on us. We need you, or have you forgotten that?"

"No sir, I haven't."

"Good, now please, keep watch."

She turns back towards the forest's edge as a number of large armored jeeps roll out from the convoy. A cloud of dead, gray dirt is left in their wake.

They're just normal soldiers. They won't be able to fend off a Guardsmen attack if that's actually what Rawlings is sensing.

"I hate when they do this," Rawlings says, following the jeeps with her eyes, her hand covering the microphone embedded in her collar.

"Do what?"

Her back to me, I see her shoulders sag. "We have about twenty other FOGs back there, but they're sending norms. It doesn't make any sense! What if they run into a group of Guardsmen? They'll be wiped out before any of us can do anything to help them," she says.

"That's normal protocol, Rawlings. We always lead with the non-FOGs."

"Are you serious?" she asks, turning to me. "Come on, Jos, they're using the norms as goddamn cannon fodder. And just look at them. The entire lot can't be more than twenty-two years old."

A sense of powerlessness hangs heavy between us as we watch the jeeps cross the distance quickly.

"Rawlings, report," Powell commands over the receiver.

Taking a deep breath, she exhales and presses the transmit button on her collar. "The scout team is almost at the tree line. No hostiles yet."

"Good. Keep me posted if any Southies bare their teeth.

"Authorize Rawlings... override master channel, set."

Good idea to give her full channel access to cut the other feeds when she speaks.

"Santos, report."

109

"Fires are out. Looks like the drivers survived, but they won't last long. They need to get back to the base for some serious treatment if they're going to survive."

"Damn it," Powell says. "Okay, getting more norms over to you. I want you and Marshall to finish up ASAP."

"It's going to take longer than —"

"When the norms get there, you guys head back to the transport."

Silence.

"Understood," David finally states. His voice sounds defeated.

"Good. Rogers, report."

"Okay... ummm, it looks like all of the trucks are now back on the roadway, but one of them's busted and won't start."

"Okay, toss it. Once you're done, get back to the transport. The norms can handle from here on out.

"The rest of you, get close to the transport. The armor will deter any snipers. We leave in thirty."

"I'm happy we didn't bomb the hill Takdeer's buried on," David says.

"I agree, but what made you think of that now? We passed that site a long time ago."

"Dunno." He shrugs. "It just popped into my mind. In fact, the whole scene popped into my mind just now. The burial, your speech, all of it. Kind of made me think about it all... the war I mean. I get that and agree."

Agree? "What do you get?"

"That I don't... we don't hate them. It was appropriate that you wished for Takdeer's spirit to move on to a happier place. You said a lot in a few short sentences."

"Thank you," I say, half smiling. "I just spoke from the heart."

"And that's what makes it so beautiful."

I nod, but smile inwardly. That was beautiful of him to say.

A sudden scream catches my attention. It was faint, distant. "What was that?" I ask, turning towards Rawlings. Her face tells me all I need to know. She also heard the wail.

"What was what?" David asks.

Again, a scream rings out. In unison, Rawlings and I stand inside the moving transport. She slams her hand down on the armrest and her panther slides out and right into her hands.

"It's from the base," she confirms. "Something's going on there."

"Ladies! What the hell? Ease down and tell me what's going on," Jacob barks, his finger hovering over the call button of his collar. Rawlings looks as if she's in a trance.

No one moves, we barely even breathe. This is the first time I'm not the person giving the warning. Usually everyone is waiting on me to report. I finally understand why other soldiers are so discomforted by rangers' abilities. I feel like I'm blind, waiting to be led by someone across a busy intersection. "That was most certainly a scream," she confirms, staring intently at Powell. "A human scream, Jake," she continues, her voice pained this time.

Powell clicks his collar. "Colonel Edington, I have confirmation of some kind of disturbance at the forward camp. Requesting clearance to send in a team for investigation. I repeat, some kind of disturbance was confirmed, requesting clearance for investigation."

"She was young," Rawlings adds.

I don't know how she is so sure the voice is female, but it definitely sounds like something horrible is happening.

"Are we close to the camp?" Ophelia asks.

Clarence pulls a small GPS from his belt as the transport slows. "Looks like it. We're only a few minutes away now."

As we come to a stop, I can see the vehicles behind us slow. Something is clearly wrong, as the ground here has already recovered from our poisons. Once again, the lush green of Keynosian plant life envelops the entire area around the dark-green road that leads to what appears to be a gigantic tree with its top removed. It's tall and wide, must span the length of three football fields across.

111

With a short huff, Jacob faces me and David. "Okay, we have a green light. Martinez, Santos, Rogers, Jackson, head towards the camp and check it out. Be careful," he says, glancing in my direction. "If the Keynosians have retaken the camp, do not engage. We can attack in unison. They'll be trapped in there, so just signal us with your comms," Jacob says, pointing to the small red button on his neck collar. It requires simultaneous activation of both the call and emergency buttons for the warning alarm to sound to the others. "The convoy will be holding this position until we hear back from you one way or the other. Understood?"

"Understood," we all say, and salute, taking off out of the transport.

"No cowboy shit either!" Powell yells after us.

They're keeping a distance. The Keynosians may not know which of the transports contain FOGs, but they don't need to know. To launch a surprise attack on our convoy in such a wide open space would be disastrous for us. We're sitting ducks out here — the only safe space would be the forward camp. The same place that might have been taken back by the Keynosians.

We keep ourselves crouched as we approach, hugging the rear of the transports and heavy carriers, cautiously peering from behind the large vehicles' charged-metal sides. Each step we make brings us closer to the amazing sight the forward camp appears to be. This is an enormous home tree. But, unlike others I've see, the top portion was lopped off and left broken on the south-facing side of the building. Yet, even in its decapitated state, it's magnificent. The scale of the thing... it's both larger and wider than any Keynosian tree I've ever laid eyes on.

Why did we leave the top portion of the tree sprawled to the south of the forward camp like that? If the Keynosians are south of us, we won't be able to see them approach. Then I see it. Our auto-cannons are mounted on the cleaved top, but they're frozen by creepervines wrapping them tight.

"What do you have, Martinez?" David asks as we move towards

the camp in a slow jog, guns at the ready.

"Nothing like the scream yet, but there are definitely people in the structure." It smells like they haven't bathed in weeks.

"Okay. Jackson, you're on point. Rogers, I need you to watch Martinez's rear."

"Absolutely. You've got nothing to worry about, Martinez," Ophelia says with a grin.

With Ophelia here, I'm positive it's not me who needs to worry.

There are many large doorways into the converted home tree. The north-facing one appears to be important, framed by natural outgrowths that curve and twist into ornate patterns. Interwoven into nature's geometry are man-made carvings that display scenes of Keynosian family life up and down its round columns. Most of it consists of women carrying baskets of goods, children playing, and men planting and trimming trees. The entire scene speaks to a very agrarian lifestyle here.

As we push on, we find our sense of smell is immediately placed under assault. The extent of the foul odors was previously held at bay by the once charged fabric doorway that now lies deathly quiet and still, made possible by the device clicking on the outside of the doorway. Each step takes us deeper, and bathes us in the aroma of filth and death.

Nothing is powered. The lights, the charged doors, they all lie dead. Despite this, the entire interior is dimly lit by daylight that streams through the numerous knotholes in the walls. It looks like hundreds of angled rods of light are stabbing into the camp. The four-point star shape of many of the openings make it appear as if four round trees grew into one massive organism. Internally, the hollow of the tree is filled with our normal military-green canvas dwellings, although on a much smaller scale. It is a forward camp after all.

I smell meat cooking. Dinner? That would make sense since the night is quickly approaching. But why didn't anyone come out to greet us?

What's that? "Activity," I announce in a whisper. I direct them to the left. There's where I hear the most heartbeats, there, in the largest of the canvas dwellings.

Taking point, Santos signals silently for Jackson and Ophelia to hold firing positions; each one moves silently but quickly, dashing ahead to stand at separate ends of the barrack's opening. He signals for me to follow him inside.

Crying... I hear someone crying, but not from within this structure. It's a woman... no, several women. "I hear crying, sobbing from the rear barracks."

Turning to me, Santos places his finger over his lips, then taps his nose. I nod. He's concerned about the smells, and with good reason. The overt scent of roasting meat is clear, but there's also an undercurrent of rot. Human rot. It can't be the Keynosians, they're all vegetarians. It has to be our soldiers, but why wasn't anyone on guard duty, why aren't any of the communications antennas up, and lastly, what the hell stinks this bad if people are alive?

David looks at me, his eyes tense as he holds up three fingers, then two and at the last, he forms a fist and dashes through the canvas flaps that block the entrance with me hot on his heels, dual pistols drawn. I dial down my sense of smell as far as possible. I don't want to pass out from the sensory onslaught.

The sight strikes me mute. Like ancient men from an era long gone, a low fire burns in the center with a spit of meat illuminated from below by lapping flames. Twelve soldiers, clearly malnourished, huddle around the cooking flesh. They turn in unison. The dim light of the fire creates deep shadows on their emaciated faces. There's an expression of surprise on their faces. That shock quickly turns to elation.

"Oh my God... you're finally here!" shouts a heavily bearded man,

114

frail and thin. The uniform that should be tailored, made specifically for each person, flaps about as the man moves. He nearly tumbles over attempting to stand.

Eleven others follow suit, shaking with excitement, but too weak to do much else. God, they smell so bad! And look at them, so dirty and marked with sores, I begin to feel pangs of sorrow for the entire lot. I can only wonder what they must have endured.

They approach, and cheer with each step.

"Down, now!" David shouts, stopping them in their tracks. His weapon is trained on the crowd before him.

"What the hell are you doing, Santos? These are our men!"

He doesn't relent. "Look at what's on the spit," David says, low.

"What, the meat?"

"Look Jos! Fucking look at what they're cooking!"

It's just a leg of meat. Maybe they captured a wild animal. Maybe their supplies ran dry and they were forced to... wait a second, what kind of animal *is* that? The shape is... oh no. Oh god no. That's a human leg. They're roasting a human leg.

CHAPTER 5

TORN ASUNDER

The abhorrent sight of the long-dead, their bones scraped clean, blackened and split, not only sends fearful shivers up my spine, but angry hackles as well. Those bones... so many, too many, piled in the back of the barracks and stacked like thin cords of ebony wood. Next to the darkened bones, piles of feces. They didn't even have the decency to bury their waste.

"Animals," I growl through gritted teeth. Are they eating the dead? Are they killing one another in some "survival of the fittest" nightmare?

The fire snaps and crackles, lapping at the dripping human fat like a hungry animal... like the bearded beasts that now face us with their backs to the cooking human flesh.

"Rogers, Jackson, get in here," David says, his voice chillingly calm. He never takes his eyes off of the filthy rabble as he walks to the spit and kicks the terrible sight away. The charred human flesh slaps the canvas wall, staining it with its grease.

Some of the men look at us, then turn back, eyes longing for the still-sizzling human leg.

Slowly, reality begins to sink in, and most drop their eyes to the dirty canvas under their feet. A few, however, do not share their shame and stare boldly, defiantly at us.

"On the way," Jackson says, his voice crisp in my ear, causing me to jump.

In a flourish of dust and a snap of the canvas flap, Ophelia and Jackson enter and flank David and me. They look at each other for a moment, then towards the soldiers we're leveling our weapons against.

"Ummm, why are we pointing our guns at our own soldiers?" Ophelia asks softly, leaning her head in my direction.

"Martinez, fill in Rogers. Jackson, you're with me," David says. I can hear his teeth grind from here. Something has him tense.

David and Jackson exit. I can hear them moving towards the rear tents in the camp. They're heading towards the direction of the crying women I heard before we entered this nightmare tent.

Are they eating the female soldiers? No, it can't be. I count nearly eight skulls, and I can't imagine any elite-norm squad has that many female soldiers in its ranks.

"Jos, what's going on?" Ophelia asks, holding her massive weapon steady, one hand clutching the top handle, the other gripping the swivel-bar that juts out from the side of the intricate, nearly human-sized machine. Despite the doubt in her voice, her arm never wavers.

How do I say this? Straight. There is no way to sugarcoat the horror. "Cannibalism."

"What?" she says, with a chuckle.

I'm not joking, Ophelia. "These men... they're eating each oth —"

"No! Never!" one of the men shouts. He quickly steps towards me.

Immediately, I step forward in a burst of speed. In under a second my pistol is nearly touching his left eye, freezing him before he can move another fraction of an inch. "Get back."

The dog snarls at me, his eyes burning fiercely.

Do it. I want you to do it. Take that step. Give me license to end your miserable existence. "Do it," I say, nearly whispering the dare.

He hesitates as if weighing his options. I nod, smiling as the pull of bloodlust scratches and claws at my reason. My hand shivers momentarily — I can't help it. The rush of adrenaline is so pronounced.

Maybe he thinks he can take me? I imagine him thinking: sure she's a FOG, but she's still a woman, right? Good. Go ahead. Do it.

The challenge is not met, and his gaze falters. Immediately after, so too does his physical resolve as he crumbles before me.

"We'd never... we wouldn't do that to our own."

"Shut up." You make me sick.

"We need a med team to our position, stat. We'll also need a stasis chamber," I hear David request over the comms.

A stasis chamber? Is there a FOG stationed here? Maybe the soldier's hurt? Could these men have actually done something to a FOG?

"You don't understand what was goin' on. You know jack-shit," one man mumbles from the back.

"What were we supposed to do, starve to death?" yet another exclaims.

"Wait, you guys were really eating people?" Ophelia says, her face still confused. She turns to me. "Cannibals?" For a second, I swear she nearly retches.

"We were starving! We had no aid, no food, no medicine... nothing! First, we were only trapped here, but then... then *he* wouldn't let us go."

Lifting her weapon up and away from the men, Ophelia steps closer, her face almost apologetic. How she's able to feel compassion for these men is amazing. "So who then? If not one another, who did you... eat?" she asks, looking past them to survey the inside of the quarters. Setting her eyes on a distant pile of bones, she gasps softly. "Keynosians? You ate Keynosians?"

How did she... oh, I see now. The clothing is woven hemp, torn and cut, it obviously belongs to Keynosian civilians, not even Guardsmen.

They ate innocent people.

It all makes sense now. The outrage that we accused them of eating Northerners. But eating the flesh of Keynosians does not make the situation any more acceptable.

"We're supposed to be better than this." Her voice cracks. "They're supposed to be the animals. Not us."

Silence. They glance at one another, each afraid to give an answer.

Then one man steps forward and clears his throat. "We were starving —"

"So you ate a person? No, not just a person, several people. You... you are the animals here. You lot are the savages," she says, her voice betraying the sadness in her heart.

"Do you even know what it's like to starve to death?" he responds, his voice exploding into a pained screech. "Do you? The pain, the desperation... how could I watch my men go through that and do nothing?" he asks, his eyes pleading for understanding.

He must be the commanding officer. I can't tell from his shredded and filth-covered uniform what rank he is though.

A faint scent of saline fills the air as the tears of the men cut through the miasma of unwashed bodies, human waste, burning flesh, and piled bone.

"We couldn't retreat. The Keynosians kept bombing, kept firing on us. They wouldn't let us leave. Then he lost it," another calls out.

"So you've condemned all your men, yourselves, to damnation? How is that the better choice?" Ophelia retorts. "God abhors such behavior! He abhors it! Do you even understand the damage you've done to your own souls?" she shouts, pointing at the pile with her weapon before training it back on the men.

I've fought alongside Ophelia for years. I've seen her in many extreme situations, too many to count. Even when we were sent to stop Frank Sun, she didn't behave like this. Never has she appeared more willing to kill an unarmed person than right now.

"Are you the commanding officer here?" I ask.

He nods his answer, his eyes locked on Ophelia. He's scared, and he should be. As he wipes tears from his face, dirt smears from his hands into black and brown streaks across his cheek. "Yes, I am," he says with a nod. "It's not the fault of these men. The fault is mine and mine alone." He looks at the rabble, then turns back to Ophelia. "I should be punished. It's my soul that should be damned by God."

"Oa... Oa, you okay?" I ask.

She doesn't look at me as she nods yes.

I sigh and turn back to the brave cannibal before us. "Didn't you have a FOG stationed here with you?"

The entire gathering of men shudder, and the officer drops his eyes to the floor. "LeRoux."

He says his name as if Ophelia and I should know. "What about him? Is he dead, injured?" I ask.

We glance at one another as they do the same, but no one answers.

"Well, where is he?" Ophelia barks.

They jump, eying the dragon rifle. "He's in the rear tent, you'll find him in the rear tent," the officer responds. His gaze drifts away slowly, headed to the ground again. "He's with the remaining captured Keynosians. You gotta understand, we couldn't stop him. He's too strong, too fast..."

"Stop him? Stop him from doing what?"

"There were women that worked here when we first took the tree home. We took them prisoner, couldn't have them signaling Guardsmen. But, just villagers that were taking care of the place, not soldiers.

"We... we couldn't stop him."

David and Jackson could be in danger. I thrust my finger into the receiver and hear it squeak in protest — I nearly broke it. "David!" I yell, hoping he hears me. I make sure not to take my attention off of the people in front of me. "Oa, David and Jackson went back there to investigate —"

"Go, Jos. Get back there and help David and Jackson. I got these monsters."

And I do. I move so fast that behind me, I hear the heavy reinforced canvas rip, snap, and clap against itself as I pass by the other tents on my way to David and Jackson's location.

It only takes a moment for me to reach the barracks, and I skid to a halt at the rear-most building. This is clearly the officers' quarters. Within I hear laughter, moans, and sobbing.

Laughter?

Bursting through with my blade drawn, I enter the makeshift foyer of the structure and I'm immediately greeted by David and Jackson, both looking morose, and with them a grinning, chuckling FOG. LeRoux, I assume. Jackson is holding his arms behind him as tight as he can, judging by the awkward twist of LeRoux's arms. Jackson broke his left arm, the other threatens to snap any moment. Still, the FOG struggles.

Then I notice it. There are tears in Jackson's eyes. Immediately I turn to David, whose face is clearly pained, his jaw clenched tight. They both look up and face me, surprised.

"Where are the prisoners?" I yell.

Mouth open, David freezes, his eyes darting away for a split second. "Martinez, get back to the others," David commands, the words rushing out.

There's someone moaning behind the privacy flaps behind them.

"Martinez, go back and guard the others!"

To hell with that. What's happened? Who's behind the flap? "Where the fuck are the prisoners?" I repeat.

"You don't need to be here, Jos. Please, head back to the others."

No.

I expand my senses. It takes only a second for me to get a lock on the prisoners, eight of them... and one other. Closer. Heartbeat erratic. The pulse is weak, and the smell of blood, tears, and semen fills my nostrils.

"Jocelyn, this is a direct order. I need you to get back to the other prisoners, right now," David says, louder than the other orders I've already ignored. That order will meet the same fate.

Someone is hurt. They're dying.

Suddenly, David softens. "Jos, you don't need to see this."

I look at the FOG, stare into his pale, dead blue eyes. "What did you do?" I ask.

He smiles at me, his teeth misshapen, some overlapping. "God commands the chosen... seeds of man, it's man's job to subdue. Do you understand?" he says, saliva falling from his mouth and chin. "Have you read the word? The good news is written in black and white, you know. I have to..." He pauses, his eyes darting around. "I don't like that look on your face! I'm not evil! But listen, I needed to repopulate the world. Maybe you should be next?" he asks, nodding his head furiously.

I grip my blade so tight, I think I may be deforming the metal handle.

"No? But maybe you're stronger. That's good," he says, leaning forward.

Jackson quickly tightens his grip further, causing LeRoux's bones and joints to creak.

"What did you do?" I yell again.

LeRoux's eyes widen in shock. "I did what God commands of his faithful! It's the... people need to want the life, do you understand? It's what..." He pauses, his angry scowl returning. "Who are you to tell me what to do? I didn't want to run... demons run, like the fallen angels. But you? You're a woman. Who are you to judge the word of God?" And as suddenly as the paroxysm of rage took hold, it recedes and he begins to grin again. "You don't even remember the words of God? Hmm, do you?"

"Jos, I need you to put the blade away," David says, his voice commanding, but calm.

This FOG... he raped someone beyond that privacy flap. She isn't the first either, judging by the scent of not only fresh, but also long-dried blood. He's been raping these women for some time now. "Where is she?" I ask, taking a step towards the doorway. In response, David steps to cut off my path to the rear of the barracks.

Don't make me go through you to get to her, David.

David shakes his head. Resigned, he steps back and reveals the thick canvas flaps.

My eyes dart to LeRoux. To this rapist. To this murderer.

"Martinez, he ain't worth it, sugar," Jackson says, sadness in his eyes. As if he's read my mind, Jackson looks back to the flap. "If you go back there... if you go and see her... his life isn't worth you getting locked up, love."

This time, LeRoux goes from anger to sorrow, his eyes tearing up. Suddenly, he's back to happiness, his expressions changing as quickly as one might switch the channel on a vid-screen. The suddenly animated madman jerks forward, wrenching his arms, snapping bones under Jackson's grip... he does not break free. His eyes are wild as he glares at me. "She was not good, you know? No... good. Look, God does not want her screams or her pain. No, that's not what God is about. It's greatness! But that is beyond her, so God didn't allow her soul to fly... do you understand?" A wave of sadness sweeps over him again, and his shoulders suddenly sag. "I had to," he mutters. "I'm so tired and there's so much work I received from God's hands, you know what I mean? That's why we can't have prayer in the Justice Department. That's why there's so much sin in the world. That's why the word of God is in there and in my heart."

I can't listen to this bullshit anymore. I should strike him down where he stands. Sever his head from his shoulders before either David or Jackson can even hope to move. Fuck the rules demanding we refrain from harming another FOG!

Yet, in this moment, I look at David, and his eyes speak to me. They beg for me to still my hand.

Damn it!

A cry slips from behind the canvas behind them, and I rush into the rear quarter of the tent and find her, a Keynosian. She's flat on her back and staring blankly into the dim, black ceiling of the tent. Good god, the girl is young. Fifteen years old, at most. Her short, bright-blue hemp blouse has been nearly ripped off. One of her nipples has been either bitten off, or torn from her body. Worse still, it is obvious that LeRoux shattered her breastplate. He crushed her young body, but didn't kill her.

Tears stream down her soft brown features as she struggles to breathe through lungs that must be crumpled and potentially punctured by crushed bone. Short shudders of air pulse into and out of her open, bloodied mouth. Her lungs are indeed damaged. Tufts of long black curly hair lie beside her head, torn from her scalp.

Why? Was it not enough to take her body? Why leave her half naked and torn, resting in a pool of her own blood?

I clutch a fistful of my black uniform, trying to grab hold of my heart before it shatters as tears stream down my face. The sense of shame forces me down, and I kneel next to her.

We did this.

"Oh my God," is all I can think to mutter. Her large brown eyes drift in my direction. "I'm," I say, my voice shuddering. I breathe, hoping to inhale some of her pain for her. "I'm here with you," I say, struggling to speak. "You're not alone."

This is someone's daughter. I could have been this girl's teacher. I could have been her mother.

Why didn't they allow us to continue to the forward camp during our scouting expedition? We could have, should have stopped this madness. As soon as communications were cut off, we should have continued on to this camp and made sure it was safe. Instead, we partied the night before coming here. I partied, laughed, and joked instead of being here to save this child.

"I'm so sorry."

How insignificant the belated apology must sound. Yet, I cannot stop myself from giving it.

Behind me I hear the man chattering on with more talk of God. But he is pure evil.

Still, some good can come of this. Justice can be served if I take the life of that psychopath! He can never be allowed to do this again.

"No... please," the girl begs the moment I release her hands to stand... to kill LeRoux. "Please... don't go. Don't... leave me," she pleads as a bubble of blood spills from her lips and more tears slide down her cheeks.

Her eyes are becoming more and more vacant as they stare into my own. She's dying slow.

"Don't want... rejoin alone. Please..." she begs, struggling to tighten her grip on my hand. "I'm scared... I'm scared. I'm scared," she cries.

125

"No, no, I'm not leaving. I'm here with you, sweetie. It's okay... it's okay, I won't let anyone hurt you aga —" My voice shatters as I struggle to say more, pushing the lump in my throat down with a swallow. "I won't let him touch you again."

"I'm scare —" she repeats, her voice fainter as life slips from her. "I want... want my mommy. I want my mommy."

My heart swells with despair. "Shhhhh, she's with you, honey. I swear to God she's with you. She loves you, sweetheart, and her love is wherever you are. She is always with you."

I reach down and press my lips against her now cool forehead.

God, please let me take this pain from her!

"We have a medic incoming for the FOG. He'll be reaching you in a moment, David," I hear over the comms.

That was Jacob. David sent a message over the private line? The direct line to the top brass? He sent a message to recover a fallen FOG, but not one to save this little girl?

I think of the trigger in my pocket. A man protecting the actions of another man. They're all to blame.

If they get that madman into an egg, I'll not have the chance to kill him, but I cannot leave this girl alone. I won't. I won't let her die scared, crying for her mother. "I'm here with you, sweetheart," I repeat, stroking her soft curly hair, kissing her cold forehead again and again.

"LaPaige, this way, now!" I hear David say, but this time, not over the comms.

He has to be a FOG to have gotten here this quickly.

"Isn't he the FOG, though?" I hear a voice ask. The familiar clang of an egg being dropped onto the ground rings out from behind the flaps.

"First things first, there's a little girl back there. She's been seriously injured. Help her," David orders, stern.

"But I was told to pick up the —"

"Hey! Get your ass in there and help that girl!" David yells. I can hear the pain in his voice.

126

There are slight sounds of a scuffle, then LaPaige appears, along with David, who's pushing him from behind.

Thank you, David. Thank you for proving me wrong.

"Oh... wow," LaPaige says, gazing at the child's sprawled and bloodied form. "I... I don't think I can help with all of this," he stutters, looking to his big white box marked with a bright red star, then the shattered child before us.

"You have to do something. You have to help her," I beg. "Please, help her."

For a moment, he looks as if he'll run in the opposite direction. But, with his lips pressed tight, he moves forward. "Okay, let me have a look." Kneeling next to her, he touches her crushed sternum, his eyes glancing down at her utterly destroyed lower half.

"She's got some serious internal injuries," I inform him.

He looks her up and down, clearly not sure where to start. "Yeah... I can" — he pauses to take a deep breath — "I can see that." He fumbles in his white box, looking, touching, and lifting before dropping the items back into the med kit.

"Well?"

He shrugs, tears welling up in his eyes.

Do something! "We can't let her die like this! Her breathing," I say, leaning down close to her parted lips. "It's getting more and more shallow."

He only shakes his head as his shoulders sag and tears drop onto his lap. Then, he stops searching.

"What?"

Moving from the entrance into the room, David falls to LaPaige's side, onto his knees. Touching LaPaige's arm, he pulls just enough to turn LaPaige to face him. "How much morphine do you have?" he whispers, looking hard into the medic's eyes.

For the first time, I see the calm and cool David cry.

127

I've finally caught up to David. Standing outside of the forward camp, nearly one hundred feet away from the entrance, he watches our techs reconstruct the sand-filled barriers that once surrounded the area. They lumber about, using small powered-suits to move the heavy blocks that fit together like a child's building toys. Nearby, just beyond the barrier, hundreds of dense plastic bags filled with RX crystals are placed in a massive semicircle to the south of the huge tree-building.

David barely appears to notice the large trucks that rumble past, causing dust to billow up into gray clouds of RX-tainted smog.

Normal soldiers who are assigned to handle the horrible toxin are generally covered from head to toe in black and gray gas suits. The young people within the vehicles, they have no protection at all. I fear for their health.

As soon as the trucks stop, men geared up from head to toe, ventilated masks and all, begin unloading additional RX from the rear of each vehicle, forming a human chain handing the thirty-pound bags to one another with a hypnotic synchronization. Above them, on the toppled treetop, other techs clamor amongst one another rebuilding and/or replacing the mechanized mortars, cannons, and stationary guns. Methodically, they clean out each unit, yanking vines from the war machines.

We are all preparing for the inevitable Keynosian attack. It won't be long before we're shelled by their seeds. So preemptively, as always, we're spraying RX a mile in all directions. It's sad. If we don't poison the land and ourselves, we allow the Keynosians to use the very earth against us. We're basically poisoning ourselves to save ourselves.

But, after my encounter with those black trees, something tells me the Keynosians may have finally figured a way around the RX. I pray I'm wrong.

After what happened with LeRoux, I have to talk to David. The entire incident sits on my heart like a ton of bricks. It slows me down, dulling my mind, making it difficult to think about anything else but that incident. Patricia and Ophelia were supportive as always, but they were not there. They didn't experience what David, LaPaige, and I did last night. I need to unload on someone who truly understands how I feel. That someone is David.

I make a beeline towards his position as he continues to stare out across the darkening afternoon sky. As soon as I reach him, I feel a swell of anger. Why didn't he let me kill LeRoux? He and Jackson couldn't have kept the death of LeRoux quiet? They could have easily given a story that told everyone of an accident or lied and stated that the man forced our hands. Why not let me kill him?

I need the answers that only he can provide.

"What the hell is wrong with you?"

He doesn't turn, he only cocks his head to the side and sighs. "Jos, I couldn't let you kill Michael."

He knows his first name? "And why not? You saw what he did. You saw how that girl suffered."

"Well, there's a couple of reasons. One: the man wasn't in his right mind. We both have experience with that.

"Two: if you were to kill him, they'd immediately charge you with murder and stick you in an egg for the rest of your life.

"Lastly, we don't need any more dead *or* frozen FOGs."

I walk in front of him, blocking his view of the construction efforts. I want to see his eyes. "Michael, huh? Is the rapist a friend of yours?" I say, feeling the venom on my lips.

"Michael was actively suffering, Jocelyn. Couldn't you tell the man needed help? He didn't need your blade," he replies, his voice listless and flat.

"Sometimes, death is all the help needed."

He looks up, fire in his eyes. "Would you feel that way if Ophelia did something heinous? Would you be so willing to put her down for doing something so far from her character that you can't imagine it was her that committed the crime?"

I grit my teeth hard. "Don't you drag Ophelia into this." The mere mention of Ophelia, my friend, in the same context as LeRoux immediately boils my blood.

He doesn't say anything, just looks at me for a few seconds before drawing his hand over his mouth. "Look, Jos, I'll never excuse him for what he did, but I can't just toss him to you so you can exact some form of revenge either. His actions were born of a broken mind, not an evil heart."

To even compare Ophelia to that animal... But, what if she takes another turn? What if her madness becomes as sick and twisted as LeRoux's?

"Ophelia is nothing like that... murderer. That rapist," I say, seething. She'll never become that.

"I'm not comparing them, Jos."

"Then don't bring her name up if you're not comparing them!" I yell into his face. "Ophelia has never hurt any of us... never. She saved lives, even when her mind failed her. She saved lives! Even when she was at her worst, she was better than most. She *is* better than most." She's an angel... my angel.

The memories are still vivid. I suffered a shot to the thigh, a pop seed that shattered my femur and almost tore the leg from my torso. Unable to move away, I caught the brunt of a Keynosian worbler-shell explosion.

The explosion knocked me unconscious.

I was awakened by the sound of my uniform being ripped from my body. Two FOGs, both tanks and my teammates at the time, dragged me away, out of sight. Their intent was clear.

If Ophelia hadn't been there...

"I'm not trying to put down your friend, I'm just saying it can happen to any of us. It's already happening to most. I know you know about all of the reports of FOGs getting so confused that they attack the wrong people, right? Then, there are those old reports of FOG soldiers lashing out suddenly in their sleep, destroying entire barracks. If it were to happen to me, would you kill me?"

"Yes. If you started raping, absolutely."

He shakes his head. "Oh, I see. You're just a cold-blooded killer. Gotcha."

She cried for her mother.

"He killed that little girl, David, all the while jabbering on about some bizarre variant of the Great Mother doctrine."

He turns back to the darkening sky. "If you really want to blame someone for that girl's death, Jocelyn, blame me." Tears well up in his eyes. "It was my call to go back to main base and report what we found. I'm the reason we didn't continue on to the forward camp. It was my call to go to that first tent instead of fanning out to check this entire base. My orders, no one else's.

"You saw her, Jos. He recently raped that girl. We were, what... five minutes too late? Less?" He wipes a hand down his face. "If I wasn't so cautious... if I'd just pushed on just a bit faster... we, we could have saved her."

"How could you come to that ridiculous conclusion? It was impossible for you to know what was going on."

As a tear falls, he quickly wipes his face again with the heel of his hand. "It was my call —"

"Stop it!" I snap at him. "Stop blaming yourself for his actions. Whatever was there, whatever was in this Michael's character, it was there before the Sacrifice turned him into a FOG. It was Michael that hurt that girl. He killed her, not you."

He continues to wipe as another tear finds its way to his cheek. "I couldn't help any of them. Richards, Hanson, Cox... none of them. That girl, she's just another person I failed —"

"Stop it, please," I say, but my heart isn't in the protest. I understand.

All of the people I couldn't save, the people I watched die. I couldn't do anything. It's not fair. So many lost, so many people I knew, gone.

"All I end up doing, all I ever end up doing is watching people, friends, die," he says, his voice faltering. "And yet, here I stand. All the people I met, the FOGs that helped me, most are either dead or trapped in eggs. But, here *I* am. The fuck, Jos, with all of this power I have, why couldn't I at least save a few more of them? Why'd they give us just enough power to watch the death of others while we survive?"

In his pained face, I find the reflection of my own failures. Like a black hole, his sadness pulls me in, causing me to lunge at him and embrace him, my arm wrapping around his neck in desperation. He pauses, then his shoulders slump down as his face lands on my shoulder and his arm grips tight around my waist. Shuddering, he makes no sound as he cries, and I can feel a familiar desperation in his embrace. His tight grip begs for a peace far beyond what I, or anyone, can provide. It's a need I understand intimately. I crave it for the safety of my own soul.

This longing permeates our ranks, taking the shape of drugs for some, sex for others, and religion for many more. For me, it takes the shape of sickening emptiness that's nestled in the pit of my stomach and claws its way to my heart. The emptiness has consumed so much of my sweetness, my softness, I wonder how any man can find me feminine. How much of what I see as being a woman is left? What have I become?

Why does David even want me if I've become this monster?

We cry together. Two of the world's most powerful living weapons that find themselves utterly impotent and broken before the horrors of war. We squeeze and claw, seeking a mercurial peace in each other's arms. It's nothing but a bandage covering a very deep wound.

It will have to do for now.

"You think anyone saw us?" he asks, composing himself with an empty half-smile as we finally separate. Reaching out, he wipes the streaks of tears from my cheeks with a frayed strip of pure white cloth taken from his back pocket.

The man actually carries a handkerchief? Who the hell does that anymore? Still, the gesture is sweet. "May I?" I ask. Taking the frayed fabric, I finish the job of mopping up the moist remnants of my grief.

I expand my senses and pick up only those few who are working in the dimming light of the early evening sun, now half hidden by distant trees.

"It's doubtful anyone is even paying attention to us. Even if they are, they probably just think we were making out."

We laugh, cautiously looking at one another at different times. There's an honesty, a gentleness to this man that I find myself drawn to. The more I uncover, the more interesting he becomes. The more interested I am in him.

"So how long do you think it'll take them to finish the defenses?" I ask as another salting truck rumbles past us, spraying toxic bright-blue crystals that stream from tubes that protrude from the undercarriage of the truck through flattened-out supra-plastic pipes.

Disgusting. I shut down my sense of smell, avoiding the onslaught of the sharp, sickeningly sweet scent. I watch the crystals as they fizz like butter landing on a hot pan; the crystals melt into a liquid and then to smoke as they make contact with the earth. The RX coats all of the green grass beneath us in a blue film and obscures the ground with a fog. By tomorrow, all of the life will be replaced with withering brown sludge.

David quickly covers his nose and mouth with his tear-stained handkerchief. "The defenses won't take long to set up. At the speed these guys are going... two or three hours, max. Our West Coast boys are pretty fast," David says, his voice slightly muffled.

Why is he covering his face like that? We're FOGs, it's not like the toxin can harm us. "By whose standards?"

He presses his handkerchief tighter to his face and coughs.

"Are you okay, Dave?"

"Dave?" he says, drawing his eyebrows down.

"What? You don't like people calling you Dave?"

"Generally no," he says. He glances away for a moment, then returns. "Buuuuut, I think I'll let it slide, just for you. It'll be our little secret. Plus, it sounds much better coming from your lips." He smiles. It's bright enough to peek from underneath the white cloth he's using as a shield from the RX.

"Let it slide?"

"Yeah, let it slide," he says, continuing to grin.

His grins are like yawns, before you know it, you're smiling along with him. "I guess I should feel privileged."

"Yes, you should. But remember, you're going to be the only one that can call me Dave, so please, let's just keep that between you and I. Deal?" He extends his hand.

"Deal," I answer, giving his hand a firm shake.

He coughs much more aggressively. It's like he's coughing.

"Are you okay... Dave."

"God, I hate smelling this crap! It always irritates my throat, gets into my nose, my eyes —"

I chuckle. "Well, just shut off those senses."

"I can't," he says, pulling his uniform shirt up to filter out the stench. The remaining larger crystals finally begin to melt away, creating a layer of sludge that resembles a polluted sea. It obscures everything below its wispy waves in a blue chemical soup.

This stuff is really bothering him. "We better get you inside... Dave."

Within the tree which we've constructed our base would normally fall into darkness as the sun drifts slowly under the horizon, but we're using hanging lights to chase the night away. Positioned haphazardly across the ceiling and strung together like holiday decorations, the lights are powered by a generator-truck that hums continuously outside. The beast is so loud I can hear it through the thick wooden walls.

Some areas are too bright, others not bright enough as the unnatural light bathes the area in its yellowish hue. It serves only to turn the once calming browns and beiges of the walls into the color of shit.

David and I walk through the rehabilitated camp. The old tents were removed, replaced with newer dwellings outfitted with air purifiers and environment controllers. It looks like a completely different place now.

But, I remember what happened here. They can't remove the past with paint, fabric, and a new set of lamps.

Across an opening, where people have been congregating to chat, I see a group of prisoners in the distance. They're seated on a row of metal chairs placed against the curved wall of the tree's interior. They're awaiting transport to the Western camp. Armed guards stand at either end of the large canopied space they're sheltered under. Shackled and still filthy, the cannibal soldiers will have to stand before the local tribunal as the military has disowned them. I truly hope they are held accountable for their crimes. They should not be allowed to see the light of day again.

As we move closer, I see the victims, seated at the opposite end of the long green tarp. The Keynosian women are dressed in our uniforms as they bolt down mouthfuls of food in quiet desperation.

I remember their faces, each one seared into my mind. The fear that swelled in their eyes when they saw David and Jackson. The relief that washed over them when they saw me, another woman. It brought me a wave of happiness. Then and there I realized one simple truth. We are women first, all under the threat of male predation. Even as a FOG, the threat is never-ending.

Despite all these women have endured, they don't look as deprived as the cannibals, although still obviously weakened. Was LeRoux feeding them in order to extend his abuse?

At least we've replaced their tattered clothing. Shackled at the ankles, the women sit together, huddling around a large electrical heater, their many hands extended to either catch some radiant warmth or grab another handful of food stacked on trays resting on the floor in front of them. They eat from anyone's tray, despite each having their own meal. Such a lovely expression of unity.

How terrible it must feel. To be surrounded by thousands of your enemies — people who've caused you and your fellow captives untold harm. Then, to be saved from that hell only to be sent to prison far away from your true home. It must feel like a cycle of endless torment. The least we could do for these displaced people is provide them with a reasonable holding station before the war ends. That concentration camp we're putting our Keynosian prisoners in is nothing more than a series of shacks atop a landfill.

Releasing what must have been a long-held breath, David gives a hard, definitive nod. "I'm going to talk to those women," he says, passing in front of me, walking briskly towards the huddled Keynosians.

"What? Why?"

He doesn't respond as he continues towards them.

I follow, but can't help but wonder what he's planning to do. "Ummm, what exactly are you going to talk to them about?"

He shrugs. "Honestly, I don't know yet," he says, partially turning towards me. "I guess I really just want to say... sorry, or something along those lines."

"That's a bold move," I reply, catching up on his right. "If I were them, I'd probably spit on you."

"So be it," he says dismissively.

"You know, you're not the spokesperson for those madmen, or LeRoux, right? You're not the one who committed those crimes against them, so you're not the one that should be apologizing. Those men are at the other end of the tent. They should have that responsibility."

He stops in his tracks, his face telling me of his annoyance. "What does this have to do with you, Jos? I'll be the one they'll be spitting on, not you. So don't worry about it." He turns and continues towards them. "I'm more than willing to take the hits for the Alliance because... well, because someone has to do it. If not me, a FOG, then who? If not now, then when?"

"The criminals that did it, that's who should be spat on. Not the guy that saved them."

"We're all criminals in war. Just because our nation sanctioned murder, that does not make killing and tormenting other people justice. It's not solely the sick of mind or screwed-up psychos that are the problem, it's everyone that's complicit in the killing. It's all of us, on both sides."

"So apologizing will make it all right?"

"Better than tossing our hands up and saying nothing at all."

"Dave, I'm pointing out to you the fact that you're not responsible. You're not to blame."

"No, Jos... no," he says with his eyes closed, shaking his head. "I'm not the person that raped her... killed her, but that does not mean I'm blameless in that little girl's death."

"So you're saying I'm also partially to blame for that girl's death?"

With a huff he looks around the cavernous forward camp. "What's with you and trying to avoid guilt, Jos? Do you want absolution? Fine, I absolve you. Better?"

"I'm not avoiding anything. I'm pointing out who the true culprits are," I say, pointing to the Alliance prisoners at the other end of wall. "And not just them. All of the people that started the war, the politicians that fed us mistrust and doubt. The hate-mongers that fed on our wealth and transformed it into extreme xenophobic propaganda. The false religious that swore to us this is God's will. All of them. They did this. The blood of thousands rests upon those hands."

"Nice speech," he says, stepping closer to me. "But it's not those people that are fighting this war. It's us. It's those men over there that are sitting and awaiting long prison sentences. It's Takdeer. It's all of the people that are out there now, fighting and waiting to fight. It's those of us that voted for the politicians who started the fighting. It's us, Jos. It's all of us," he says, motioning with his finger between him and me. "We're destabilizing their country. We've opened the door for this, all of this. Shit, we're still doing it and will probably do some more of it tomorrow and the day after."

His words sting. I don't want to feel this guilt. I don't want it. I don't deserve it.

"Jos?" He steps even closer to me. "I understand what you're saying. I get it, we didn't make those decisions for those soldiers. We didn't force anyone to rape or kill. But, it's the Alliance, the country itself, that hurt them. And guess what? We are that country. We are the Alliance. Our body, our blood, our bones... our choices. We are *all* responsible."

I want to scream at him about how wrong his stance is. But I can't. I can't because it's not wrong. The Keynosians point their weapons at a soldier and call her Northern. They're not addressing that individual, they are addressing a nation. They are addressing the Alliance as a whole. And it goes both ways. At no point did I see the Guardsmen as anything more than enemies of the state. I didn't see the individuals. I saw only the enemies of my tribe.

I glance past him to see one of the Keynosian women touch the hand of a younger one. Their eyes meet, and the older woman nods reassuringly, struggling to coax a smile from the younger one's dry, chapped lips. Another, with the black sleeves of our uniform shirt rolled up her bony forearms, reaches around to rub the girl's back.

Her eyes meet mine, and she smiles. She remembers me.

They're just like Patricia, Ophelia, and me. Sisters bound by the horrors of war and tragedy.

"You're right... you're right," I say, punctuating my words with a slow nod. I grab his hand, much to his surprise. "Well, since you're committed to going over there, I can't let you do it alone. I'm coming with you... just in case. Okay?"

"Just in case?"

I shrug. "I don't know... just in case something happens and I need to intervene."

He chuckles. "Thank you. I appreciate that."

A twinge of nervousness strikes my chest as the older woman, my age it appears, stares at us warily. She taps two others, who turn, in unison, to watch our approach. A deep, welling sadness builds in my heart as soon as it becomes clear to the women that we are here for them, and their eyes widen with hints of fear.

Without speaking a word, David kneels before the women, bowing at their feet.

Shit! I didn't think he'd do that. Should I follow suit? For some unknown reason, it feels wholly appropriate to do so.

So now, I kneel, head down and tense, preparing for any coming blow as I am completely and utterly defenseless before them.

"On behalf of the Alliance, I am so very sorry for your suffering," David says in a clear voice. "I'm so sorry... I'm sorry I couldn't... I couldn't stop —" is all he's able to get out before he's suddenly overwhelmed. Grief crushes his ability to speak.

I think to speak, to say something that would show these women what's in our hearts, but the growing lump in my throat prevents me. It halts my voice, but not my body. I place my hand over my heart as tears fall freely. I have no idea what they'll do. At this point, I no longer care. I'm willing to take and accept any retribution they're capable of dispensing. In resignation to this fate, I close my eyes and wait for judgment.

I hear them move about us. Surrounding us, but no words are spoken. I can feel the pounding of their hearts. What are they waiting for? Just get on with it.

For God's sake, do it already!

Seconds pass, and still nothing. A minute, then two (I think), and still I feel no attacks come, and no insults are cast upon me. What are they doing? Unable to resist my curiosity, I open my eyes and am greeted by a circle of silently crying Keynosian women. The older Keynosian, her gray hair dense and thick, places a hand on the top of my head. She smooths down my hair and brings her hand slowly around my head, down my temple, stopping at my jaw in one continuous motion. "Thank you," she says, lifting my eyes to meet hers. Beautiful, clear dark eyes, which belie the horrible treatment she experienced, greet me with tenderness. Her eyes sparkle, reflecting the brightness of the fluorescent light behind me and the orange glow of the heater. "But, like us, you gotta let it go." She turns to David. "You both gotta let it go. It won't be easy for any of us, but know this truth: dirt held in the hand grows nothing."

She takes my hands into hers and gently kisses me on the apex of my head. I feel the dryness of her lips on my scalp as they press soft into my hair.

We look at one another, quietly, gently, like sisters seeing one another after years apart. A lifetime of separation. Giving my hands a firm squeeze, she releases them and smiles as she closes her eyes and begins to hum. The sound... it's so warm and rich, I feel it in my heart, touching my soul. It's a simple tune, almost childlike, but there's something more that flows from the notes. It's something wonderfully human, something loving.

As the melody repeats, the others join in, adding their warmth to the soothing sounds.

I expected vengeance and received... What did I receive? Is it peace? Is it a release from guilt? Is it the touch of humanity in the most inhuman of circumstances? Whatever it is, I'll take it, given from the hands of people we deemed savages.

They are not my enemies. They are me, on the other side of a coin we call Earth.

Ophelia and Patricia staked out our section in the tiny women's barracks as soon as its construction was finished... as far away from the exits as possible. With 170 or so women, FOG and non-FOG, officer or grunt, being given only this one small barrack, there's no room for well-mannered patience.

Standing in the dimly lit female quarters, I was surrounded by the other women, who'd gathered the moment I began telling the tale.

"And not one of them spit on you *or* David?" Patricia croaks loudly. "Did they at least kick David?" she asks, her hair still wet from a recent, short shower.

"It took me by surprise," I admit. "I was fully prepared to get a smack in the mouth or something. But honestly, they were... incredible women."

"And they just sang and cried with you guys?" Ophelia says, her hand flat on her chest, clearly preparing to shed a tear. "Ohhh, I so wish I was there. They deserved such a heartfelt apology from every single one of us."

With a grunt, Patricia flops on her bunk, her mouth twisted. "I damn sure wouldn't have done it. I have enough scars already, and I don't need to give some Keynosian chicks the chance to mess up this face," she says.

"Oh please!" Ophelia moans as the others laugh. "You always act tough, but really... you're just a sweetheart," she says, winking.

"You better stop hitting on me, Oa. I may take you up on that.

"And who's to say sweethearts like me aren't tough too? Shit, if you really think about it, it's those Keynosians who are way more sweetheart-ed than me. To survive what they went through and still be forgiving? Those are definitely tough women. They're damn sure tougher than I am, 'cause I wouldn't be forgiving of any one of you if that happened to me. I mean, really? The girl's mother had to listen to her only daughter being raped and beaten," Patricia says, breathing out sharply. "It don't get much tougher than that."

"Lord, I can't, I won't imagine it, in fact," Rawlings says, running a brush through her thick silver mane as she looks into a small mirror affixed to the green canvas wall near her bunk. "I assuredly would have lost it after that. I really can't understand how that mother is even beginning to deal with that kind of trauma. In fact, just thinking of losing my daughter, it hurts my heart."

"I wonder if she actually saw it happen?" Barbara, a young FOG, asks.

141

She's such a nice girl. Like most weaker FOGs, she's been fighting as support, mixed into the ranks of non-FOGs to bolster their combat power. Even so, she's still managed to amass scars virtually everywhere on her body. Clear evidence of her bravery and how weak her actual healing ability is. She and the others gathered look at me for the answer.

I can only shrug. "I don't think so. They were being held in a different barrack most of the time. But, if they didn't see it, they knew. They had to know."

"The screams must have been heartbreaking," Ophelia says, pulling her knees up to her chest.

"I think I would have killed myself," Rachel adds. "Slit my own throat or something. End it before allowing myself to be raped to death like that."

Rachel is not fighting on the front lines. She, like LaPaige, is a tech. Rachel chuckled and shook her head when I told her of LaPaige's behavior in the tent. She explained that he's a "by the book" kind of fellow, but he also has a really big heart. It's not that he's inept, but he freezes in unexpected situations. He's first and foremost a scientist, not a soldier. Saving a dying girl was something well beyond his capabilities to address on the fly.

"What about the FOG that starved those norms? He's to blame, not those soldiers. They shouldn't even be prosecuted for what they *had* to do," a non-FOG says from behind Rawlings.

"They ate people, and we actually have laws against that kind of thing," Rachel says, with a sarcastic snicker.

A young lady steps out in the open from behind Rawlings. A bunk over, she walks around and moves closer to the small gathering of FOGs and Patricia. "That FOG took all of the supplies," she says with a frown. "It was that *FOG* who killed and raped those prisoners... and probably who knows what else. He's to blame."

The blond, short and stocky, places her hand on her hip. "What I want to know is, why didn't you lot just kill that rapist instead of sticking him into an egg? Why is he even being allowed to continue to serve?"

I can sense the tension mounting as the other women in the barracks begin paying attention to the conversation.

"What the fuck are ya'll taking about? To even imply that the cannibals shouldn't be charged... Are you even trying to be serious? Those bastards ate people. They don't deserve a free pass for that," Patricia barks back at the husky woman.

Surprisingly, she does not back away.

"No surprise you'd side with the FOGs, Patel," someone else says from behind the husky blond.

Patricia freezes at the comment, clearly taken aback and upset by it.

She jumps up from her bunk. "First, who the fuck are you?" she says, pointing, jabbing her finger in the general direction of the comment. "And second, what the fuck is that supposed to mean, 'No surprise you'd side with the FOGs'? I've been in the shit from jump, have you?" Patricia steps towards the non-FOG, glaring. Her damaged arm shows how tight her fists are clenched, as the muscles under her paper-thin skin ripple, tendons pulling taut. "Where the fuck have you been? Did you get nearly burned to death saving your platoon? Huh? No, all most of you've done is shoot from the back of *these women*. Just watching *these same women* here run right at the bullets to protect your sorry asses." Suddenly she stops her approach and appears exasperated. She turns her back to the non-FOGs and sighs, closing her eyes.

Not finished with her rant, she turns back to the group. "Listen, just don't start that shit comparing FOGs and norms, okay, because I'm not trying to hear that noise. If anyone's been giving their lives to this war, it's them. They've given not only their lives here on the front, but they've given their lives back home as well. They'll probably end up being monitored for the rest of their existence. All this for home and country. How about you?" she says. No one responds. "No one? Yeah... I thought not."

I fight back a grin. She stalks back, getting near to me, and I touch

143

Patricia on her arm and coax her back down, encouraging her to sit on her bunk and relax. "Calm down, Patricia," I say. What I really want to say is, that's my girl! But she knows my heart enough. I don't need to speak the words out loud.

"I'm calm, Jos, but what the hell is wrong with them for even trying to make that distinction?" She's still fuming despite having said her piece. She has good reason to feel such anger towards the comment, just as the comment warranted being said. We are all supposed to be equals on the field of battle, yet that's never been the case. From the automatic sergeant rank we FOGs receive, to the vast amount of leeway we're given in regards to fraternization. While I agree it's not fair, it's certainly understandable, as Patricia so eloquently pointed out. Without us, without our bravery on the field, the Keynosians would have won a long time ago. We may be less likely to die out there in the field, but that does not mean we're not taking a lot of hits. We still bleed. We still feel pain... lots of pain in fact. Just because we can survive an acid-seed attack does not mean the ordeal doesn't feel like we're being burned alive.

Still, just because their feelings make sense, doesn't make it right. "Pat... they have a point," I tell her. She greets the comment with a look of annoyance. "A crime is a crime, regardless of the reason. If no leniency can be allowed the normal soldiers, why is it given to us FOGs?" Pat, you weren't there. You didn't see what he did. He tortured, then murdered some of those women. He raped and murdered that girl. Once LeRoux was done, he gave the corpses to his fellow soldiers like they were sides of beef. What could they do against him? What could they do with those corpses when faced with starvation? Michael, the rapist, may not be as strong as Jackson or Ophelia, or as fast as me or Rawlings, but he's still much more powerful than any of those cannibals were.

Sucking her teeth, Patricia sighs. "You can't be serious," she responds, looking disappointed in my comments. "That asshole was out of his mind, sure" — she gestures, flicking her hand away from

144

her own temple — "but... wait a second." Suddenly she shakes her head and raises her hands. "I don't believe ya'll got me defending a rapist! This is nuts. Matter of fact, I'll just add this, they should just cut off his twig and berries while he's in the egg. Fuck him. That should be the first step. But, still..." She pauses to glance at Ophelia. "Remember, the guy's mind was totally shattered. Matter of fact, what soldier in this damned military is going to walk away without some kind of screw loose? Hell, I grew up in a family of soldiers and there ain't one of them that isn't just a bit lopsided."

"So should the cops just allow FOGs to do whatever they want and only receive a slap on the wrist?" Ophelia asks Patricia.

"No, but that isn't the point I'm trying to make. At least we non-FOGs can hide how broken we are. Deal with that shit in therapy or something. But you FOGs... ya'll can get so fucked up..."

"What should be done then, Pat? To FOGs if they do something criminal?" I ask.

"We need to help ya'll. Shit, we broke it, we should fix it, right?" Patricia takes a moment, looking at the crowd, now transfixed on her. "Look, if LeRoux is to be held accountable, what about the bastards that created him, huh? What about those guys who knew the process was dangerous but let it go on anyway?"

"Created us?" Ophelia says. She rises and stands closer to the FOGs. Closer to me.

I suddenly get the feeling that Patricia's concern is mostly about Ophelia and me. There's something in the way she's looking at us, a tenderness in her eyes. "Pat, I know you're not saying a FOG shouldn't be held responsible for terrible actions, but I'm just saying we can't completely excuse his behavior as the misdeeds of a broken mind. He may be suffering, sure, but what's going to happen if he slips again? Do we, as a nation, simply turn our back on what he did? He committed those acts. That was him, not solely misplaced synapses." As I speak, the non-FOGs, minus Patricia, nod in agreement. "At the very least, he should be kept in confinement and

145

if released, remain under constant watch. And we still don't know what happened to the three female soldiers that were stationed here."

Stepping forward, Rawlings waves her hands in the center of our gathering. "So what about us, Jocelyn? What about people like Ophelia and I? I had my time in the egg, as did she. What will you do with us if we suddenly snap? Should we also be locked in eggs forever?"

My eyes instantly head to Ophelia. "So what exactly do you recommend?" I reply, turning to Rawlings. "Should we do nothing about them? Or maybe we should simply wait for them to do something even more heinous?"

"Wait for us," Ophelia adds.

"Wait for us, what?"

"Wait for *us*. You said them. It's not them, it's us. It's Polly, Rachel, David, all FOGs, including yourself. We have names, and you have a name as well."

"Look, I know it's us, Ophelia." But it's not me, and I pray it'll never be me.

"Then say it, Jocelyn. You're going to have to face the fact that we are all potential ticking time bombs," Ophelia adds.

She's right. The only FOGs in this room that aren't on medication are Rachel and I.

A smile appears on her face. "What's funny is, I do agree with Jos. A true God-fearing nation can't do *nothing* about us FOGs going all crazy. The fact that we're going to patch that guy up with drugs and send him right back out into the field... well, that's just plain wrong. There are some crimes man can't sweep away. Yet, crimes like The Sacrifice, just like Patricia mentioned, we have stood idly by while tens of thousands die. All for the sake of increasing the nation's power. Is that really any different than us being okay with murder? Even the good book has specific laws against that kind of thing, and since we're a pre-dominantly Godsoul believing nation, those are the things we should draw the line on, and not just when it's convenient." Lifting her head, Ophelia looks past us and into the crowd of non-FOGs. "For me and my beliefs, cannibalism *and* rape are unforgivable offenses, FOG or not."

"Even if the person was forced to be a cannibal?" the tough blond asks.

Ophelia shrugs. "God gave us all free will, and what God has given, no man can take away. We always have a choice."

"Their choice was death or cannibalism."

"That's a choice, isn't it? We have to choose to obey God and be given a seat at his table, or we can disobey his word, even if it means our death to obey it. Death in the here and now, or eternal bliss with the keeper of my soul. I know what I'd choose," Ophelia says matter-of-factly. The crowd stands silent as she points to the blond. "What's your name?"

"Me?" she asks, but Ophelia only continues to hold her stare. "Coraley, Katherine Coraley," she answers. "But everyone calls me Kat."

Lighting up at the name, Ophelia grins. "That's a cute name. Kat... I like it," she says. "Look Kat, it's no secret that I'm a very religious person, I don't hide that. Even so, I'd never consider myself some kind of scholar of the word of God. But, I do know one thing... we all have free will. That free will was given to us by the divine, and no one can ever take it away. But with that power comes a price. The cost is that Point of Decision, where all of our souls will be tested.

"It's said that we each have a different Point of Decision, a crossroad. We each make a choice once that point comes, to choose either salvation or damnation. I believe, for those soldiers, that incident was their Point of Decision, their souls' crossroad. It was their time to choose damnation or salvation. They could be damned by committing utterly evil acts that would forever haunt them, dooming them to hell, or they could choose salvation. Salvation in knowing that even with their deaths, the enemy, the true enemy, could not win. Even at the cost of their mortal lives, they would not allow themselves to be broken by fear, overcome with sin that caused them to run away from the one true God. Those men chose damnation in both the hereafter as well as in the here and now."

147

"To die for the glory of God, is life itself," Rawlings adds.

"Amen."

The thudding sound of Keynosian bombs hammers the camp, sending shudders through the earth all around us. The eyes of everyone in the barracks dart towards the green canvas covering our heads. The sound of our own shelling soon begins in earnest as a response.

"Looks like it's starting," Barbara casually states, taking a deep breath as she pulls her black uniform top from the hanger positioned to the left of her cot.

There's a collective sigh as we each head to our respective spots and gear up for eventual combat, choosing to sleep in uniform.

Looking around at my comrades, I notice too many FOGs, far too many of us, grab opaque amber pill bottles and take a dose of medication. They need to be ready to fight.

I wonder... am I next? Will it be me who's next to receive the diagnosis that's ruined so many? Will it be me who has to swallow a tiny red pill to stave off complete madness? Will that madness lead me towards that eternal damnation Ophelia spoke about?

I could be next.

CHAPTER 6

BALANCING ACT

I hate this waiting crap," Patricia says, her voice muffled by the contoured gas mask strapped tight to her face. Her uniform covers every inch of flesh. Even her hair is held down against her skull with the smooth, matte black of her gear.

Our ten-man team has been sequestered to a hazmat wait-station — a fully encapsulated tube — while the techs RX bomb the area yet again. But, even in the wake of an RX bombing, many of the vines inch inexorably past the doorway — slowed but not stopped.

"I think I can say with confidence that none of us like the wait," I say, grabbing the back of her wrapped head.

Jacob strikes Petersen's thick metal shoulder harness and glares at the bright red numbers counting down the level of RX still hanging in the air outside the base. "Okay, boys and girls, get your gear in place. We have to have the base's defenses fully operational ASAP. Without those turrets keeping the Southies honest, we'll end up trapped in here like the previous crew. And that, we can't afford. The lives of the soldiers in here depends on us ensuring our supply line stays intact." He looks around at the group assembled, and nods. "Alright, as soon as we get out there, I want a standard formation on the doorway. Every eye needs to be on the lookout for scouts, no matter how unlikely it is they'll make an appearance. We'll be sitting ducks past this doorway once it seals behind us.

"Now, I want Martinez and Rawlings to stay in tight with your escorts, and don't wander. We can't afford to lose either of you ladies this far into enemy territory. You're both indispensable."

"You don't have to worry about Rawlings, Jake. I won't let her out of my... where she'd go?" Clarence asks, looking around for Rawlings, who moved so quickly he didn't notice. She's presently standing on his right, ducking behind the thick metal scaling of his harness. Its plates rise an inch from his shoulders and link together into a rigid band once it's under a charge. They need it. The kickback on dragon rifles during firing is pretty intense. Without the harness, I'm sure Clarence and all tanks would have to grip their weapons so tight they'd deform the metal.

We all laugh at the sound of Rawlings smacking his rear end hard enough to lift him to his toes.

"Looks like you've got some competition on the speed front, Martinez," Clarence says, rubbing his buttocks with one hand and trying to grab the elusive Rawlings with the other.

He only manages to catch air. She is fast, and seems to revel in that power. It's understandable. It must feel like time has reversed itself and given her a renewed sense of youth. Age doesn't matter very much when you're in a FOG body.

"You're going to have to do better than that, Marshall," David says through a gas mask. He's the only FOG in the team with one on. You'd think he'd be able to withstand the poison being as strong as he is, but you never know. Every FOG has at least one chink in their armor.

"You talk... wait until you see Martinez move," Clarence says.

A round of "ooohs" fill the air.

"I have Marshall, remember? I watched her move in a fight."

"I'm sure you watched her move in a fight, out of a fight, walking around, eating dinner, etc," Dougie quips, and the ooohs become mmhmms.

"I'm telling you, guys, Martinez is insanely fast," Clarence continues, clearly trying to get us riled up.

"Are you saying I'm not fast?"

"No, you're fast... but are you Martinez fast? I dunno," he says with a shrug, while checking the ammo in his backpack.

"Really now?" Rawlings says, taking the bait. "Looks like we're going to have to settle who's the fastest FOG today." Rawlings presses her thumb against her chin and squints, her eyes narrowed into black slits. "So, what's a suitable challenge?" she asks herself.

"Twenty on Martinez, whatever the challenge," Petersen says, turning to Rawlings. "I've seen her move. Sorry, Rawlings, you're going down against this chick."

"Seriously, Gerard? You're going to bet against me?"

Petersen answers with a shrug and smile. "Hey, this is about the cash, Polly, and I'm a gambling man."

"Not possible. No one is faster than Rawlings. Shit, I'll take that bet." Dougie joins, pulling out a wad of bills. "Double or nothing!"

"Alright guys, enough!" Powell snaps. "Now's not the time to pull out your money. We've got to get our heads ready, and I've yet to see all of you even check your gear completely." Startled by the outburst, our mouths begin to sag at the edges, until Powell's face softens. "We'll collect the winnings afterwards. Fifty on Rawlings!"

The tube explodes with bets, boasts, and the overall brouhaha of warriors.

The tension in the tube has become palpable, nearly audible. The timer is getting close. At 32, we go and it's currently at 36 and falling rapidly. The auto-launchers stopped functioning last night, and I truly doubt each of the thirty turrets we have mounted were hit directly and jammed by vines. Not even Guardsmen are that good firing from long range.

The digital numbers above turn from 33 to 32, and the hum of electricity stops. The once-rigid mesh flaps on either side of the wait-station tubing whip out, forced open by the tube's pressure. I feel the change inside of my ears as the machines at the other end of the tube whirl on briefly before shutting off, giving us all a quick rush of air before it all goes totally still.

151

The dead flap begins to softly sway back and forth, moved by the breeze that carries hazy-blue wisps of the poison that undulates around the edges of the forward camp's main entrance.

"On my mark, Jeffersen, Marshall, and Rawlings, left of exit," Powell says, his voice echoing through our earpieces, his hand raised high so we can all see the visual signal if we can't hear it. "Next, Jackson, Rogers, and Martinez, right. Last, Santos, Patel, and me. Petersen, secure rear flank."

Tense seconds pass in complete silence, and I begin to push my senses. The familiar tingling flows down my spine in waves, like rivulets of water flowing from my crown towards my lower back area.

I can feel energy pulsating all around me from the machines at the rear of the tube and even more so, from the powerful heartbeats of the soldiers around me. Like waves flowing outward at each beat, heat laps at my skin from all directions. I can't help but respond. My blood, pumping hot, rushes through my frame as my body tries to match the rhythm of those around me, especially Ophelia and Patricia. There's a wanting, a desire to be close. I'm sure it stems from the time when we were apes needing the warmth of other apes to chase away the chill of night air. There was a time when I mistook that pull for sexual energy. That wasn't the truth. It's the longing for human connection, a wanting that's intrinsic to humankind. A desire for community emanating from our very bodies. It's beyond lust, beyond the desire for sexual contact. It is what we are.

In my opinion, loneliness is one of the most painful feelings a human can experience.

Next, I listen. The breathing, the heartbeats, tapping of fingers, grinding of teeth, the sounds of gas in digestive systems, it's all an endless litany of notes in the song of life. It now completely surrounds me. It's a most beautiful song. Even the sounds of wet eyelids sticking and sliding over tired eyes sounds sweet in the midst of corpses. But now is not the time for such "happy thoughts," therefore these are the things I force out of my mind. The symphony

152

of life is too much noise, too distracting to think on in the face of war. So, I focus past it and allow the sounds of the humanity close to me to fade into useless background noise, like the whisper of wind we don't notice until we focus our attention.

I smell the stench of Petersen's feet, the nearly overpowering aroma of Clarence's cologne, the faint aroma of blood that surrounds Patricia, and the breath mint clicking in Rawlings' mouth. These are just a few of the smells that fill this tube. They're all stuffed in here, packed tight, pushing against the transparent plastic walls of this tube it seems. Even the acrid smell of those antipsychotics Ophelia pops into her mouth like candy and the scent of Clarence's pheromones as he frequently glances at Rawlings' rear end... the dirty boy. Despite the smells that mask normal human aromas, like perfumes, they still emit scents that are unique to each of them. It's as if I "see" their fingerprints with my nose.

I really enjoy the smell of David. Musky, masculine, and never hidden by cologne. It's peaceful in its simplicity. It fits him.

Enough of that... focus on the task at hand, girl.

I gather my senses and push them further outward, beyond our hazmat cocoon. I push them outside, past the now flaccid mesh-metal flap. The first things to welcome me are the eerie sounds of scraping. Creeper-vines and black-worm seed roots frantically search for fuel through the haze of RX gas. Under normal circumstances, creeper-vines would search out victims for twenty-four hours straight, attracted to the specific smell all humans share. The RX gas renders them virtually powerless — they're too weak to threaten anyone now, but that doesn't diminish their hunger for human flesh and blood.

Slowly I kneel, pressing my hand firmly on the tightly compacted earth, listening, feeling intently for any sign of danger beyond the dying vines. I search for human life, for any hint of Guardsmen. Their woody smell, the sound of their thundering heartbeats, the vibrations of bipedal movement on the ground. Anything I can use to keep my tribe alive.

"Into position now," Jacob says, his eyes fixed on the swaying mesh barrier.

An ambush seems so unlikely. We blanketed the area with RX. I can't imagine the Keynosians would throw the lives of their Guardsmen away by sending them into so much poison. But, that didn't stop Takdeer, did it? Something has changed I think. The aggressiveness of their attacks last night, the black bullets, that oddball tree surrounded by Northern munitions, all of it speaks of a kind of desperation on their part. They are willing to toss away their future to secure the now.

I guess it's no different than what we did when the Keynosian military took over nearly half of our country, prompting us to create FOGs. A process that killed tens of thousands.

Desperation creates the most abhorrent behavior.

"Team 1, go," Jacob says calmly, dropping his hand.

David pulls back the flap, and the first group takes off in a flash.

Even after so many battles, I still feel a rush of nerves before heading into potential danger. I barely look at Jacob as I tense myself, preparing to run out into the open. My eyes meet David's and we smile in unison.

There's no cover out there. Just our backs to a wall of wood and before us, the top of the massive tree home strewn out across an open field. I can't shake the feeling that something is going to happen. We've backed the Keynosians into a corner, and anything backed into a corner will fight at its fiercest.

"Team 2, go."

Jackson, Ophelia, and I bolt out, weapons at the ready.

We are led by Jackson, and automatically we all head right, with the bright sun at our backs and the hovering blue RX gas lingering about an inch above the dying earth at our feet. At the southern-facing wall, we're greeted by a maze of branches jutting out from the fallen treetop. Some of the branches burrow into the ground, carving deep crevices, while others reach for rays of sunlight that struggle to filter through the canopy above. Like a checkerboard, the ground is covered by sunlight and tree shade, but past that, the illumination becomes less and less frequent. Near the fallen trunk, no light enters. But, that's where we need to be.

Jackson and Ophelia level their weapons towards the horizon, moving quickly towards our defenses mounted on the fallen treetop, which is lying on its side like a toppled building. Their thumbs are poised over the triggers of their weapons.

"Rogers, Martinez, channel 5-5-3," Jackson calls out.

We quickly turn the tiny knobs on our neck receivers to dial in.

"You're running this show, Jackson?" I ask.

"We are on the Western shore, my town, so yeah," he says, turning to smile at me.

"Thank goodness," Ophelia sighs. "If we let Martinez run the show, there's no telling what she'll do." Ophelia chuckles, her words not a joke despite the humorous expression. She's concerned I'll take, what she'd call unnecessary, risks with my own life.

"Thanks for the vote of confidence, Oa."

"Love you too, Angel Jos." She beams.

Annoyed as I may be, her calling me Angel Jos softens the criticism. I love calling them my angels, and I hope they feel the same. This is, of course, Ophelia's idea. But Patricia cannot let such a thing stand unchallenged. So, she created our 6-6-6 channel, dialed in reverse, started by turning the tiny dial left instead of right.

Ophelia hates dialing into that channel, but does it nevertheless.

"Okay, since I'm leading this little outing, can you give us a reading, Jos?" Jackson requests, swinging his dragon rifle in a wide arc spanning forty-five degrees, stopping at Ophelia's vector, where she picks up the motion and carries it another forty-five degrees, lifting the barrel out of the way of errant branches that jut towards us like sharpened stakes.

"Nothing so far that my senses can pick up." But, that doesn't mean they're not out there.

"Clear," Ophelia chirps.

"Clear here as well. Jos?"

"Just dying roots and vines, nothing more. Clear, Jackson."

"Awesome. This is turning out to be an easy assignment. Going to check in with the others."

There's a click over the receiver, telling us Jackson has left the channel. Another click signals his return. "Got the all clear. We're heading to the perimeter I think... yeah, the perimeter, wherever that is." Jackson shoots Ophelia and me an awkward look. "Oh right, I'll go first."

"I assume the perimeter would be just beyond this branch? On top of the fallen tree trunk?" I say as if asking. Of course that's where it is.

He nods. "Makes sense... let's do that then."

I like Jackson a lot, but clearly he doesn't have the experience or confidence to be in charge.

A look and then a silent, long inhale from Ophelia confirms she agrees with me. I may be reckless, but no one dies when I run the show. The only life on the line is my own.

A sudden buzz in our receivers alerts us to a group-wide message.

"Ladies and gentlemen, it appears we're seeing the same thing. All clear, no activity. Still, I want everyone to stay sharp. We all know what Guardsmen can do with enough time and preparation. With all of the hidey-holes they can be in around here, I wouldn't put it past them to advance on our location, just out of the RX range, to launch a few creepers when we least expect it.

"You've all got your assignments. Signal back as soon as we're good, and I'll make the call to operations to start the secure and repair procedures."

"A babysitting mission, Gunny?" Petersen questions.

"Would you prefer a front assault?" Jacob replies.

There's a moment of silence. "Hell no."

"Good, now let's get this done ASAP."

"Turrets, turrets... where are they hiding those things," Jackson says under his breath, his eyes scanning the shaded landscape. "Okay, so where's the first defense turret?" Jackson asks, stepping forward, weapon sweeping the area in front of him. Ophelia follows next, her weapon spanning the area to our left and behind.

With her eyes at our nine, Ophelia leans towards Jackson. "First one should be at the far end of the treetop." She nods her head up into the branches.

"Ah, gotcha. Makes sense. Okay, ladies, follow me." We crunch our way forward, stepping on dry, writhing vines, passing under the thick shadows of branches above.

Again, pushing my senses reveals only the sound of burrower beetles, bioengineered Northern weapons, feeding on the tree's carcass. They are the only insects that can consume plants tainted with our poisons.

"I don't think Guardsmen would actually come this close to RX," Jackson says, keeping his eyes forward, then turning all the way to our three.

"That may be, Jackson," Ophelia responds. "But both Jos and I can attest to Guardsmen doing some amazing things. Even in clouds of RX."

"Amen to that," I add. I've witnessed Guardsmen continue to fight even after being completely disemboweled. I personally slashed a Guardsmen so deeply across the neck, I struck her spine. Still, she had enough strength left to fire off many more rounds into the group of norms I was protecting. We FOGs may generally be stronger and faster than the average Guardsmen, but they are certainly tougher than we are, especially when armored.

"There's our defense batteries," Jackson says, turning to grin at Ophelia and me. He points up, into the shadowed treetop.

I see them as well. Tubes, six feet in length, flanked by smooth wheels sitting on the nearly one-hundred-foot-wide trunk of the felled treetop. Their thick circular bases, adorned with a strip of bright blue sensors, are strewn with clinging vines, clearly gumming up the weapons' motors.

157

Clinging vines. I hate those things. They were a favorite of the Keynosians during the early half of the war when we were still trying to use a more mechanized force. They used them to stop vehicles, helicopters, missile launches, and basically anything that required the use of mechanical technology. One Guardsmen with a handful of those vine seeds could easily stop a tank, and often did. A few clinging vines and our multi-million-credit weapon would be completely useless, irreparably damaged.

I didn't know they were firing them from cannons nowadays. They used to deliver them by hand.

I look up at the turrets and see them struggling to turn, their motors emitting a low whine. Wait... they're all trying to turn left?

Shit!

"Let me get into position so we can start clearing that crap. You ladies stay here. This should only take a few minutes." With a powerful push, Jackson launches himself high in the canopy near the long-guns.

"Jackson, stop!" is all I get out as he leaps, and instantly shots pierce through the shadowy canopy. Struck several times, Jackson is launched back and into the tree stump base's moss-covered walls.

He lands with a thud, nearly upside down, against the trunk. I hear him grunt as he begins to fall. But, catlike, he twists and turns himself, landing gracefully on the hazy forest floor with his rifle trained on his assailants high in the brown-leafed canopy.

"Contact! We've got contact! Right side! Martinez, Ophelia, get some cover!"

Shaking off the shock of seeing Jackson land so gracefully after taking those shots, Ophelia and I dash backwards towards a nearby alcove created by the once great tree's roots.

"Jackson, this way!" I yell, withdrawing my pistols to lay down some cover fire for him and Ophelia. The loud boom of the dragon rifles Jackson and Ophelia wield sound like a baritone voice yelling the word "doom" over and over again. Its massive explosive shells hammer the thick branches above. The dense wood turns into clouds of dust with each pounding shot.

"Contact left side! They were waiting for us!" Rawlings yells. "Fuck, Dougie's down! I repeat, Dougie's down!"

"Rawlings, Martinez, tell me something," Jacob orders.

Ducking into the alcove, I go into action immediately, trying desperately to tune out the firefight, and focus instead on the distant noises hidden in the canopy. It's clear they have the high ground. I don't need my senses to deduce that. But the count and location, that I need to figure out before we're all slaughtered.

It's as if the Guardsmen know how to blind runners. They shoot in turn, each volley bleeding into the next, sounding like unending fire. Each shot echoes painfully across my temples, and I struggle to push beyond it all.

Gotcha! "I have five... no, six heartbeats, erratic. I'm just getting so much info, I can't get a fix on anything solid."

"Same here on the left," Rawlings reports, her voice strangely calm. She sounded the same earlier. Her calm is unnerving.

"Shit, they got us pinned, we need backup now!" Petersen yells.

"Not gonna happen," Powell barks. "If anyone comes out of *any* exit, they're dead. The Guardsmen have both the high ground and the angle on the doorway. David, Patel, and I can confirm that. It was all a setup. How the hell did they get past all of the RX?"

"Patel, give me some good news!"

A sudden, single crack comes from above, near the doorway. "One," Patricia announces. "Looks like we have only a few of them running around right now."

My angel... best sniper, period.

"Hold your fire, Patel, we need to coordinate and keep our aces protected."

Breathing heavily, Jackson leans towards the alcove entrance. "Sounds like you've got a plan, Gunny. Good, 'cause we're pinned down over here," Jackson says. He winces and shuffles backward as a bullet ricochets off of the opening of our hiding place.

Black FOG blood seeps steadily out of Jackson's wounds. I quickly assess him: one shot went straight through his thigh, another passed straight through his upper arm, just missing his bone.

I look closer and see one of the slugs. The charged metal didn't stop it, but the underlining ceramic plating that all harnesses are affixed with did. Even that barely stopped the bullet. As he turns, another impossibly black slug dislodges from the deep small hole it created along with pieces of shattered plate. Wait... black slug? "David, it's a black bullet!" I say, bringing my shoulder up to say the words clearly in the receiver.

"They're using black bullets again? Fuck guys, don't let that shit hit you," Petersen barks.

Gritting his teeth, Jackson tears a piece of fabric from his uniform top. "Too late for that, sweetheart," he chuckles softly. He quickly ties the fabric over the holes left by the bullets in both his arm and leg.

At least they cleared his body completely. I have no desire to dig another bullet out of a tank.

I grab the fallen slug and glare at it. Something is different. This is not what we encountered before. "They changed it. This isn't the same thing we encountered at that village. This one doesn't sparkle, it's just utterly black, heavier as well."

"Now's not the time to turn scientist on us, Martinez! Concentrate on getting a fix so we can start dropping these Southies!" Powell says. He's right, they take priority at the moment.

As I begin to focus again, the opposition cuts loose, sending streams of whatever that crap is they're using for ammo towards our team.

"We have to shut them down, Jake. We gotta get our people out of here or they'll eventually get those black shots into all of us," David says.

"Tell me something I don't know, Santos... Rawlings, I know you got something for me."

I hear her exhale hard over the receiver. "I think so. Damn it, we gotta get Dougie some help. He's not recovering... the shot struck him in the forehead I think."

"Get it together, Rawlings! We can't do shit until we stop them from locking us in here, and it won't take long before we're all stretched out with bullets to the brain box. So come on, Rawlings, focus... Can you get a fix?"

The comms go silent for a few tense seconds. Can Rawlings actually get a lock with all of this background noise? If so, she's amazing.

"They're scattered... two are moving to my left... they're coming around. Most are right downrange of you and Santos. A few more are headed towards Jackson's group."

I don't believe it. She's doing it. She's actually doing it despite the deafening rifle fire.

"You sure about that?" Petersen asks, his tone sharp.

"Alright, Petersen, lay down some cover fire, now! Short and sweet!"

"Damn it, Gunny, I don't wanna be shooting at nothing again... Is she sure about this?"

"Petersen, fire now!"

Again, the dragon rifle belches out rounds of apocalyptic fire, slapping ordnance hard against branches as wide as two full grown men. The thick branches are great cover for the Keynosians, but that won't last long. Each bullet cuts deep into their shelter, shattering some in half and splitting others into huge fragments.

I hear someone or someones in the distance running into the fray, towards the enemy. By the speed, I assume David and Jacob are on the move, going forward with an attack plan. Glory hogs.

Still, this attack by the Keynosians... It makes no sense, or does it? They can't hope to win this minor skirmish. Even if they can keep the exits locked down for a while, it'll only be a matter of time before they run out of ammo and the surrounding area is laid to waste by the RX. It's been our go-to weapon for over a year now, created to not only deforest an entire swath of land, but also greatly weaken any Guardsmen that come into contact with it for any length of time.

The potent neurotoxin overtakes their nervous systems, reducing their strength, speed, and agility to that of a normal person. At that point, they are far from a match to even the weakest FOGs.

I can't imagine the horror they must feel at the idea of being captured by the North. The things we do to them for even the smallest amount of information. It's not right, but neither is allowing them to kill more of our people.

An image of Takdeer flashes before my mind's eye.

Wait, could this be another weapons test?

"What's rolling around in your head, Jos?" Ophelia asks, adjusting her dragon rifle for full automatic fire. With a click, her cooling system hums to life and puffs of white smoke ooze from her rifle barrel.

"This is all reminiscent of the encounter we had at the village. In fact..." With a few clicks, I'm back in the main team line. "David, this is all too familiar to be coincidence."

"How so?" he grunts. I can hear the rattling of rifle fire through my earpiece.

"Takdeer, his suicide run, remember?"

"Not a good time for twenty questions," he says, his breathing telling me he's in the midst of a fight.

"I think they're trying to test again, the bullets I mean. How else are they going to know they work if they don't test them?"

"Why is this important right now?" Jacob asks. I can hear his breathing over the comms — he's on the move as well.

"I just recovered one of the slugs they're firing at us. It's very similar to the slug Petersen was struck by. That slug slowed down his healing," I say, rushing to get the thought out. "Petersen continued to bleed for far longer than he should have, but the worst part is, it really made it hard for him to recover."

"Jackson and Jeffersen are in serious trouble. We need to get both of them inside ASAP. Jeffersen especially. If he got hit in his head... I think it's going to kill him if we don't get that bullet out." We don't have a moment to spare. Jackson could actually bleed to death, and

Jeffersen could suffer serious brain damage and die if we don't get them both into either stasis or surgery.

"What? How?" Rawlings asks, her voice ringing a tone of disbelief. "Jeffersen's been with me for over a year. The man's recovered from far more serious injuries than this. I've personally witnessed Dougie —"

"Fuck, Rawlings, now's not the time to reminisce!" Petersen barks. "Martinez is right this time! I've experienced one of those fucked up bullets myself. If they made it better, Dougie ain't gonna heal through that shit until the slug is pulled out. Even with it out of my leg, it still took hours for me to heal."

My thoughts then turn to David and Jacob. "David, Jacob, don't get hit. I know you're both used to taking punishment and fighting anyway, but this time, you can't let any of those bullets hit you. One hit could equal death."

"Ummm, FYI, guys... I can confirm. I'm not feeling my normally... vivacious self," Jackson says, his voice sliding downward.

I turn to see him slumping against the dark tree bark inside the nook, his dragon rifle slowly falling to the ground. It's as if he can no longer support the weight of even his rifle.

Suddenly, as if overcome, he and his weapon fall with a thud into the blue RX mist, the poison half covering his face.

"We've got a man down!" I yell.

"Holy shit... Dougie? Dougie?" Rawlings screams.

"Jeffersen's down, folks. I mean really down. I don't think he's getting up. Gunny, he's starting to twitch over here," Marshall says. "Come on, dude, stay with us."

The sound of crashing cuts into Rawlings' sobs. I look up to see David clutching the ankle of a Guardsmen, using him as both a blunt instrument and a shield against one of his countrymen. Jacob, on a branch below, fires shots upwards, to an area just above David's head. He's keeping the other Guardsmen at bay.

"Patel, smoke 'em if you can!" Jacob yells.

Her Suzy-Q cracks in response. "Two."

I catch of glimpse of Jacob tossing his rifle over his back and donning his knuckle-dusters. "Martinez, Rawlings, get the wounded back inside ASAP. Rogers, tear their hidey-holes down if you can!"

On cue, Ophelia cuts loose into a full sprint towards the fallen treetop, firing on full auto as she goes. The stream of explosive shells sends shudders up into the branches as large chunks of dense wood spray everywhere. She heads towards the widening opening her gunfire is creating. Then, with all of her might, she slams herself into the trunk, splitting the fallen section in two and knocking two of the turrets down. The vibrations from the force of her attack send David to the ground, but also reorient the severed treetop. The Guardsmen and Jacob do not fall under her attack, but it does cause them to stumble out into the open.

That's all Patricia needs. Suzy-Q cracks twice more. "Three and four," she says, her voice scratchy and stoic, completely devoid of any of the humor that usually graces her speech.

Two Guardsmen fall from the sky like dead leaves, their faces showing the same woody protrusions that afflicted Takdeer. One of them, clearly a man in his thirties, has an entire face of them, a large one seemingly coming from out of his left eye.

This is a suicide mission. These are Guardsmen on the verge of dying.

Grabbing Jackson, I take off towards the door. "We can't let any of them escape. We have to find out exactly what they're up to," I announce over the comms. Jackson's large frame is awkward to carry and made even worse by the slippery blood that continues to gush from his wounds. "Whatever they're experimenting with, it's worth letting these men give their lives for it."

"Good point," Jacob says as I watch him kill another Guardsmen, thrusting his rifle through his target's forehead. "Clarence, Petersen, keep those that are still hiding honest. Toss some metal their way. David and I are on the way to your location."

Opening an eye, Jackson looks around as if surprised. "You're carrying me? Hell, I should be carrying you."

I chuckle and continue to make my way to the base entrance, ducking in and out of deep crevices in the wooden wall. "Don't be stupid, Junior. I'm a FOG, just like you." I keep having to reestablish my grip on his uniform. It makes moving difficult.

There's no snappy comeback this time, only a hard grimace. "It burns, Jos... these damn bullets burn like hell," Jackson says, his voice still smooth like silk, but weak.

"Don't you worry, Junior, you'll be good as new before you know it."

"Great... that's really great... tired of staining my only uniform."

Rawlings reaches the base's entryway, the same one we first emerged from, before me. I can hear the force she's using as her fist pounds the door, Jeffersen over her shoulder. The blows shake the surrounding structure, which holds the charged wall in place. They better open that goddamn door or we'll take it off its fucking hinges!

As if aware of my thoughts, the flap goes flaccid just as Jackson and I reach the opening.

We blast through the door. Neither of us stop at the plastic tube. We rip right through it and alarms go off in an instant.

"We need a medic now!" Rawlings screams as flashing red lights roll over the four of us from behind.

"I'm here." It's LaPaige barreling towards us, carrying two gurneys. Behind him, I see a host of other medics hauling eggs behind them on a lift-suit. Was he listening in on our team channel?

Before another word is spoken, LaPaige places the gurneys down hard. "Get them strapped in, now."

We do as instructed, and both Jackson and Jeffersen are sprawled out on heavy metal gurneys. Quickly, LaPaige begins wiping away the river of blood streaming from Jeffersen's forehead. "Rachel!" he calls over his shoulder. "I need you to work on getting that bullet out of that soldier." LaPaige nods in the now-unconscious Jackson's direction.

She arrives in a huff, running at a pace that's far slower than most FOGs, but definitely faster than a normal person. She's carrying a stasis chamber over her head as if it's simply a beach ball.

"I'm going back out there," I say.

"I'm right behind you," Rawlings adds, quickly giving Jeffersen a peck on his forehead, smearing blood on her lips. "They won't escape. Not a single one."

It doesn't take long before we're back into the fray, but this isn't what we left behind. There's open fighting now. Our small crew is standing down what looks like twelve remaining, dying Guardsmen, all moving slower than normal, clearly affected by the RX exposure. Shots are ringing out from both sides.

The occasional crack of Patricia's rifle rings out, followed by her current count. Seven I think she's at.

As another Guardsmen falls, the man standing next to him looks up towards Patricia's position. In a flash, he digs his gloved fingers into the wooden walls of the base and races to the top, sweat dripping from his face. He's headed towards Patricia. I've can't let him reach her.

"Headed to you, Pat," I say, leaping from branch to branch with all the speed I can muster. The toppled top's branches will get me there faster than scaling the side of the base along with him.

"Got a bogie coming my way?" she asks, reloading, her voice calm.

"Oh yeah. Coming in hot."

It's a good thing these Guardsmen aren't nearly as fast as I am, especially when weakened as they appear to be. With my blade drawn, I reach Patricia's location just as the Guardsmen decides to take the final few feet in a single leap. He lands without his left arm or either leg attached. My blade makes certain of that.

He flails his remaining arm about, trying to catch something, anything. "Prisoner acquired," I announce as another shot rings out from Patricia's rifle, Suzy-Q.

"Eight."

"I need some... ugh!... I need some help here!" Petersen yells over the comms.

"I'm good here, oh angel of mine," Patricia says with a smile, her eye focusing through her large scope.

"Right, headed to the next target." With a wink, I step off of the branch and fall into the sea of smoky blue.

Three Guardsmen are beating Petersen's ass; one looks to be wielding jet-black knuckle-dusters and the other two are using their weapons as clubs to batter him with. They're out of ammo? Why are they using their weapons like that?

Petersen's too slow to keep them at bay and gets cracked across the jaw just as Rawlings appears, her rifle in a cradle hold. She runs at them full speed, her weapon firing as she approaches. But, even at that speed, with her rifle firing full auto, she only manages to clip one woman on top of the head. The shot stunned her, but it'll only take the Keynosian a moment to recover from such a blow.

I'm amazed watching our enemy evade these attacks. They have to be reading our minds. Each one moves before Rawlings even levels her firearm in their direction.

"Muthafuggers!" Petersen mumbles, flaying at the two Guardsmen with his dragon rifle, attempting to ward them away with the weapon's barrel. Obviously undeterred, they rush him, intent on beating him to death it seems

Again, I push myself hard to intercept one, aiming to remove an arm. I only remove the man's hand. He pulls away, but not fast enough to avoid my blade completely.

Crack! "Nine."

Before I make another high speed slash, the knuckle-duster-wielding Guardsmen's skull explodes in front of me.

Before the body can hit the ground, I rush to Rawlings' side and cut nothing but air as the smirking, one-handed Guardsmen pulls a sidearm out of his side holster and brings it to bear on Petersen.

"Eat it!" I hear from behind. It's Petersen. I turn to see him holding a thirty-foot section of hardened bark. Rawlings and I drop to the ground immediately.

The Keynosian's eyes widen. He makes a futile attempt at running away, but to no avail. It crashes into the Guardsmen. I hear it crush him. As it slides away, a single brush stroke of blood paints the ground.

"It ain't that easy to take out Gerard Petersen, bitch!"

Crack! "Ten." The female Guardsmen is stretched out, facedown in the blue RX mist.

Crack! "Eleven."

The RX is taking more and more of their speed. They're getting slower by the second. If this wasn't a suicide mission, the Keynosians made a terrible mistake attacking us like this.

"David, get some cover, they're firing again," Jacob says.

The sound of crushing wood rings out as the broken section of tree Ophelia created begins to shake violently. It's Ophelia again, and somehow she's rocking the gigantic treetop. Her hands are clamped so tight on the tree, it appears as if she's squeezing a massive pillow. The bark deforms and tears away in huge splinters the size of her entire body.

She's rattling the remainder out of the hiding spots they've retreated to.

Crack! "Twelve."

I can hear Ophelia's heart beating so violently I wonder if it'll burst. Despite that, Ophelia moves the treetop over and over again. Twisting it, snapping the sprawling branches that stretch out across the blue-smoke filled area. Sweat saturates her face, gluing her hair down around her brow and cheeks like wax.

From where I'm standing, about two hundred feet away, I hear the sound of her tendons snapping under the strain. If it were not for her ability to recover quickly, I think she would have died already many times over doing acts like this.

No FOG has ever displayed such strength. No stories, no rumors, nothing even comparable has been said about another soldier being capable of the feats she's preformed. No one has ever shown the power Ophelia possesses.

Crack! "Thirteen."

"That's enough, Rogers!" Jacob yells. Dropping from the foliage above, Jacob looks around at the devastation Ophelia has wrought. "Shit," he chuckles, looking at her across the field, through the branches, blue smoke, and wood dust. "Don't kill yourself for this rabble."

She does not return his glee, releasing the trunk with a crash and falling to her knees.

"Patel, what you got?"

"How many prisoners do we need again?" she asks.

"One is more than enough," Jacob says, signing the fleeing duo's death warrants.

"Goddamn, Jackson, how much are you gonna eat?" Petersen jokes as Jackson, seated at the end of a long branch we decided to have our dinner on, digs into another full tray of food.

Chuckling, his steel tray close to his chin, Jackson shovels heaps of fortified mashed potatoes into his mouth. "I'm starving, man. Getting shot by those black bullets takes a lot out of you."

"So, LaPaige, what's the lowdown on those bullets?" Jacob asks, placing his tray atop the pile of other used trays.

LaPaige is here because Powell asked him to show. I guess we're getting debriefed finally. But why just us? I assume the other FOGs would need to know this information as well.

"It's strange," he says, shaking his head, eyes drifting down to the desiccated gray earth. "The bullets are made of some kind of composite metal as far as we can tell, yet they seem to react like compressed ironwood. The thing is, it looks like it's alive... or was alive at some point. The stuff has cells like a plant, but altered in some strange way."

"How is that possible?" David asks, taking my empty tray from me and placing on the pile.

Ophelia looks up and smiles at me.

"It's not possible for metal to have cells... but this metal does... we think. If that is the case, it's not a form of life we're familiar with. But that's not the worst of it. The biggest conundrum is the fact that the bullets appear to absorb all energy they come in contact with.

169

Absorbing it, eating it somehow," LaPaige says, his eyes gliding over our gathering.

"So what the fuck does that mean, Gerald? Is Dougie gonna recover or what?" Petersen asks.

I may not like him, but he does have a way of getting straight to the point.

Taking a deep breath, LaPaige sighs. "We retrieved the bullet, but that wasn't enough to get him in the clear. The bullet killed every cell around the point of penetration. Literally sucking the life out of everything it came in contact with."

They are made of death. They are made for us. "Are you saying it absorbs even our cellular energy?" I ask.

"That's exactly it," he says, excitement in his voice. "It's absorbing our cells' energy into itself, effectively killing them. It's brilliant. It's stopping all cellular production, and thus, prevents our healing."

Jackson pulls his arm out of its sling and tears off the layer of gauze covering his wound. The entry point and all the surrounding tissue appears to have died. Black and seeping, the hole still oozes pus. "See that? That was bigger a few hours ago. I really thought I'd lose the arm."

LaPaige points and nods at the wound. "The wound actually started getting infected. Can you imagine that? Eventually the cells are replaced and the dead tissue reabsorbed, but it takes some time."

"Are you saying Dougie... are you saying Jeffersen's dead?" Rawlings says softly.

"No, no. He's not dead. We've got him in a stasis chamber now. We're hoping to keep him just above cryo, cool enough to prevent him from dying, but not so cool that the surrounding cellular activity stops. Hopefully, given enough time, he'll completely recover from the injury, just like Jackson over here."

"So basically," David says, his expression showing his exasperation. "Petersen took a shot to the leg and didn't recover for nearly twelve hours, but his injury didn't look anywhere near as bad as Jackson's. That would mean they're improving it, mastering it even. The crap we pulled out of Petersen had shards of sparkling crystals in it. This new bullet, it's got to be the deepest black I've ever seen."

No FOG can take a bullet like this in any vital organ and hope to survive out in the field.

Powell stands and walks in front of us, his back to the base. "David's right, they've obviously been working on this weapon hard and fast. That was also confirmed by the captured Guardsmen... the one Martinez so lovingly left with no legs and one arm," he says with a nod. "The gimp gave us some interesting information before he died. This new weapon is high on their priority list. Real high. The bullets we've taken so far are definitely part of a new ordnance created exclusively to kill us, but they're not able to mass produce. Not yet anyway."

"Maybe we can wear some armor? What about that heavy ceramic stuff?" Ophelia asks.

"Good point," LaPaige says. "We've tested it to see if the bullet can penetrate our charged fabrics first. That's not looking good. Even when we increase the charge, that bullet goes right through. Our ceramic plate armor seems to fare only slightly better."

"Yeah, one shot shattered the ceramic under my harness like it was made of glass."

"But it *did* stop it. Saved your life to boot. So, do we even have ceramic armor here?" Jacob asks.

LaPaige sighs. "Doubt it. It's so much heavier than the F-Tech armor, I can't imagine we'd spend the credits to make enough to protect everyone, not to mention the resources to lug that stuff. The cost would be far too much."

"Wishful thinking. Goddamn those Southies. It makes so much strategic sense to send some soldiers to test it, soldiers already knocking on death's door, before pooling all of your resources to produce it," David adds. "I can't imagine any soldier turning down a mission like that. It's reasonable to give them one last shot of taking down the enemy."

"That's what I'd want," Petersen says, nodding in agreement. "One last shot to even the score."

Sliding forward, David stands, squinting at Powell. "So, what's our play here, Jake? I know you didn't invite us all here to just shoot the shit and bitch about the situation."

Petersen rubs his still-bruised jaw. "Yeah... that's not your style, Gunny. What gives?"

Jacob smiles. "Ahhh, you guys know me so well. What gives is we need to shut them down before we're all toast. Our prisoner gave us the coordinates to some kind of laboratory near the western shore, tucked away underneath one of the mountain ranges there. He believes that's where they're making those —"

"And you need us to go and shut it down," I interject.

Tight-lipped, Jacob grimaces. "ASAP."

Nothing is ever that simple. "There's no way the Keynosians will let us get close enough to take out their best chance to win this war. Certainly not without major resistance. It seems obvious that any small group headed that way would be killed. Such a run would be a suicide mission."

"Which is why we'll send in a small unit, us, while our main force will go full bore to the stronghold directly to our south. Hopefully, that large of an all-out assault will draw any reinforcements away from the target facility. Without that stronghold, they won't have the manpower to stop us from taking the sole resistance they have left."

Pulling her thumb and forefinger from her temple, Ophelia opens her eyes and raises a finger. She's trying to get Powell's attention. "God willing, that will work and end this conflict, but what makes you think that pulling such a stunt will be successful?" Ophelia questions.

She's been massaging her temples off and on for hours now. In fact, she, Clarence, and Rawlings all seem to have a constant headache. That's not the normal sign of a FOG slipping into madness. What's going on? Is this new medication causing new issues?

Nodding, Powell draws his mouth downward. "That Southern stronghold is their last hope. Without it, they lose. Period. They'll have to send whatever forces they have at the facility to that base. We don't know why they don't just move the base to the facility, and we don't care. They screwed the pooch on this, and we're going to take advantage."

"I'd like to ask an off-topic question," Rawlings says, standing then walking towards Patricia. "How the hell did you shoot all of those Guardsmen? I ran at them, full auto, and could only clip one. But you? You were able to snipe... what, twelve Guardsmen within a few minutes. Sure, they were slowed, but all head shots? That shouldn't be possible, weakened by the RX or not, that special ammo you snipers use... still impossible to hit so many in so short a time period. So spill it, how *is* that even possible for you to do? No other sniper has ever been able to do what you're doing."

All eyes instantly slide to Patricia. "What do I do?" she asks rhetorically, taking a moment to breathe in the right words. "Well, I don't see myself as trying to kill anyone. I mean... in my head," she says, pointing to her temple. "I don't think of it as trying to kill my target."

"What are you doing, taking their picture or something?" Clarence says with a chuckle.

"Yeah, that's it. That's exactly it."

"I was joking," Marshall clarifies.

Her expression flat, Patricia looks blankly at him. "Okay, but I'm not."

Ophelia and I turn to one another and grin. We've heard this before and still find it hard to conceptualize.

Taking another deep breath, Patricia looks at the group and shakes her head. "Here's how I see it. If a Guardsmen can read minds, not saying they can, but what if they do? I mean think about it, each time we come at them, trying to cause harm, they move. So it's got to be something about us that they're picking up on. Hell, I've been thousands of yards away, totally hidden, and they still moved as if they knew exactly where I was aiming."

"That's not news, Patel. We've all experienced that. The question is, how do you manage to hit them?" Jacob asks.

"I stopped trying to hit them.

173

"Look, I know it's hard to believe, but that's how I feel. That's how *it* feels, I mean."

"They won't understand unless you tell them when you starting getting hits, Pat," I say. I didn't understand until she gave me the whole story. If these guys are going to understand, she'll have to do the same for them.

Patricia glances at me, annoyed. Then, with her eyes downcast, she frowns. "I gave up, totally and completely. They were slowly wiping us out after killing the FOGs we had with us. My old squad that is. They were slaughtering my unit. Shit, it was only two of them, but goddamn were they doing a number on my crew. Soldier by soldier, they'd avoid everyone's shots, mine included. In fact, they completely ignored me and the other two snipers and continued their slaughter. At some point, I dunno, I said fuck it and gave up. I couldn't hit them. I couldn't even clip one. I felt totally useless. It got so bad, I even thought about killing myself simply to not give them the satisfaction of killing me themselves. Then, for some reason, it happened. It was the emptiness. It must've given me something, an edge I guess. I hit one, and then another.

"After I put them both down, I figured it had to do with my giving up. But I couldn't repeat that feeling over and over again, now knowing that I could actually get kills.

"So, I had to let it all go. I had to try to get empty again. Release the need to kill. Once I was there, in my mind I mean, they stopped moving before I could pull the trigger. But you can't pull a trigger and not think about what you're doing. So I needed to think about something benign. It was only when I thought of it as simply taking a picture that it started to click again."

Shaking her head, Rawlings holds her hand up. "You're being serious? So when you're out there putting slugs in the heads of our worst enemy, you see yourself not shooting people in the head, but taking their picture?"

"You're making it sound weird. It's not weird."

"Are you kidding me? That's shit's weird as hell!" Petersen says, chuckling bitterly. "You're out there taking glamor shoots of Guardsmen while FOGs are fighting for their lives."

"You gotta admit, hon, that is some strange info," Jackson says, adjusting his leg slightly with his hand.

"Petersen, why do you make everything confrontational? You act like you're not happy Patel dropped twelve Guardsmen," David says in Patricia's defense.

"Look, I don't give a fuck what you think about me, Petersen," Patricia says calmly. "I have a job to do out here, and I'm going to do it to the best of my ability. And, if I have to think of them as cute bunnies, dancing kittens, ex-boyfriends, or even members of my family, I'll do it. All that matters in the here and now is keeping those bastards from killing my people."

Looking a little embarrassed, Petersen can only nod at Patricia.

"So you think they're reading our minds?" Rawlings asks.

With a shrug, Patricia shakes her head. "I don't know what it is. I just know the moment I stopped thinking of their death was the moment I was able to hit my targets. If it's mind reading, some weird sensory awareness, or just them smelling my hair spray, I couldn't tell you."

"Maybe that's how David and Jacob are able to connect their blows?" Marshall asks, his large brown eyes wide.

Jackson nods. "David and Jacob keep talking about combinations of moves, but that doesn't mean anything if you aren't fast enough to pull them off."

LaPaige steps closer, nodding along with Jackson. "There is some evidence that Guardsmen are able to perceive external threats. We can't explain exactly how it's done, but we believe it may be related to an ability to see in different wavelengths."

"That still doesn't explain how they're able to know where attacks are coming from," Rawlings says.

"I'm baffled you even use a rifle, Rawlings. Aren't you fast enough to overwhelm them with your blade?" I ask.

"I may be able to move my body fast, but my eyes and awareness aren't able to keep up, especially in such highly active and obstacle-rich battlefields. You on the other hand do seem to be able to remain fully aware of your surroundings."

Suddenly, Petersen snaps his fingers. "Oh! I think I just won some money!"

"What, how you figure?" Jacob replies.

"Rawlings just admitted that Martinez is faster than she is," he says, pointing his finger at a smiling Rawlings.

"I don't believe I said that, buuuutt I will concede. Martinez is certainly *functionally* faster. She has both the physical speed and the best spatial awareness I've ever seen in a FOG."

"Ha! Pay up, Gunny!"

Throughout the night, the thumping sound of RX canisters being launched systematically over the countryside echo throughout the camp. Like the heartbeat of a sleeping lover, the steady *thump, thump, thump* is rhythmic and strangely comforting in its predictability.

I lie awake, with my eyes closed, listening to the melody. Then I hear her. I stir before Ophelia reaches me, letting her know I'm not totally sleeping. Her skin still hints of the machine oil the tanks coat their dragon rifles in.

Quietly, Ophelia kneels next to my bunk.

I don't turn around. I don't need to. "What's up, Oa? Going out for a late night stroll?" I whisper.

"No. I just need to ask a favor of you."

I turn over to face her. Whoa, her face is flushed red. "Oa? What's wrong?"

"This pain... is getting worse and worse each day."

Oh no. "We need to get you to the infirmary. Maybe they need to adjust the dosage or —"

"That's not why I'm here," she says, waving my concerns away. "I need you to promise me something."

"Whatever it is, hun, it can wait. We —"

"Jos, listen!" she says, her face no longer calm.

I look around the barracks quickly, seeing if anyone was awakened by her loud whisper. "Sure, Oa."

"I need you to kill me —"

"No!"

"Jos, stop and listen for a moment. Please."

"I won't kill you, Oa. I won't. I can't."

"If things go badly out there. If I lose it, if I'm hurt bad... bad like Jeffersen, don't let them bring me back. Don't let them freeze me, store me like some unspent bomb until they can find some use for me. Find some new war to throw me into. We're not supposed to exist for those acts. God didn't spend millions of years making us just so some stupid scientist could cheat me out of my purpose, cheat me out of meeting my savior, cheat me out of being with Chad, in glory."

Is she sliding down again? That must be it. "Maybe you just need a higher dosage, Oa," I say.

She closes her eyes, her face sagging with sorrow.

Something has to help her. Having Patricia and her with me for so long has been wonderful. I don't want to lose her again. "The techs in the infirmary can evaluate you. Maybe prescribe something."

"Yeah, maybe," she says, dejected. With a painfully forced smile, she casts her eyes downward, then directly into mine. "But, if they can't, I'm suffering and it's my time to... don't let me suffer, Jos. I don't want that. Just bless me and send me on my way."

"Oa, I can't —"

"If not my sister, then who? David? Jackson? Maybe I should ask Pat to end it all for me if she can?"

"Damn it, Oa, why are you doing this?"

She only smiles, as if preparing to laugh. "Because I know you love me. Because you're my angel. Because I know Pat doesn't have the power to do it alone. She would if she could, but she can't. So, I only have you, Jos." Reaching out, she wraps her pale hand around mine.

177

"If not your sister, then who?"

"If you were suffering."

"You have to promise me."

"If there was no other way."

"Promise me."

I clutch her hand tight in return. I know the truth, and if it were me suffering or headed to an eternity of stasis, I'd want the same. "I promise." There's no other response I can offer that would honor my friend, my sister, and the love I have in my heart for her.

She smiles, wider than before. "I knew I could count on you, Jos."

"So, can we go to the infirmary, now?" I pressure.

She sighs and nods. "Although I doubt they can help. It's just... ahh..."

"Are you alright?"

"I'm... aarrggh!" She doubles over, her hands pressing tight to her temples.

Suddenly, as if on cue, the other FOGs with amber bottles on their nightstands begin to groan and yell out.

"Oa! What's going on?"

As if frozen in place, she stops, her body stiff and still as a statue, her eyes wide as saucers. Then suddenly, shudders violently shake her as blood seeps from her nose and her eyes roll up into her head. With a thud, she hits the ground like a marionette without its strings. The sound echoes as the bodies of other FOGs do the same.

CHAPTER 7

UNHINGED AND SHACKLED

Ophelia slowly pushes herself up from the gurney she's resting on, pulling tissue paper out of her nostril and an IV out of her arm. Gingerly, she removes two round white digital monitors from her temples. "I'm fine," she continues to insist with some frustration, despite the persistent flow of black blood from her nose.

"Rogers, please don't get off the table," LaPaige says to no avail as the monitors each flatline in turn.

I glance at the digital time display above the monitors. We've hit the better part of an hour, and LaPaige has provided no explanation as to why Ophelia collapsed. In fact, he's provided little more than grunts and random sounds of discovery.

"Why not?" she asks innocently. "You said my scans are normal, my blood doesn't show anything out of the ordinary, and even if you did find something, you're not even sure you can help me with the equipment you have on hand here."

"Normal is a relative term, Rogers," he says.

His nervous chuckle only adds to the tension in the room. Patricia, Ophelia, and I, all visibly annoyed, glance at each other before throwing him a heaping pile of shade.

LaPaige may not be a fount of information, but I'd still feel better if Ophelia were kept overnight. "There's nothing normal about having a seizure," I say. "And you've given us nothing but more questions, sir. So, do you or do you not have something definitive to tell us?"

"I'm sorry, I only have ideas of what may be the cause," he says, his pale blue eyes glued to the dull illumination coming from his hand-held pad. He nods and runs a finger across the screen. "More tests are probably needed to make 100% certain of the cause or causes. For all we know, this could be some spontan—"

"Oh come off it!" Patricia barks, cutting him off. "There's nothing spontaneous about this. Those new pills are the cause, or at least some kind of combination of chemicals." She points at a large glass cabinet standing across from the gurneys. "What more evidence do you need than damn near every single FOG suffering from nosebleeds, headaches, and vertigo *after* taking the pills?"

LaPaige looks up from the neon glow of his pad, the fire in his eyes mirroring the flashing lights on the flickering screen. "And what would you have me do, Patel? Hmmm? Do we allow everyone that's suffering to have a complete psychotic break? The stasis chamber and those pills are the best treatments we can provide right now. If you take away the pills..."

"Look, I just don't want to hear about this being spontaneous, especially when we know for damn sure that there's a connection between the antipsychs and these new symptoms," Patricia growls.

"Look, we're at the cutting edge here. We're making advances daily. Stuff that should be happening over decades is taking months to achieve.

"I realize that a growing number of FOGs are showing signs of what can only be considered schizophrenic breaks since the Sacrifice, with the vast majority of sufferers experiencing debilitating auditory hallucinations. But think, these new antipsychs seem to silence those hallucinations completely. Imagine the implications for treating all types of mental illnesses back home. We could be on to something here!"

"That's great, for those people, but what about now? What about her?" Patricia points to Ophelia, her face awash in pain. "What about these FOGs suffering today? Huh? Just take a look back there, man," she says, turning to point at the line of FOGs. "LaPaige, there's nearly one hundred of the Northern Alliance's greatest soldiers, all messed up. Without them, fully capable of doing what they do, there won't be a Northern Alliance to go back to."

I can't hear LaPaige grinding his teeth, but his face does show his obvious frustration. "Again, what would you have me do? I can't pinpoint the problem with the new drugs, so I can't recommend a fix. Even if I could pinpoint it, I don't have the ability to actually fix it here, and those that can wouldn't be able to get us an updated version of the drug for weeks even if they knew what the problem was."

"But you know what you can do? You can tell them what you *do* know, give them something to hold on to, instead of that fucking blank look you're giving me right now. That's a start," Patricia says, her voice growing grave as she looks back into the faces of the many disturbed FOGs awaiting a treatment that isn't available. "All you and the brass do are divvy out information in tiny portions. Drip, drip, drip," she says, squinting her eyes as she holds her fingers like pincers. "I may understand why *some* stuff is kept quiet, but this stuff... the stuff that affects our health? The stuff that keeps these heroes in uniform and not on ice... that should be given freely.

"You say you barely know what's happening? Well, we know even less. So stop hiding whatever it is you're holding on to in that big head of yours, and tell us something."

For a moment, LaPaige's eyes widen and his heart rate increases.

He knows something, and he's purposefully keeping quiet about it.

Ophelia dismounts, her bare feet slapping the white plastic that covers the floor. "If there's nothing you can do, then I'm going to take my leave." Pulling an amber bottle from her pocket, she holds it up to the light. "I'll need a refill soon."

"What? I just told you those pills are the cause of that seizure you had hours ago. Did you forget that already?"

181

"I know you mean well, Pat, but these little red pills... they're doing their job for the moment. They suck. I mean seriously suck. They taste horrible, get stuck in my throat, and turn my urine brown, but they've also kept me in the here and now for way longer than anything else has before. Heaven knows, I've tried every pill you guys have put out previously, all with terrible results," she says to LaPaige. "So, if all the new antipsychs give me are a bloody nose and the occasional collapse, fine. I can deal with that."

"You had a *seizure,* Oa," Patricia says. "That means those pills are doing something that interferes with your brain functions."

Looking Patricia directly in the eyes, Ophelia shrugs. "Nothing will ever mess with my brain as much as the Sacrifice. And, in any case, I can probably heal any damage a seizure would cause, so no big deal."

"What if it causes something worse than what the Sacrifice did, Oa? What if —"

"What if this, what if that... what if it solves all of my problems and only causes a little nosebleed? Heck, I've dealt with bleeding on a monthly basis for years now," she says with a pitiful chuckle.

"That may not be all it does, Oa," I add. "LaPaige here is hiding something. I heard his pulse." I turn to LaPaige. "So, out with it, FOG."

"What?" he asks with a half-smile. "I don't have anything —"

"Stop. We both know what I can do. When Patricia said you're hiding something, you reacted instinctively. You think forcing your vitals back down can fool me when I'm standing this close to you? Just tell us what you're holding back."

"Shit... okay, well, here it is... I think the RX is part of the problem. Days ago I put forth a recommendation to the brass that every FOG wear gas masks in the field, and if they anticipate more than a few minutes of exposure to the herbicide, really they should wear a full hazmat suit as a general rule. I've yet to hear anything back, but if my theory is correct and RX is the issue, simply limiting exposure should be the most effective method of prevention."

Patricia nods. "A powerful herbicide, powerful antipsychs, yeah that could be the root cause. Drugs do have a propensity for dangerous interactions, just like alcohol. Although, convincing all of the FOGs here to don that much protective gear is going to be difficult. There's still resistance even amongst the normal soldiers to wear full protection."

Pat's right, if RX is indeed the problem, we're going to need more than just a suggestion to convince FOGs to wear hazmat suits nearly 100% of the time. We coat pretty much everything with the stuff just before we advance on any target.

"There's something else... something worse." After taking a long, slow breath, LaPaige presses his lips tightly together as he looks past us and at the line of soldiers at the entrance. He moves in close to our trio. "Okay, here are the facts as I'm aware of them. The disease that keeps pushing FOGs into madness is a direct result of The Sacrifice. It changed our brain chemistry in order to enable us to be what we are. But the process wasn't as elegant as it could have been."

"We know that much," I say.

"What you may not know is the Keynosian Guardsmen go through a similar process. The side effect they suffer from appears to be those prominent skin calluses we've been seeing amongst their ranks. But instead of driving them insane, it causes them to die early."

I think of Takdeer. "So that's what those lumps were about? We're seeing so many Guardsmen covered in them nowadays."

"Yes. Guardsmen are meant to have a fairly short lifespan. That's information we've had for years now, since even before the war started. But we believed we could improve on that part of their process. Surprisingly, we succeeded. In fact, we did so well, the Sacrifice quite possibly has made us immortal."

Immortality? Immediately my eyes meet Ophelia's. She'll never get to heaven. She'll never see Chad again.

"At the rate we renew cells and rid ourselves of toxins, it's likely that FOGs will never age, at least not like any other life form on the planet.

"At first the scientists assumed the Keynosian process was flawed, that they didn't understand how to eliminate that problem. Today, many are thinking differently. Personally, I think the short-life-span mechanism was put there on purpose.

"I'm sure you ladies noticed that all of the Guardsmen in years prior were older men and women. Not a single one of them was under forty. Nothing like our soldiers. We didn't start seeing younger Guardsmen until this year. So I believe that as veterans have died in battle, the Keynosians have turned to younger men and women to replenish their ranks."

"Oh my god, just get to the point, LaPaige," Patricia complains.

"The original Guardsmen, the soldiers that were active in the first year of this shitty war, were chosen because they were parents."

"Okay..." Ophelia says with a shrug.

"All Guardsmen are sterile. Every single one of them."

"Sterile? But you just said they had children."

"They had children *before* they were turned into Guardsmen. You see, only a small fraction of Keynosians are born empowered. And only an empowered can become a Guardsmen. So, we believe that empowered are encouraged to procreate — to create more empowered and populate the Keynosian army. All this *before* joining the ranks of the Guardsmen."

"What does that have to do with our guys?"

"We modeled the Sacrifice, the procedure itself, on every known aspect of the Keynosian process of transforming an empowered into a Guardsmen. But we never accounted for the first step in the Keynosian process — sterilization. We just didn't know that was their initial step. Somehow, shutting down the reproductive function acts as a counterbalance to the metabolic transformation that the Guardsmen undergo.

"Because we skipped this important first step in the Sacrifice, we have these mental imbalances. Since sterility is key, only those that were already sterile before undergoing the change will remain stable. Every other FOG will go completely mad."

I need to clear my head.

The green leaves around us catch the wind occasionally, swaying our branches together and apart, like dancers on the wind. Perched on the thick branches of the severed treetop some one hundred feet above the ground, we've been ruminating on the revelation. So far, not much has been said.

The area was saturated with RX days ago, leaving the ground a desert of dead vegetation. Sad gray rot now creeps up the trunks of the trees, threatening to consume them in another day or so. Our home tree, the largest in the area, clings desperately to life, its crown still lush and verdant despite being separated from its root system and doused in a powerful herbicide.

From this height I have a bird's eye view of the area for miles around. I push my senses and see a line of massive black trees about ten miles away, standing guard like sentries. I suspect that beyond their border lies the Keynosians' final stronghold.

"How can we be so sure he's right?" Ophelia asks me, a tremor in her voice. "We know what's in store for me. But for you, Jos, I have to believe there's still hope."

I think of the growing number of FOGs taking antipsychs just to stay coherent. It seems inevitable that I'll join them. "Well, I knew my time would come eventually." I shrug.

"Neither Powell or Santos are taking any medication," Patricia adds.

"See, there *is* hope," Ophelia says, plucking a partially green leaf from its branch. "I still hope for you."

She smiles at the word hope. Even when she herself is utterly hopeless. Personally, I find little inspiration in the word as I look down at the dead earth.

Hope. That flighty bitch hasn't been my, or any FOGs, companion during this war. Acceptance... she's a far better friend. She's always present.

"You know, if I fell from this height, I'd survive. Possibly suffer a few broken bones, but ultimately, I'd survive," I mutter. "Even if I landed square on my head and cracked my skull... I'd most likely wake up tomorrow with a headache as the only evidence of my stupidity.

"From the moment we emerged from those pods, I felt virtually invincible. It was like nothing on the planet could possibly kill me. But my God, if LaPaige is right, we've been doomed to an eternity of madness." A sad, angry chuckle slips from my lips. "It's funny... right now all I can think about is how hard it would actually be to end my own suffering. Could I physically kill myself or would I heal through any damage?" I look at Ophelia, feeling more compassion for her than ever before.

"Would you please stop it?" Ophelia asks, her voice sounding more like a command than a request. "You've got to have faith, Jos. You have to keep hoping that God's mercy, God's direction, and God's love will provide the help we need." She crosses her legs and grins. "God has a plan. He always has a plan. So there's always something to hope for."

"Is that what you're hoping for? God to reveal his plan to you?" I ask.

She chuckles and shrugs, before looking up at a group of clouds moving on the wind. "He brought me you two." She looks at me and winks before turning to Patricia. "He granted me my own personal guardian angels. So yeah, I'm going to continue to trust."

How can she continue to believe in a God that is allowing her to slowly go insane?

Patricia sighs. "Good luck is always the work of God and bad luck is always the work of the Shadow, huh?"

"I don't see meeting you guys as luck. That was God's plan. Spotting your keys on the floor of a cab just before you get out, that's lucky."

"And that's where we differ from you, Oa," I say, glancing in Patricia's direction. "In our world, you running into two crazy chicks that just happen to love you is totally dumb luck. It was luck that you and I reached the Sacrifice line at the same time. It was luck that we both got Patricia as our operator. It was even more luck that she was willing to keep watch over my locket, which caused us to reconnect after we emerged from the egg. And so, it's nothing more than pure luck that I'm not currently taking pills from a small amber bottle or locked in some stasis chamber with no chance of recovery.

"God's plan, if I believed in God, it should have been for me to suffer with that mess, not you. You deserve better than that. If there was a God, you'd be home with Chad, having a beautiful baby. If there was a God, you never would have met me."

Ophelia's eyes drift back up to the clouds. "But, what if... what if it was God's grace that guided me to you? Isn't that just as plausible as luck? And what if there's something I can only see through my madness? What if this is a gift, a lesson or trial that only I can undertake? It is written in the Great Book that many men go through terrible suffering in service of a higher purpose. They are shining examples for the world. Doesn't that make the pain worth it?"

"Tell that to the little girl we found when we arrived at this camp, who was raped to death."

That wasn't fair of me. I can see her bristle at my mean-spirited comment. I can only shake my head at my own callousness. "Wow, I'm sorry, Oa. That... that was neither right nor fair."

"No, no... it's fine. We don't have to understand all of the Creator's plan for it to still be working for the greater good. I know I've had my faith tested over and over again in this war. Still, I know there's a plan for all of us because I choose my faith and love of mankind. God is love. Love is freedom. So I choose to be free, I choose to feel love, and I trust in the Lord."

"You were this close," — Patricia brings her fingers within a millimeter of each other — "this close to being locked away like Sun. This close," she repeats, her jaw tight and eyes squinting.

"And being locked away means I'm not free?"

"Uhh, yeah. That's exactly what it means."

"Oh no, sis, no," Ophelia chides, placing her hand on her chest. "Freedom is in your heart and your spirit, it is not in the flesh.

"I know my spirit is free, even when I'm in stasis," she says, her chest rising as her smile widens. "Even when my mind is raging, my spirit remains, and that will always remain free. I know because I can feel the presence of love the very second I'm brought out of stasis and think of my sisters."

Looking at our silent faces, Ophelia places her head against the dying tree. "Jos, there's a plan. There's always a plan. God will provide the path. You just have to follow it."

Such an impassioned plea, stated beautifully. But I don't accept that this is God's plan. I don't even accept there's a God. "If God's plan is for me to go mad, then I refuse to accept it. I reject it with all my heart," I say, feeling myself get emotional, angry at the idea that her God wants me to suffer forever in madness. As much as I love you, Ophelia, I cannot and will not accept your God if that's his most fervent wish. "I don't deserve that. You? You for damn sure don't deserve it."

"Martinez!" I hear someone call from below. The voice, it's David's. "May I join you?" he yells.

I look to Patricia and Ophelia, questioning if either has an objection. They shrug. We'll have to table this discussion for later. "Sure," I yell down.

In a few powerful leaps, David reaches us, standing next to the seated Ophelia, his eyes never leaving the ground below. "Good to see you ladies." He nods, keeping a tight grip on the large branch at his side.

Patricia nods back. "Hey."

"It's good to see you too, David," Ophelia replies, nodding in response.

"How are you doing, Rogers?" he says, genuine concern in his voice. "I heard you had a rough time last night."

Ophelia's face registers surprise before she grins. "News travels fast, eh? I'm doing much better, thank you for asking."

Okay, enough of that. He's getting a tad bit too comfortable with Ophelia. I clear my throat. "So, what brings you up here?"

Hello, green-eyed monster. I check my irritation — he's only showing interest in my sister's wellbeing after all. He's also not your property, Jocelyn.

"Santos, you're not going to sit?" Patricia chuckles, looking David up and down. It's becoming obvious that Santos isn't comfortable with heights. "What, are you afraid of heights?"

"No. I'm not afraid, per se. I'm what you'd call, *concerned.*"

"It's not like falling from this height will actually kill you, you know," Ophelia adds. The fact is clearly lost on him right now.

"It's just... we're up really high."

"You'll work through that fear before you know it," I comment. I remember he came in the second Sacrifice, so he missed out on many of our initial drone helicopter and cargo plane drops.

I stand and "accidentally" bump my foot against the branch Ophelia and David are on.

He digs his fingers deep into the wood as the branch moves slightly. We all laugh, even David, who glances at me warily, his nostrils flaring.

"So teach, what brings you up here?" I ask.

"I um, I have a question for you Midwest ladies regarding Dougie's... I mean, Jeffersen's replacement. Since he's going to be down, locked in stasis for God knows how long, another FOG from the Midwest was brought out of the deep freeze to take his place. Some guy named Sun, Frank Sun."

Sun... NO!

My blood freezes, and by the looks on Pat and Oa's faces, theirs does as well.

"What the fuck is wrong with them?" Patricia questions vehemently.

"They can't be serious, can they?" Ophelia asks, her eyes wide as dinner plates. "Did the brass forget what that man did?"

Taken aback, David's brow furrows. "None of this is sounding good to me." Again, he lifts his eyes from the distant ground to see our faces. "That bad, huh? I mean, I thought I'd ask to get a heads-up on a new teammate, but I wasn't expecting this reaction."

If only you knew just how bad this replacement will be. "It's terrible news, David. Absolutely terrible. Of all of the crappy decisions made, this has to be the mother of them all. Frank Sun is a ticking time bomb."

"What do you mean... what'd he do?" David asks, glancing at each of us.

I stand and jump over to David. The shaking causes his fingers to reflexively burrow even deeper into the wood, his fingers now so far down into the wood, only the last knuckle is visible. "Too much, that's what. He did too much for anyone to even consider him an ally to the North."

"He was like... well, like dropping a bomb on the battlefield. He killed everything," Ophelia says.

"And when she says everything, she's being literal," Patricia says, shaking her head. "The man killed every living thing in his path until he was stopped."

"But, with the new drugs, he should be much more stable, shouldn't he?"

He doesn't get it. He has no idea how powerful Sun is. How utterly insane he is. "Possibly, but what if they don't keep him subdued for long?"

"Then we stop him, like we do all FOGs that are actively suffering."

"No, you don't get it." Patricia chuckles, her hand stretching across her eyes.

"Okay, what don't I get?"

"Sun is possibly the single most powerful FOG ever. He's as fast as a ranger and stronger than most tanks. The man is a juggernaut. Most of the gains we made in the Midwest were because of him," I say.

"He also caused a lot of Alliance casualties. He's like a whirlwind of destruction," Ophelia says, gesturing with her hands by twirling them and extending her index finger.

"David," I sigh, walking along the branch to stand closer to him. "It got so bad the entire Midwest forces began calling him 'Fallen

Sun.'"

"It's a take on the fallen angels from the Blessed Book," Ophelia explains.

"Yeah, I get the reference. The Fallen Son, the first born of God's angels who took the side of the Enemy, the Great Darkness."

Ophelia's face lights up. "You know your scripture."

"Then I really do understand why they're reviving him. We can just launch his crazy ass right into their stronghold. Turn him loose on them."

"Then what?" I ask.

"Then what, what?"

"Someone will have to stop him. His madness won't be satisfied. It's never enough for Sun."

"Okay, once the war is over, we stop him. Jake and I have taken down a lot of our *lost* men and women. It's how we got to know each other so well —"

"You don't get it! Sun was only stopped because he wanted to be stopped. They sent Ophelia and I out to cut him off, halt his progress before he reached a Midwest town called Waverly. It took him only a few seconds to shatter my left arm and jaw. The man nearly choked Ophelia into unconsciousness with one hand. That's when Ophelia began reciting the Great Mother's prayer," I say, a hand on her shoulder.

"He's that strong?"

"Stronger," Patricia sighs.

"David, I have no idea how we can put down 'The Fallen Sun.' But I can tell you this — Sun scares me. Really scares me. And, if he comes for us, and I guarantee you he will eventually, we're all dead."

The flap softens, but the humming of electrical current continues. The room, mostly made of charged fabric, has become a prison, and the gate is now open. As we pass through the white material, I find myself struggling to handle the sight of him. Sun. He's here, alive. Sitting there in the middle of the room on a small metal folding chair, his hands folded neatly in his lap, wearing a cavalier smile.

Why would anyone drape such a man in white? His very presence soils the air around him.

He looks around, his eyes dark and lifeless, like dull coal, and studies the charged white room. Machinery surrounds us, and vid-screens are hooked on the buzzing material like pictures on a living room wall.

"Oh my god. Jocelyn, isn't it?" Sun exclaims, excitement filling his face.

A chill runs down my spine. "Yes," I reply, hating that he remembers me. I hate that I'm even here preparing to address him. I glance nervously at this dumb pad, filled with handwritten questions, prepared by LaPaige. I take a deep breath. Bastards shouldn't have ordered me to do this interview. Sun and I have history. I tried to kill him, and still want to.

He rubs his bald head and smiles. "It's so good to see a familiar face, I tell ya. It feels like I've been living in a fog for like, a week or something. And by fog, I don't mean FOG!" Sun says, laughing at his own stupid fucking joke.

"Keep engaging him, he needs to remain calm while the drugs work on his system," I hear LaPaige advise over the receiver. He's obviously watching us from behind the tent's wall. Safe.

Is he simply a psychopath? Is he using the affliction so many are dealing with as a cover? Those are the questions we all should be asking ourselves.

David and Jacob are waiting in the wings as backup, just in case things get out of hand. They're probably here to stop Ophelia and me more than anything else.

Sun's eyes light up when he turns to Ophelia. "Oh, I know you too!

192

Hi... ummm, Ophelia, right? Ophelia Rogers! I never forget a face."

"Yes, Frank, it's me, Ophelia." Her voice is stern, cautious. We're both ready to fight... or turn tail and run. The latter probably being the best option of the two. Neither of us will do that though.

"Some guy told me to wait in here a moment so two soldiers can come in and welcome me from stasis, but I wasn't expecting two lovely ladies! That's a big bonus." His smile is genuine, honest, and very disarming. The smile of a murderer.

"So... why are we still here? I'm starving!"

"We're here because any soldier coming out of stasis for as long as you've been in should be greeted by a familiar face. And since there are only a few of us from the Midwest, the brass requested that Ophelia and I evaluate your status."

His smile lessens ever so slightly.

"It's not much, just a few questions we're supposed to ask you."

"Sure, okay. Well, can we get this started? I'm ready to get out of this place. Everything smells of RX!"

Why are we even doing this evaluation? This man is a mass murderer. Insane or not, there's something dark in him, something evil.

I force a smile, in spite of my blood boiling. "What's your full name?"

"You know my name."

"We have to ask. Just to make sure you're still all there."

"Oh, well, I guess that makes sense. My name is Frank Sun, but everyone just calls me Sun."

He strangled more than twenty innocent refugee boys who were holed up in an abandoned factory. After the slaughter, he piled their bodies up like a stack of dirty clothes, then wrote their names in blood on a nearby wall. It took us weeks to find him, despite a massive manhunt. He showed no remorse.

"Your age."

"Well, now that I know today's date from the screen over there, I should be just shy of thirty-three. My birthday's coming up in a month."

193

He stormed a hospital containing wounded soldiers and locked them all in with him. He hunted them throughout the huge medical facility for days, like a sick game of hide-and-go-seek. He sexually abused every male soldier he *decided* to find, then brutally assaulted them. Even going so far as to castrate a few of the unlucky ones... with his mouth. Luckily, those men died. The others are forever scarred both mentally and physically.

"What high school did you graduate from?"

"Oh, Eastmore High! It's just on the outskirts of North Brimmton. I was actually on the chess club. I won every match we had," he says, wagging his head.

Emma. She was another FOG, his supposed girlfriend. He demonstrated his love by twisting her head completely around — dozens of times — shattering her spine over and over again. He knew she wouldn't die from her wounds and carried her around. He forced her to watch him hunt, brutalize, and eventually kill any soldier, Keynosian or Alliance, he could find. She watched it all. Heard it all.

Emma had three children back home, one of them a newborn. She was a lost soul, driven insane by the Sacrifice. Nothing like Ophelia; Emma barely knew what she was doing half the time. My gut tells me that's why he wanted her.

I can still hear her screams in my mind. She screamed the entire time we carried her from that pile of bodies he dumped her on, paralyzed from the neck down, to the moment her egg was closed.

Fuck him.

Fuck them for bringing him back. Fuck their plans and everyone who's complicit in this act of utter folly. "Do you feel any remorse for killing those boys?"

A deafening silence fills the room.

"What the hell! Martinez, what are you doing? Don't provoke him. The drugs are still working their way through his system," LaPaige yells over the earpiece.

I couldn't care less.

"W-W-What? What are you talking about? Boys?" Sun stammers, his face awash in shock.

"Martinez, what are you doing? Stick to the fucking script!" Powell chimes in, loud enough to cause me to wince.

"Yes. The boys in the orphanage, don't you remember?" Ophelia adds, circling to the other side of him. She's nearly in tears. As am I.

He chuckles nervously. "What? You guys know me... I, I would never hurt kids. So, maybe you should just stick to the script like that guy just said," he snaps, his pleasant demeanor disappearing in a flash, exposing a deep anger. Then, as quickly as it rose, it falls, returning to neutral.

The madman is still in there, I know it. He's not suffering. He's a mass murderer with the power to carry out his sickest desires.

"So you don't remember what you did? What do you remember of trying to kill Ophelia and I? Anything?" I say, pushing. I feel myself growing more and more angry as the seconds tick by, as he looks at me innocently.

People I knew... people I liked and cared about. They're dead and worse because of him.

The flap flies open and Powell storms in, his face flushed red. "Get out, now! Both of you, OUT!" Powell orders.

I don't turn around. "What about Emma? You said you loved her, remember? She had a family, a husband that didn't know she lost her grip on reality. He didn't know she lost her sense of self, her ability to control actions. She trusted you to take care of her, and instead, you took advantage. You tortured her. Why? Why would you do that?"

His breathing becomes deliberate as he clenches his jaw tight, the muscles flexing and pressing against his skin like a pulse. "Emma? Is she here? Did she make it?"

He's lying! He's a goddamn liar! The bastard is playing us for fools. Enough of this! I hurl my small pad at him as hard as I possibly can.

He catches it and calmly reviews the questions before dropping it on the floor.

195

Bastard! I grab my blade and push myself so hard I start to vibrate. But, before I can rush him, I feel arms around me, holding me tight.

"Jos, chill," David says in a loud whisper, his lips close to my ear.

Lord he's strong, much stronger than I am. And so, I struggle in vain. I could kill Sun now. He doesn't know how fast I've become. He doesn't know what I'm now capable of. I have to stop him before things get out of hand, again. "David, it has to end now... he can't be allowed to leave here," I growl, trying desperately to twist away from him.

David gives me a shake. "Come on, calm down. It's done, Jos. It's been decided already by the brass. This isn't a fight you can win."

"Whose side are you on?"

I almost feel him bristle. "I'm on all of our sides, which is exactly why I'm taking you out of here. So come on.

"Damn it, woman, stop struggling so much."

With me tight in his arms, David starts to walks backward, and I watch Powell stand in front of Ophelia, cutting off her view of Sun and pointing to the exit behind us.

She doesn't move. "And on the third day, the sky fell black as obsidian, the winds stopped blowing, the rain did not fall for many days as the dirt lay cracked and wasted.

"On the final day of drought, rain as red as blood fell from the sky and within the storm, a dark star landed up on the earth. 'Lo, behold the Fallen one!' the voice of God called out as the sound of many instruments. 'He is the end, he is the final punishment, the Death. The final seal has been shattered and the fallen son of God is set loose on all of mankind.'"

A stunned look flashes across Powell's face. For a second he falters, his shield cracking under the weight of Ophelia's recital of holy scripture. His hand begins to drift downward as if second guessing himself.

"Jacob, you have to listen to reason," I call out, trying to meet Powell's eyes. "Sun can't be set free. Not after what he's done! For

God's sake, there's a reason he was called Fallen Sun, there's a reason we can't trust him!"

Powell's eyes reach mine and he regains his composure. "And you know this how, Martinez? Please tell me how the fuck you know anything about the efficacy of the new drugs. Tell me how you are so certain about the extent of our brother's disease, even after months in stasis? Hell, how do you even know Sun or anyone will suffer again? How the hell do you know anything more than our scientists know? The fact is, you don't know shit!

"And don't think I didn't hear about your tirade against LeRoux. I heard exactly about how much you wanted to kill him. You wanted to commit one of the biggest offenses we FOGs have, killing one of our own!

"Just... just get out of here, both of you. Fuckin' go, now." Turning Ophelia by the shoulders, Powell pushes her toward the exit.

He doesn't have to push her hard. She's said more than enough.

Behind Powell, Sun shrugs. "Can someone tell me what's going on?" he says, dumbly looking around as if the walls, the wires, or the machinery will answer him.

Bastard. That evil, sick bastard.

"Jos, stop fighting and let's get some air," David requests as we pass through the flap, his arms loosening enough for me to twist free. I turn, feeling rage building in me.

He greets me with a compassionate gaze, raising his gloved palm to my face. I could easily get around him, but for what purpose? I can't kill Sun with David and Powell fighting alongside that maniac. The way he snatched that pad out of the air, it was as if it were merely sitting on a shelf, waiting.

I guarantee this, if he slips, even for a moment, he dies with LeRoux on the battlefield... One way or another, I'll find a way to end them both.

David continues to follow Ophelia and me as we storm away from that makeshift prison, leave the compound, and walk north.

What the hell does he want? "Don't ever grab me without my permission again, David. Do you hear me? Ever," I warn, my fingers a mere twitch away from the hilt of my blade. At this range, he could never stop me from unseating his head from his shoulders.

No... stop it, Jocelyn. David was trying to help you. He doesn't deserve this anger or your violence.

Wow, look at me. When did I become so bloodthirsty?

I swallow my venom. It sits in my stomach like a hunk of coal waiting to be set alight. "Look, I'm sorry, David —"

"Don't, it's alright," he says, giving a light shrug. "I agree with you and Rogers."

"You do?" Ophelia says, as shocked as I am.

"Yeah, I do. I read the guy's files. A good person, good in their heart, would regret their actions later. Especially when they're under the effects of the antipsychs. This Sun character" — he pauses to shake his head — "he never showed any remorse on those sky-eye tapes. Not an ounce. Nothing like LeRoux."

My face twists in anger.

"Wait, before you go off on me, listen. I wanted to take LeRoux apart too. I really, really did. I knew the man in basic, but that, the guy that hurt that girl... that wasn't the LeRoux I met back then.

"It took everything I and Jackson had not to take his head off and report him dead before we got there. So, I don't blame you for acting like you did with LeRoux, and definitely not with this Sun guy. Hell, your reaction makes more sense to me than putting that sicko back into the field."

"Then why didn't you just let me kill him?"

"Because to do so would put you and Ophelia in stasis, forever."

"Powell would just love that, I'm sure."

David slowly shakes his head. "As closed-minded as Jacob appears to be, he is not a monster. Truth be told, he was also against awakening Sun. Jake fought damn hard to stop it from happening, but the orders came from above, far above him in fact."

"Generals?" Ophelia asks.

"Prime Minister and his cabinet from what Jake told me."

Ophelia gasps at David's revelation. "Why? What's so important about Sun?"

With a frown, David steps closer. "What do you think they'll do with the greatest weapons ever created, once they no longer need them?" he says, ending the words with a long sigh. "What's to stop someone like Sun from wreaking havoc on Northern territories once this war is won?"

"The less of us the better? Is that their plan?" I muse out loud, knowing full well what the truth is. They're scared of us.

They should be scared of us.

"All of this, the raid, the revival of stored FOGs, the blind and stupid frontal assault on the remaining Keynosian stronghold, it's all an effort to... *decommission* us, I think," David says. "I mean, just look at the skies nowadays. The spores are gone from a lot of the airspace. We could launch missiles now and probably wipe them out."

"So, they're hoping that Keynosians wipe out the FOGs and vice versa? By the Great Book, how could they betray us after all we've done?" Ophelia asks. "We're a godly country... aren't we?"

For the first time while she's sane, I hear Ophelia express doubt of her purpose here. Doubt, not just in the government, because we all know there are fools in power, but in the clergy as well who serve as close advisors to the Prime Minister and his cabinet. It was the church's support of the war effort coupled with the death of her fiancé, Chad, that inspired Ophelia to enlist in the first place. But if that's all a lie, what does that mean for her?

"I doubt God had anything to do with this decision," I say. But I remember seeing the highest members of her church on screen, lauding the virtues of this righteous war. They guilted many of us who were found to be positive matches for genetic manipulation into signing up for the Sacrifice. Guilted many others to take up arms for the sake of our nation. So many dead because of guilt, god and patriotism.

199

Look at us now, you goddamn, hell-bound sycophants! Hundreds of thousands dead for the glory of your god. A god that has nothing to do with the divine and everything to do with amassing trillions of credits.

"I agree with Jos. They don't represent our nation, we do. We are the blood, we are the flesh... us," David says, nodding at Ophelia.

"We should gather everyone, tell them all to refuse this mission, force them to —"

"No," Ophelia interrupts.

"What do you mean, no?"

"I mean no, Jos. We do the mission. We end this war."

What? "Don't you think others have a right to —"

"How else are we going to kill Sun?" she asks, her eyes angry. "I don't think anyone here can stop him alone, and if he's not stopped here... now, it's truly the end of time, and the Great Darkness wins. This war must end, Jos, and the Fallen Sun cannot be allowed to run loose on this earth."

It's cooler up here at the severed treetop, under the bright lights of the moon and stars. It's hard to see these sights back home. The only illumination I could see on the roof of my old building came from planes, the moon, and the glow of civilization below. A sad replacement for the beauty of the star-filled sky at night.

David wraps up the remnants of our dinner into a plastic waste bag and pulls it tight. "What's on your mind?" he asks, tapping me with his elbow.

He and I are alone for the first time. I'm actually nervous! "What isn't on my mind," I reply with a chuckle, turning to see his half-smile. "I called you up here because I wanted to talk to someone I don't have ties with."

"Ouch?"

I laugh. "It's not like that. Normally, I turn to Ophelia or Patricia, but they're my friends. No, they're more than friends, they're my sisters. And that's the problem. They're biased, as anyone would expect, so asking them certain questions won't get an honest response."

"What makes you think I'm not also biased, in your favor, of course," he says, leaning in closer.

"I don't know why, but you're always so damned levelheaded."

He laughs. "Sorry to disappoint you with my levelheadedness. But, since I'm here, give it to me. Tell me what's on your mind."

His voice is so comforting and personable, but I hear something different in his heartbeat. He's not as relaxed as his expression would suggest. The organ thumps at each shift of my body, each touch from my hands.

"What do you honestly think of this plan to storm the enemy's fort like some medieval combat vid? Seriously, what do you think about this strategy?"

"I think it's stupid, but necessary."

"Necessary? Really?"

"Do you ever look at the faces of the FOGs and norms? The fatigue and war-weariness? Most of us, especially the FOGs, have been fighting nonstop for years... and that's just in my Sacrifice group. Those in the first wave," — he pauses, tilting his head to meet my eyes, and smiles — "you, and those who were in that Sacrifice group, you've had enough. I think that you, personally, have had your fill of this idiotic war. So, the sooner it ends, the better."

"Far more will die in that kind of assault."

"And if it drags out for another year... Jos, we have a suicide rate that's beyond reason amongst the norms. Many more of them are dying from RX-related diseases. Hell, we may not have any more soldiers to take the last Keynosian stronghold in a few months. Not to mention the fact that the Southies now have those black bullets, which can take the most powerful FOG down instantly. Without us, do you really think the North can stand up to a reconstituted Keynosa?"

He's right. Damn it, he's right. At the speed the Keynosians can clean up the RX today and grow new weapons, they'll easily outpace us in an arms race.

"No, I don't think our country can stop the Southies if the war draws out for another year. They couldn't do it before they created the Sacrifice, that's for certain. But boy, it's just... tiring knowing that so much is dependent on us. Where's our break? Where's our opportunity to capture the dream?"

"No rest for the weary, huh?"

"No, I guess not."

He inches towards me, rocking back and forth, deliberately so, moving from butt-cheek to butt-cheek. It's pretty comical. I struggle to repress my smile.

"Think of it this way, you'll get to go home with tons of awesomely fun memories to fall back on," he says.

Again, he leans in to bump himself against me. I know what he's about to do, and he does nothing to disguise it. He cocks his head to one side, blinks slowly, and delivers a bright, toothy smile.

"And what memories would those be?" I ask, accompanying the question with a knowing sigh.

"Memories of this moment, this time, and all of the times that were good. Times that were fun, exciting, and happy."

As cute as he's been, as comfortable and safe as I feel with him near, I'm still on shaky ground with all of this. It all feels... silly, and selfish. What right do we have to happiness when so many, on both sides, suffer? What right do two government-sanctioned murderers have to enjoy life?

"And what makes you think this moment will be fun and exciting, as you say?"

"I guess that depends on what we turn the moment into."

He always has an answer. Damn fool. "Oh really?" I say with another chuckle, keeping my eyes diverted towards the large, concentric, industrial saw marks running across the starlit treetop. It's as if we're sitting on the surface of the moon, surrounded by nothing but flat emptiness all around.

I feel the warmth of his skin, his breath, close to my face. He's all desire and want. Everything about his body says he wants to touch me, to kiss me.

"Yes, really," he says, with equally annoying and appealing calm.

He's closer to me, his lips too near. I turn. For a moment, I'm frozen, captured in his gaze. Our eyes connect and the warmth of his breath, light and pleasant, reminds me of how wonderful love can taste. I want to feel love again, with this man. With David.

He moves his lips closer, slow, grinning and knowing I want him back. A stirring builds in my stomach and I feel myself drawing into the touch of his tongue against mine.

Warnings and wishes mix as our lips touch.

God help me, I want more. Like a snake sliding up my side, his hand creeps gently against the roughness of my black soldier attire. He has strong, but gentle hands.

What will this become? What will this experience amount to against the bloody background of war?

Should I even care?

Yes, I do want this. I do want to enjoy this short moment, this tiny extraction of time, before the pleasure is all washed clean by blood in the coming days. "Take off my top," I order softly.

I'm taking this moment for myself. I do deserve a glimpse of happiness. Isn't that what we're fighting for? And right now, in this space and time, I'm happy here, with him. I'm happy to imagine myself loving and being in love with this good man.

On the other side of the fallen treetop, the entire fighting force has assembled. Like multicolored confetti, the leaves that once hung on the branches have begun falling. It's as if autumn has finally arrived.

RX-contaminated dust and bits of broken leaves swirl around the wheels of our massive vehicles as we prepare for a final confrontation with the remaining Keynosian forces. Cheers and prayers fill the air as thick and pernicious as the exhaust from our lumbering trucks.

Patricia's backpack lands with a thud near my foot. "I know that look," she croaks. Her smile is mischievous.

Impossible. There's no way she knows I slept with David last night. Except, there's a grin on my face that crept up like a thief, robbing me of my privacy.

"What? Something wrong with Jos?" Ophelia asks, turning to get a good look at my now purposefully stoic expression. "Are you feeling okay?"

Sidling up next to me, Patricia bumps her hips against mine. "Oh, I'm sure she's doing more than just okay. Ain't that right, Jos?"

"I have no idea what you're talking about, Patricia," I lie.

Her eyes go as wide as her smile. "Ohhhh, it's Patricia now, is it? Thanks for confirming why you were so late getting back last night, I mean this morning... and why you have that silly grin on your face."

"I'm lost. What are you talking about, Pat?" Ophelia asks, half smiling.

"I think Jos got herself some of that sweet David action."

"Oh my goodness, really?" In an instant, Ophelia swings her rifle to her side and flanks me. "Was he nice? Did you have fun?" she whispers, hunching her shoulders up with obvious glee and coy discretion.

I take a moment as flashes of his hands caressing my neck, my thighs, and everywhere else crosses before my glazed eyes. I turn to face them each in turn. Patricia is nodding incessantly, and Ophelia's expression is akin to hopefulness. I can't keep this from them. "Yes."

Ophelia's hand slaps across her lips. It fails to hide her huge smile. "Oh my god, that's so awesome!" she cheers with a bounce.

Patricia shakes her fist and whispers a long "yes" through lips pressed tight against her teeth. "About time you got yourself some."

"Yeah, you deserve it, Jos. Oh my God, I'm so happy for you!" Ophelia grabs me into a tight hug as she bounces up and down a bit more.

I can't help but laugh. "Ya'll really need to calm down," I advise, returning her hug and scanning the area for nosy eyes and ears.

As soon as she releases me, I look for a secluded spot... there, behind that cargo transport. I nod in its direction. We start out walking casually. But that ends quickly. Ophelia and Patricia break out into a near jog with me trailing behind.

As soon as we are out of a sight, I turn. "Okay... was he nice? Yes. Did I have fun? Definitely," I answer as we huddle together conspiratorially.

"You have no idea how many women were after him, Jos. Rawlings has been telling us about all of the other chicks he could have banged, but didn't," Patricia says.

"'Chicks he could have banged.' Why do you have to talk like that, Pat?" Ophelia says.

"What? It's the truth."

I wave my hand dismissively. "I couldn't care less about other chicks. David... David's a good person." Yes. That is the best way to describe him. He's good in a world where being good only makes one appear weak. Somehow, he's made that goodness a strength. "He's also honorable. You know what I mean?"

"You're thinking about the incident with those Keynosian women?" Patricia says. She's been studying my face, reading me as if she's looking to find honest happiness.

Yes, it's there, sis.

"It's that and everything else he's done. At no point did he comport himself as anything less than a true gentleman."

"And being cute helps," Patricia adds.

"Oh, it absolutely does!"

Again, we laugh like children.

"I'm so happy for you, sis," Ophelia says, her hands on her heart. "It's stuff like this... those moments of happiness, that fill us with love."

Love? No. "Well, we're not in love."

"Yeah, Oa. Little nookie isn't enough to turn *like* into *love*."

"Oh lord, you girls are so anti-love! And, I wasn't even talking about romantic love, I'm talking about human love. Like the love of all humanity. That kind of love."

Patricia crosses her arms and smiles. "Well, that *is* true. Some good sex can definitely renew your faith in humanity!"

With packing done, we walk through, around, and in front of the flowing, winding lines of Alliance soldiers boarding long black-painted trucks. It's early still, but many of our forces are beginning to move out. Equipment, food, and medical supplies are in abundance. We control our supply lines these days. The Southies are more interested in holding on to their last stronghold than in trying to disrupt our pathways of support.

We're still too far away for me to spot the Keynosian stronghold, but it's obvious where it is. The end of this war hides behind those black trees in the midst of our enemies' home field, where they'll have the biggest advantage.

I, we, need this war to end.

"We were supposed to be at the transport already," Patricia complains.

I couldn't care less. "They can leave us if they're in that much of a hurry."

"We're not late at all, Pat, see?" Ophelia says, pointing to a digital readout atop a towering pole. "You just like to be early."

"No, I just like being where I'm supposed to be, and on time."

"You want to run ahead?" I say, purposefully conveying my annoyance. If she wants to maintain her reputation for being completely prepared at all times, she's free to go.

Patricia sucks her teeth. "That's not a bad — is that David coming this way?"

My heart bounces at the sound of his name. I snap around and expand my senses as quickly as possible.

I see him, hear him, smell him, but there's trouble etched across his expression.

"Okay, let's go, Oa," Patricia says, locking her arm under Ophelia's just as David reaches us.

"Morning, ladies."

"Hi, David," my sisters say in unison. Their eyes shift back to me.

Ophelia winks. "See you at the transport."

"Wait," David says, nearly jumping out at them.

"Are you okay, Dave?" I ask. Clearly something isn't right.

"I'm good, but I'm more worried about you ladies."

"Worried? Why are you worried?" I ask with a chuckle.

"It's Sun. He's going to be in the transport with us."

CHAPTER 8

ALL'S FAIR IN WAR

Ophelia, Patricia, David, and I sit, crammed together, thigh to thigh, with barely room to breathe, in a norm-soldier transport. Every inch of real estate is occupied by either a body or a bag. The chilly, bare metal floor of the cabin is covered with thin green blankets that barely keep us warm, and reek of blood.

The cabin floor fails to cushion us from the harsh ride caused by the transport's poor shocks. Still, despite the rough ride, the stench, and lack of personal space, we find ourselves enjoying the company of the other soldiers. There's something grounding about connecting with them. They laugh unguardedly, smile from the heart, and talk honestly without fear of injuring one another with their words. They are truly like a family, while we FOGs readily form small cliques and backbite whenever the opportunity arises. That's the reason I only associate with my two sisters-in-arms.

"What company is this again?" I ask a handsome young grunt. He stares out of the back of the vehicle, eyes glued to the fleeing ground beneath us.

He turns, faces me, and smiles. "27th regiment, ma'am," he answers, glancing at David quickly. His smile fades under David's gaze.

Although never in an aggressive way, David made sure to lay claim to me the moment we entered the transport. He started by simply helping me into the transport. Then, he boldly placed his arm across my back and planted his hand down near my buttocks, all the while leaning into me as we jostled against one another. No one dares get too personal with me as he's marked his territory quite clearly. He amuses me with his high-school antics.

Still, there is some benefit to having a strong man around: repelling unwanted advances being one of them.

"Martinez, if you ever get tired of being around those stuffy-ass FOGs, we'd gladly take you, and the rest of you folks, into our crew," Sergeant Polk says, pointing from behind a gaggle of her men. She's resting her arm atop the head of a happy, but rough looking kid who can't be more than nineteen years old. She looks like she could be around my age, her head completely covered in premature silver.

"Why thank you, miss," I say with a nod.

She smiles. "You're quite welcome. As much as we enjoy ya'lls company, I gotta ask... why are you FOGs even here? It's gotta be a lot more comfy in the transports they give ya'll."

As if preparing to recite rehearsed lines, David chuckles and raises a finger to get everyone's attention. "Since I know all of ya'll are probably thinking the same thing, I'll explain.

"It ain't easy getting comfortable when there's *someone* around that rubs you the wrong way. Know what I mean? Kinda like havin' your back to an open door," David says.

One of the men to our left, wearing a flag pen with the colors of the Midwest force on his helmet, leans forward knowingly and says, "Sun." A chorus of "yeahs" follow as the soldiers nod in unison. The flag-wearing young man grins. "I told everyone I could about Sun. Saw him passing by."

Among these men and women, David's demeanor and speech seems to change. It's like he's taken off a mask, and I see a glimpse of his past. He's so at ease with the soldiers, as if he belongs amongst them. Most of these soldiers come from poor families, I'm guessing, since the majority of norms enlist for an opportunity to work their way out of poverty. I wonder if that's how David grew up? Polk did say that she went to the same secondary school as David, a few years ahead of him.

"Hey, David, you remember me?" a young man says, pulling his helmet off and holding it to his chest as if addressing a dignitary. He leans out from behind a few guys and into full view. Rays of sunlight filter through the ripped green fabric above our heads and bathe his fresh face in a warm glow. "We met during the Barron Springs raid. Well, hard to say 'met' in the midst of a fight, but you and Gunny Powell were wounded and we were trying to get you guys outta the area. At least far enough away from Southies so ya'll could recover."

For a moment, David looks unsure, his face blank, his eyes squinting ever so slightly as he leans towards the young man. Lips pressed tightly together, he frowns. "We lost six from your company that day. Six dry-boys, right off the line. Hell, their feet were still cracked and ashy they were so new... but damn, were they brave. I wish I knew the name of the guy who grabbed the worm seed and tried to toss it away."

"Billy. Billy McDonnell," the young man answers.

"Billy," David says. "He saved my life."

A collective sigh flows through the transport as heads nod in acknowledgment. Sacrifice isn't foreign to these soldiers. Sacrifice isn't foreign to any soldier.

"Yeah, he did." The young man beams. "If it weren't for Billy, Gary, and Pete, we'd never have gotten ya outta there. But damn it was a blessin' when you and Gunny Powell finally recovered. Without ya'll, we'd never have stood a chance of takin' back that city," the young man says, his voice ringing with a deluge of unspoken emotion.

There's a sense of pride and camaraderie flowing through these ranks that at once moves me and sickens me. They lack so many resources — are given our leftovers — and still see the FOGs as perfect and unsullied. The entire armed forces see us as the very pinnacle of Northern power... because truthfully, we are. But with all the adulation comes the forgetfulness of blind patriotism. Our accomplishments are praised, but the atrocities of our broken are brushed under the rug.

If we win, how much of our suffering, and the suffering we've caused, will the Alliance wipe clean from history?

"That was the first time I ever saw David and Jacob in action," the young man continues. "I mean, it ain't like I never saw a FOG fight, but most of them ain't nothin' compared to you two."

"I've actually never had the chance to see a FOG like David in action. But I heard they're really somethin' to see," a voice sounds off from the rear, close to the transport's fold-down rear door.

"Pffft! Something to see? It's more than that!" a smiling woman, a girl really, shouts.

"I'm glad you're on our side," a man adds, his smile glittering like a beam of sunlight.

"Hey... hey, let's not get crazy," David says, raising his voice over the swelling praise. "We're not doing anything more or better than what you guys do. In fact, we're doing less, far less. It's ya'll," David says, pointing over the tight-pressed crowd of bouncing heads. "It's you folk that are taking the real risks. All of you who run out there, without advanced healing, without enhanced strength, and without superhuman speed." He shakes his head from side to side. "Real bravery? That's not what FOGs have. It's you guys. Each time you risk your asses on that battlefield against foes that are clearly far more powerful than yourselves, you teach us what real courage looks like." A big smile spreads across David's face. "Y'all have no idea just how proud I am to be here with you."

The receiver crackles over the nonstop din of the transport. "Attention, FOGs, we'll be commencing with bombardment in a few minutes, so be on high alert."

David, Ophelia, Patricia, and I turn to look at one another in turn.

"Something happening?" Polk asks, noticing the shift in our expressions.

Instantly the old transport falls silent as everyone waits for the response.

"Yes... yes, something's happening. We just received word that we're going to start the RX bombardment," I reply.

"Alright, soldiers, you heard the lady, gear up! We don't need you scabs having your lungs conkin' out on us before you get them filled with tasty weeds," Sergeant Polk commands. As soon as the words are spoken, they react. Bags are opened and containment suits appear. It takes only a few moments for the entire battalion, still packed tight in our current confinement, to be draped in the black, protective garments, Patricia included. I'm now surrounded by faces covered with respirators. All of the once-familiar eyes are hidden by streaks of white light that dance across the clear polymer lenses.

There's something about Patricia in the company of... normal people, that's comforting to watch. They see her and connect to her in a way that's normal, human. We FOGs, on the other hand, are treated as glorious statues. No, massive weapons, used to protect — and once declared useless, placed in an egg, stored for future use.

But Patricia, she's their sister-in-arms. They lean on her, tug at the straps on her backpack, and slap her on the shoulders. They touch her. They see themselves in her, a woman who's killed more Guardsmen than any single FOG.

Good. I'm happy they don't fear her. I see the hope and promise of normalcy for Patricia. She can grow old, fat, and happy with her children and grandchildren playing about, providing enough distraction to help her forget the horror of this war. If she survives this, she'll be able to slip right back into the world.

As much as I envy her future, I'm also very happy for my beautifully flawed, completely perfect sister.

Patricia turns, catching me staring at her. "Did *we* miss something?" Patricia asks, her voice muffled through the respirator's filter. "I didn't hear the command for the FOGs to gear up."

"That's because it didn't come." I barely conceal a look of disgust. The chain of command still hasn't informed the ranks about the possible interactions between RX and the new antipsychs. "Oa, you should put on your gear," I advise, tugging on Ophelia's small backpack, trying to open the flaps.

"I can't fight with all of that gear on."

"Well, you need to —"

"I don't know how you fight with that crap in your lungs," David interrupts, lifting his hand. "Maybe you can at least try the mask? I wear it all the time and it's never been a problem for me."

She stops for a moment and looks around at twenty or so soldiers whose eyes, peering through thin plastic windows, are currently glued on her. "Sure, I guess. The mask doesn't seem so bad."

What's going on with her? She seems so melancholy. I reach over to her, patting her leg. I nod and smile, and she returns the expression, albeit with much less vigor.

"I thought FOGs didn't have to worry about the RX?" one of the soldiers asks. I think his name is Pietro... or Peter.

"Personally, that shit makes me choke," David says, placing his hand around his throat. "I can't be in that crap for more than a few minutes without coughing up a lung."

"He was wearing his mask back in Barron Springs too," the young soldier says. His name is O'Connor, I think. I hope they don't expect me to remember all of their names later on.

"Yeah, I'm consistent that way."

We fall into the steady grind of war preparation, transfixed by the thick blue smoke before us as we prep our equipment and set up quick-tents. We move in and out of the equipment truck, like ants devouring a piece of food on the ground, purposefully and inexorably consuming the contents before us.

The particularly loud thump of an RX launcher causes me to wince and dial back my hearing. The bombardment is well under way. Each thump spews a tall tower of noxious blue vapor into the air, which stands momentarily, marking its location. Then, as quickly as the column rises, it falls, like a tower of soft clay collapsing under its own weight.

We all watch the poison slowly seep into the beautiful greenery of these Keynosian lands. The substance undulates in the breeze, but only slightly — enough to prove itself to be gaseous. In my heart, and the hearts of many, RX is like a virus, a disease. It kills not only those it's directed against, but all, even those that willfully spread it. It won't be long before the black trees fall. It won't be long before all life here falls under the RX spell I suspect.

"What the hell is going on? So many of these FOGs aren't wearing any gear," Patricia groans through the mask. It causes her already coarse voice to drop another octave.

"They're not wearing their gear because they were not told about the potential danger of mixing RX with the new antipsychotics," I reply, still staring at the RX-filled forest before us.

"It is possible that they choose not to wear the gear, ya know?" I hear from behind us. It's Clarence. "That gear is stifling, hot, and really stiff. Even though it's formfitting, it bunches at every joint. I can't stand it."

"Come to pay us grunts a visit, Marshall?" I ask.

"Well yeah, that too," he laughs. "But seriously, I'm here to support you ladies. Powell is sticking at least two of his 'speartips' in each of the forward quadrants." He points behind himself to a large supply transport, at the top of which stands a circular speaker.

"I want a perimeter established ASAP!" Powell yells, standing on top of the transport. He's shouting orders instead of using the comms or the speaker above him.

"You, Harlson! Reinforce quadrant 4. I think they need at least one other FOG to balance them out. We can't have any weak points on our flanks."

215

I'm not surprised that my trio will be sent to the 9th quadrant. I think he wants us as close to the danger as possible. Is it because of our actions with Sun?

We've been here for over an hour, and I've yet to lay eyes on Sun. I don't know whether to be angry or joyful at the fact.

"Hey, Jos," Ophelia whispers, swiveling her massive weapon to one side. "Have you seen Sun?"

No surprise we're thinking similar things. "No, I haven't seen him or LeRoux. And I'm not looking forward to seeing them either."

Patricia pulls a bottle of soda from her lips and stifles a burp as she pushes the respirator resting sloppily on her cheek toward her ear. "If you guys really want to know, I've already spotted both of them. Got a good look through Suzy-Q."

"And you didn't fire?" a voice says from a few yards away. Again, it's Marshall. "But seriously, ya'll need to leave this one alone and let Powell handle it."

"Are you kidding me? If anyone should be on our side, Clarence, it's you," I say, extending my finger in his direction.

"Come on, Marshall," Patricia says, pointing her open bottle towards Clarence. "Are you telling me you want to just drop it? You want us to ignore all of the shit Sun did back in the Midwest? You were there, man. And from what I heard, he did some terrible things to a few of your buddies."

"I'm telling you guys, Powell's got this covered," he says, conveying greater confidence than I could ever muster for that man. "He may be all gung-ho, captain hero and shit, but he's actually a good guy underneath it all. He moved Sun and LeRoux to the 7th quadrant to back up the norms there."

Ophelia drops her bottle into a plastic bag dangling from the rear fender of a transport. "Out in front like us, huh?" she asks.

"Yep. He wants them right in the thick of things. They're leading the charge over there with the lower-level FOGs. Either he's looking to see them die or hoping Sun lives up to his rep," Clarence nearly whispers.

We wouldn't want to let the so-called lower-level FOGs know what we higher levels are up to. Damn, Clarence, Powell's got you hook, line, and sinker.

"That's a stupid plan. If anyone can survive this, it's Sun, and with all of us gone, he'll have free reign."

"Jos, at the very least, we can hopefully kill two birds with one stone. At worst, Sun is either outright killed or he kicks the Southies' asses. Sounds like a win-win to me."

As Patricia spits a short stream of water from her mouth, I echo the sentiment. "I'd prefer the Southies to Sun."

Waiting for RX to work is tiresome, boring in fact, particularly after the initial salvos are launched. It lies about like an old, dying dog unable to find a place to finally rest peacefully. These moments of waiting feels like the calm before the storm, where everything is quiet as soldiers mill about trying to pass the time. Most lie about, but many others gamble, betting on the few items of comfort they've accumulated during the war. Items that fit in their long, formfitting backpacks but have absolutely zero value in combat.

It's noon and warm. Warmer than it should be. Draped in our tight protective gear, the heat and the boredom feels like some form of medieval torture.

Marshall, who's been stationed with us in the 9th quadrant, yanks on a strap hanging from his backpack and smiles. He presses his hand to the receiver in his ear.

I could eavesdrop on him, hear what he and Rawlings are talking about — I assume it's Rawlings he's talking to — but it seems like far too private a conversation, not to mention the fact that it's none of my business. I wouldn't want people listening in on a private conversation of mine.

"Rawlings gives her love to ya'll," he says, beaming a bright smile.

"Aww, that's so sweet! How's she doing?" Ophelia asks.

"Good! Better." He grins, even as his words trail off. With a stillness I'd never associate with him, Marshall stares off into empty space. "She's much better than yesterday, that's for sure. Dougie's... *injury* really hit her hard. They were really good friends... both of 'em in the war from the first Sacrifice, like us. It's hard to lose someone you've grown close to. And then, to be taken down by something as stupid as that weird seizure crap... I think it's all been pretty tough on her. I guess it shows just how vulnerable we actually are, ya know?"

Raising one of her eyebrows, Patricia turns to look at me, then Clarence. "You know she's like, in her fifties, right?" she jokes.

It's obvious he's no longer the Clarence we knew just a few days ago.

He laughs. "Yeah, and? Age ain't nothin' but a number."

He has no idea just how arbitrary age is to FOGs now.

"In any case, we spoke about that and it's cool. Nothing that can't be overcome."

I give Clarence a firm slap on the back. "Don't tell me the great player Clarence Marshall is *gasp* catching feelings for someone? Stop the presses!"

We may laugh, but I feel a weird sense of pride looking at Marshall now. My god, the man is growing up right before my eyes. He's always been like a perverted little brother, as strange as that may seem. I'd like to think I had a hand in his recent development, but Rawlings probably had more to do with it than me parrying his many advances.

"Well, yeah... I am sorta enjoying my time with her. She understands... you know what I mean?"

"I think everyone can understand that," Patricia says. "Soldiers understand soldiers."

"Naw, I mean it's deeper than just two soldiers enjoying each other's company. It's... it's two high-level FOGs getting into one another. Our experiences aren't the same as even other FOGs that rank lower. It's like a brotherhood, within a brotherhood, within an even deeper brotherhood for FOGs like us?"

With a hand on her hip, Patricia gives Marshall the side-eye. "What, so I wouldn't understand that?"

"Awww, come on, Patel, you're practically a FOG, been that way for a while now. Hell, Powell even acknowledges you as a member."

I find my mind drifting away and wonder where David is. He doesn't have to stay in the quadrant assigned until the new prep order is given. Why isn't he here with me?

"It's been a few hours already. They're going to be giving the prep order soon," I announce, cutting into the friendly conversation to everyone's annoyance.

"Why aren't you wearing your gear, Clarence?" I ask. "I'd suggest you put it on this time, at least the mask. There's some... potential danger with the RX and the antipsychotic meds you're taking."

"Potential danger? Like what?"

Patricia pulls on her mask as if preparing to don it. She flanks Clarence's side. "RX affects the nervous system, just like the antipsychotic you all were prescribed," she says, lifting her eyebrows as she nods.

"Okay?" Again, he shrugs.

He's not getting it.

"Okay, think of it like this... just like they say don't drink and take a sleeping pill? This is the same. RX and the antipsychotic mixes and certain chemicals are amplified," Patricia whispers.

"It's no coincidence that Ophelia and Rawlings were the first to collapse along with the FOGs assigned to watch duty," I add.

"So, what? Only the folks that're fully geared up will be okay?" Clarence asks.

"Dunno. You FOGs can get rid of toxins so fast, it may only be a problem if inhaled directly. There's just not enough info, but better to be safe than sorry, right? Anyway, I think LaPaige would be a better judge on that. I haven't really done any research on RX and its interactions with other chems," Patricia answers.

219

Ophelia gets up on her tiptoes and looks about. "Where is LaPaige?"

That lab rat won't be here. Hopefully, he's working on improving these drugs. "Probably back at the main base, diddling beakers."

"Naw, Jos, LaPaige is here," Clarence says.

What?

Clarence laughs. "That's exactly what I said! Come to find out, the dude asked Powell for a spot on our team. That little guy really wants to be here for this fight. In fact, he was sitting in your seat on the transport, Jos.

"Oh, by the way, Patel, he asked about you," Clarence says, grinning and elbowing Patricia. "Looks like someone's got a crush on a certain nearly superhuman sniper."

Patricia only chuckles. "Picture that! As much as we'd fight..." She looks at us for a moment. "So, what'd he say?"

"Dude just wanted to know what was up with you, is all. So, don't be shocked if he comes strolling up here with flowers in his hand or some shit," Marshall answers.

Patricia smirks and shakes her head from side to side.

She's interested. That fake dismissal doesn't fool me.

"And where's Santos?" Ophelia asks.

I realize my eyes have widened in interest.

All three look directly at me. "He's right by Powell's side in quadrant 5, of course. From what I understand, those two have been fighting together ever since Santos cracked his egg. He's like Powell's right arm."

"I figured that was the case. Especially after seeing them fight together," I add. "They fight like they're extensions of each other."

I wonder how much damage the RX has done so far.

A long beep sounds over the comms, interrupting our conversation. "Northern Alliance patriots, may I please have your attention. This is General Sanford and I'm addressing you this day to tell you how proud I am of you, the true Patriots of the Alliance."

Wait, the trees... they're not dying. They're not even weakening.

"Today, this day, will be marked in history as the moment you, the patriots of the Northern Alliance, faced and defeated the worst scourge the world has ever known... the Keynosians. No longer will we of human decency and kindness be subjected to their backward, violent behavior. No longer will our southern border be controlled by sycophants and extremists. Today, we liberate not only ourselves, but the world, of this blight on mankind. The nation of Keynosa will fall today, and forever!"

"Does anyone else see this? The trees, they're still there, still strong!" I yell. If we cannot bring down or at least weaken their main weapons, our assault will be met with far greater resistance than we're prepared for. We cannot face Keynosa on fertile soil.

"She's right. Goddamn it. Jos is right." Patricia levels her weapon on the distant southern horizon. "There's no way we survive running through a still-living forest."

"Heroes of the Alliance! I ask that you do one thing and one thing only... I ask that you, my brothers- and sisters-in-arms... GIVE. THEM. HELL!"

The entire Northern forces gathered release a powerful yell, shaking the desiccated ground beneath us. It's a yell that contains more than just the patriotism General Sanford is trying to invoke, it's filled with a sense of finality, the great sense of wholeness one experiences after the completion of a long, arduous journey. We've reached the end, but we've also reached our final roadblock.

It is a roadblock buttressed by those large, black trees.

"And what will you have me do, Martinez? Call off the attack? After what the general just said, do you really think that any of the calculations will change?" Powell says, standing in small clearing at the rear of our forces. He sounds tired, exhausted. I may not like him very much, but he does appear to be dedicated. I respect that, so I respect him, mostly.

221

He faces North and laughs with his back to me, his eyes to the sky, a glowing thin-pad in his hands. "Oh what the hell, Martinez, after the general of all of the armed forces has sufficiently blown an acre of smoke up our collective asses, I'll just call it all off and utterly embarrass him. No, we push. That's the plan and that's what we're going to do." He turns back towards me and David, his eyes burning with conviction, just as they scream for rest. "No, Martinez, the Northern Alliance military structure doesn't work like that. We are soldiers. We follow orders, and whether you like it or not, you are a goddamn soldier, just like the rest of us grunts."

"Even to the death?"

"Fucking stupid question... yes, of course, Martinez. Even to the death. How many others have run towards danger to save your ass and protect our nation? How many times have you? It's what we do. So, gear the fuck up. We got a stronghold to take down."

"This is insane. David, are you really going to go along with this?"

"Why do you assume that no one but you understands the situation, Jos? Sometimes, things just have to play out and we pick up the pieces later. That's war... that's always been war."

Betrayal. He's betrayed me. He's actively betraying me. What the hell is wrong with me, trusting another man with my heart?

"No, it's what we're making it," I say, anger burning in my chest. "Nothing is the way it is by happenstance. We make it what it is. So, please, spare me your half-assed history lesson."

"Excuse me, Gunny, but why aren't those trees dying?" I hear from behind us.

That voice... Sun.

Powell leans to his left to look past me. "We don't know yet, Sun. LaPaige said he'll get back to me within the hour. Now head back to your quadrant, soldier."

I turn quickly.

"Oh, hi Martinez." He waves.

I feel my muscles tense. How dare he even speak to me. I don't respond, I just stare at him blankly, wanting desperately for him to do something that will warrant my blade to be drawn. If he thinks an encounter between me and him will end like the last one, he's sadly mistaken. I'm not the same woman I was back then. I'm stronger, faster even. I won't hesitate to kill him.

"Hello? Martinez?"

"Sun! What did I just tell you? Get your ass back to your fucking quadrant! I'll let you and everyone else know what's going on as soon as LaPaige gets back to me."

"Yes, sir. Martinez, I don't know what I've done to make you so angry with me, but I'd like us to at least find a way to peaceably fight together. Is that possible?"

"I have nothing to say to you, Fallen."

"Fallen?" he asks, looking around as if confused. "Are you talking to me?"

All I have to say is written boldly on my face. I want so much to kill him now, my hand itches.

"What the hell is wrong with you, Martinez? Are you off your meds or something?"

"Sun! Back to your quadrant, or back to your fuckin' egg. Your choice," Powell yells, pointing his pad forcefully. Another inch and he touches Sun's face.

Please don't obey his direct order. Give me the opportunity to execute you, here and now.

Sun's face changes, his expression becoming empty, cold, utterly devoid of life. I've seen that look before. Clearly, Powell's disregard for Sun has altered the landscape. Powell even turns his back on him. Does he not know that he's offending a madman? Sun's hands, balled into fists, shudder at his sides.

If I were Powell, I'd watch my back.

As Sun turns to walk away, he smiles wide. I think he's actually happy.

Yes, Powell should definitely watch his back.

"Martinez, back to your quadrant too," Powell orders with far less anger than he used on Sun.

"I'll walk you back," David, who's been standing at my left, says softly in my ear.

Powell turns, still annoyed. "David, I need you here, with me."

"I'll make it quick."

There's a moment, a very tense moment, as David and Powell look at one another.

Powell breaks the standoff with a loud sigh, and turns back to his pad. "Whatever, just make it quick."

"Did you see him, David? Did you see Sun's expression change? The man is a threat to everyone here, especially Powell after the way he spoke to him."

"Yeah... not much daylight between the way Powell spoke to him and your behavior towards Sun. So, I need you to be careful too, Jos. You can't keep poking this tiger with a stick. That's not a healthy interaction."

Now you're on my side? "I can take care of myself, Dave. I don't need you, or any other of Powell's lackeys, looking after me."

Taken aback, David stops and touches the hollow of my elbow, turning me gently. "Whoa there, I'm still on your side," he says, his face expressing confusion and anger.

"Really? You could have fooled me," I snap back. "Why didn't you back me up there? You know this is a bad idea, especially since the RX has absolutely zero impact on those black trees." I turn to look at the distant forest. I push my eyes, telescoping my vision to get a look at the trees. "What the hell?"

"What... what's wrong?"

"The RX, it's gone."

David turns as well, squinting. "I don't believe it. Did the ground absorb the RX that quickly, or did the trees... shit, look at the base of the trees," he says, pointing. "The ground around them, it's littered with huge stacks of... is that charcoal? I could have sworn the ground was clear just a few hours ago."

They were right. David, Powell, the brass... they were right all along. "They figured it out. Goddamn it, they figured out how to stop RX contamination. David, what are we going to..." I turn to see his eyes downcast, his expression grim. "David?"

"They've finally adapted to the RX. Jake showed me the reports, but I still had a hard time believing it."

No more RX? "Maybe we can redo the formula. We can head back to the base, gather more intel. Maybe we can —"

"Jos, come on," he says with a sigh. "If we wait any longer, we guarantee the Keynosians a chance to get stronger and turn the tide of this war back in their favor."

If we attack them on fertile ground, every weapon they have will be far more powerful. The black-worm seed alone could take half of our force down before we even reach the gates of this supposed stronghold. "God, David, look around here. Look at their faces. They're mostly children. They won't survive this."

His shoulders sag. "I came to fight because of the kids, and if the Keynosians are allowed to continue, they're going to win, Jos —"

"I can't believe you."

"And if they win," he continues, "*we* won't have a classroom to go back to. *We* won't have a country of our own."

"It won't matter if we're all dead, now will it?"

"We *may* die, sure, but if the Keynosians win, it's guaranteed that we won't have a country at all. We are both witnesses to what they did to South Wynd, to West Kingston, to Walton, and to so many other areas. We can't afford to stop and wait this one out. We don't have the luxury of time. Especially now that they can stop any and all RX contamination with those black trees.

"We both want to save as many people as possible, but this is war, Jos. People die."

How dare he lecture me. "What? You think I don't know that? Who do you think you are? Who the hell do you think I am? Look, you condescending asshole, I've been fighting this goddamn war longer than you, so don't stand there and talk to me like I'm some dry-back rookie, Dave."

"So what should we do, Jocelyn? Huh? If we wait, we can be damn sure they'll take us down, especially with those black bullets they've developed."

At the mention of the new Keynosian ordnance, a murmur passes through the ranks. The words "black bullet" echo through the rows of waiting soldiers — spines stiffen as fear and doubt take hold.

They should know. They should know that their Fingers of God, the Alliance's unstoppable, unkillable soldiers, can be taken down with a single bullet. Without their saviors, will they lose the will to fight?

"I'm waiting for your answer, Jos. What should we do?"

"I'm thinking! Goddamn, David, let me think."

"And that's the pressure Powell is under. Death now, or death later.

"Now add to the mix the fact that the brass is forcing Sun down Powell's throat. Do you think Powell is unaware of that guy's history? Of course not! This is the hand he has been dealt, and he's doing his best to make a winning hand of it... for everyone's sake."

"He should have let me kill him."

"If you killed Sun in front of Jake without just cause, he'd have to put you in deep freeze, immediately. We can't afford to lose you." He steps forward, close, too close, near enough to kiss. "I can't afford to lose you."

In the middle of the camp, in the midst of hundreds of soldiers, David takes my face into his hands and kisses me.

God, I want to be mad at him, to hold on to my anger, but with the touch of his lips, a fire of a different sort takes hold of me, and I surrender to his embrace.

Moments later, buzzing voices, low like whispers, begin to swirl around our heads like hungry mosquitoes — annoying reminders of where we are and the impossible mission ahead. I pull away, my hand on his chest. "You should go back to your quadrant. Powell is waiting," I say, patting him, gently pushing him away when I only want him near.

He doesn't budge. "I need you to understand something, Jos. I

226

need you to understand that I've found myself in a really unknown emotional space with —"

"Shhhhh!"

That buzzing... what is that? I look towards the sky. That looks like an Alliance rocket.

"Wha' da, did you just shush me?"

"They're attacking."

"What? Who?"

"Oh my God... they're using Northern tech to attack us." I hit my comm. "Powell! Order everyone to get cover, we've got incoming!"

"Back up now! Find cover!" David yells, waving frantically for the surrounding crowd of soldiers to disperse.

We have less than thirty seconds to get them all to safety. Impossible.

"Find cover now! Use the trucks! Clear out of quadrant 5!" Powell all but screams into our collective ears. "It's an air-razor! Get under the trucks!"

So this is what they were up to back at the village we scouted. They were studying our weapons, learning to make them and turn our tech against us.

I take quick inventory... there aren't enough trucks to protect us all. Anything standing over three feet from the ground will be slammed with a massive shockwave of concussive force, and it'll happen in the next ten seconds. The distinctive whine of the incoming air-razor missile is now becoming nearly unbearable.

So many non-FOGs stand, frozen in fear or run far too slowly to escape death. I can't save them. There are just too many.

David places his hand on my back and pushes. "Run, Jos!" he yells.

So, I run.

Air-razors are designed to cause serious damage to anything standing three feet above ground. They detonate just before impact with the earth. The sound that they make as they slice through the air can best be compared to the hiss and wail of a cat in heat, magnified a thousandfold. To defend against these, and most of our guided missiles, the Keynosians launched spores, barely visible to the naked eye, into the air, which triggered early detonation for most long-range ordnances. The spores rendered our guided missiles useless, so the majority were decommissioned very early on.

I never experienced an air-razor in actual combat, yet I never forgot the sound of it in basic training during a simulation of friendly fire. I scoffed at the technology initially. "Why build a missile that announces its own approach?" I asked. The instructor's answer: "Because it's terrifying."

She was right.

The sound alone is debilitating, and then the concussive force it can generate is metal shattering. Yet in a clear swath of land, one could theoretically lie down and avoid injury. The problem with the theory is that the force of impact transforms all items not nailed down into deadly shrapnel that shreds all within its path.

Most of our FOGs are able to get far enough away to avoid death, but still many in the 5th quadrant are injured. Our non-FOG brothers and sisters, on the other hand, aren't fast enough. We lose nearly a fifth of our soldiers in a single attack. The field that was once our staging area is now a gigantic graveyard.

Here I am, sitting in a massive trench with others who are wounded — physically or mentally — staring at dirt walls as we pray for a quick recovery and Keynosian mercy.

"Why did they only launch one attack?" Ophelia asks. She's keeping pressure on the wound of a woman whose arm was severely damaged by shrapnel, just below the elbow. She's going to lose that limb. A nearby medic quickly arrives and stabilizes the woman, allowing Ophelia to finally release her vise-like grip. Wiping the bright red blood from her hands, Ophelia turns to Patricia and me.

"They could have done far more damage than this. It doesn't make any sense to stop the attack."

"Maybe they want us to back off. Maybe they didn't know exactly how much damage the AR would do. Maybe they only have limited resources and only built the one. After all, they're basically working with stolen technology and trying to reverse engineer the weapons. Or, maybe they just thought it would be fun to see us running, dying," Patricia answers, peering from the top of the trench into the line of black trees standing in the distance.

"They're mounting an offense," I mumble. It's the first thing that comes to my mind.

"An offense?" Ophelia asks. "I dunno... it just seems like they're... I mean, the Keynosians almost never use weapons like this. Why change now?"

"They're losing. So now, they're adapting. Just like nature." The moment I say the words, I know the truth of it. "They need time to adjust. These weapons, our weapons, are probably still a little strange to them. They have to learn how to use them properly. They have to test them out and see what's possible — who better to test them on, than the enemy?"

Patricia nods. "Wow, makes perfect sense," she says, a hint of amazement in her voice. "They're being methodical in their approach, just as they are with everything else they do."

The sudden crackle from our earpieces causes many to jump, myself included. The reaction shows we've not completely healed from the attack. "Prepare for our response," Powell warns. He's not wasting time, and now I finally understand why. He was right. David was right. The longer we wait, the more opportunity they have to adapt.

Phoomph! Phomph, phomph!

Our projectiles whizz through the air, towards the edge of the black forest. It's a flailing attack. We have no idea where the Keynosians are. But, it doesn't matter, those black trees have to go. But this time, unlike our initial RX bombardment, there's utter silence as we collectively watch and wait.

"It has to work," Patricia grunts, "It has to."

She's doubting, as am I. The earlier failure of the RX has diminished our confidence greatly.

In flashes of white light, our missiles, nicknamed hotplates, detonate just above the ground. For a moment the world goes black.

When the light returns, the trees greet me, waving their singed tops at the North's military might. Billowing black soot strikes us in a gust, rushing away from the huge, black centurions. These wooden soldiers just will not bow to us.

At the point of impact, a tree or two are split and splintered, their tops ripped rudely, exposing bright green inner bark.

With her arms stretching wide, Patricia groans. "What the fuck are those trees? They're tougher than ironwood."

"Plus, they appear to absorb RX," Marshall says, shooting his hand up to wave at the approaching Rawlings. David is following close behind.

"So good to see you ladies!" Rawlings says, nearly running into Ophelia, with her arms spread wide. After a tight embrace, she moves to Patricia. "I missed your presences on the transport ride. It's tough enough being a ranger, but to also be stuck in a transport as the sole woman with all of those men. Ugh." Finally, she gives me a quick, tight embrace before reaching her final destination, Marshall.

Tenderly, they mutter words of concern for one another. Words I make a point to not listen to.

Cautiously, David approaches me. "I'm sorry I bolted on you like that. Powell —"

"Stop. You're safe. That's all I care to hear from you right now." We cling to each other.

Phoomph! Phomph, phomph, phomph! Phoomph!

We all stop and watch as a second barrage of missiles take off. They don't look as hard and straight as they did initially. Disappointingly, they reach the peak of their arc and slump pitifully towards the forest.

We'll have to fight them on their ground this time, on their terms.

"What if they respond?" Patricia asks. The answer to her question is already piercing the sky.

"Incoming!"

The word jerks though our bodies. I watch the second Keynosian attack cut through the sky. It's off. The trajectory isn't correct and falls far short of our current position.

"Their launching system looks to be about the same range as their other attacks," David suggests as he peeks over the crumbly gray dirt. "Back at that village, they only disassembled the actual weaponry, probably from undetonated ordnances. Shit... there's more incoming! These aren't ARs."

"Incoming!" Someone yells.

"I think this one's a salamander. I could see the markings," Patricia says, holding her rifle tight.

The flash from the salamander is immediately followed by a wave of heat above our heads. We used salamanders extensively in the beginning of the war, to fry both electronics and flesh. That is, until we discovered that the Keynosian weapons of choice consisted of living, breathing human matter. Furthermore, burning their plant life or their Guardsmen was pointless because of the speed with which each could regenerate.

The scent of our burning dead's flesh fills the air.

"Those poor souls. I'm going to give them their last prayer before the Southies attack again. Someone's got to help them on their way to Paradise. I'll be right back," Opehlia announces and bounds up and away.

"Wait! Shit... we can't let her go alone," I say, leaping up onto the trench's edge.

"Don't worry, Jos. I've got your back," David says, rising with me.

I smile and nod as we head out onto the scorched earth above.

"You just had to give David our channel info, didn't you?" Patricia complains, her eye pressing into her scope as she surveys the trees in the distance.

"It was a rush decision. Sorry, Pat."

"You two could help with these last rites, ya know?" Ophelia says, standing over a dead soldier's charred black flesh.

We can't even identify these bodies that appear as smeared charcoal etchings on the ground. There are no remains to send home. The families will receive only a pittance of financial restitution, a funeral, and a salute for the lost life of their child. Little consolation for grieving parents.

Ophelia is right. Someone has to honor these people. "What do you need me to do?" I ask.

Ophelia instantly beams a smile. "Really?"

A chuckle slips past my lips. "Really, Oa. What else am I going to do? Pat can handle —"

"Pat *and* David can handle the lookout stuff. Is that what you were going to say?" David responds over our private comm channel.

Patricia rolls her eyes.

"Welcome to our private channel, David," Ophelia says, giving me an exasperated look. I put my hands up and mouth "sorry."

"Don't worry, ladies, I don't plan to stay long."

"Well, let's get this party started," Patricia says.

"Jos, here." Ophelia hands me a small, fat book. It's a copy of the Holy Book.

"Turn to page 312. We'll be reading verse 23."

The faux leather covering the tiny version of the Holy Book feels flimsy. The pages feel too thin, too fragile to hold ideas that have shaped much of our world, from the Alliance to the Central Union.

As instructed, I turn the pages, find the verse, and see the first word, love. I look up to see a tear slide from Ophelia's eye. "Thank you so much, my angel. Thank you."

With her hand outstretched, she reaches for mine and pulls me to her side, gently placing her head on my shoulder. She takes a deep breath.

"Love," we say in unison.

CHAPTER 9

THE COMING DAWN

We've found a way to mimic many of the Guardsmen gifts, but one of their attributes has continued to confound our scientists. They seem to demonstrate a kind of precognitive ability during battle. They seem to be able to predict an opponent's movements so accurately that they can deflect any blow and even dodge bullets. No one knows for certain how they do this, but it gives them a decided advantage. Even outnumbered sixty to one, the Guardsmen have single-handedly kept the Alliance forces at bay for the last two years. Generally, an Alliance soldier, FOG or not, simply cannot take them on if they reach melee range. It's only through strategic teamwork and sheer overwhelming numbers that we've been able to stave off Guardsmen assaults and overwhelm those precognitive abilities.

Many of us have learned to fear them. Even the strongest FOG is on shaky ground when engaging in hand-to-hand combat. Even I, whose speed has proven to be my only effective tool, still feel a moment of fear when I face a Guardsmen. On more than one occasion, I've missed nearly every slash and swipe of my high-speed attacks only to be saved by a single final blow.

Thankfully, we've discovered a chink in the Guardsmen's armor — although they are strengthened by the sun, they also grow sluggish in its absence. As such, our biggest wins are during the coldest of winter nights.

Today, winter's too far away to hope for, but the cool night wind and the bright full moon urge us to combat. We are no longer in a rush. Instead, we march cautiously and approach with great care as we head into that mass of trees where we are no longer afforded the protection of RX.

A few shattered trees, whose bright green hearts seem to glow with some strange bioluminescence, mark the area where our missile attacks struck. It's those broken trees that will be our entry point. They're the only things we've managed to kill so far.

"Slow down and let the norms sweep and clear the way first," Powell says over the private mission channel. "I don't need any of our raiding crew getting killed here. Once you're at the facility, then you have permission to die."

I want to protest, but to what end? The non-FOGs quickly advancing ahead of the main force are trained to "weed" out the Keynosian mines and plant traps. Tanglevines are the most frequently used hidden weapon the Keynosians have. One step on the thick clump of roots instantly sends thin, sharp stakes through even a reinforced boot and up into the horrified victim's foot. The living weapon then uses said victim as fuel for tendrils of vines attached to its root system deep under the ground. Those tendrils grow at an amazing rate into the victim's body, tearing their internal organs apart, feeding on its nutrients. Eventually, they blast out in all directions, killing their host.

Each subsequent person struck by the vines that explode out becomes the next launching point for the vine's continuing assault. The chain reaction happens so quickly, so fast that no one caught in its grip has time to respond. They hear their fellow soldier scream, then turn to see themselves stabbed and infested as well.

If a FOG is the victim, it can be a catastrophe. Our bodies' fuel is far more condensed, which greatly increases the number of tendrils and the speed of their movement. Many a platoon has been laid to waste with just a single tanglevine trap.

234

Then, there are the black-worm seeds. They aren't actually seeds as the name implies. They're more akin to pods. These pods are generally littered along some piece of fertile land, looking very much like diminutive peanuts, barely above the earth's surface, but their roots can extend for several feet in all directions, holding them in place like an anchor. The seed pods store an enormous amount of energy, and they grow and compress hundreds of seeds within. Once the shells are crushed underfoot, they break, popping and spraying the area with a small cloud of seeds. If the black-worm's progeny touches flesh, they sink into the pores and begin to take root. Their entry is barely noticeable at first — written off by most as a bug bite when they're first encountered. That is, until they begin to grow above and below the person's skin. The contaminated host becomes the plant's new, very large, seed pod, eventually exploding and contaminating everything within thirty feet of its corpse.

Removal of the seed is often very painful; most of the afflicted are left to die painfully or mercifully killed by their brothers- and sisters-in-arms. That only applies to non-FOGs though. The immune system of a FOG, enhanced far beyond that of a normal person, can fight off the infection, slowing its spread enough to give others time to remove the weapon's head and the source of its internal attack. No, it won't kill a FOG outright. Instead, it'll give FOGs the distinct pleasure of watching others die slowly around them as they suffer.

Ophelia screamed terribly when I found a black-worm head in her back and started pulling on it, drawing out the long thread-thin roots. The extraction had to be done slowly so that the roots would not break under the pressure. It took hours to get those blood-red monsters out of her.

I cried with her that night. I cried because I became the cause of her torment, as well as the cause of her relief. But there's little joy in being the savior if the saved suffers so much they crack their teeth from biting down so hard.

"Hey, Martinez, are you here or what?" Clarence asks from behind.

"Yeah, I'm good," I lie. I'm not good, but I need to be. I have to get my head in the game here, not dwell on the pains of the past.

"Looks like you were zoning out on us," Clarence says. "By the way, Powell's telling us to hang back... the four of us are way too far forward."

I look back and take in the tragedies that lie behind us. Those were people once. People with families and friends. Now, they are dust strewn across a vast field in enemy territory.

"We're too far ahead?" Patricia says with a bitter chuckle. "They shouldn't be sending so many people straight into that potential shit-storm. Two, maybe three at a time at most," she complains. "They have thirty mine-scanners up there. That's way too many."

Slowing with us, Ophelia sighs. "There's no *potential* about it," she states, her jaw tightening. After praying over so many corpses, she appears spent. "I'm sure we're headed towards another tough fight."

"Just be happy they're not dropping more of our own bombs on us," Jackson says.

Haven't gotten the chance to speak to him, but it looks like he's finally recovered completely from the black bullet. Good, we're going to need his strength.

I wonder where David is now. I wish he was here, with us. With me. I assume he and Jacob are busy formulating plans of attack with the other commanders. I just wish he could do that without leaving my side.

"Think they may have blown their wad on that last barrage?" Clarence asks. "It isn't like they've had tons of time to manufacture those weapons."

"Probably, but better to err on the side of caution," I hear in my ear. "We suspect they're waiting for us to make it through this forest so they can get us out in the open again." It's David. He's listening over the receiver.

I want to tell him how much I miss his presence, but I can't do that, not over this public channel. I'm left with only the hope that David stays safe.

Despite the damage, the struck trees still stand in clear opposition to us. Broken but not beaten, just like the Keynosians... just like us.

The first line of soldiers silently enters the dark forest. Only the red light of their night-sight goggles and faint beeping of their mine-scanners hint at their presence. The soft sound of their searching is both comforting and unnerving. These sonar devices look like nothing more than long sticks attached to flattened tire-sized disks, but they are our only defense in this foreboding expanse of forest. The intermittent beeps send sound waves into the warm, rich earth beneath the black trees, in search of dangerous plant life. They're moving too fast for my liking.

"Team 1 is in. Scanning for signatures," a voice calls over the public channel in a hushed tone. "So far so good."

"Team 2 is also in. All's quiet here as well. Nothing coming up."

"Team 3's in, scanners showing nothing so far either. Seems like —"

BOOM!

The explosion is deafening... but I shouldn't be hearing an explosion from a Keynosian mine. The sound of a tanglevine is more akin to the rustling of dried leaves. Even their somewhat explosive sun mines emit nothing more than a loud hiss.

That isn't Keynosian ordnance at all. It's another one of ours.

"What the hell was that?" Powell yells as bodies fall like rag dolls against the trees at the forest's edge with a series of sickening thuds.

There was no flash of light, which marks the explosion as a nightshade. "They're using nightshades. Our nightshades," I reply over the comms.

There's silence as our forces try to gather their wits. It only serves to accentuate the screams that begin breaking through the tree line. Despite our collective shock and terrible pleas that start slow and built into strings of obscenities and begging for help, no one moves. Thousands of black shadows with flashing red-dot eyes stand in silence while our brothers and sisters die just a few yards away. We can't enter and they can't leave. To do so would only put more people at risk. So, we are left standing here, listening to the horror as we struggle to contain our growing grief.

"FOG platoon 4, get out who you can, but don't go any deeper if possible," Powell orders, his voice now monotone.

Quickly, a five-man group dashes into the foliage.

"Okay... do we have any *standard* mine-searching equipment?" Powell says over the general channel. "Anything that can detect not only Southie plant life but *our* technology as well?" No one says a word. "Come on, people, we need an answer ASAP!" Powell yells, the frustration evident in his voice. He and everyone here knows there was never a reason to bring scanners for Alliance weapons. But without them, we'll never make it to the other side.

"Anyone? Supplies?" he asks, pausing for someone, anyone, to comment. "Come the fuck on, people, we have soldiers dying in there!"

"I think I can jerry-rig something, Gunny," a voice replies, finally. A rather familiar voice in fact.

"LaPaige?" Powell asks.

"Yes?"

"Alright. Do it as fast as you can," Powell says. "Take whatever and whoever you need to get the job done. We're pissing the night away, and we can't afford to do that. We need to hit those damn Southies as soon as possible, because come dawn, we have to assume hell is waiting for us."

"Give me an update, LaPaige," Powell orders for the umpteenth time.

"Okay... okay, Gunny, I think I got it," LaPaige replies, his voice nearly gleeful. Sounds like he's actually enjoying himself. It must be a challenge for him to create such a thing on the fly.

"With our current seeker scanners, I was able to use our charged-armor tech to alter the signals using the composites charging —"

"LaPaige, I don't need the details. Okay? What I need is for you to tell me it works."

238

"Yes... yes, well, it should work."

"Does it work?"

"I'm sorry, Gunny, but I can't give a guarantee. It's easy to operate —"

"Good, go try it out," Powell orders.

"What, me?"

"Yes, LaPaige, you. Who else here is qualified to use your contraption?"

Don't we need LaPaige's brain for the factory mission? Still, he is a FOG and if there is an explosion, he'd likely survive it even if he's on a lower power tier.

For a minute or two, there's utter silence. A lone, shadowy figure walks out into the open and heads towards the tree line. The glow from a pad attached to a scanner hauntingly illuminates LaPaige's boyish features. Wires dangling and bumping against his thighs, he cautiously moves forward, disappearing into the tree line.

"Amazing he did that so fast," Patricia says. "I bet he found a way to enhance the sonar scanners by adding an electromagnet of some kind."

"A magnet? He's using a magnet to find the metal?" Ophelia asks.

"I assume so. It definitely makes the most sense." Leaning forward, Patricia chuckles. "Still, to use charged armor like that as a bridge. Brilliant. I hope it pays off for him."

Seconds tick by and become minutes as thousands watch and listen for the slightest indication of success or failure. Myself included.

Will he die? Chicken out? I give my senses a push, focusing solely on the distant sounds coming from the forest. It's easy to pick up on his feet crunching the thick, black bark those trees shed.

The sound of movement stops.

"So ummm, what happens after you find one?" LaPaige asks over the comms.

Laughter and cheers erupt as dark figures shake their fists, point, and jeer, taunting the black trees.

Finally, a much needed win, delivered by the one person I'd never expect such bravery from. We can do this. It's not a hopeless cause.

Powell chuckles over the comms, encouraging even more laughter. "LaPaige, man, I gotta hand it to you. Bravo.

"Now, can we get teams 1, 2, and 3 over there ASAP? LaPaige is going to need a lot more armor and scanners. We'll need to hustle if we want to reach those Southie bastards before dawn!"

"Three cheers for LaPaige!" someone yells out. Three cheers is what LaPaige is given.

We're coming for you, Southies... and this damned war will be ending one way or another. It has to. I don't think either side can endure another year or even another week of this.

"This is taking forever," Patricia repeats as she walks beside me. It's been her common refrain of late. The laughter we enjoyed hours ago has faded into slow sighs and whispering complaints.

Five wide we span, meandering through the dense forest. LaPaige could only make five more upgraded scanners in the timeframe he was given. So, as they struggle to avoid mine after mine, defusing or setting off controlled explosions, the six soldiers in the distance work desperately to help us outrun the coming dawn.

We're not going to make it in time.

"I'd rather we go slow than hurry and get a bunch more people killed," Ophelia says, no longer holding her weapon at the ready. It sits behind her, resting quietly on her back as the harness does its job of putting the weight on her shoulders and hips. Not that the weight is at all important to someone as strong as she. "I get the feeling this is going to be a tough fight, and we'll need as many as we can get."

"With their use of our tech, maybe our toughest," I add.

"Now that's saying a lot, Jos," Patricia says, a frown weighing her features down.

Doom! Doom! Doom! Doom, doom, doom, doom!

The sound hammers through the forest and into our ranks.

"Who's firing?" I yell. That sounds like a dragon rifle.

"Who's firing?" Powell yells, unknowingly parroting my words.

Doom, doom, doom, doom!

Again, the distinct sound of the Alliance's most powerful assault rifle can be heard in the distance, and nearby screams follow close behind. The attack isn't coming from within our ranks.

"What the fuck, everyone down!" Patricia yells, dropping immediately to the dirt.

A dollop of dark liquid hits her in the chest with a slap, and the headless body of a soldier drops right in front of her face. She does not close her eyes.

What the hell is going on?

"Take cover! Everyone take cover now!" Powell yells.

Lifting my face from the cool earth, a sickening realization dawns: the Keynosians have developed a dragon rifle of their own and are firing it against us.

Foolishly, spooked by the sound of FOGs attacking, black-clad bodies scatter into the forest, desperate to get behind the safety of the tough black trees that we once tried to destroy.

Dragon rifle fire — the sound of doom — sprays the area, boring into our forces.

Quickly, I take inventory of myself. No, I wasn't injured.

Why the hell are so many soldiers running so far into the forest? "Stop!" I scream out. Don't they realize the area is heavily booby-trapped? "Goddamn it, stop! Don't run into the woods!" I call out again, frantic.

As if on cue, explosions rip at the edges of our fracturing ranks.

"They can't see us, just get down!" I scream in desperation, feeling my vocal cords strain.

Damn it. The main comms. I need to repeat this so everyone can hear. My fingers flash to my mic and quickly press down... far too hard. The call button crunches under my hasty, panicky attempt to reach the masses. "Fuck!"

241

Ophelia's head whips around. "What's wrong Jos?" she calls to me, her words spilling out, hurried, as if the three were hinged together. Her eyes scan me, fearful that something more than a broken mic is the issue.

"Get me some eyes on these bastards, ASAP," Powell yells to our panicked soldiers. "I need eyes so we can take them down."

More explosions, more screams, then dry leaves — tanglevines — rattle through the air and tear into whomever the lucky ones will be. It only takes a few fools too scared to drop to the ground to cause tanglevines to lay waste to hundreds.

"Oa, tell those idiots to stop running into the tree line!" I yell. "Do it now."

She nods, then takes note of my broken comm. "On it," she replies. "Stop running into the tree line! You're triggering traps!"

"Tell them to get low. They can't see us."

"Get low, they can't see us in the dark," she repeats.

"Everyone, do as Rogers says," Powell orders. "Stop running into the goddamn forest! You're just killing yourselves and everyone along with you!"

I calm myself, coiling my muscles and pushing my senses outward, preparing for combat. I see the tendrils of vines fly out of the midsection of soldiers, hear their screams.

It's our turn now. I see my first target, nestled a few dozen yards away, firing from behind a tree. "I'm going," I announce to Patricia and Ophelia.

Rising quickly to her feet, Ophelia whips her weapon around into firing position. "I'll cover you," she says as I run towards the opposition.

As always, Ophelia's weapon hammers the trees in a wide arc, just barely ahead of me in perfect synchronization with my movements. She knows me so well.

The Guardsmen can barely see me in this dark forest, but he responds nevertheless, anticipating where I'll be. He'll be too slow. As I pull my blade free, he lifts his weapon in an attempt to block the bite of my blade.

You can't stop me.

The first slash splits through the bicep a second before he can move the homemade dragon rifle into the blade's path. My second pass goes completely undefended. With little more than the sound of a breeze, my blade slices through his neck. I don't wait to check him, I don't need to. The thud is evidence enough, and right now, I need to find cover and prepare for the remaining members of his team. No time for gloating as the sound of exploding shells sweep into the trees around me.

Now that they know I'm here, they move into strategic positions, an attempt to triangulate their attacks, to trap me. Hiding behind a tree, and now pinned down by dragon rifle fire, I cannot use my speed to overwhelm the other Guardsmen. I chuckle at the realization that these bastards know how to deal with rangers. How long have they been at this? Their proficiency aside, if they're focused on me, then they can't trap my brothers- and sisters-in-arms any longer.

A powerful crash echoes northwest of me, and the body of a Guardsmen is tossed out of the clustered trees. The body tumbles and spins a few yards before landing on a mine that tears the man to shreds with the force of its explosion. Like an echo, another crash erupts from the east.

"Move outta there now, Martinez," Powell barks. "We're going to open up hell on these bastards!"

"I'd hate to be on your bad side," David quips. I can hear the smile in his voice as he emerges from behind a very large tree, his mace thick with black blood.

The remaining Guardsmen quickly realize they've lost the advantage and turn their weapons towards the multitude of soldiers who've begun to return fire. First, in only a few cracks, but now the tempo is increasing with each passing second, forcing them back.

Then, in perfect union, they disappear, turning and running deeper into the forest. They move in a confusing hopscotch manner that's so fast, it's impossible for anyone to follow. They know exactly where the traps are set, going from sprints to leaps as odd intervals. It's as if the area was marked for their eyes only.

243

Once again, we are left battered and confused as the Southies score another successful attack.

Amidst calls to regroup, the low groans of the wounded haunt the forest. Clouds of dust, brought up from the shattered bark of the black trees, fill the air. Many are coughing profusely. This dust is terribly irritating.

"FOGs, status report now. I want numbers on the dead. If injured, I want wait times for recovery or, for the norms, when they'll be ready to return back to base. We have to move out ASAP, ladies and gentlemen, so let's move with some purpose!"

I look up and sigh at the sky, now turning from black to a dark blue. The sun will be rising soon. Our advantage is lost. Again, they've outwitted us. At the advent of the war, it was we who confounded the Guardsmen, turning the tide of the battle in our favor. We've held that tenuous advantage for nearly two years, but that edge may be evaporating.

Soon, if we don't change the direction of this fight, it'll be us who are retreating.

"There's a clearing," one of the men scanning for mines shouts.

They've done an amazing job reconfiguring more of the scanners with LaPaige's help. We're now able to make progress at breakneck speed, clearing what must be hundreds of mines. The main person clearing has been LaPaige, pushing himself and the norms scanning with him hard. They've had a tough time keeping pace with him, barely managing to clear half as quickly.

I wish we had him during the retaking of Steel Harbor.

Still, despite our progress, the Keynosians are slowly and steadily reducing our strength by taking both lives and our will to fight with each encounter. We're fearful, checking each shadow and movement as we march forward. They're chipping away at our resolve, taking apart our power base, the vast number of norms.

Winning is no longer our driving force, because no matter who wins, neither side will be the global power it once was. It's impossible for any nation to lose a generation and remain strong.

The sun's up. I can feel the power of the sun's rays in the air around me and smell its effect on the plant life, although I barely see it through the dense foliage covering the sky. It'll be a cloudless day, hints of clear blue peek past the dark green canopy above.

"Just focus on the end," a gentle voice calls to me.

David! I whirl about to find him walking right by my side.

Patricia grins. "She's been zonin' out again, David," Patricia comments. "I don't know how much cheer you're going to get from her."

I restrain a happy chuckle. "She's right ya know. There's no telling if you'll be talking to the happy-go-lucky Martinez or a brooding killjoy," I say, smirking at Patricia. Casually, I slip my hand into his and take a half-step closer. "It's good to see you made it, Dave."

"Well, someone's got to make sure you don't go running off again like that."

"Oh yeah? Are you here to stop me?"

He laughs as he pulls his head back. "Like I could. No, I'm here to help you run off, but just a bit more strategically this time."

"It's not just Santos. We're all here." That's Jackson. As I slip my hand from David's, I turn to see him, Powell, Petersen, LaPaige, and Rawlings come up from behind, a smile on each of their faces. It feels like some sort of family reunion.

Even Powell greets me with a nice smile, for once.

"Slow down a bit, guys," Powell says, his eyes scanning around, his arms waving us in. Slowly, casually, we increase the gap between us and the rest of the soldiers marching in front.

I feel the warm grasp of Jackson's hand on mine as he flashes me a huge smile. "Jos, you might like to know about a little birdie. This little birdie, she's such a chatterbox. You see, she goes from person to person, repeating things. Well, in this little birdie's travels, she stumbled upon a man named Frank Sun," he says, tilting his head towards me. With a grin, he leans in closer. "The birdie sat on Mr. Sun's shoulder and told him LeRoux considers himself the 'main man' in this and every quadrant." With a shrug, he turns forward. "I wonder what'll happen there?"

Powell glances at me, his mouth tight, and nods. Did he cook this up? In any case, I do hope LeRoux and Sun kill each other, but I doubt they will. LeRoux would be nothing more than a plaything for Sun. He isn't powerful enough to pose a real danger. Only the people in this group are capable of that.

Still, if Sun takes the bait... I wish LeRoux a long, painful end.

Powell, checking to see if forces in front of us take notice of our absence, keeps his eyes looking straight ahead but crouches over a little. "Martinez, Rogers, and Patel will lead the charge," he says softly. "You ladies have been working together and are the most effective team. I trust you can start us off on good footing."

"Why?" I ask, turning to face him. "I thought you wanted to save the rangers? Keep us protected? Then there's Patricia, arguably your ace in the hole —"

"I want to win," he says, turning to me. "Moreover, I want the Northern Alliance to win. I want our country to survive this. I want that more than I want anything else.

"I watched recordings of your battles, Martinez, and again you confirmed it during the assault at the confiscated base and finally back there in the trees. There's no one as fast as you. No one. That being the case, you'll draw fire and keep our main forces from receiving focused fire. I need you focused on staying alive more than attacking.

"Then there's Ophelia. Clearly one of the strongest FOGs, right up there next to Marshall and Jackson, if not stronger.

"And finally, there's Patel. We've all seen you in action."

"So, I'm your distraction, your bait?"

246

"No, you're THE distraction. You're the main bait. And with Ophelia and Patricia supporting your attack, your group can single-handedly turn the tide of a battle, but only if you're careful and cautious. So, as soon as they begin to triangulate your movements, I'll need you to fall back and actually let the others take up your slack for once. We can't have you dying, at least not until after we've taken down that weapons facility.

"That being the case, Santos and I will be offering our support when things get sticky... and they will."

"What about me?" Rawlings asks. "Since you're giving her my former role. Unless of course you're planning on having me sit this one out?" She grins.

Powell chuckles. "Not a chance, Rawlings. Martinez is faster, but not as gifted in scanning. Plus, there's no one I trust more than you. So, I want you, Marshall, Jackson, Petersen... and finally LaPaige to focus on clearing a path to the facility."

LaPaige clears his throat. "Great. More mine clearing."

"Looks like LaPaige is our other ace in the hole after the grit you showed back there. So everyone, keep an eye out for the nerd." Powell offers LaPaige a cool grin. "You can tell us what the hell we're after once inside this mystery weapons facility. You know more about Keynosian technology than anyone else. It's just an added benefit that you're a FOG."

LaPaige only chuckles as a smirk slips across his face. "Score one for the nerd."

"So the facility is over here?" Ophelia asks, pointing westward.

"More like southwest," LaPaige corrects, adjusting the direction of Ophelia's hand with a tap.

We reach the clearing. Slowly, the crowd ahead begins to spread out, checking the sea of green through the cover of the trees.

"They're stopping. Hold here," Powell orders us, keeping our group a healthy distance from the larger force ahead.

Reaching the clearing is not the joyous moment I thought it would be.

No soul takes a step beyond the once-loathed trees, which offer far more protection than the open field ahead. Ankle-high grass covers the expanse, but not a flower is in sight. Strange.

The flat clear area is perfect for stopping a much larger advancing force in their tracks. Their firing sights are completely unobstructed, and they can simply stand behind the trees and fire into our ranks. Even a barely competent sniper would have no trouble picking a large number of us off. They'll be shooting fish in a barrel.

Finally, I see the fort, our main target, standing in the distance, its base hidden by another forest of black bark. Its top, a single massive tree with nearly transparent leaves, gives the sunlight filtering through a green hue.

Powell takes a deep breath, his eyes fixed on the goal ahead. "Stay on mission. All of you, stay on mission.

"This isn't going to be a pretty battle, far from it," he says, grimacing hard. "So, I need all of you to focus and make sure you stay alive, don't deviate... you got me, Martinez?" Powell says, turning to give me a suspicious stare.

"Don't worry, Gunny, I'll stay on mission," I lie. Well, it's not actually a lie, at least not until there's reason to make a liar out of myself.

"What about Sun?" Ophelia asks, her thumb rubbing her temple while her other hand shades her eyes. Headaches again.

Powell nods. "He's going to lead the secondary charge, probably disrupt a lot of the Southie plans. But, he's also a wildcard. As the most powerful FOG we have here, he can actually make or break the entire assault if he goes berserk and targets our forces."

"And if he decides —" Clarence asks.

"He won't."

"If he does?" I push.

I can see the annoyance on Powell's face. "If he becomes a problem, David and I will handle it. Bottom line is, we'll cross that bridge when we get to it. As for now, we go forward as if he'll do as told."

248

I don't believe it for a second. In fact, I don't believe he believes what he's saying. The brass has no idea what they're dealing with in Sun. And if Powell thinks he and David can take him, he doesn't understand the thing Sun has become. Those two won't be able to stop him alone. That's fine, I'll have to be the insurance. I may not have their strength, but that's not what's going to stop him. Sun has faced down Ophelia and lived, so no, strength won't be enough.

I once had the opportunity to end him. I was the only one to get close enough. But I hesitated. I couldn't imagine ending someone I used to look up to, someone I saw as a mentor... someone who saved my life.

That was then and this is now. I won't hesitate again.

"You all know what to do, so keep your mission channel open. If things change, I need all of you in the loop and ready to be fluid."

Suddenly I remember my carelessness in pressing my receiver. Shit. "I umm, I broke my receiver," I say sheepishly.

Powell looks at my neck and sighs. "How the hell?" he asks, confusion blanketing his face.

"How'd you do that?" David asks, smiling.

"That's not the first time she broke her receiver," Patricia offers. She motions towards me, her hand palm up. "When was the last time you broke it, Jos?"

"Throwing me under the bus?"

She chuckles along with the others.

"Okay... fine. Can you still hear?" Powell asks.

"Yes, that I didn't break."

"Good. Well, we can't replace it right now, so you'll just have to listen." With a slow realization he begins to smile. "I guess it's not that bad of a situation after all."

It doesn't take long for the Keynosians to line the opposing side of the field. I can see their weapons, and they all resemble Alliance machinery. The sizes are similar. The general shapes match as well. They're wielding what looks like dragon rifles, harnesses and all. They also have a good number of shoulder-held launchers resting in their hands. All small arms, meant for mid-range combat. Perfect for this exact scenario.

"Are they waiting for us to attack?" Ophelia asks.

"Yup. They're waiting for us to charge them, and run directly through this field to do it," Patricia answers. "That's what I'd do if I were them. We want to get to them, not the other way around." Her rifle in her lap, Patricia checks her magazine. "Plus, why spoil all those lovely mines they've most likely littered this field with by launching a barrage of shoulder-fired arms at us? The moment we try to get at them, that's when the fireworks will start."

"So, how are we going to start this?" I ask, looking around at all of the young faces in the 27th, 14th, 2nd, and the 9th regiments, as well as a substantial contingent of lesser FOGs who're waiting anxiously behind the non-FOGs.

Damn brave of the 27th to request this detail as soon as the offer came up.

Patricia turns. "Sarge, what do you think?" she asks Polk, who's standing just behind us.

Looking through a pair of binoculars, Polk scans the field of play. "Patel is right. It'll be impossible to make a charge. It'll be suicide."

Ophelia nods, walks over to a tree, and taps the bark. "What if I could help with that?"

In a slow, relaxed motion, she takes off her harness and rifle, places them on the ground nearby, and hugs the thick, black bark of a nearby tree. The tree is so wide, her arms can't even reach halfway around, but that's all Ophelia Rogers will need. Slowly, she squats down, her arms growing tighter around the tree, crushing the bark.

In a slow exhale, she squeezes into the black bark, creating puffs of gray dust all around her. Slowly she begins to rise, and terrible sounds pour from the ground as roots snap and groan in protest, clinging desperately to the earth underneath.

With a final wrench, Ophelia drops an entire tree down in front of us.

The 27th regiment stands stock-still, every mouth sagging open, speechless.

Pushing the tree forward with her boot, she moves it to the green field's edge. With a smile, she throws her hands on her hips, breathing labored, and turns back to face Polk. "Okay" — she huffs — "you guys can follow me from behind the tree. I figure if they can stand up to one of our bombs, they can stand up to a few mines and some dragon rifle fire long enough for us to reach the other side."

"Oh my god." This gives me an idea. If I can use this to protect me on the other side... "Patricia, can you call Petersen over here?"

"What's up?" Petersen says, his voice and face betraying his annoyance.

He looks down at the uprooted tree in shock. "Damn, Rogers, you tore a tree outta the ground?"

Ophelia nods, her eyes closed and finger again on her temple. "It wasn't so difficult. I don't think the roots are that deep."

She's not looking well. Just like back at the camp before she collapsed. Those new pills are more trouble than they're worth it appears.

I notice Patricia shooting me a glance. She picked up on the frequency Ophelia has these headaches as well and gives a nod toward her. "You okay there, Oa?" she asks, taking a step towards her.

"Yes."

"You don't look too goo —"

"I'm fine. Can we get on with this?"

Again, Patricia shoots me a concerned look.

"I hope you didn't call me over here to brag about how strong Ophelia is?" Petersen asks Patricia.

The man frowns so often, I'm beginning to think it's his default expression.

"Of course not," I reply. "I asked you here because I have a request." Slapping a smaller, nearby tree, I turn to them. "Can you and Ophelia toss a tree over the entire field and into their front lines?"

Ophelia looks at the ground for a moment, then across the wide green space. "Together maybe?" she asks, turning to Petersen. "I mean, if we coordinate it, I think we can do it. What do you think?"

"Sure, sure. If I take the center, keep it stable, ya know?" he says, walking to the edge of the forest and the green field. "You take the rear, using those rocket-fuel arms, I think we can get it over."

Ophelia nods. "Yeah, I think we can." She smiles back to me, slapping her hands on her top, making a cloud of dust. Her hands, darkened with soot from the tree bark, stain everything she touches. They've already given her once-black uniform a dull gray appearance.

"But why do it at all? You want us to throw trees at the Guardsmen?"

I walk over to the tree lying on its side, prop my boot up against its sparkling black bark, and stare out across the field. "I think I can run it."

"Run what?" She walks to my side, pointing across the sea of green, and she looks at the side of my head. "You mean run across that field?"

I nod and meet her glare. "Yeah. It wouldn't be the first time. I mean, that's pretty far, but I've been able to outrun a lot of things."

"Wait, wait, Jos. The last time you pushed that hard, you nearly passed out," Patricia says.

"No, she didn't *nearly* pass out," Ophelia adds. "She absolutely passed out. You dropped so fast, I thought you were shot."

"That was a much farther run, and it was for a way longer period of time. This? I could run this in a few minutes max."

"I dunno, Martinez, this seems a bit sketchy to me," Petersen says.

"I agree with Petersen wholeheartedly," Polk adds. "We need all of the FOGs we can get to make it across there."

"Look, how else are we going to get this done without taking on far too many casualties? Even these trees aren't going to last under focused fire. We saw how they splintered back there when the Southies were firing on us. A whole line of them... with sidewinders and halo missiles? They'll get around the trees more sooner than later." I pause for a moment, surveying the faces of those gathered. "Nothing? Okay then, here's my plan. I'll run across the field and engage the enemy there with a few hit-and-run tactics. They can't ignore me, especially when I start dropping people."

"If you don't pass out," Patricia says.

"I won't pass out, Pat."

"How do you know?"

"Because I know my own body. How many times have you personally watched me do this? Forcing them to fight faster than they can compensate, even for just a few minutes, can be a huge asset."

Patricia sighs loudly. "Okay, but then what? Do you think the tree, the one that Ophelia and Petersen toss all the way across this field, will be a *distraction* while you go in and draw their fire? Come on, Jos, that's insane," Patricia says, shaking her head.

"Look at them, Pat," I say, pointing at the soldiers standing behind us. "You don't think we'll get full fire the moment we step into that field?" I move in close to her. "No one will make it across. They'll all die even with these trees as cover. They have way too many weapons," I whisper. "Even if there's the odd chance of a few people making it to the other side, then what? Our numbers would have dwindled so much, we'd be dead soldiers walking. Not to mention we'd have Guardsmen, well-rested Guardsmen, standing in full sun I might add, bearing down on those lucky few who actually make it across.

"We must get them off the line, or to back off or whatever. Something has to change. If we don't make that happen somehow, we lose. So, someone has to do it. Someone has to keep them from pouring all of their firepower at us when we approach."

Patricia huffs. "Just stop it, Jos. Okay?"

"Just stop what?"

"Stop treating us like we're your responsibility! Everyone here is an adult. You think we don't see that this is a shitty situation? You think we don't see the obvious? You think we don't know that we'll most likely die on this field?" she says, her voice nearly cracking. "We are each other's salvation, Jos.

"Remember back when Powell was telling us the plan way back at the forward camp? Remember that? Well, I think you got it screwed up in your head about why some of us were angry at Powell. Speaking for myself, I wasn't angry because he didn't give us this or that important information. No. What made me mad was he actually believed we'd run away. He calculated that it was necessary to keep that information secret to keep the number of soldiers high. He believed we, warriors that have already risked our lives countless times, weren't ready to die for the country we love after all we've been through."

"And you don't give us the credit of caring about you. Caring enough to die for you, same as you feel for us," Ophelia adds.

"But you don't need to throw your lives away for me. You have families, you have futures, you can —"

"Goddamn it, you can be so stupid sometimes," Patricia says, shaking her fists at me. "Dying for you, and for all the others standing with us, *is* dying for my family. *You* are my family, Jos."

"And here's what you don't seem to get, Pat. Me dying for you, for them... that's me dying for my family as well. I'm willing to die for the only family I have left." Even as the words leave my lips, my eyes begin to well up with tears. As do hers.

"Yet, the difference between you and me is I don't presume to take the full burden of your life onto my shoulders. We both choose. That's how I see it. I would never tell you to sit back and let me risk my life. I'd ask that we make a plan and we do it together, just like everything else we do. We do it together, and we do it together because we love you enough to die with you, not just for you."

I get it. I love you too, Patricia, Ophelia.

"Just think about it, Pat, okay? I am fast enough to avoid getting caught in the explosions. You know that. You've seen me evade them before. I'm the only one that can get us even a sliver of wiggle room. I'm the only one capable of providing the necessary distraction."

"But you don't have to do it alone. Give us a choice for once instead of trying to steal our right to choose for ourselves."

Petersen clicks his tongue. "I gotta admit, you've got some serious balls, Martinez, but even I think it's a dumb idea. They'll have you surrounded and dead in seconds. You can't keep that many Guardsmen back. No one can do that alone."

"Well that depends," Polk interjects, coming up from behind us. "We norms may not have super-duper hearing, but we're not deaf, either. So while you ladies were debating, I was collecting mini-mines." She pulls a line of mines and their detonators, taped to the front and back of a long, black leather belt. "Now, if you pick a corner — like there," she says, pointing to the edge of the Keynosian line. "With one of these tough ass trees positioned between that cluster... hell, you can set up a bulwark of sorts. You get tucked away in there, you could toss mine after mine at them and force their right flank off from their firing line. Plus, considering how much they love going after rangers, they're bound to try to put you down. Then, as they break rank, we can use that hole as an entry point and keep the log angled so it doesn't take all direct shots."

"Keeping the log angled? Why would that help?" Patricia asks.

Polk chuckles. "Looks like the old dog knows a trick or two the young ones don't. The ammo for dragon rifles was first used on strike jeeps and hovers. They're meant to penetrate the enemy's armor first, then explode. We created them after the Westonia War. Those bastards had some bizarre armor that took a long time to get through."

"You served in that war?" I ask.

"I did, yes. Those desert rats would be a welcomed sight right now."

"But in regards to the angle, what most don't know is the bullets aren't pointy, they're round at the tips because the Westonia armor couldn't be cut into, it had to be punched in. So due to the tips, if you can hold armor at a good angle, say thirty to forty-five degrees from the shooter, you can cause the bullet to pop before it gets full penetration."

"Didn't know that."

"Now if you've noticed, those Southies have packed themselves up in one location, facing the bulk of our forces in sector 8 which isn't in a direct line to us. So, all we have to do is keep the log angled and it's possible to get them completely across. They won't be able to get full penetration, they won't be able to cut through these hard ass trees as fast and we'll be able to basically use the logs as shields the full way across.

"Now I know you FOGs are badasses and all, but we men and women of the 27th damn sure ain't helpless either. We have enough strong backs to push a few logs along the way ourselves. That'll add some additional fire support for you folks."

I take the belt from Polk and look it over. With this many mines, things could definitely get interesting over there. "How many mines are attached to this belt?"

Polk shrugs. "I dunno, about thirty or forty. The point is, if you can actually make it across, you'll be able to stay hidden behind those trees for some vertical protection, using the trees like a trench. But it won't work until we make damn sure they can't draw you out into an open area and time you. So with you pickin' at them and us marching quickly towards them at a good angle, we can probably make it across this butcher's table in one piece."

Petersen shakes his head. "Doing that will still make her a sitting duck, just a duck trapped behind a bunch of trees."

I look at Patricia. "That's why we have our fellow soldiers," I say, with a grin to my friend. She's right. We need one another. We always have.

Patricia nods. "Ohh, just had an idea... if we push more than one along the ground, we can force the tanglevines to trigger between the logs, rendering them harmless."

Polk nods. "Still, she'll have to hold that position for a while. That's a damn long time to wait with Guardsmen gunning for her."

"We can use our med range ordnance to give her some cover and time," Ophelia adds. "We still have those."

"This all hinges on Martinez not passing out, right? I don't think Powell will be happy if we lost you on this shitty field, Martinez," Petersen says, giving me a suspicious glare.

"I can do this. We can do this. Hell, we have to do this or scrap the mission entirely."

"I think you should wait for reinforcements," Petersen says.

"We need you to keep at them once you're on the other side, force them off balance," Patricia says, ignoring Petersen, holding her lips tight as she stares blankly across the green gulf. "So, even though you're good with those mini-mines, I don't see it being enough. The entire group here will have to keep too many of those from focusing on you. Black trees or not, if they keep firing on your position, they'll cut right through those bad boys after a while." Patricia turns to Polk. "We'll need a firing crew. As soon as we're in range to fire, we have to start cutting loose. No delaying."

"I don't believe this shit. You chicks are really thinking of doing this?" He looks at us, and no one relents. "Well, I'm gonna have to let Powell know what's goin' on."

"Ohh, I have another good point," Ophelia chimes in. "Since we'll be using two or three trees, that'll keep the shredder rockets it looks like they have from spraying us with shrapnel. I mean, they only have a short range on that nastiness, right? So, with these tough trees in front and us remaining down, that'll be enough to keep the majority safe."

"Oh that's true, I didn't think of that." Patricia nods. "Plus, if we make sure not to roll the one we're hiding behind, and keep some of that nice thick foliage, I can easily take position on the log and assist Jos from range."

I turn to Petersen. "You know what, Petersen, that's a great idea."

"What idea?"

"Telling Powell. Maybe he can offer some assistance or additional suggestions?"

In disbelief, Petersen chuckles. "Yeah, okay. We'll definitely see what assistance he gives."

"Great. We'll have to move really fast to get into position and hold them off," Polk says with a smile. "So everyone will have to push like hell, right soldiers! Can't let a soldier like you go down." As her people shout a cheer, she pulls out a sleeve of ammunition from around her thigh for my pistols, and hands it to me. "You're going to need all of the ammo you can get."

Eying the top of the black tree sprawled out on its side, Patricia grins. "Just don't push too fast or make any sharp turns. Don't want to slip out and into the open with those guys firing at us with freakin' dragon rifles."

Ophelia giggles, her hand on one of the fallen black trees. "I can't promise you on the speed, but I do plan on going straight down their throats."

I nearly busted out in laughter when Petersen tells Powell about our plan over the facility mission channel. He sounds like a child tattling on a sibling. Clearly he expects Powell to take disciplinary action against us, but instead, he does nothing but offer praise. He even has Jackson, Petersen, and Clarence rip up a few more trees to speed up our preparations.

"If it succeeds." Powell repeats a few times too many, to my great annoyance. Still, he's far from a fool, despite his youth. The man knows we need as many people as possible to survive this death trap if we're going to win this.

Behind me, the snapping and ripping sounds have finally lessened on the black missile of a tree Petersen and Ophelia are preparing.

"Not the most aerodynamic missile in the world, but it should fly pretty good," Ophelia says to no one in particular. I don't know what's going on with her now, but she seems to be much better than before. It's like a veil has been lifted and she's back to her normal self again. No headaches, nothing as of yet. Good. If there's anyone we need to survive this, it's her.

Covered in fine gray soot, Petersen drops a thick branch down with a thud. "We're still going to have to really put some 'umph' behind this to get it over to the other side," he complains. "I'm probably gonna have to push myself past my limits — hurt myself — so I'll be worthless until I can heal."

"Yeah, probably," Ophelia says, barely listening as she stares out across the area, streaks of dust painting her face. "I assumed that was always what we tanks did."

So many people are coughing now. It's the dust from the bark. It's on everything. Every soldier working on limb removal is covered in soot.

"Keep a few branches for me," Patricia calls out. "Keep this one... and that one there," she says, pointing to a short, thick branch covered in leaves. "I want that large one to remain in place too, just in case I need some stronger coverage." As she approaches the location she designated as perfect, her face mask in place, she slings Suzy-Q over her shoulder. Deftly, she hops onto the trunk of the tree and crouches down, using the limb and foliage to hide her presence. "Yeah, this'll do."

She has the right idea with the mask. The thin film of dust hovering in the air is causing a lot of people problems.

Damn the sun for being so high and bright today. Everything is working in favor of the Keynosians. They have the bright cloudless sky, warm sun, fertile earth, and the combined tech of Keynosa and the Northern Alliance at their disposal. If they were even close to us in number, it wouldn't even be a fight.

I need to prepare for this run. I quickly open my backpack and grab a few fuel-rich MREs. I glance up as I stuff one in each breast pocket. I check the distance again... yeah, I'm sure my muscles will run out of fuel before or just after I hit the far forest floor, pushing at my max. I'll need to keep myself calm and relaxed and try not to burn any more energy than is completely necessary once I get there.

Ugh, I hate the taste of these peanut butter flavored MREs. I think Ophelia has the chocolate flavored kind. I look up to ask Ophelia if she'll swap a peanut butter for a chocolate and notice she's staring blankly into nothing. Then, for a single solitary moment, I swear I see her lips move in silence.

As if shocked that I noticed, she turns to me with a start. "Oh, Jos. I think we're ready." She glances around for a second, nodding. "Yeah... yeah, we're ready."

That didn't look good. "You okay, Oa?" I ask, handing my backpack to a nearby soldier.

"Me?" she asks. "Oh, yeah! I'm good. Just ready to get going, yeah... get going."

A cool chill crawls up my spine. Is she slipping back into psychosis? She took her medication; I saw her take it. Could it be the RX contamination wasn't fully cleared by the black trees? Maybe her dosage needs to be increased?

The receiver crackles in my ear. "Martinez, where are you all with the prep?" I don't respond, because I can't.

I hear Patricia laughing. "This is Patel. Yeah, we're ready, but shouldn't we wait for nightfall? It's not going to be pretty if we attack at high noon."

"Patel? Oh right, Martinez broke her mic button. Great work there, Martinez," Powell sighs. "Anyway, that's a negative, Patel. We can't wait. I was given the order to attack an hour ago."

She shakes her head. "Roger that, Gunny."

The common channel crackles and everyone working on the trees raises their head in unison. "This is Gunny Powell, first-gen FOG. Most of you know me, know the things I've done. So I'm sure you all know, I am one of you.

"As much as I don't want to attack in broad daylight, as much as I think this entire plan to attack the Southie stronghold is bullshit, as much as I want to save each and every one of your lives, I also have my orders. So, as all shit rolls downhill, you now have your orders to partake in this rolling shit feast." The gathering chuckles and nods knowingly.

"Here's the thing. I had a soldier a few days ago request that I tell you, all of you, everything. This soldier asked that I play it straight with my brothers and sisters. At first, I declined, as I was ordered to do. They gave that order because they weighed the risk and rewards and didn't see the reward in it. They gave it because they couldn't imagine that we'd fight, despite the odds. They actually think many of you will run if you know just how hard this battle will be. Well, I say they're wrong." The murmuring of the men and women begins to swell. "I know you're going to ask, 'Hey, Gunny, you're a grunt, soaked through and through, how are you going to square not telling us?'" Heads nod, of course. "I have to admit, that would be a fair question. So I'll answer... it doesn't. There ain't no way that shit'll EVER square. You can't square bullshit." The crowd smiles.

"The task they're asking of us is hard, damn hard, but I was there on Black Rock Steepe when we pushed back these bastards and retook Sandtown. That was hard. I was there when we held Bowling Downs and when we beat impossible odds on Windfall Mountains. That was hard too. I was there, same as you, and I know what we're capable of, even when shit gets hard. So, despite how hard the fight, I believe in us. Goddamn it, I believe in us!"

This isn't like the pep talk given by the general, no. Powell is truly one of us. A soldier who's been in the muck, who's been in the worst of the worst and has come out on top. He may be manipulative and a politician at heart, but he is definitely a soldier.

"I'm not going to lie, and I'm not going to hide it anymore. That shit ends here and now. We are going to suffer casualties. Probably a lot of casualties. Even with the idea of using these tough trees as shields, once we reach them, we'll have to engage with fighters that are incredibly tough. But, fighters that we've also beaten before. So, I won't tell you to charge out there with a promise that you all will be fine. I can't even assure you we're going to win this one.

"So, let me tell you what I do know. I know we've faced worse. I know we faced down hell itself, and we *won*.

"So here's *my* deal for everyone who doesn't have the balls to continue... run. Fuck it, if you're too afraid to fight for your country... run! No one here will stop you, I'll make sure of it. I damn sure won't report you. So, if you're a coward, go ahead and take off.

I'm okay with it, because right now, the Northern Alliance doesn't need cowards. Not today. Today, the Alliance needs real soldiers who are willing to do the impossible, again. So go ahead, now's your chance, cowards."

For a long moment, silence stalks our ranks and all that moves are eyes. Eyes that have seen things they wish to God they had not. Eyes that have seen the worst in both the Northern Alliance and Keynosa. Eyes that have stared down death. But above all, eyes that see themselves as true Northerners.

"Good, the real citizens of the North are here. The heroes of the Alliance, the true blood, the true flesh and the true bones of our great, great nation. That's who stands with us now. Patriots.

"So, let me ask you a question," Powell says. "What will you die for? Hell, I know my answer. I will die for my country. More than that, I will die for you. I will die for the mothers, daughters, the sons and fathers who stand proud in front of me today. Those same people we are protecting back home. But, I won't ask that of you 'cause I don't know what you will die for. I only ask that you remember. Yeah, that's right, remember. Remember the thing that you *will* die for, and hold it tight. Because today... everything is on the line. Everything that you hold dear is in jeopardy, as this fight determines what the future holds for those we are protecting here and back home.

"So, grasp that thing in your mind, and remember why you're here. Because today is the beginning of the end for this shitty war. Today is the day we stop those motherfuckers from taking what's important to us! Today... today we stomp a fuckin' mudhole in those Southie bastards!"

"Are you ready?" Petersen asks Ophelia, his back to her. She shifts and squirms under the thick black tree she has perched on her right shoulder.

Her lips move silently, barely visible under the shadow and dust of the tree. She nods at Petersen's back. Does she not realize Petersen can't see her?

"Hey, ugh... sound off!" Petersen yells to her, sweating streaks of muck down his temple and cheeks.

"I said I'm ready!" Ophelia snaps.

Oh my god... it's the bark. The bark! How could I have missed it? The entire tree is coated in RX. That's what's been causing the coughing. That's what's been causing so many people to have headaches. I reach for my mic... damn it. I broke that. "Patricia!" I yell.

She waves behind herself in my general direction. "I'll be fine, Jos. You should be more concerned about —"

"It's not that... it's the trees. The damn trees! They're all coated with RX residue!"

"Go," Powell barks out the order over the general channel.

With a loud grunt, Ophelia and Petersen launch the tree in the blue. It rockets off like a missile. Even from here, the sound of their tendons snapping is distinctly audible.

I turn back to Patricia, who glances down at her gloved hands, which are now a dull gray, just like everyone who assisted in the process of uprooting these poisoned trees. Looking up at me, her expression turns severe, pained with the realization that a new, greater problem now brews.

What are we going to do if our soldiers pass out or, worse, lose their minds?

"Jos, now!" Ophelia yells over to me.

I see the tree they threw angling directly where Polk pointed out. It'll make it across, but that was only a distraction and cover for me. I've got to get there as soon as possible. I've got to run!

Running is not just in the legs, it's a whole body experience. The wind presses against my face, whipping my hair as the very air becomes a barrier to my moving. Behind me are the sounds of explosions and rustling leaves. I run hard, as hard as I ran when I carried Patricia to safety after the acid-seed attack. It's not that I'm outrunning the dangers themselves — no, I'm outrunning the mechanisms that trigger the dangers. Everything moves a second or two behind me. And everything behind me wants me dead.

I'm effectively outrunning my own death.

"Go, Jos!" Marshall calls over the mission channel.

"She's going to make it. That crazy bitch is going to make it!" Rawlings adds, her voice giddy with laughter. "Run, girl!"

Quickly the edge of the second forest and the end of the odd, green grass flies to me. Just as quickly, my body begins to give away and I feel myself losing balance. These bursts of speed, for all they are worth, consume all my body's available fuel. Fatigue quickly sets in with a pounding ache as I crash into the root-strewn forest floor. I tumble headfirst, scraping against hard wood roots and the soft earth. Painfully, I skid to a thudding halt against the tree meant to be my shield. My arm scrapes the black bark so fast, I feel the skin of my upper arm give way. If it were not for my uniform's ability to avoid tearing, the muscles of my left arm would be exposed.

It doesn't take long for the Guardsmen to turn their attention to me, the invader. I hear the doom of their rifles and feel the crashing of the bullets against the outside of the tree. It all feels like a dream.

Quickly getting to my feet, I rip out one of the MREs and jam it into my mouth, nearly gagging myself on the dry, overly sweet and crumbly faux-food.

Then the world tilts.

At my back, I feel the hammerfalls of dragon rifle bullets as they strike over and over again against the tree.

It feels as if I'm missing moments here and there.

Clouds of dust rise up from the bark in plumes of gray. I gulp hard, choking down the MREs. I'll need fuel, but they won't provide that energy right away. I feel my body fat reserves and muscle mass decreasing, loosening my uniform.

I feel by body falling slowly as I reach in my backpack for the mini-mines. It's as if I can't straighten myself.

Explosion after explosion rings out, shaking the vertigo from my mind, and in the distance, I hear Ophelia. She and a few others are moving to my position as the mines in the field go off and rocket fire slams into the trees they push. They're moving quickly, just like the Guardsmen coming my way. I'm sure they'll be vaulting over my makeshift shelter in mere seconds. I need to act.

Again, I push my muscles hard, moving out from behind the log to attack. In quick succession, I throw mine after mine towards their charging forces. I don't look, I don't have time to as they force me back down into cover. I go down the line, pressing the triggers and causing a series of explosions in their general direction. Smoke quickly follows and floods the area. Perfect. I have a few more moments.

I hear the crack of Suzy-Q singing out her single note ballet.

Patricia's covering me. I better make the best of it.

Blade drawn, I leap up and target the closest Guardsmen who's struggling to peer through the smoke and fighting off the stun of the explosions. Another diseased Guardsmen. His eyes enlarge the moment I make my decision to attack. But, by the time he realizes, I'm already on top of him. Three slashes and I only manage to cut off his right leg at the thigh. Before I can turn to face the other Guardsmen I hear barreling towards me, gunfire pours in my direction as well as the hiss of a shoulder-fired missile. Damn it! I race back to the log and duck just as the rocket hits.

Again, the world tilts on its axis more than it should as more rockets explode against the tree, forcing it to slide into me and knock me out into the open. Quickly, I scramble back under the clouds of shattered bark to the protection of the tree, which is no longer jammed amongst its sisters. Bearing down with my legs, I push back against the tree with all of my strength. Explosion after explosion slams the log against my back over and over again, forcing me to push down with my legs so hard it feels as if they'll snap in two.

This is too much... I'm burning energy too fast. Between my attack and now my feeble defense, all I can do is continue to push with my legs and keep this log in place.

Please, don't pass out. I can't let myself succumb to the darkness.

I shake my head and realize just how far from the log I am now.

More moments lost! Desperately, I scramble back into the tree's dark cover. Not good.

Where the hell is my team? The Guardsmen are close and getting closer by the second. This tree will not last much longer under their barrage.

They're coming. I hear them. I hear their calm hearts beating hard, but steady. I hear their bare feet stepping on dried leaves and twigs. I hear the clink of their metal harnesses against the cooling cable. I hear them whistling out commands to one another, the sound seeming to come from all around me.

I grit my teeth, clutch my blade, and wait. It won't be long before they get over this log. Maybe a few more seconds. Good. Let them come. I'll make damn sure they lose more than they gain to take me.

Wait. What's that? It's a soldier. Carefully, but very quickly, he runs along the same path I took, carrying two large branches on his shoulders. The lone soldier leaps over massive holes in the earth and the starburst pattern of green vines left by spent tanglevines. Suddenly, the figure jumps into the smoke and into the fray.

Is that David? A FOG with his face mask strapped on tight. That has to be David!

What the hell is he doing?!

He hurls one of the large removed branches, a slab of black wood that's the length of a large jeep, into an approaching Guardsmen who can't avoid it due to its sheer size. I sit up, looking over the log to watch another branch speed towards our enemies. The Guardsmen seem to know exactly where to move, and this time only one or two are clipped but not stopped. Most evade the branch completely, but it stops their advance on my position as they've turned to fire at him. With a final push, David tumbles over and skids to a stop at the end of my protective log, bullets snapping and exploding just above his head and into the top of the log.

He looks up, and despite the cover of the mask, I can tell that he is smiling brightly. It's like he's having fun.

I must have passed out. I must be dreaming. Has the fog of

266

unconsciousness crept its way into my dreams, my fantasies? No, I'm not done yet. He's actually here!

I find myself both happy and angry to see him.

Scooting on his butt, he twists onto his hands and knees to crawl rapidly to me, his rear end chased by more exploding shells thumping the end of the fallen tree. He bumps into me and peeks up above the log before quickly dropping again as more bullets graze the top of the battered wood beam.

Slightly winded, he smiles. "I saw you on my way here and thought, 'Hey, that pretty lady looks lonely.'" He laughs.

"So you thought to join me? Is that it?" I ask.

"Exactly." He pulls his mask down, his teeth shining through the dust and frequent spray of black and pale brown fragments that splinter up from the flesh of the rocking tree. With one leg, he braces the tree against the attacks with ease.

He looks around and nods as if inspecting the area. "Not a bad spot you got here. Mind if I hang out with you for a little while?"

This is absurd. I'm spent and weak. We're pinned down behind a tree that's being torn apart by advancing Guardsmen attacking us with Northern arms. Through it all, knee deep in chaos, he grins with his head hunched down, nearly hidden by his shoulders.

I explode into laughter. "You're an idiot!" I yell, trying to regain my composure.

It's just so absurd.

Why is he laughing?

Why am I laughing?

"I can be that sometimes. Ouch," he complains as a spray of particles tear past his face and neck. "But, if I didn't come here, how was I going to save you from being utterly bored?"

I wipe a tear from my eye. "You're right about that. I'm definitely not bored now."

I feel the slow building of my strength as the spots begin to recede. He saved me, providing just enough time for me to recover. But, in doing so, in saving me, did he also doom himself?

"So... what now?" He laughs.

Again, I burst out laughing. I want to grab his face! "Damned if I know. I thought you'd have an answer to that question."

He's perfect. I reach over and plant a big kiss on his lips, even as the tree is whittled down, slowly disappearing above our heads. I know I want to be with this man.

I feel the vibrations increasing at the center of the log. Soon, our main source of protection will be shredded, and we'll be left completely exposed. Fine. At this moment, as my lips and tongue caress his, all feels right with the world. I'm at peace in his embrace.

If this is indeed my end, this will be a most pleasurable end indeed.

CHAPTER 10

PROMISES TO THE LIGHT

They attack in perfect synchronization. Every angle is covered by waves of dragon rifle fire, keeping David and I pinned to a spot behind the fallen black tree. The Guardsmen have no intention of letting us out without exacting our blood and flesh as payment. I listen intently for gaps in the rifle fire, any path or pattern that'll give us an opening, but as soon as I turn in a direction, the Keynosians intercept.

I better eat again. Whatever I do, I'm sure it'll ultimately require a lot of energy. Quickly, I cram another K-bar into my face, choking down its dry and gritty smash of sugars, proteins, and minerals. With effort, I swallow as much of it as possible in one gulp. I'll need all the help I can get.

"I don't think now's a good time for a snack, Jos," David says, taking hold of his mace. "Sounds like they're regrouping and ready to make their move." He tosses another mini-mine over the log and detonates it in the air. Hopefully it buys us another moment before we're riddled with bullet holes.

With another hard swallow, I get down onto my elbows, avoiding the spray of wood from the explosion and the Keynosians' return fire. I nudge closer to David, who's now nearly flat on his back, his chin pressing tight into his chest. They've whittled away half of our log so far.

"We have to attack," I say, loud and close to his ear. His head is propped up against the crumbling black bark, and above it, the exposed iridescent green tree core gleams. "Waiting here is going to get us killed."

"Agreed," he says, ducking even lower as a sudden explosion slams the battered tree into us again. "So, if you have a plan of attack, feel free to share, 'cause right now it'll be hard to mount an offense without both of us getting shredded by these assholes."

These Guardsmen, split off from their larger group, have clearly been given the sole task of killing David and me. They make no move to fire on the approaching logs of our fellow soldiers, moving across the green expanse at a very good pace. Right now, they have us pinned and are doing all they can to keep it that way. Wisely, they've spread themselves out, hidden by the trees to avoid possible return fire.

"We go together. You attack, I defend," I say.

"That's a good plan, but you've got it flipped on who should be the defender. You're much faster than I am. You should attack and I'll defend. My slow ass will make a much more appealing target."

"Can you... ack!" A spray of wood slices across my face, and warm blood seeps from the cut. "Can you see attacks coming from multiple directions like I can?"

Pulling his mask down from the top of his head and into place, he gives me a quick no head shake. "But I can take more punishment than most. My healing is probably far better than yours," he says, his voice muffled by the mask. "They can't keep up with your —"

"Do you want to live?" I interrupt. We don't have time for this debate.

He gives me an odd look, before wincing at the sudden explosion behind us.

"Do you want to live?" I repeat, grabbing his hand tight.

"Of course, but —"

"Then do what I'm asking! I can see everything... everything, for a short period of time. I can isolate my eyes, speed them up, make the bullets appear to slow down. It'll enable me to block incoming fire."

Of course, that's before my eyes give way, blinding me. "I can protect you while you attack. All we have to do is stay alive for a few more minutes. By that time, the others should have made their way across the field."

"What the hell are you talking about, blocking bullets? No one can do that!"

"I can, Dave, and I will. So, are you ready?"

"Damn it, Jos," he complains, glancing at each end of the log. "This isn't going to work that easy, I need —"

"Three!"

His eyes widen. "What are you... Jos, don't you do that! Don't force this!"

"Two," I say, pulling my blade from her sheath, my eyes locked onto his.

"Goddamn it you're a stubborn woman!"

"One!" I get into a crouch, making sure to keep my back out of the line of fire. I'm going with or without him.

"Shit!" He quickly follows suit.

"Go!"

He goes to the end of the log, near the forest edge, moving as fast as he's able. With his mace in hand, he charges the first Guardsmen he sees with me close behind. I begin forcing my eyes to move faster, forcing my brain to process the images they're receiving. As my body begins to vibrate, my perception changes. It's as if someone has put a vid on slow motion. The world appears as if it were dropped into a vat of gelatin. Everything slows to a crawl. David running, the Guardsmen emerging from behind nearby trees to fire on us and the bullets... they aren't all that slow. Their speed is different, faster by a wide margin. Yet, I can see them like falling rain as they speed towards our slowed bodies.

I watch David charge our enemy, his muscles bulging, his face hardening as he approaches. Turning his body, he moves to strike the Southie with a backhand. As always, the Guardsmen reacts as soon as David turns, and begins to duck under the strike. David will miss him completely.

271

Suddenly, as if he were aware of his coming failure, David ducks down and whips his mace through the rich earth beneath his feet, spraying the Guardsmen directly in his face with clumps of dirt.

Both the Guardsmen and I are shocked. He actually manages to catch a Guardsmen by surprise. The Keynosian reacts instinctively, drawing himself up and swiping the dirt out of his eyes and off of his face.

David immediately follows up, planting his foot with a stomp and whipping the mace onto the side of the Guardsmen's head.

With a crunch of bone, the man falls completely still.

For a second, there's utter silence on both sides. Then, the sound of a Guardsmen's body plopping face-first into the dirt breaks the spell.

Immediately, the other Guardsmen respond with a series of whistles as they raise their weapons, their sights on David, as one. In slow motion, they all press their respective triggers simultaneously. I see the rifles pump their ordnance at us in a spray of fire and smoke.

As if there are no bullets headed his way, David charges into the fray, running full tilt at the enemy. The man is brave, I'll give him that.

Time for me to act. Moving close to his side, I lock on the incoming bullets. I've done this one other time, defending Patricia and Ophelia, so I know it'll work. But I've never had this many targets, never had to defend against dragon rifles.

I have to plan this perfectly in order to deflect these bullets. Each move, each block has to be strung into a single, smooth motion, carrying each one into the next. One wrong twist, one wrong swing, and I won't be fast enough to adjust and keep David and myself alive. As fast as I can move my arm, bullets are still faster.

I see it. I see the pattern. Yes, I can do this.

In a single motion, I feel the first, second, third, fourth, fifth, and all the subsequent shots pang against my blade and explode barely a foot from our bodies. Thank god they are all on full auto and not moving. The pattern simply repeats over and over again, allowing me to continuously deflect the bullets.

The strain... it feels as if I'm tearing my body apart.

David closes in on the next Guardsmen. He appears to feint to his left, as if preparing to strike the Guardsmen with a left hook. Instinctively, the Guardsmen reacts by lifting her arm to block. Instead of striking her folded arm, David brings his mace down on the Keynosian's shoulder so hard, the woman's body seems to fold around the metal. As David withdraws, he follows up with that left hook both the Guardsmen and I were expecting to come.

Another enemy falls.

It's as if they're not able to see the first move. I know David explained it, but to see it in action is amazing.

If the Keynosians were shooting in bursts and continuously adjusting their angle, we'd be dead now. They haven't learned to do so yet. Dragon rifles are not a weapon they are familiar with, so they're simply unleashing streams of metal by holding the trigger for as long as they still have ammunition. Good for us. But I don't know how long my eyes are going to hold up. They're burning so much it's getting hard to see through the tears streaming from them.

David charges another Guardsmen.

Something in my arm snaps and screams in pain. Shit, I can't keep this up.

Crack! "One," Patricia says calmly over the receiver.

The Guardsmen drops before David can reach him.

Thank you, Patricia. My sisters are getting closer.

Even as the number of Keynosians tasked with killing us dwindle, they seem undeterred. They're focused on putting us down, unwavering in the face of their people dying. They may yet succeed, as I start feeling and seeing the edges of my vision weakening into a blur. We need to find cover before I burn my eyes out completely.

Then I see it... black bullets. I have no idea where they're coming from and I can't worry about that right now. Divert them. David and I can handle the others shots hitting us, but those black bullets take priority. They have to be stopped.

As David runs to the next Guardsmen on his left, I spin around him and raise my blade to deflect the bullet.

Pang!

It hits the dull edge of my blade and takes a bite out of it. Shit! I can't afford to lose my blade. Not here, not now.

Three more black bullets appear, bearing down on David, and again, I move around him.

Pang! Pang! Pang!

Damn it! Where are they firing from? We reach the next Guardsmen just as he releases his clip and tries to slam another in. David will take him — I have to make sure those terrible bullets never hit us.

The next volley of black bullets is already incoming.

I push hard again, boosting my overall speed. Quickly, I move in between David and the Guardsmen. In one motion, I grab the Keynosian by the collar and use my hips to throw the soldier up, over, and in front of us, dropping him directly into the path of the black bullets.

I don't hear the bullets strike, but I see the man shudder.

As the Guardsmen falls, I notice blood through the blurriness at the edges of my vision. Please don't let it be a black bullet. Anything but that. I turn to see chunks of flesh blown off of his thigh, upper arm, and calf. The result of dragon rifle explosive rounds. Thank god for small miracles.

"Fuck!" In a quick push, using his only functioning arm, he hurls himself behind a tree just in time, avoiding five more ebony shots.

I look down and see the Keynosian, dead. That shouldn't be. It was only three shots. I've seen Guardsmen take hundreds of rounds and walk away with a grin so long as they were never struck in the head. Whatever those bullets are, they're not only lethal to FOGs, but to Guardsmen as well.

I look up to see streams of bullets coming for me. Using the Keynosian as a shield once again, I lift the dead mass into the path of the incoming bullets. Quickly, I follow David behind the tree and toss the body to the wayside.

Good god, it feels as if my eyes are going to explode. "How are you doing?" I ask, scanning his wounds.

It's happening. The light is slowly fading from my eyes.

Blinking hard, I look again at David's injuries. He's done for now. The injuries are not superficial. He'll need at least an hour to recover from so much — wait, is he healing already? The river of thick black blood that was spilling from the wounds has already quieted. In a steady creep, pink flesh begins to rise up and around the empty space that was in his thigh. The same goes for the other injuries. He's replacing flesh in seconds, something that should take far longer to happen.

He wasn't joking when he said he heals fast. I've never seen anyone heal so quickly.

Then something painful snaps in my eyes. I know what it is — I'm going to go blind in a few seconds, but it's just too soon.

"How am I doing? How are *you* doing?" I hear him ask, grabbing my shoulder.

I can barely make out his features. "I'm fine... I'm fine," I say. "How much time do you think we have?"

"Fine? Are you serious?" I see his head as nothing more than a dark blob flopping back and forth.

I feel his hands on my face, forcing my eyes open. They must look terrible.

"God damn, your eyes look like they've been dipped in blood. Can you see, Jos?"

We should have waited at the log. I'm going to get both of us killed. The thought brings tears to my eyes. "I can't see very well, no. But... but, I can make out shapes still. I can —"

"What the hell are you talking about? Your eyes are bleeding!"

"I can see your body! It's just... the details. I can't see detail right now." Even as the words leave my lips, my sight darkens even further. Images that were once shadows and black silhouettes fade into nothing more than blobs of space surrounded by hazy light, and even that continues to fade.

275

David grabs my hand and pulls me close to him. Suddenly a wave of fear strikes as the rest of my sight slowly recedes and the world turns into absolute night.

If I've killed him with my bravado... Don't let him die because of my stupidity.

The idea of being blind, permanently so, frightens me much more than the bullets ringing out. I stumble into him, arms stretching wide to feel for something other than empty space. I feel him tug me in a different direction. Did I just wander out into the open?

"Stay calm, Jos. The others are only a few seconds away. We just need to hold on a bit more."

But it would only take a few seconds for the Guardsmen to kill us. If we die... "David, I'm so sorry."

"Sorry? What are you talking about?"

I know my eyes are open. I know it. I can feel the very air whisking across them, feel the particles of dust sticking. But, there's nothing. All that lies before me is an ever-present absence of light. I can't defend him. I can't defend myself. "I'm sorry..." I feel my voice crack as a well of emotion bubbles up from my core again.

I feel the warmth of skin, his fingers wiping away my tears. I grab his hand, desperately so.

"Don't be silly," he says softly, close to my ear. I can barely hear him above the explosions, the screams, and the thunderous call of doom. He's close enough to kiss. "I'm here because I choose to be. I wanted to be here with you, understand?" he says, a smile in his tone. "I *want* to be here."

A pulsing warmth envelopes my heart and body as his words wash over me. I see his smile in my mind's eye.

Then suddenly, the world around us goes quiet. The gunfire, the whistles, the shouts, all of it stops in an instant.

"What's happening?" I ask, grabbing David's arm. I focus in and catch the sound of running, the sound of bare feet not moving towards us, but running away... again.

David huffs. "I have no idea." He leads me away from the tree, and I instinctively reach back for its familiarity and safety. Blind and exposed is all I can feel now. "The Keynosians, they just... well, they just cut and ran."

"Ran?" They had us. We were trapped with nowhere to go. Why would they do that? "They had us —"

"Jos!" It's Ophelia. "Jos, are you alright?" she yells.

"Oa!" I call out, waving my hand in the direction of the call. "I'm here with David!"

"I see that now... and you can stop yelling," she says, her voice giddy as she snatches me to her. "I told them you'd make it, but no one believed me. I told them and here you are."

I feel her tears on my cheek.

"I believed it," a gruff female voice calls out. "Jocelyn Martinez doesn't die, she just multiplies!" Patricia and her jokes. Still, her scratchy voice sounds so sweet right now. "Hey, are you alright, Jos? Something wrong with your eyes? Oh, you burned them out again."

A small hazy bubble opens slowly at the center of my vision, allowing the light to seep in. Pawing in her direction, I sigh. "Yes. I burned them out keeping David here alive."

David rubs the base of my spine. "Yeah, that's definitely true. She kept me alive. Don't know what I'd have done without you."

The mission channel beeps. Goddamn, it never stops.

"Just heard that you made it, Martinez. Good work. Reckless sure, but good work nonetheless," Powell says. "Listen up, folks, we're close to ending this shit-storm, so keep your head in the game and focus on the task."

"You're insane as hell, Jos, but I love ya!" Jackson cheers.

"FYI, gang, before you start handing out medals, there's a potential wrinkle in our plans," Powell injects. "Sun and LeRoux... both men are now missing. I just got word."

I told you so. I fucking told you so!

"We have to get them," Ophelia barks.

"We will, Rogers. We will."

It's begun. Just as I warned. The Fallen Sun is back.

A young FOG, no more than eighteen years old, stands in front of Powell, squirming.

Powell's appearance is off-putting. His face is soft. It would be far softer were it not for that long scar that cuts across his features, aging his appearance by a decade. It gives him an eerie ruggedness. His expression stern, he glares up at the young man before him. "I put you in charge of watching them, Chan, so please explain to me how they got out of *your* sight," Powell says, his hand covering his forehead.

The entire spear tip, as Jacob called us, is here. We've formed a circle around this frightened boy. I can understand his fear. The most powerful FOGs that remain, most of us anyway, are standing before him, demanding answers.

"Gunny, that Sun guy was too fast! I tried —"

"Keep your voice down," Powell barks, turning subversively towards the main group ahead of us.

The young man nods, trying to peer over Powell's shoulder, past us, and into the gathering of soldiers only fifty feet west of us. "Sun is fast. I mean really, really fast," he says, now whispering as he takes a moment to glance my way. "Before I knew it, he had that LeRoux guy on his shoulder and took off to the east, hanging along the edge of the forest."

"Damn," Powell growls, turning eastward. "Okay, I think we'll…" He pauses and glances at Chan. "You can go," he says, dismissing the young man with a wave.

After a nervous salute, Chan quickly walks away from us and Powell's eyes give chase.

"Okay, as I was going to say, I knew we'd have to deal with Sun at some point, but the question is, do we do it now? Is this the right time to go after —"

"No," Ophelia says.

"No?" Powell responds.

"No."

The group turns to Ophelia. They're surprised by her outburst. I am not.

"What'd you mean, no?" Powell asks.

Ophelia doesn't even glance in Powell's direction; her eyes are fixed towards the east. "What I mean is no, I'm not continuing on with this mission until we stop the Fallen Son."

There is no sense of anger, or even a hint of discontent, just the sound of a determined woman taking a stand.

"Fallen Son?" he says, his face full of confusion. "I don't think you understand, Rogers. This isn't a request, it's an order. We can't spare —"

"No!" she says loudly, turning towards Powell, her face stoic and sure. "It's you who doesn't understand. This is exactly what he wants. This is exactly what the Fallen Son will wait for. This moment in time where he can fade away. He wants us to forget, to be relaxed. He wants us to deny the truth. He is the Great Evil. Although he wears the face of a child of God, his heart is a stone of darkness." More scripture.

"What the...? Are you off your meds or something, Rogers?"

There's a moment, a second of hesitation, as we all turn to look at Ophelia and wonder... has she actually slipped into madness again?

"She's right," Patricia says, breaking the awkward silence. "This is his MO. It's always been that psycho's strategy to run off and come back only when he thinks no one will be concerned about him, or when we're too busy fighting a war. That's how he was able to cause so much trouble back east. He runs, but he never runs too far. He always stays close enough to terrorize. He always stays close enough to take more victims."

Turning to LaPaige, Powell frowns. "Is that true?"

Almost reluctantly, LaPaige nods. "Well, the reports did say that Sun frequently returned to get a, ummm, *fresh* victim after a few days. So yeah, there's evidence that Sun will stay nearby, just within striking distance of our forces or any people for that matter."

"Okay, but will he interfere with us?" Powell asks again.

"I don't think he cares about any mission other than his own sick one," LaPaige answers. "But what they do say is... he often focuses on the men he thinks are the strongest. Which, coincidentally, is everyone in this group."

"Wait," David interjects, raising his hand towards Powell. "Are you seriously thinking of leaving without dealing with this psycho?"

Powell gives a grim nod. "We might have to. Look, the guy's not as important as shutting down that facility, as least according to the brass. They want that mission done first. We can focus on Sun afterwards."

Shaking his head, Jackson shrugs. "I dunno, Gunny, this guy raided a safe zone building and did things... he hurt a bunch of little boys. Now, I don't mind so much if we lose a soldier or two, fighting men and women that signed up to be in the shit, but I'm not willing to risk him heading back north and attacking civilians."

"Willing?" Powell responds with a laugh. "What are you guys talking about with this 'willing' stuff?"

"I'm with them, Powell." Even Petersen? "We're out here to save the North, man. And there's no guarantee we'll all survive that facility. If we don't, who's going to stop that guy? I know for damn sure people like Chan can't get it done. Hell, we're the only ones that can even stand a chance against that retard."

Powell's eyes scan each of us, moving across the circle we've made before they fall to his feet. "Okay... well, we all can't go after him."

As the words come out, faces begin to change from doubt to relief. Powell's going to defy the brass.

"I'll need half of you to continue forward and support the attack on that fortress." Dropping his head, Powell places his hand over his chin and bottom lip. After a moment he looks straight to Ophelia. "Okay then, Rogers and Martinez have to go after Sun. They're the only ones who've fought him before. Patricia, David, and I will also go. The rest will move forward and attack the fort. Rawlings, Jackson,

I'm going to need you two to hang back with LaPaige. Keep his ass safe."

"Yes, sir," the trio says in unison.

"Rawlings, Marshall, focus on cutting a path to the west... by any means necessary."

They look at one another and nod.

"Patel, I need you to keep some distance between yourself and the four of us. But, if you can get a shot, drop the bastard."

"Why do you want me to hang back?"

"You're our ace, as always. I can't pull you out at the first play."

"Yes, sir," Patricia says, her gaze fixed on the path east. There's genuine malice in her eyes, something I almost never see from her.

"Okay, that's it," Powell says, giving a slight shrug. "We get it done and meet back up at the mission objective. Martinez, once he's dead, move ahead of us and join Rawlings and Marshall."

There's a moment of solemn silence in the circle. It's as if we're saying our goodbyes with nothing more than our eyes.

This is the end. One way or another, this will probably be the last time we're gathered like this. I say my goodbyes with a grin and nod to each person. They respond with a similar gesture of sad appreciation. We are the strongest FOGs alive, the world's most powerful living beings, and we're coming to terms with our own mortality, to the eventuality... no, certainty that not all of us will be returning home.

"Okay, stop it. I'll make sure to buy everyone a strong drink when we all get home, got me? So pull it together, people, we're going to have a lot of work to do. Move out and keep your comms open. We need to be able to coordinate if things go south for us. No pun intended."

Not long into the night the screaming starts. Primal and raw, the screams are without restraint. Pure horror. Pure agony. It's difficult to hear.

What's obvious to us all is that LeRoux is not enjoying his alone time with Sun. This is one of those moments where our ability to recover from the most grievous of injuries is not an asset. Sun will draw the torture out as long as possible, and poor LeRoux will heal over and over again.

When it started, I told myself that LeRoux brought this on himself. After the first five minutes, I focused on what he did to the girl. I tried to convince myself that his actions were utterly deserving of this punishment. But, after two more minutes of his piercing cries and pleas for mercy, I stamped his debt as paid in full. But Sun, he shows no mercy. Even hours later, as LeRoux's garbled screams of incoherent words rip through the night sky, I find it difficult to understand why any human would continue to inflict more injury, more grotesque violence on another. I'm left only with the question: why?

My blade would have been far more merciful.

"What the hell, why does he keep changing position?" David asks, turning to me.

"He knows we're following. He knows we're looking for him, but he's not done with LeRoux. Also, there's the added pleasure of allowing his pursuers to hear what's in store for them."

"And when he's done with LeRoux, then what?" Powell asks.

"Well, he'll probably come for us."

Powell laughs. "More distinctly me, I'd think. I'm betting that psycho thinks he and I have a score to settle." He's held a look of grim determination the entire time we've been on this hunt. I wonder if it's finally sinking in that this is all his fault. Does he now take responsibility for LeRoux's torture?

"So you meant to antagonize Sun?" Ophelia questions. It's odd to see her go into a fight without the bulky harness and her dragon rifle. She abandoned it before we left. It'll be too cumbersome in a hand-to-hand battle, just like it was the first time we fought Sun. And with

Sun, you can be assured the fight will come to that.

"Yeah. I figured it was the only thing I could do to stop him from taking people at random if shit went haywire."

"Which is why Jake kept so many of our crew with him," David says.

With a smirk Powell touches his temple, then points at David. "Exactly. Much easier to defend a target if you know what the target is. But, this whole LeRoux thing... that was on the fly. I fully expected him to ignore that crap altogether and come after me regardless."

With a pained expression on his face, David sighs. "Lucky us... he only took LeRoux."

Powell runs his finger along his scar and exhales sharply. "Well, LeRoux was going to get put in stasis, probably for the rest of his life." He turns to me. "Yes, Martinez, there is some justice out there. The brass couldn't let him come back home, at least not alive and well. It was going to be either a body bag or an egg. I figured I could use him for another task."

The screams continue, and the group is taken aback by their renewed force.

"Over here... found another body part," David says with a long sigh. He points just south of us. "So he's now armless, legless, and lacking certain... equipment."

We keep discovering bloodied remnants of LeRoux's body as we follow Sun. Some are hung luridly from the trees, and others strewn grotesquely along the forest floor. They lead us, like a trail of breadcrumbs, eastward. We found evidence of his castration at the foot of a large oak. His legs and an arm were found in quick succession thereafter. It's clear that LeRoux initially fought, struggled, and grasped at anything within reach. That's made evident by the bloody claw marks that paint the ground, trees, and brush around his dismembered parts. But, as we've come across his left arm, it seems the struggle is going out of him. Perhaps Sun is losing interest.

Powell partially turns to me, his eyes still scanning east. "How far now?"

"Same. He's staying about a quarter of a mile out of our reach."

283

Even if we push and run, Sun will do exactly the same thing. Of course, it's possible I could catch him, but I'd have to do it alone, and I doubt I could kill him without the others, especially if it's a standoff.

"Goddamn it... Sun! Sun! Stop so we can get this over with!" Powell screams.

There's a moment of eerie silence, as if the earth herself is waiting for his reply. Then, as if in response, we hear renewed intensity in LeRoux's screaming.

This game Sun is playing, as sadistic as it may be, probably has a purpose behind it. We're just not privy to either the rules or the point. To us, it's pure madness. But, what's clear is he's leading us to somewhere. A somewhere he thinks would be advantageous to him. A somewhere he could kill us all in peace.

"Look, we're approaching the edge of the forest," Ophelia says. "It looks like a Keynosian town up ahead... or what's left of it anyway."

"What do you have, Martinez?" Powell asks. The man's focus has been unwavering.

With a quick push, I assess the area. The village is empty, ravaged by RX. Massive trees, hollowed and wasted, slump over rotted cores. The stench of fetid plant material fills the air. Perfectly symmetrical streets stretch out evenly in rectangular blocks of living quarters and fallow farmland.

They left our lands and towns covered in life. We've made large sections of their country wastelands.

"Sun is in there, somewhere." A fitting place for him to call home and tomb. Fallen lands for a fallen man.

I start stuffing my face with MREs. I won't be low on fuel for this battle.

"Anything else, Martinez?"

"Other than a dead town, no."

"Just... I just wish he'd stop playing whatever game he's got going," Ophelia says. "I don't have time for it all."

"Well, it looks like we're about to get our wish. Sun is somewhere in here. Waiting for us, I'm sure."

Powell, stopping at the edge of the town, nods. "If he's waiting for us, great. Everyone, stay alert. We have to..." Powell pauses, turning his ear towards the main road before us. "Do you hear that?" Powell asks, pausing, his eyes rolling from side to side, his index finger pointing forward.

I push my hearing. I pick up nothing but the sounds of life beyond the death before us.

"Hear what? I don't hear anything," Ophelia says, looking around as well.

"And that's what's so interesting. LeRoux has stopped screaming and Sun has stopped running."

David responds to the information by grabbing his mace.

"Going for a deep check." I search, filtering out the nighttime noise. The entire area is a dead zone... save the steady rhythm of one heart. It's him, Sun. I know it. Like David, I pull my blade free. It won't be long now. Sun will come, and I pray for David and Gunny. Sure, they may have watched or read about Sun, but to actually experience such a monster is something different entirely.

"LeRoux is dead, and the only heartbeat I hear is straight ahead, about five of these Keynosian blocks and to the left."

"I've finished with this toy!" Sun's voice screams from ahead of us, breaking the oppressive quiet. "And so, I welcome the arrival of my new toys!"

"Fuck you, psycho!" David replies, his calm demeanor now gone. "Why? Why the hell would you do this to another human being?"

Silence answers David.

"Don't allow the Fallen Son to turn you from the light, Santos," Ophelia says, her voice calm. She looks around as her lips move in silence. Even after taking a double dose on the way here, she still appears to be slipping away from us. How long before we have to deal with her?

She notices me looking at her and presses her lips tight. "There is no love in the heart of the Fallen One," she says softly, almost to herself.

"Are you saying he hates everyone?" David asks.

Ophelia looks to the sky. "Hate is not the opposite of love, brother Santos, apathy is. Sun is empty. There is a void where his heart should be. A dark place that only leads away from the one true God."

"So why? Why do any of the things he's doing if he doesn't care? Why do the things he's done?"

I told you it would come to this, David. You and Powell should have heeded me earlier. Better yet, we should have killed him in his egg. But, I guess in the eyes of our leadership, that would have been a waste of a great weapon, a waste of government property.

"You're trying to attach logic to the illogical. It doesn't work that way, David," I add. "Do you really think the reason he killed LeRoux was because he raped those women, or because someone claimed his strength was greater? No. Sun doesn't care about that. Sun knew you wanted him to attack LeRoux, just as he knew we'd come for him. He wants to show us just how powerless we truly are. This entire game, this whole hunt is nothing more than Sun's invitation to our funerals."

"So, my protégé has come as well. Good. And that was a very good observation, Jocelyn. You are correct, of course. I wanted Powell to come. In fact, I wanted all of the so-called best of the best to come so they may witness and be a part of the main event. I'll start with Powell of course. He's a proud man, a brave man. I'll really enjoy breaking him!"

"Them come out and do it, Sun!" Powell yells in reply. "I'm right here. Come out and face me, you fuckin' psycho!"

Again, silence.

"You're a coward, hiding and running. Come out, you goddamn chicken-shit bitch!"

Silence.

"Don't waste your breath," I say. "He's in the building ahead. We'll see him soon enough."

We cautiously approach the corpse of a huge home tree. The massive tree is similar in size to the home tree that serves as our base. But, this one is completely rotted. The flesh of its thick branches sags and sloughs off under its own weight, hitting the ground in wet smacks of brown, liquefied wood. Soggy gelatinous leaves lie all around its base, covering the ground for nearly two blocks. This tree was clearly the focus of our RX attacks.

This place reeks of death.

"Anything, Martinez?"

"He's upstairs somewhere, but there's something else... someone."

"Someone? Is LeRoux still alive?"

"I didn't say that. It smells more like what's left of LeRoux," I say, pointing in the direction of the foul smell, a mix of blood, feces, and semen.

As we step into the building, we quickly find the remains. Sun, using LeRoux's intestine, hung the deceased FOG soldier's corpse like drying laundry on the exposed rafters of the home tree. His head dangles a foot above the body. Sadly, all of his wounds were healed or nearly healed at the time of his death.

The head stares at us. Sun removed LeRoux's eyelids. He didn't even allow him the luxury of darkness, forcing LeRoux to see the horrors being inflicted on him.

"We should have killed him in his egg." I have to get in a little, I told you so.

"Now's not the time, Martinez," Powell growls. "Just work on giving us a status of his location."

Can't even concede to being wrong, Powell?

The sight of LeRoux's remains has finally cracked Powell's veneer. He's nervous judging by his heartbeat, but we all are at this point. If Sun manages to defeat us, the fate of LeRoux will be our future as well. I wonder if he'll keep us alive, just like he did Emma. He kept her around for weeks, forcing her to watch what he did to the men he captured.

I'll kill Ophelia before I allow him to hurt her like that.

287

I hear him. "He's a few floors above."

"How many floors?" Powell asks.

I can only shrug. "Can't tell exactly." There's too much background noise from this building, which is literally melting around us.

"So, did you enjoy my artwork?" Sun yells out.

Got him. "He's four floors above us... more or less." Judging by the level of vibrations and distortions.

"You can't give us an exact floor count?" Powell asks.

"If you wanted that, you should have asked Rawlings to come along. She's better at sensing than I am."

"Over here. I see the stairs... or what's left of them," Ophelia says, nodding towards a sinking door frame to our right.

We stop at the wall as David peeks around the corner. "I'll take point," he announces. "If that's okay with you, Jake?"

"Yeah, okay. Good idea. Martinez, follow in close to Santos, I'll be behind you. Rogers, you got the rear guard."

Good idea. Give the object of Sun's wrath — or affection — the most protection. If Sun can snatch Powell and leave, he will.

Slowly, we march up the stairway, single file. If Sun thinks he can take the four of us straight on, he really is insane.

"The Fallen Son," Ophelia says to Sun as he sits on a windowsill, turning to stare out into the coming night.

The last vestiges of the day's light give his face an eerie illumination.

"Good to see you too, Ophelia Rogers. Judging from your herky-jerky movements, you're on your way back to an egg," he says with a smile. "Ah well, at least you're free."

David stops and moves ahead of the group. I flank his left and Powell flanks his right. Ophelia, standing to Powell's right, has held herself together rather well so far. I'm proud of her. If she's still suffering from delusions, she's making a point not to show it.

"I have to thank you for the nice long rest," Sun says, stretching and yawning as he stands. I assume that's LeRoux's dried black blood that coats his mouth, chin, and chest.

"Turn yourself in, Sun. Killing a FOG is a serious offense," Powell orders, stepping forward.

Sun doesn't even acknowledge the statement, turning back to look out over the dead village.

"The day I turned myself in, the day you quoted the divine scripture to me, Ophelia, it all instantly made sense. The death, the resurrection... everything, it all fell right into place. You see, there are too many FOGs out there," he says, raising his voice. "So I figured, what if? What if I was put on ice for a few years, decades even. Eventually, the powers that be would bring one of their greatest weapons out of the deep freeze, right? The North's love of war would demand it even!" He chuckles, turning to face our group again. "There's always a war those bastards want to be fought. A war the weak can't fight on their own, a war that needs the strong to handle it. So, it was only a matter of time before I was dragged out of my egg and back into action."

"Sun, I need you to turn around and kneel," Powell says. "You can go back into the freeze, back into stasis."

"You can imagine my surprise when I woke up and we were still fighting the Keynosians! I mean really? You'd think we'd have won this war by now." Sun's face tightens into a snarl. "Then, I remembered just how weak the world is. How weak the North is." Just as suddenly as the sneer formed, it melts away. "You needed a man like me then, like you need a man like me now and like you'll need a *me* in the future. But the difference between you and I is I'm free and you all are slaves. I'm done taking orders from people that can't fathom how powerful I am. I'm a fuckin' god compared to you!" he says, letting out a forced laugh.

"Frank Sun! Turn around and kneel!" Powell repeats. The words lance out like a spear.

Powell slides his left foot forward, preparing to fight. I can feel his heart pounding in his chest, the nails on his thumbs scraping the handle of his knuckle-dusters. There won't be another request to surrender.

"You think I've gone mad? No. NO!" Sun screams, his eyes wild with excitement. "For the first time in my life, I'm free. I'm free of being concerned about what others may think. Free of hiding who I really am. Free, and through the Sacrifice, powerful enough to take my rightful place as the lord and master of all men, of all lands. It's time the world saw that Frank Sun is their GOD!"

That's my cue. I push my body immediately, forcing my eyes to work harder, enabling me to see as much as possible. I don't push too hard this time. As fast as Sun is, he isn't a bullet. Still, the strain causes my eyes to ache.

With just a glance, from Powell to David, an order is given. In an instant they move as one, hard and fast like two sides of the same coin.

They're going to flank Sun on both sides. Yet, Sun smiles. David and Powell are fast, but Sun is faster and probably just as strong of either of these soldiers. He goes for David first, striking him across the face so hard I can hear the bones shatter.

Clack!

The surprising sound of David's mace making contact is broadcast in the space. Sun's right side buckles instantly, and he screams out in pain with a high-pitched yelp as his ribs collapse under the attack, his body nearly swallowing the mace within the folds of flesh and cloth.

Unbelievable. Was David expecting to be struck? He must have braced himself perfectly. I noticed he planted his right foot back and twisted as the blow landed. He rolled with the punch, sucking away much of the force. So, instead of the punch taking David's head off, it only shattered his jaw and cheekbone.

David drops to the ground as Sun stumbles towards Powell, moved by the mace strike.

Before I can make a move, Powell is on top of Sun. As if practiced, Powell is in position to catch the stumbling FOG. Fear fills Sun's face as Powell launches a blow towards his center. Wisely, Powell didn't go for the head shot; instead his punch hammers Sun's sternum. It propels him backwards and into the nearby wall just left of the window. He slams against the wall so hard it nearly shatters. Powell has no plan to relent. He follows and delivers another body blow that crushes Sun's right side, pushing him further towards the corner.

My turn. I push hard, moving so fast I feel the air itself scraping against my face.

I'm going to take his goddamn head!

"No!" Sun screams, raising his hand defensively as he cringes, attempting to block my blade with flesh and bone.

As fast as I am, I am not fast enough, and all I've managed to take is his hand and a section of scalp and hair.

BOOM!

The area fills with a wet haze as Ophelia hammers her body into Sun's, crashing him into a wall.

I can't see him. Where is Sun? Instead of seeing my target, I find nothing but a hole in the wall.

"Damn it," Powell yells, echoing my sentiment. "We fuckin' had him!"

"I... I didn't know the wall would give," Ophelia says, sticking her head out of the massive hole and down towards the ground, where Sun hits the gray dirt with a thud.

"Didn't know the wall would give? You can lift a tree the size of a building and you didn't think a rotting wall would give way?"

"Shut up. We need to focus here," I say, stepping in front of Ophelia and Powell.

Teeth pressed hard together, Powell punches the wall, widening the opening. "We can't let him get away. Everyone get down there so we can finish this shit," Powell says, leaping out of the window.

I turn to see David gripping his jaw before charging to the hole in the wall, following Powell down.

"No! Get away!" Sun screams below. Ophelia and I follow Powell and David down.

Sadly, I see Sun run away a split second before Powell lands, moving so fast I wonder if I actually am faster than him.

Powell doesn't immediately follow. He faces the direction Sun escaped to and waits for the rest of us to hit ground. Smart man.

As I land, Powell turns to me. "Where is he?" he barks anxiously.

Behind me, I hear the thud of a body hitting the wet ground. I turn to see Ophelia's face against the diseased earth.

Is her balance failing her as well now?

"What the hell, Rogers! Have you lost your shit or something?" Powell yells at her. "Maybe you should head back, get some egg time before we head to the final assault. Let the rest of us finish Sun."

"Are you okay, Oa?" I ask.

Then I see it, her eyes roll into her head and back again, struggling to focus. Blood drips from her nostrils. It's just like before.

It's this place. This entire village is spoiled by RX, swimming in the toxin. That must be why she's starting to fall apart.

"I... I'm... I'm fine," she says, struggling to stand, stumbling into David as if intoxicated. She looks at each of us in turn. "I'm fine!" she yells, her eyes struggling to maintain their hold on the surroundings. "We... we can't let him get away."

Powell glares at Ophelia. "Martinez, which way," he asks again.

It doesn't take long to hear Sun, mumbling to himself, whining about how unfair our attack was, how he'd win if it were a one-on-one encounter. He's reassuring himself of his self-proclaimed god status.

He's truly a madman.

"He's at one o'clock," I say, chopping my hand in the direction.

"David, you okay for point again?"

With some clicks, David realigns his jaw manually and tests the fix by opening and closing his mouth a few times. His cheekbone slowly knits itself back into place before our eyes. "Yeah, I'm good to go, Gunny."

The man is too tough for words.

At David's reply, we sprint off. I don't know if we'll get a better chance to kill Sun than the one we had. He may be insane, but he's not a fool.

In a second or two we're at the mouth of another dilapidated, rotting tree. Stopping in the entryway, Powell stares into the structure's dark interior. "Sun! Sun, come out now, you fuckin' coward! We're not done with you!"

"I'll rip you to shreds. I'll rend you limb from limb. You're not the better man, Powell. YOU'RE NOT THE BETTER MAN!" his voice screeches. "You're not my superior. I'll kill every one of you. I swear I will. I WILL KILL YOU ALL!" His voice cracks as if he's on the verge of tears.

"That guy's a straight-up lunatic," David says.

Powell remains facing forward, his eyes fixed towards the tree's entrance. "Martinez?"

"Yeah, he's in there. Not sure how far up though. Again, it's hard to tell with so much background noise."

As we walk in, I can hear the sound of wet material squish under our boots.

Wiping the still dripping blood from her nose, Ophelia looks around, moving like her body is stuttering.

"Good god, Rogers, you're looking like shit," Powell says.

Ophelia reaches into her pocket, grabs a tablet, and swallows it. "We need to finish this. We need to keep going," she says, nodding a bit too much as she gulps a few times, pushing the pills down her gullet. "I'll be fine, okay. Let's just keep moving, keep going."

We should go back, get her some help. All of the RX exposure may be overwhelming her system. If we return, maybe they can help her, stop her from the inevitable crash she's careening towards.

"Oa, you should head —"

"No, Jos. NO," she nearly screams, causing everyone to jump in shock. Noticing the reaction of the group, she swallows and inhales deeply. "This is my fight. This is the fight I was sent here to have. This battle against the Fallen. This is God's fight, and I must be here for it. The Fallen Son must be stopped so the world can be saved. So you and Pat, so you both can be saved."

293

My eyes well immediately, even as her shuddering slows. The drugs aren't stopping her drift into madness, but they appear to keep her going. It's like she's on the precipice of total madness, clinging desperately to reality solely to complete this mission.

David turns and leans in, close to Powell's ear. "Gunny, maybe you should order Rogers back to —"

"You heard her, Santos," Powell interrupts. "She said she's fine for this fight." He looks at Ophelia from head to toe. "So, let her fight. And despite her prior screwup, she's the only one here that can match or exceed Sun's strength."

It takes only a moment for a FOG to win a fight. All we need is a moment's lapse in our opponent's concentration to change the course of a battle. And, it takes little more than a fraction of a second for this fight to take a dangerous turn. In the blink of an eye we hear a pop. I turn to see that the sound was of Ophelia's neck snapping. Like a brick, she falls to the ground beside us, screaming. David and Powell whirl around to see Sun glaring at us from behind.

Just as his name flashes like a neon sign in my thoughts, a sudden kaleidoscope of dulled color and bright pain envelops me. I feel my body thud against a surface, but I'm not sure which direction I've been thrown. What I do know is, I have to fight the encroaching unconsciousness. I can't allow Ophelia to be left helpless and in the hands of Sun!

Quickly, I look around to get my bearings. I'm inside the building, in the dark. I turn towards the exit, and I begin to realize the team's situation through the flashing lights popping intermittently in my vision. Ophelia's down, hurting, her body convulsing on the ground. Her head... it's turned the wrong way. Sun broke her neck.

David is out it appears, and Powell is in the process of being choked to death. He's struggling mightily, but it's clear his fighting is futile.

Then the eyes of madness, Sun's eyes, focus on me.

I push my body just in time to evade his attempt to strike me with Powell's thick frame. I can hear the man's ribs shatter under the impact.

Get out... get Ophelia... regroup somehow.

I yank my blade free from its scabbard, and immediately Sun draws Powell in front of him. The stump of his severed hand presses against Powell's cheek. The bleeding has already stopped. Clearly, he almost entirely healed from the previous attack.

"Take the others and go, Martinez. You, Rogers, and that other guy, whatever his name is. I'll let ya'll go for now... even though you took my hand," Sun says, his face transforming from calm to madness. "You took my hand, you stupid bitch. You stupid fucking bitch!" he yells, spittle spraying the side of Powell's face. Then, as quickly as it came, the storm recedes and he dons the calm veneer once again. "You know me, Jocelyn. We've fought together, I even saved your life. You remember, don't you?"

I barely hear him. I need to be ready to strike when the opening appears.

"You can go back and say you lost track of me, say you couldn't find me after I took Powell. No one would know. Just let me have this piece of meat. And, and don't worry about the hand. I'll... I can get it back. Just... just leave now. Okay? Leave now while you still have the chance!" he barks, shaking Powell's unconscious body like a rag doll.

If I push hard enough, so hard that I tear my body to shreds, I'm positive I can end this in a moment. But, should I cut through Powell to get to Sun? I may not like the man, but I can't leave him to Sun. Ultimately, it would be merciful to kill him. Leaving him here would be a far worse fate than death.

Sun moves closer, walking into the dark interior of the tree building. He holds Powell up like a shield, peeking over his shoulder, making sure to keep an eye on me. "Oh yeah, I see. Yes, yes, I see what you're thinking. You want to cut through him to get to me, right?" He laughs. "Yeah, you do. I can see it in your eyes. You changed.... yeah. Changed. You're colder, harder. So go. Go ahead and do it," he says, sticking Powell's limp body forward. "Go on. You fancy yourself to be faster than me? Guess what, you're not. I'm the alpha, Martinez. Me! So you... you just run along for now, okay? I'll find you eventually. I'll get you back for —"

Without notice, the upper left side of my face, directly over my eye, is showered in a spray of blood followed by the sound of a bullet striking the wall behind me, spraying my neck with wood fragments from behind.

Suzy-Q. Patricia! I forgot she was following us.

"Now, Jos!" Patricia yells with a gasp over the receiver.

His eyes vacant, Sun slowly lowers Powell's now stirring body just enough to expose the nickel-sized hole left by Patricia's well placed shot. My target has presented itself!

With a hard push, I soar towards him.

His eyes fight to focus as I approach. Wordless, he watches as I pass my blade through the top portion of his skull. I push so hard I don't even feel the drag of his skull against my blade.

In a skid, I stop myself and turn to see blood seep down the back of his head, exposing the location of my strike. I can't let him heal.

David and Powell rouse themselves just in time to see me kick the top of his head off.

It's done. Finally, it's done.

Ophelia.

Twisting backwards, her face in the fetid earth beneath us, Oa's body convulses violently. The tragedy of Emma is revisited in the here and now... in my Oa. In my sister.

"Goddamn it, Oa," I say, falling to her side. Slowly, I turn her body, moving her face out of the brown, rotten material that covers everything. "Oa, we're going to get you back, get you better," I say as she gasps for air.

Contorting with pain, she looks past me and into the sky, her mouth and face covered in filth. "It hurts, Jos. It hurts so much," she mutters.

She'll live. Just like Emma, she'll survive this and heal. "You'll be okay, Oa, just relax okay? Just relax."

Emma is alive, but she's not well. The last time I saw her, she was in constant pain. But Ophelia, she's a better healer than Emma. She'll be okay.

She has to be okay.

I turn to Powell. "Call someone. We have to get her to an egg!"

Startled, Powell jerks his eyes away from Sun's corpse to look at me, then at Ophelia. He nods. Turning away from the scene, he presses his mic. "This is Gunny Powell. Lock in on my location and send a med team ASAP. We have a FOG down. I repeat, we have a FOG down."

"No, Jos, no," Ophelia mutters low. She moves as if to touch me, but grabs nothing but the rotten matter she lies in. "You promised me... you promised," she says, tears flowing from her cheeks, her body jerking awkwardly with sobs. "Please, Jos... please. You... promised!"

"Shhh, no. Don't talk like that," I whisper. "We can help you, Oa. We can save you. Hold on just a bit more, okay? Just hold on."

I hear my receiver crackle and ring a tone, indicating our private channel. "Don't you do it, Jos!" Patricia's crackling voice calls. "Don't you fuckin' do it!"

I hear her moving in the distance towards us. She must have run the entire way, struggling to keep up with us. I smell her sweat, see her face glisten in the dim twilight.

Her hand shakes in exhaustion as she trains Suzy-Q on me.

Ophelia, her crying more intense, turns her eyes to me. "Mercy!" she screams. "Mercy lord. It hurts so much. It hurts!" she screams to the sky.

Then, her eyes train on me. "Jos, let me go!"

"We need some morphine!" I yell. Someone has to have something!

"Martinez! Get away from her," Powell orders. "We have a med team flying our way. We can save her, Jocelyn."

David looks at me, his eyes pained, his face wet with tears. How long has he been standing there, crying silently?

"Martinez!" Powell yells, pulling my eyes back to him. With a deep breath, he softens. "Look, we can take care of her. Just like Emma.

You remember her, right? She's alive and doing well, real well."

I can't help but huff at this comment. "Don't be an idiot, Powell. Ophelia and I saw her. She's not... don't lie to us, Powell."

"Martinez! I'm telling..." He sighs. "Jocelyn, I'm ordering you to stop and back away. If you do what I think you're going to do, if you do what she's asking, ...I'll have to arrest you."

"JOS! IT HURTS SO MUCH! PLEASE! YOU PROMISED ME! PLEASE!"

I look up to see Patricia through the haze of tears. Her body shakes with her sobs. She begins to move her lips, her head nodding as Suzy-Q's barrel falls to the ground. "Run, Jos. Do it and run" are the words I see. She's telling me to do it.

She's telling me to kill an angel. Our angel.

I love you, Oa.

The sound of her skin, her tendons, her flesh tearing cuts into me. My heart shatters as I pull her head off.

I've broken my heart with one single act of mercy.

And so, I run.

CHAPTER 11

FACING THE SUN

I have no idea where I am. I've been running west I think, although I'm not sure if I've held that course over these hours. Nothing looks, smells, or sounds the same as before; wherever I am, this place is completely new to me. Unlike the RX-dusted areas that I've grown accustomed to, this pristine forest is buzzing with life. But in my state of high alert, I find the noise in my ears, and my head, to be deafening. I can only quiet the external noise. Even when I withdraw my senses, I'm left with the shrill sound of shame.

I killed Ophelia.

I killed my friend.

I killed my sister.

The mountains in the distance signal water nearby, the ocean according to the maps Powell showed us. If I am close to the ocean, I must also be close to the facility we were going to raid. I turn north and see a massive cluster of trees, black trees, tightly packed around a massive home tree. The Keynosian fortress. I'm south of the Keynosian fortress.

I could have waited, gotten her help.

I killed Ophelia.

I killed my friend.

I killed my sister.

Damn it. I can't ignore the intrusive thoughts that have plagued me any longer.

Why didn't I wait? She was just experiencing mental breakdown. How many times before has she returned renewed after a few days in stasis? Twenty times before? Thirty? I've lost count.

Yet, how could I ignore my promise to her? How could I ignore how she begged, how much pain she was in? Maybe she didn't know what she was saying?

Maybe she knew exactly what she was saying.

Did I fuck up? Did I kill my friend when I could have saved her life?

Damn it, Jos, focus on where you're going. Everything looks the same no matter what direction I turn. Should I continue west? What if I come across the facility? I should probably avoid it altogether and keep a healthy distance from it and my team. My former team.

No, I can't go back, not without being charged for killing a fellow soldier, not without being charged for killing my friend. There's no worse offense. For most, it means life imprisonment. For a FOG it means being stuck in an egg and put on a shelf. They're going to —

I killed Ophelia. I'm guilty of killing Ophelia. I deserve to be in stasis forever.

Stop! Don't think about... please, don't think about her death.

I need to focus on my next steps, and getting captured and placed into stasis is not a good plan. The only way to avoid that is to get off of this continent. What's keeping me here? All of my family is dead. Ophelia is dead. Patricia, she'll be fine. She's probably better off without me. So, I'll keep running northwest, continue giving the Keynosian base a wide berth, and hopefully miss the weapon facility as well. I'll try for the coast, swim to an island or something just to get started. I can survive for months with very little sustenance.

I see her face, twisted in pain. Ophelia, her head twisted and her body writhing in agony. Her face, it was serene when I...

"Goddamn it, stop! Stop tormenting me!"

The smile she wore when I first met her. The elation we felt when we finally got our bodies under control. Our tears after Ophelia learned her mind was fracturing. Her frozen, sleeping features behind the thick glass of the egg. Her laughter. Her smiles. My angel.

She's gone forever, and it's my fault. I didn't have to honor that promise. She wasn't fit when she asked me to... "Why didn't I wait?" I killed my friend.

The weight of grief drags me down like an anchor. It stops me dead in my tracks and again bombards me with images of Ophelia. It hurt to see her in so much pain.

I deserve the egg.

I deserve stasis.

Ophelia was supposed to survive this war, not me. She didn't deserve that end. I did... I do.

The tears have ceased for the moment, and I take the opportunity to gather the broken shards of myself. I have no idea how long I've been sitting against this strange tree, sobbing. This place is odd. The tree, which has held me up during my emotional collapse, looks like it's absorbing a smaller one right on the other side of it. In fact, many of the trees in the area appear to have saplings melding into them. The saplings are all tilted towards their elders, as if pulled by invisible ropes. Thin webs of green filament cover some of the saplings, attaching the smaller to the larger, binding the younger to the older.

What possible reason would the Keynosians have for developing these trees?

A familiar crackling sound pops into my receiver. "Jos? You there, Jos?" Patricia!

Do I want to talk to her, hear her curse me for killing Ophelia?

Oh, right, I can't. I broke my mic.

"Damn, you broke your mic. Forgot about that," she sighs. "Look,

301

I just want you to know that I know. I heard her. I heard Ophelia... begging," she says, struggling to say the last portion. "It also sounded like she made you promise something pretty fucked up. That wasn't fair of her, but you should have told me, we all could have talked about it."

"I didn't think, Pat. I never thought it would come to this," I mutter to myself.

She's crying. I hear it in her voice. She quickly clears her throat. "You did what you had to do, Jos.... You did what you had to do. Okay? Ophelia, she deserves better than what Emma got stuck with. She deserves better than everyone in this shitty war." Again, her voice trails off, the pitch peaking at the end. Her muffled sniffles fill in the silence. "Goddamn it," she says with a chuckle. "I wish you were here. I wish I could just hear your voice. I wish you didn't have to run for ending Oa's pain. It's funny, I never thought I'd lose either of you... I thought it would have been me that got myself killed. But god, it hurts so much more to lose someone."

Even in this drizzle, I feel the flow of my warm tears running down my face. "I miss you too, Pat... I miss you so much right now."

"No matter how much I miss you, I'd rather you be free. You hear me, Jos? You don't deserve punishment for doing what's right. You don't deserve the charges Powell brought up against you," she says, her voice angry but stifled.

"And FYI... LaPaige told me to tell you that you're sterile." There is a moment of silence on the line. "Jos, did you hear me? You're sterile, probably been sterile your entire life. You'll never go insane like the others.

"Maybe... I thought maybe they'd think differently if they knew you weren't going to get sick. I was hoping Powell would put what you did aside for the greater good, or whatever the fuck that even means. But instead, he's affirmed how much of an asshole he is. He just said some crap about needing to follow the letter of the law... like that means fuck all when your friend is screaming for mercy." Again, her voice catches in her throat. "But, you know what, sis, you don't need this military. In fact, you don't need this fuckin' country. Fuck us!" She laughs. "Get your ass outta here, you hear me? Be free! Hell, I'd say you served your time, paid in full with blood," she says with a chuckle.

I chuckle along with her. "I wish I could take you with me, Pat. I wish I didn't have to do this alone." I know she can't hear me, but maybe she can feel my earnest wishes for her. Maybe across the miles, she can feel my love.

"Look at me, happy for someone being sterile! What kind of shit is that? But, damn it, I'm loving this news for you.

"Oh, you know what else he told me? LaPaige I mean. He was actually ordered not to tell anyone about the link between sterility and sanity for the FOGs or that most of you are destined for life in an egg. Can you believe that shit? They didn't want you or any FOG to know what was in store for them. How fucked up is that?"

"Utterly fucked up."

"Anyway," she sighs. "Call me in a few years when all of this is old news and I'm some cranky battle-axe so I can live vicariously through you. I... I just want you to be a part of my life, sis." She pauses, giving me time to think about how much I want the same. "Just make sure that when you do call, you're on some hot, sunny beach in the middle of nowhere. Oh, and make sure you're sippin' on something strong and sweet too... and no, I don't care if it gives you a buzz or not.

"I love you, Jos. Don't you dare forget that, okay?"

"I love you too, Patricia." Again, tears fall from my eyes.

"Now, take care of yourself. And unbeknownst to the powers that be, I'll be keeping this channel open for as long as possible. Whatever I can find out, you'll find out. We can't let that 'by the book' dickhead Powell catch you." She laughs. "All this cryin' crap and I almost forgot about the other person waiting to talk to you... well, talk at you, since we can't hear anything you've got to say.

"Numbskull, breaking your damn mic..."

The line goes silent. Has to be David.

"Jos, it's David."

I laugh. "Hi, David."

"I want you to know something. What you did was the right thing to do. Fuck the law, fuck the rules, fuck Powell. What you did was love, plain and simple, so don't beat yourself up about it. This is coming from a person who knows.

"Finally... I know you and I just met, basically. And, I know you've got more important things on your mind than some middle-aged teacher pining for your attention. But I want you to know that you're very special to me. I don't know what it is, what *this* is, I mean, but I'm willing to wait until the day we can meet up again. I'd really like to nail down exactly what this can be. I mean, if you want to know what this can be."

"Damn it, you're going to make this hard on me, aren't you, David?"

"I'm kinda rambling now." He sighs. "Boy, it sucks to not hear your response to what I'm saying. I have no idea what you're thinking, so I'm going to hope you're smiling right now."

Smiling... check.

"Hell, you could be laughing at me hysterically for all I know," he says, the smile in his voice evident. "But, whether or not you're laughing, crying, or just plain ol' indifferent, I want you to contact me when you're safe.

"Okay, well... I don't have much else to say, so I'll make my closing remarks.

"Just keep your head low, please. I think the Keynosian spores that kept our aircraft and sky-eyes downed will dissipate completely once this conflict ends. And you know, once the sky is filled with those eye buggers again, it'll be hard for you to stay hidden."

Impossible is more like it. It's looking more and more likely that I'll have to leave the entire continent to escape my own country.

"I look forward to hearing from you, Ms. Martinez, so don't take too long to contact me. I can only hold out so long. Maybe a few decades, but that's all." He laughs.

"I'm looking forward to it."

It feels like I'm going in circles. At the border of the strange cluster of trees, I find a string of repeating flatlands and forests, one after another. I could run, but it's probably best to conserve my energy for now. I may need it for whatever I'll have to do, or face, once I hit the beach.

The stronghold is no longer directly north of me. That's good. I don't need to get unintentionally spotted by Guardsmen or FOGs.

I am getting closer to the mountains. I can feel the change in atmosphere. I've been going uphill for some time. Progress? I hope so. At least I know I'm not back where I started. I may not have the best sense of direction, but based on my proximity to the mountains, I can safely say I'm headed the right way.

The ocean will mean escape from the land I've called home my entire life.

The terrain changes from the soft, fertile earth I've grown use to and becomes much rockier. The area is still beautiful, I wouldn't expect less of Keynosa, but the signs of life have diminished significantly. Gone are the constant sounds of birds, animals, and insects scuttling here and there. Life feels more spread out, porous. I find myself missing the frequent distractions of life. I guess I've crossed some unknown barrier.

Wait... what's that? I'm picking up the faint scent of food cooking. Vegetables, potatoes, hints of a wide array of seasonings. The aroma wafts gently along the late-afternoon breeze. There aren't any villages nearby that I can see... so where is it coming from?

I search for the source. There. The smell is coming from a mountain cave hidden amongst an outcropping of massive rocks.

I inhale deeply, filtering the air for the tale-tell scent of Guardsmen. They all carry hints of mildew. Nothing. If it isn't Guardsmen, then it must be refugees.

305

That smell's got my belly's attention. I wonder if the people cooking will be willing to share. More likely they'll be more interested in bartering. Keynosians love to haggle I've heard, and since we're this deep in Keynosa, trading with refugees might be the best way to fill my belly. After all of the energy I burned fighting Sun, killing Sun, and subsequently running away, I need something more substantial than my two remaining ration-bars.

Stuff to trade... what the hell do I have that's worth trading? I still have a bunch of odds and ends tucked into my uniform, so I do a quick inventory. A flashlight — which is of zero value to me — could be used by a Keynosian. Guns, I wouldn't trade to a Southie. I wouldn't be able to live with myself if they used it to kill someone I knew.

Someone's there!

Quickly, I duck behind a tree and remain as still as possible.

Focus on the person.

With senses open, I take in the measure of the body moving in the distance. It's a female, Keynosian, judging from the scent. She's not close, and in the setting sun, I'm probably very hard to see at this distance. I take a peek.

She's young, in her twenties I think. Looks as if she's foraging. I wouldn't be surprised if there are many pockets of Keynosian communities still living off the land out here.

I continue to watch her and wonder if she's with the group in the cave.

Her eyes scan the rocky landscape close to a large outcropping of mountainous stones that tower over the nearby trees. She walks calmly around the base of the granite monoliths, craning her neck to and fro, clearly searching for something very specific. Hmm, her face is strange. The markings that most Keynosians have are symmetrical, running along both sides of the face with complete uniformity, mirror images of each other. But this young woman, she has an asymmetrical mark that covers her left eye, like someone splashed her with green paint and never got around to folding the paper.

What is she picking up? Is that a small mushroom? She turns it over in her hand before dropping it into a pocket... no, a satchel resting flat on her hip. It's so close to her body it looks like a part of her pants.

I should get closer.

Before I can even move, she suddenly goes stiff and turns in my direction.

Did she see me? No, that's impossible. I'm much too far away for even a Guardsmen to spot me. I've been on enough scouting missions to know that, but still, it's like she sensed me regardless.

Could she be a Guardsmen? She doesn't have the scent of one.

She picks up her pace, her heartbeat quickening. She's not running, but definitely concerned and moving accordingly. If she were a Guardsmen, she would be moving with far more speed than she's displaying.

I glance from behind the tree again. From over her shoulder, she continues to look in my direction as she heads back towards the cave. Somehow, she knows I'm here, or she knows *something's* here. I guess from her perspective, I could be a predatory animal, but that doesn't explain how she's aware of another living thing this far away.

I continue to follow her, keeping my distance and only moving when she turns away.

I give her a closer look, pushing my sight as she cranes her head as she walks, trying to spot whatever disturbed her earlier. She has one light eye, hazel in color. The other is as dark as midnight. If it were not for that mark on her face, she would be a very attractive girl.

She's strong. Broad shouldered and thick limbed, and she moves like an athlete despite her rather buxom build. She leaps over rocks and climbs a steep incline with ease. Not Guardsmen levels, but still the entire display is impressive. Her strength reminds me of Patricia.

She reaches the mouth of a cave and throws one last look in my direction, squinting hard against the fading light. She struggles to catch sight of me one final time before dashing into the dim entrance.

She may have led me to food, but will I be allowed to eat?

She's not alone. There are children and another woman in the cave, judging from the smattering of chatter and the sound of various heartbeats. Hmmm, there's something off with the smell and sound of the children. I don't think they're healthy. A few have very labored breathing, and all are carrying the scent of disease or some kind of sickness.

"Jeevan's back, young ones," the other woman announces. "And it looks like our stew will be complete, mostly."

"Yes, I found a few hindor mushrooms, but none of them were mature."

"How many ya get?"

"Five or six..."

"Hmmm, that's good enough, I think.

"You lookin' troubled there, Jeevan. What's wrong?"

"I dunno, Giaan, something was weird out there. I did as you taught and I thought I sensed something was following me. It was weird."

"Weird like what? Dangerous weird or the weirdness that comes from the death of earth?"

There's a pause as neither the women nor children speak.

"No, it wasn't dangerous I think, but it was something... I don't know how to describe it. Mmmm, sadness?"

Sadness? What is this girl talking about?

"Maybe it was a sick animal? With all of the toxic garbage them Northerners been droppin', sickness has become the norm, and with sickness comes pain... then sadness. Remember, there's a host of sensations you probably gonna feel... hmph... that ain't no animal. Someone's out there."

What?

"Someone? I didn't see anyone," the younger woman says defensively.

"Whether you see 'em or not, someone's definitely out there." Another silent pause. "It's not a Guardsmen, it's something else entirely. Something unnatural."

"Grammy," one of the children says weakly, "it's a Northerner, I can feel her."

That's impossible. How could she "feel" me?

The sound of feet scrambling and the rustling of fabric quickly begins to grow. "Okay, gather your stuff, we have to leave," the older woman says. "We can't let no one find ya'll. If the Northerners catch us... we don't want them to catch us, not like this."

I can't... I don't want them to leave.

"It's coming!" a child chirps weakly.

They must have some form of ESP, but regardless, I have to tell them I'm no threat despite my uniform. I run, pushing only enough to get me there in a breath or two. Surprisingly, the two women greet me at the mouth of the cave, rocks gripped tight in their hands. Brave.

"Stop right there!" the woman named Jeevan says, her left hand outstretched, the large rock cocked back in her right, ready to be launched.

The other is a beautiful brown-skinned Keynosian woman. Despite her baggy clothes, her shapely body is clearly displayed. Everything about her exudes a youthfulness, a glow. If it were not for the way she spoke, I'd assume she and the younger woman were close to the same age.

The older woman slowly drops the arm holding the weapon and nods. "You're scared... ain't ya?" she says to me, her thick, curly black hair resting on her shoulders. There's a strange blankness in her eyes, as if she's not really looking at me.

She moves in front of Jeevan, who drops back and stands in front of a gaggle of pale, gaunt children, all of whom are huddled together near a fire. They're terrified of me. Me, who was once a teacher of children their age.

A pang of shame strikes me.

"I'm sorry, I don't mean you any harm," I say softly. Putting my hands up, I crouch slightly in supplication.

"I know that, girl," says the older woman. "You may not be here to harm, but you're definitely here for *somethin'*. Mother wouldn't bring you here if you didn't need to be.

"Is that why you're afraid? You think that somethin' you need, we ain't gonna give?"

"I'm just looking for some food and shelter for the night. That's all," I announce. "Umm... look, I have stuff to trade if you like?"

She laughs. "You wanna trade? You come all the way out here to trade? Is that what you think?"

"No... I'm, well... it's a bit complicated. What, what do you mean is that what I think? I came here for food."

Again, she chuckles. "Okay," she says with a smile. "How 'bout you can come and sit by this here fire and tell me what you got that you think is worth tradin'?"

The crackle of the fire seems to enhance the sleepy children's laughter. This woman... I can't describe her in a single word, she is so many things.

Loving.

Wise.

Maternal.

Warm.

Insightful.

Haunting.

These are just a few adjectives that come to mind as I look into her dark eyes.

"Alright, miss Jocelyn, tell us what's really staining your spirit, hon," she says, caressing the hair of a young sleeping girl no older than twelve.

Holding a wooden bowl of delicious, bright-red stew, I give a shrug of feigned ignorance. "What do you mean?" I ask, moving another spoonful to my mouth. "Stained spirit?"

"Miss Jocelyn, the pain on your heart is written on your face as clear as day, baby. No different from these here children."

"Baby?" I say with a huff. "It's been a long time since I was called baby by anyone that wasn't trying to..." I glance at the children and think better of my choice of words. "Well, that wasn't a man, let's say."

I swallow the mix of herbs and vegetables, handpicked from the multitude of bushes along the mountain trail.

"I'm fifty-two years old, hon. What are you... thirty something?"

She's in her fifties? I try to wipe the shock from my face. "I'm forty-two."

"Well, to me, you a baby, okay? Now really, what's hurtin' you, miss Jocelyn? What's the real reason you here?"

"I'm running," I blurt out. I speak before my brain can come up with a suitable lie. No... I don't want to lie. They invited me into their midst, so at the very least, they deserve my honesty.

"Who ain't!" she says, laughing. The girl in her lap stirs. "Awww, shoooo. It's alright, sweetie. It's alright. Momma Giaan is here with ya."

"If you're lying, Giaan will know," a boy says, shuffling about collecting the empty bowls. "She's magic 'cause she's a seer."

"I already told ya, ain't no magic in this world," Giaan responds immediately. "There's only life. It's there for all to see."

"Like the life growing in you, Giaan?" I ask, unable to repress a grin. She's not the only who can sense things.

A look of shock washes over the faces of the others in the room. "Ooohh!" the children say in unison as their shock folds into smiles.

She meant to keep that secret.

"Looks like you've got something special 'bout you, eh?" she says, bringing back her grin.

Whispered calls to listen to her belly bubble from the children, quickly followed by a harsh shush from Jeevan.

I'm sterile. Looking at Giaan, a woman far beyond child-bearing age by Northern standards, I find my mind working hard to banish pangs of jealousy and the momentary pain of loss. I'll never give birth, ever. I'll never have the chance to hold *my* baby.

311

There will never be a "my baby."

I feel even more broken.

"Ya'll listen to your auntie Jeevan," Giaan whispers. "Too much noise and we'll be right back where we started, tryin' to put the young ones to sleep, understand?"

The children nod, their smiles intact.

"Good. Anyway, ya'll won't be able to hear nothin' no-way. She's... yes, she, is too small to make any noises for ya. Understand?"

"So this group's running as well?" I ask.

Giaan nods. "Sometimes, the right thing to do ain't following along, but standin' up, right?"

"Right," I respond. I look into her eyes and see a knowing that makes me nervous. How much *does* she see?

"Look here, Jocelyn," she says, scooting over to me. "I can see that pain as clear as I can see this here rock. It's paintin' your soul, like ink on a shirt. Course, you ain't gotta tell me anything. You could hold it all in if you like." She shrugs.

Taking a deep breath, I try to steel myself from the swell of sadness I'm keeping trapped in my heart. Nothing will allow me to forget, will it? "I had to kill a friend." The words spill out, and despite myself, tears fall. "Wow, I guess that river hasn't run dry yet," I chuckle.

"You loved that friend?"

"Yes. Like a sister."

"Then you go on and let them tears honor her, baby. Just don't you forget that whoever she is, she's in the arms of the Great Mother now. Ain't no need for you to feel sorry for her. Never forget that, you hear?"

The words tear at my heart, and my face twists in grief despite my efforts to tamp the expression down.

Again, Giaan chuckles. "Girl," she says, grabbing ahold of my hand, "there ain't no shame in tears. The shame is bein' afraid to allow 'em to fall."

Placing her warm hands on my face, she guides me to her comforting shoulder.

Memories of my mother...

"What's your friend's name?" she asks, her breath warming my forehead.

I gulp hard, struggling to answer. "Ophelia."

"Blond little thing?"

Again, something cracks and a deluge of tears stream. I nod.

"I feel her with you." She laughs. "Woo, by the Mother, she loves you too."

I can't stop my shoulders from shaking.

"Guardian angel... you were that for one another in life, huh?"

I don't know if she's asking or not. I no longer care. "Yes," I croak out, my tears moistening the shoulder of a woman I would have once seen as the enemy. How foolish this war feels now.

"Freedom. That's what she wants for you in this here life. Freedom."

"Freedom?"

She nods, placing a finger under my chin. She gently lifts my face so our eyes are looking directly into one another's. "Now I know what you're thinking, but she don't mean death. She means the freedom love brings, do you understand?"

No, I don't. My face continues to contort with grief. I must look terrible now, just as all eyes become fixed on me.

"You don't? Hmm, okay. How do I explain it?" Closing her eyes, Giaan tilts her head to the cave's jagged ceiling. "Oh... okay, I'll ask."

Ask?

"What did you do before becomin' a soldier?" she questions.

It takes a moment for me to compose myself. "I was a teacher," I answer.

"Did you love teachin'?"

I nod. "Yes, very much."

"Did you feel confined and trapped when you was teachin'?"

"No, never."

A wide, bright smile fills her face. "Well, that's the freedom of love for ya! Even when you're doin' somethin' for hours, under a huge amounts of stress, there's just somethin' about love that makes it all energizin', makes it all seem worth it."

313

The sleeping girl stirs. "I'm thirsty," she says, her beautiful large brown eyes wide and fixed on Giaan. Her breathing is the most labored of all the children here.

"I'll get it," Jeevan says, standing quickly.

Giaan tosses her hand into the air. "No... no, you got it last time, remember? It's my turn this time."

Still standing, Jeevan glances at me, her face flashing anger. "Giaan, you're busy and pregnant. You should rest."

"Sit, girl. Talk to our guest," Giaan orders.

Even her order is given with a smile.

In a huff, Jeevan sits, her face turned towards a sleeping boy. She gives me the impression that she doesn't like me, or more so, she doesn't like what I represent. The enemy.

"Is there anything I can do to help?" I ask, trying to wipe my face dry with my uniform sleeve.

"Naw, hon, you gathered all that food, turned a small meal into a feast. I ain't done much else but get that girl there to sleep. Nearly put myself to sleep doin' it too," she says. "No, you just rest here. I won't be but a minute." With both hands, she swats the dust from her backside and walks towards the night sky. "You stayin' the night with us, Jocelyn?"

"Yes. If that's okay, I mean," I say meekly. I shouldn't. I should head out, make my way to the ocean. My stomach is full and they can't help me... I have no reason to stay. "I'd like to stay."

"'Course. But we ain't done talkin', you hear? Our talk will be what you gotta trade. That's the payment you gonna have to make."

"Sure." I smile, but as I look at Jeevan, I wonder if she'll suffer me to remain in her presence for long.

That girl's been making a point, a huge point, of avoiding me in every possible way. The five minutes of Giaan's absence feels like an hour around this frigid woman. Honestly, I can't blame her. I'm the face of the North. Hell, I wear the uniform of those that have killed and imprisoned so many of her people.

I still hope to get to know her. Somewhere inside, I hope she can forgive me.

Okay, I'm utterly sick of this tension. "So, what did you do before the war?" I ask, leaning back on the heels of my hands.

With a slow open-mouthed breath, Jeevan turns to me. "I know what you are. Giaan does as well."

I'm a FOG. I'm the very reason your people were pushed to the edge. Still, my expression hardens. "Oh really?"

"Yes... really. You're Undying. She may act like she doesn't know, but she does. We all do."

Takdeer emerges in my memory — he used the same word to describe FOGs. But from his lips it was spoken with a sense of respect. This girl, she soils it with anger and disgust. "Undying. There's a term I haven't heard in a while," I reply, unclenching my teeth, making an effort to retain my calm. There's no benefit in matching her anger. I'm a guest here.

The awkward silence between us continues as we take turns looking towards the dark cave walls.

Instead of focusing on Jeevan, I turn my attention to the youths. The peaceful faces of children sleeping, there's nothing like it.

I'm glad I stayed.

"Healer," she blurts.

"Excuse me?"

"I was... I *am* a healer."

"Healer? You mean like a doctor?"

"No, I don't mean like a doctor. A healer cares for the overall health of a person, spirit, mind, and body."

I thought doctors did that. "Oh, I see. So, are you the *healer* for these children?"

Again she sighs. "I'm not the healer for these children, no — well, yes I am, but I wasn't initially."

I lean in, cautiously checking to see if any of the children are being stirred by the conversation. "What's wrong with them?" I ask in a whisper.

Jeevan pulls back as if surprised by the question. Her eyes scan the six as they breath softly. "They are... they are exhausted, drained, but hopefully not beyond help."

"They seem so ill."

"They are." She nods, her eyes gentle. "Terribly so. The spirit can only take so much before it can no longer sustain the body."

Jibberish. I understand the words, but none of them make sense to me in the context they're being used. Are we really that different? "I don't understand."

Another annoyed sigh as Jeevan looks up to the ceiling.

"They are special," Giaan answers from behind. Slowly walking in from the cave's mouth, she's illuminated by the fire and framed by the shelter's darkness. She holds a small, but plump, hemp sack as she passes behind me and towards the child. "As you Undyin' must know, being special can be a terrible burden, yes?" she asks, sitting next to me.

"What are they capable of?"

"You ask many questions, but offer little," Jeevan interjects.

"There's no reason to be defensive, Jeevan," Giaan says with a smile. "We both know she is not an enemy. That bein' the case, you need to learn to recognize the energy being brought before you, go from the inside out, not the outside in."

What's the energy I brought? Assuming they're talking about me, of course. "It's alright, I understand. I mean, look at me. I'm the chief weapon of your enemy."

"No," Giaan snaps, placing the sack down with more force than needed. It gently undulates like gelatin. "Unless you lied to me earlier when you called yourself a teacher. Did you? Are you a teacher or a weapon?"

The glee gone, Giaan nearly glares at me. I cannot help but wither under both her gaze and the question.

What am I?

I am a teacher. "I'm a teacher," I say.

Giaan raises her eyebrows. An unspoken call for me to repeat my claim, but this time with conviction.

"I'm a teacher," I repeat with assurance. A response that softens her expression, returning the grin to her face.

"Good. You have to remember, Miss Jocelyn, they can't take what you don't give. These children, they ain't yet able to know that fact, so they did what they were told to do. Good kids. Sadly, those in power were willin' to ask for more than these young spirits could bear. If they weren't removed, they would have given their lives, for the sake of death.

"But you... you grown. You, Miss Jocelyn, should know better. And if you don't, I need you to realize that can't no one take more than you willing to give. No one."

"I understand," I say. "Well, about me, I understand. But for these children... what are they, some kind of weapon?"

"Something like that, yeah. You see, these six are all that remains of the Keynosian weapon program," Giaan says, her voice soft. "All of the weapons, the ones I'm sure you Northerners fear the most, are made from their flesh and the flesh of children like them. And I ain't speakin' metaphorically. Those weapons are pulled from these young bodies. They gave birth to the first of them, the seeds, and the rest are propagated from those first-born."

Jeevan shakes her head. "You telling this stranger too much, Giaan."

Giaan chuckles. "She don't understand no way."

She's right. I don't understand.

Turning to me, Giaan nods. "But, of course you wouldn't, you ain't a Keynosian." Pointing across the sleeping young bodies, Giaan presses her lips tight. "There are those with a special connection to Mother, to the earth." Her hand hovers just above the thick layer of leaves we rest on. "That connection, it's strong in them, stronger than most. That connection, it gives them the ability to bring forth creations from within.

"Ya know, it's said that the mark, the first mark that is, was created by such a child." She brushes her finger along a green mark hidden behind her ebony curls.

317

"So those aren't tattoos?"

"Nope. They're a gift from Mother, passed from mother to child."

"And these children, they can create plant life directly from their bodies. But, that process of weapon development, it drains them," I say, finally understanding the circumstances. I hope. "And your government was willing to drain them dry, work them to death, quite literally, in an effort to defeat the North?"

With a sigh, Jeevan and Giaan nod.

I can only laugh. "Then we are the same, those children and I. North, South, it's all the same it seems."

"How's that?" Giaan asks, somewhat confused.

"To create us, the Undying, the Fingers of God as we're called up North, our government sacrificed thousands."

"By the Mother," Giaan exclaims.

"Every single one of them were sacrificed to create only a few hundred of us."

"Then why?" Jeevan asks. "Why would you say yes to such a thing?"

"How could I say no? I believed that our way of life was under threat. That is what we were told, over and over again. I was scared. We were all scared."

A chuckle burps from Giaan. "Ain't that the way? It's always the responsibility of the poor and lower castes to secure the country for those at the top. Bunch a' bullshit if you ask me.

"It's always easy to send someone else's child to die. Harder when it's you and yours."

Is that Ophelia?

She stands in the distant, rain-soaked field... but something is wrong. Not only wrong with her, but wrong with me. I don't feel the same. I try to enhance my vision, but nothing occurs. I try to run to her, but my muscles don't cooperate. My movements are oppressively sluggish, as if I were drugged. Then it occurs to me... I'm no longer a FOG. I'm just Jocelyn Martinez, the teacher, the divorcée, the lonely spinster who dedicated her life to teaching children she could never have.

Maybe the Sacrifice never happened? Maybe Ophelia's not dead? "Ophelia?" I yell, but no reaction is returned. She just stands there, staring away from me, away from the low sun at my back and towards the dark and distant horizon ahead of us. Her hair, long once again, lies flat from the rain and plasters her head.

I run towards her, slowly, weakly, like any other normal human. Too slow. She's so far away. I'm barely halfway to her and each subsequent step begins to slow, as if ever-increasing weights are being added to my legs and feet.

"Ophelia," I call again, nearly gasping, tired from dragging my weak human body to her. She's only a few steps away now, but my lungs are burning so fiercely I'm unsure if I'll even make it to her. "Are you" — I gasp — "alright, Oa?" Damn, so tired.

"You owe me, Jos," she says, but her voice is strange, vacant, devoid of the life that once animated it. The life I took from her. "A life for a life," she says, almost sighing the words out. "Isn't that the proper payment of such a debt?"

"Oa, it's me, Jos." Why doesn't she turn to look at me? I reach out to touch her shoulder... no. Please, no. Her head... like a doll abused by a bitter younger brother, it has been twisted around... just like it was before I... took her life. My heart sinks as I realize she didn't escape death. She's still a FOG. She's still broken, just as I am, shattered by the knowledge that I took her life.

Weak. I'm so very weak.

I see her eyes open, the whitest of white and the bluest of blue, staring at me from behind wet and matted golden blond strands. "Stop looking in the wrong direction, Jos," she orders.

"They can help you, Oa, keep you alive if we can get you in stasis!" I should have left her alone, let her live. She wasn't in her right mind when she begged for death. Maybe... maybe she would have wanted to live once she recovered, despite the constant pain she'd have to endure.

If only I didn't rush. "I'm... I'm sorry, Oa," I cry. I want to touch her, hug her, but... suddenly, I'm afraid. "I should have waited. I should have been stronger."

"Jos. Stop looking in the wrong direction."

"What?"

"Stop looking in the wrong direction. You're looking the wrong way. You owe me your life. Stop moving forward while staring behind yourself, hoping to reclaim what was lost. You owe me your life. Debt must be paid. You owe me."

Does she want me to kill myself? "I'll pay any debt, I accept any punishment," I stammer out, my heart racing at the idea of suicide, at allowing her to take my life.

I deserve punishment for killing my sister. I deserve to die.

"Live, Jos. Live. Be free. Live. You just have to look in the right direction."

"I don't understand. What do you mean, live? I don't —"

"Love is freedom. Live free. Love is freedom. You owe me your live. Live free." In one quick motion, she turns, spinning her face away, sloshing water into my face as she grabs my head. "Love is freedom. Stop looking in the wrong direction," she says, her voice growing louder.

Her grip tightens as she turns my head to the left slowly, steadily. God, she's so strong!

"You're looking in the wrong direction. Live. Love is freedom."

It's hurting. She's hurting me! "Oa, wait, stop!" I yell, trying to twist away, to pry her iron grip loose.

Her fingers do not budge. She only pulls me close to her, thrusting my face into the back of her head. I feel my neck reach as far as the vertebrate will allow, but she doesn't stop twisting. She's going to break my neck!

"YOU'RE LOOKING THE WRONG WAY!"

With a start, I awake to the sight of Jeevan's single hazel eye, illuminated by the still-crackling fire. She glares at me, her finger resting in the center of her full lips.

I forget where I am. Looking around the damp cave, the pieces begin to slide into place. I'm in the company of Keynosians. Good people who allowed me to spend time with them. Allowed me to eat their food and spill my pain onto their shoulders. I look at the children in the circle as they sleep. Jeevan shakes her head at me before lying back down.

How is this fire still burning strong? What kind of wood keeps it burning like that? Whatever they're using, it's obviously as effective as the thick sheets of massive leaves that cover the thin hemp blanket beneath us, used to soften the feel of the hard ground. A twinge of guilt hits me as I find myself resting my head comfortably on a bundle of leaves given to me by my once enemy. I would have tossed these people into a truck to be transported to a massive concentration camp just days ago. Yet they show me nothing but kindness. We are no different, merely birds of a feather who've found themselves flocked together by circumstance and chance.

"Jos?" I hear over my receiver. "It's me, Patricia."

Her voice breaks me out of my restless thoughts.

My finger, responding instinctively, lands on the broken receiver. It's then, as my awareness catches me, that my hand slips slowly to the hollow of my neck.

"Jos, it's me, Patricia."

I know, Pat. I'd know your voice in the midst of any raucous party, in the middle of a firefight, and probably in a hurricane. Sometimes I think I know your voice better than I know my own.

"I keep expecting you to say something," she says with a grunt that was quite possibly meant to be a giggle. I see her shaking her head in my mind's eye, annoyed. "Dumb I know, right?"

Strangely, I'm happy to hear that tinge of sadness in her voice. I imagine it confirms her love for me.

321

"Anyway, I just wanted to tell you to be careful. We're about to engage the Keynosian stronghold, since it's night and all. So, I'd strongly suggest, if you're headed west that is, you keep a good distance away from this place. If you're not, feel free to ignore the warning. But, if you are actually heading towards the ocean, keep an eye out for us... and stay away.

"I know you're aware by now that Powell's cut you off from all the known channels. That's standard procedure, of course, for deserters."

A tingle hits my spine at the word. Deserter. It's a synonym for coward in my mind.

"That's bullshit, Jos. You're not some goddamn deserter. That fucking guy made you a deserter by threatening to arrest you for doing the right thing," she very nearly yells.

I hear her breathe deep. "He's definitely not happy about what happened with... what happened before."

I killed Ophelia.

"As soon as we got back and started assessing our next play, he started whining about us not having the fucking muscle to force the facility open if it's locked. Of all of the things to bitch about, ya know? I mean... Oa died! If that's your biggest complaint, then you're just a callous asshole.

"Seriously, how the hell was I ever interested in the guy?"

"Anyway, if Marshall, Petersen, and Jackson aren't enough, I can't imagine how tough he thinks this gate is. We should have enough muscle to open pretty much any and everything on God's green earth with just those three.

"Oh! I have a message from David," she says, then pauses. "I know you want to hear it. I'm just pausing to build tension." She chuckles.

She clears her throat. "He says, and I quote, 'Tell her that I'll come running. Just say when and where.'"

The man is certainly persistent.

"I know you're going to contact him, right? Right?" Again she laughs. "Whatever freaky stuff you did to him, you definitely broke that man. So, when you get settled, you can call me so I can learn that shit. You must make it vibrate or something."

I fight hard to stifle my laughter. God, I miss you, Pat.

"Oh, and don't think I'm making it up either. David would have contacted you, but Powell has been keeping a close eye on him. I think Powell is wondering if David is going to bolt and attempt to find you. Powell's probably got the right idea, 'cause David's been walking around camp with a really sour look on his face, staring south the entire time.

"By the way, I think Powell's starting to realize that we must have some private channel. Duh, 'course we do. Shit, who doesn't?

"Well, I'm out of things to update you on. But, as soon as I can get some more info, you better believe I'm going to let you know.

"I love you, Jos. I may have three sisters, blood sisters, but I've never felt as close to them as I do to you, as I did to Ophelia. I really want to grow old with big sister Jocelyn in my life. Please make sure we can make that happen, okay?

"I love you. Stay safe."

And with that, the line goes dead.

If I push hard, I can hear the fighting from the cave's entrance. It won't be long before the mission team heads towards the research facility. Towards us. When that happens, we can't be here.

"Giaan, may I have a word with you?" I call, turning back into the dim cave.

She nods and finishes folding a huge hemp blanket into a rather small square. The same thin blanket that covered the floor for all of us is now folded so small it fits into a makeshift knapsack. Quickly donning the bag, she runs her hands through her curls and walks over to me near the cave's entrance. "Yes?"

"We can't stay here for long."

"Is that why you all fidgety? Was wonderin' what got you so riled."

"There's a huge force of Northerners headed close to this location."

"They fightin' at that big ol' encampment to the north, right?"

"Yeah. How'd you know that?"

"There ain't but one place left to fight. Well, there and the weapon facility south of us."

"And that's my main concern, the weapons facility. There's a group of FOGs, I mean Undying, that's going to storm that place. They intend to destroy it outright."

"Okay. If they find us?"

I can only shrug. "I have no idea what they'll do."

"But they'd only want you, right? You're a deserter," Jeevan questions, her intent clear. She wants me specifically to leave.

"They won't have time to split off a group to capture me, so I doubt I'll draw them, but they are on the lookout for ambushes. I would be. So most likely they'll shoot first and ask questions later. Hell, they may not even ask questions. They're on a timetable, so they'll spray the area with rifle fire, possibly toss a few grenades and move on.

"Again, that's what I would do."

Walking towards Giaan and me, Jeevan looks at me, her expression heavy with suspicion. "You know all of this how?"

"Because I was going to be a part of that team." No point in deceit. I think we're past that now.

With a deep breath, Giaan walks swiftly back to the gathered children. "So, since we're all just a bunch of runaways, we need to start runnin' away. Your people are on the way, you're not 100% sure, but I'm certain that a group of Guardsmen will come for these children."

Jeevan's eyes widen with a sudden, fearful realization.

"It's that bad?" I ask as Jeevan steps quickly to the huddled group of children.

"Come on kids, we've got to go, right now," Jeevan barks.

"Yes, it's bad," Giaan answers. "If that facility is attacked, the weapons facility that is, our people are bound to call for reinforcements. A lot of 'em. And since it's their last hope to win this dumb war, they'll come from everywhere."

This is it, the final battle.

"If they find these kids, they'll take them back to the facility. The same facility we... they are going to destroy?" I ask.

"No, hun. They ain't gonna take them back, these children are spent. If they find these kids, they gonna kill each and every one of 'em."

CHAPTER 12

CARRIED BY THE WIND

There are no accidents Giaan assures me. According to her belief system, if we follow the will of this "Great Mother," all things flow as they should. She doesn't believe that life always follows the path of least resistance. She believes that life follows the willful intent of itself. Humanity, and the Earth itself, is simply fulfilling its own collective will. From the inception of life, to man creating bombs to destroy it, our progress, oftentimes messy and difficult, is the result of Earth's desire to reach this point and beyond. And whether we know it or not, in following our collective will we are indeed following Mother's will. We are the Great Mother. Mother is the collective consciousness of the living Earth and all that resides therein.

Giaan seems to delight in sharing her beliefs with me, and they are indeed fascinating. The idea is that death is nothing more than a change of existence, a rebirth of sorts. Our energy, the life force that animates all of mankind, will always be recycled for the next generation. The process is not so different than the cycle of renewal that water undergoes. Evaporation begets clouds, clouds beget rain, and rain begets water on the surface, only to be evaporated again. It all repeats infinitely. It's all within the Great Mother's plan.

To the Keynosians, the concept of heaven and hell is foolishness.

Of course, Giaan never says that, but her expression exposes her heart. The idea that anyone or anything could become stuck forever in a singular form is abhorrent to her. It's a perversion of their cycle of life.

Man simply forgot the truth that we are the one and true God.

And here I thought they just worshiped trees.

"Miss Jocelyn?" Dhann, the eldest boy, calls to me as we walk. Even though sickly, there's a lovely quality to him. He has a way of being that's warm and nurturing, a way that the other children gravitate towards.

"Yes, Dhann?"

With a glance to Jeevan, he moves in close. "Can I hold your hand?" he asks, his voice soft, nearly pleading.

"My hand? Well... sure, sure."

His hand, soft and cold, clings to my fingers. He pulls himself close, pressing his body against my leg and torso. Memories, long forgotten, pop into my conscious mind. Memories of children I taught in days that feel so very long ago. Images of children who lacked parental affection. Hurt children, who needed something only love could supply.

But I'm not his mother, I'm no one's mother, and I never will be.

I look up and see Giaan's smile. "What?" I ask, smiling.

Working her way over a steep incline, Giaan lifts a small girl, her hair bone-straight and jet-black, up and around onto more level footing. "Oh, nothin'. Just seein' a fellow traveler get back on the right road." She winks.

I know what she's saying. I also know Dhann has no idea what the metaphor means. He only grins, content to swing his hand wrapped in mine as far up as it can go. For the first time today, he wears the brightest of smiles. We both do.

The group moves at a slow, but steady pace across the mountain range. This pace is about to be disrupted. Ahead there's a break in the ridge, offering us a difficult but passable path westward.

"How are we going to get across here?" Jeevan asks, peering over the side of a steep drop-off carved abruptly into the rocky terrain. She sighs and glances up and down the gash in the earth. "We have no mountain climbing gear, and even if we did, how do we get the children down to the bottom and then back up across the gap?" Her body language yells defeat as she begins directing the exhausted children in the opposite direction.

It's not that far down or across. I'd easily survive the fall if it came to that. Probably wouldn't even break or tear anything in the process. Getting back up would be more difficult, but I should be able to use the various crevasses to jump and climb back up on the other side. I could take one or two across at a time and repeat the process until we all made it to the other side. How long would it take? Or better yet, could I jump the chasm? Yes. I think I could. It'd certainly save us a ton of time.

What's that? Ah, a very familiar sound... the sound of combat. The whispers of war, carried on the winds, echoing against the stones surrounding us. It's too faint for the average person to hear, but all too easy for me. Far too easy.

How long have they been assaulting that Keynosian stronghold? I guess it is indeed a fortress.

Our group of runaways is steadily turning north, looking for another way across. "I can get all of us across," I say.

I look over the edge and see a small river flowing at the bottom of the gorge.

"Really? How you gonna manage that?" Giaan asks.

"I'll jump."

"Jump?" Jeevan asks. She thrusts her finger at the distance. "You're going to jump this?"

Clearly, she doesn't believe I can do it. "Yes, jump. As in run and leap. It isn't too far for me."

"You can really jump across this?" she asks again, pointing at the daunting chasm.

I can't help but laugh. "Yes, I can. But, the real question is, how many can I carry while doing it."

329

"Ohh, can I go first?" Dhann asks, nearly bouncing up, his hand raised in a flash.

This brave boy. "No Dhann, I'm sorry but you're too young," I say, dropping to one knee. "I don't want to risk something happening to you." I look around the group for a moment, before finally stopping at Jeevan. "Jeevan, are you willing to try it first? If you can trust me, that is."

Jeevan says nothing as her eyes glide to Giaan, then the children, then back to me. With a sigh, she nods. "I know why you're asking me," she says with a frown. "I'm the only other adult here that's not pregnant."

"Is that a yes?"

"You Northerners use that word so freely, but trust is something earned, not given willy-nilly," Jeevan says, walking right up to me. She turns and points a steady hand towards Giaan. "I trust Giaan without question. I trust her. We've been through a lot, and despite my situation" — she drags the back of her fingers along her cheek, stained dark green from the half-mark adorning her face — "she took me as her pupil when no one else would.

"So, if she's willing to risk her life and the life of her unborn for you, so am I. Yes, I will be the first, because I'd rather die than let harm come to my mentor."

More explanation than I needed, but I'll take the yes nevertheless. "Good. Let's get started."

I take position a few meters away from the ledge, with Jeevan holding onto me from behind. Her legs, wrapped tight and high around my upper waist, are sufficiently out of the way. Her arms are doing their best to choke me as she grips as tight as she's able.

Speed will be important, more so than anything else. If I jump too high, the landing could jar her loose and cause injury. She might be strong enough to hold on, but I doubt the same to be true of the children. Of course, not enough speed and I won't make it across at all. But, that shouldn't be a problem. I'll make the jump and have the speed to do it. I just need to be careful with my cargo.

"Jeevan, I'm going to need you to stay as still as you can and please keep your legs high on my trunk. If you bump your legs into mine, you could potentially slow me down, and that's not good." Or cause me to break your leg with the force of my upward thrusts.

"Legs high. Got it," she says, her voice nervous. I can feel her head nodding against my hair.

Why is she holding her back so straight? I'm not a horse. "Jeevan, please lean in and get your body as close to mine as possible." I can feel the thudding of her heart in her arms. She's terrified.

Gulping audibly, she nods again. "Okay… sorry."

I stifle a chuckle. Not so tough now, are you? "No need to apologize. Just stay as close to me as you can and hold on tight. I'm going to start a little slow. I don't want to break your hold on me." I grab her arms just above the elbow. "But, once I start moving fast, I need your grip to be as tight as possible. Don't worry about choking me. You can't. Once we hit the lip of the gorge and I leap, the force could pull you loose."

"I'll be closin' my eyes, so can I start holding tight now?"

I laugh. "Yes, that's probably best."

Ahead, the rest of the group moves to the side, standing as tense and tight as Jeevan is clutching my throat. I can see the hope in their eyes.

"Thank you, Jeevan," I say.

I don't wait for a response. I just run. Jeevan, to her credit, doesn't scream, she only gasps and clings as tightly as humanly possible. The edge comes fast and with a forceful push, I soar. As I drift, so too do my thoughts.

Love is freedom. Freedom from what? I've never experienced love as anything more than a prison of emotional and/or legal bonds. Every romantic relationship I've ever had was wrought with pain and bondage, warfare even. Intellectually, I know that's not really love. People who claim to know what it is have explained that to me. But, what is love, if not that?

Except, David doesn't give me that feeling of fear and tightness. I don't find the need to cling to him, I don't need to do that. I feel at ease with him. Is that how true love begins? Free, like the feeling I'm having now, soaring through the air. I'd like that.

The ground on the opposite side of the gorge approaches quickly. I adjust my eyes, slowing down the world so I can catch the ground easier, matching my foot speed to the speed of my landing.

With a jolt, we're across. Success! I come to a halt, and Jeevan gingerly relinquishes her grip.

"Unbelievable."

"Not so unbelievable. The Undying were created after researching Guardsmen. Your people."

"Really? But I've never heard of Guardsmen being capable of such feats."

The smile on my face fades and my expression drifts into a grimace. "The cost of that power was the death of tens of thousands. Power has a price. This power came at a terrible sacrifice."

Her eyes downcast, she tightens her full lips. "I'm sorry."

The comment was genuine. "I am too."

For the first time, Jeevan smiles at me. She's a lot prettier when she smiles.

"Okay, so we know it'll work. I'll go get the others and repeat the process."

I head back a few meters.

"Jocelyn," Jeevan calls as I prepare to leap again. "You are indeed a blessing. Thank you."

"You're welcome."

"I can feel the saltwater!" Dhann says, tugging at my hand, urging me forward. He has a good nose. I assume he can smell it although he clearly said "feel," but even then, the ocean must be a few miles away. We're still surrounded by the sparse vegetation and rocky landscape of the high mountains. It'll take quite a while to walk these children down from here and onto the beach so they can start their trip north.

They *want* to be in the concentration camp. They *want* the anonymity that comes with imprisonment amongst strangers. These children can't even be free amongst those that call them brother and sister. What right have I to complain? I had the opportunity to be a teacher, to get married and have a life of my own. They will grow up under the control of their enemies both outside and potentially within their own culture. Still, I guess that's far better than dying outright. You have a chance when you're alive.

I watch them. They're all walking with much more vigor as the sun warms their jet-black hair. It seems Dhann and the rest of the children have regained a measure of their youthful strength. Even the worst of all of them, Surat, the sickly girl who needed a drink, now skips, kicking small rocks as she walks.

Hope is a dangerous thing, yet it grows as I watch these beautiful children.

"Girl, you are always in la-la land," Giaan says, her arm over Surat's shoulder, playfully pressing down on the child's torso in mock need of support. The game elicits more than a few giggles from the rejuvenated, gifted Keynosian girl.

"I have a lot to think about," I reply.

"Like?"

"Well, losing my country for one, and now having to find another, if that's even possible. I'll be hunted by the Northern Alliance for the remainder of my days, which could very well be a very long time. What I did to my friend —"

"Sounds like you got a lot on your shoulders," she says, cutting me off.

"It certainly feels like I do."

Getting another giggle from Surat, Giaan turns to me and smiles. "Carryin' the past around all day, every day... that's a tough haul. Why would you choose that?"

Choose? "I don't choose to carry the past around with me."

She raises an eyebrow.

333

"Your past is always there. It's not like I can discard it."

"It's always there, sure, but the past is only a place to launch yerself from. It ain't a place to hang your hat."

Again with the gibberish. "What do you mean?"

She lets out a sigh. "There's an old Keynosian saying, 'dirt in your hand grows nothing.'"

I don't even try to hide my bitter chuckle. "So, you're telling me to let it go? Just let it all go? Just like that? What, I'm supposed to just act like the past never happened?" I say, feeling a twinge of anger. I did kill Ophelia. My heart was indeed broken, more than once. My country is actively betraying me by hunting me down for committing an act of mercy. Those things did happen, and I have to deal with them. None of those incidences are questionable, they are all facts.

Her chuckle, once pleasant, is now annoying. She bounces her head from side to side as if formulating a response, weighing the respective pros and cons of her thoughts. "Now I ain't said nothin' about actin' like it ain't happen. 'Cause I assume you're right, and they did indeed occur, but there's a difference between not forgettin' and languishin' in stuff you can't undo. Look, you gotta take your past as it is, the past. It's static, unmovin', but *you* still gotta keep movin' forward. 'Cause each step we take, it's a step from the past, through the present, and into our future. The future we gonna... we hafta choose for ourselves.

"Look," Giaan says, reaching over and placing her hand on my shoulder. "Turn 'round here and look at that," she says, pointing up towards the plateau we recently left. "We don't concern ourselves with the base of the mountain while we climbin', do we? Ain't no one here dwellin' and worryin' about how far we had to walk, or how hard it was to get around that steep pass, or how sleepin' on a bed of leaves wasn't the best. You know why? It's 'cause we're past that trial. It's gone and done. So, we just keep goin' forward, leaving each of them moments behind us, but recognizing that without those steps, we wouldn't have made it this far."

334

Her words strike a memory. The dream of Ophelia I had last night. "I'm looking the wrong way."

She nods. "That's right... you looking the wrong way. That's a good way to put it. 'Cause you can't get nowhere far if you keep walking backwards, eyein' the past. Ain't that right, Surat?" she asks, giving the girl a tickle.

The girl smiles, the excitement of youth in her eyes. "I can walk backward really far. Wanna see?"

Giaan and I laugh as Surat looks on, completely serious. Stopping the girl from turning, Giaan kisses her forehead and chuckles. "I'm sure you can, sweetie. How about we try it later? I'd love to see that."

Elated by the challenge, she lights up. "Okay!"

Going back to her previous game of weighing Surat down, Giaan turns to me again. "Now, unless you're Surat, you ain't gonna get too far walkin' through the rest of your life watchin' the past replay over and over again."

For a moment, no one speaks, but we all keep our heads forward as we walk. No one dares to look back.

"Look, Miss Jocelyn," Giaan says, taking Surat's hand. "I'm guessin' you done seen it all, you bein' a soldier and all. You probably got a world of hurt in your head that's just eatin' at you sometimes, huh? Hell, I ain't even a soldier and I have regrets from petal to root, but understand this... you can't keep that dirt in your hands and be happy. You got to let it go so it'll grow somethin'. And maybe, just maybe, what grows from mess will put a smile on your face."

"I should learn from my past, that's what you're saying."

"More than learn, hun, build. The past will always be there. In fact, it's the past that makes your foundation strong. 'Cause for damn sure there ain't no foundation more solid than past experience."

She looks at my hands, taking my left palm in hers and rubbing it with her thumb.

"All that hurt you got in you, all that pain... that's knowledge. Each piece, each moment is another rung in your ladder, it's another brick for your foundation. Ya'll Northerns do use bricks, right?"

335

Fortified concrete. "Yes, we do."

"Look, all you gotta do is keep climbin', lookin' up and movin' towards the sunlight. Towards love."

"Love is at the top?"

"Well, there ain't no top, there's just the climb. But, when you headin' in the direction of your choosin', you find freedom. Freedom in the climb and the progress. Freedom is love. The rest, that's just the shit you had to step in to get there."

The host of children gasp, some chuckle.

"Ohhh!" Dhann says, his hand covering his mouth as if the words were his.

"Oh hush!" Giaan says, laughing. "Ain't like you never heard that word before."

Surat swats her on the hip playfully. "You're bad, Auntie Giaan!"

"That's true," Giaan replies, her eyes meeting mine.

"I can hear them, they're getting close," Dhann says. His young voice is low, echoing in the small alcove of rocks we're tucked behind. I've pulled a section of stone and shrubbery over the entrance, blocking all sunlight from reaching us. We were lucky. If the Guardsmen had reached this flat plateau a few minutes earlier, they would have spotted us easily.

"You can't hear them, Dhann," Jeevan corrects. "You feel them, very different than an Undying. Guardsmen are a powerful force, a force you gifted are tuned into."

"He's right about one thing, they are getting closer to us, and coming at a good clip," I say. "They'll be reaching us in a few minutes."

For the first time, Giaan's normally jovial expression turns to concern. I can smell her fear. "If they happen to find us, you should run, hun," she says to me. "Ain't no reason for you to die here.

Maybe you can take Jeevan and the kids, get yerselves out of here? There ain't no reason to give —"

"Stop it," I say, interrupting her. "You don't tell me what I'm willing to die for, okay?" I say, allowing the anger I feel to put a sharp edge on my words.

Didn't Patricia say something similar to me? I don't think I received it well back then, but now I see why she said it. It was the truth, and I didn't want to accept it.

"Jocelyn, you don't understand," Jeevan says, touching my arm. Her eyes are blind, staring up, wide and hungry for a small glimmer of light. Yet, she is still able to find my arm with ease. "These children, they're like a beacon to Guardsmen. They can feel each other. Feel the other's life force."

I am a teacher. I've wanted to work with young people, to educate *and* protect them, for as long as I can remember. I cannot... I will not sit idly by and allow these children to be harmed. "I don't care about the reasons. I can't turn my back on these children." There must be at least twenty Guardsmen heading south, towards the facility. Patricia was correct, they've sent reinforcements to protect their weapons, some of which I have with me now.

"I'm going to help you to continue your trip north, to the concentration camp. When you guys are safe, that's when I'll leave."

"Noooo," Dhann groans.

"What? What's wrong?"

Tears well up in his eyes. "I don't want you to go," he pleads, his eyes begging in the darkness.

I don't know what he had to endure, but whatever it is, I'm sure he didn't deserve it. "Dhann," I say softly, my hand on his cheek, "I can't stay. I can't go to the camps because they'll arrest me, sweetie. Do you want me to be arrested?"

"I don't want you to go."

"And I don't want to go. But, do you want me to be arrested?"

He pushes himself closer to me.

He needs someone in his life. I wish I could be that someone.

"Okay, everyone quiet. They're getting closer," I say as the rumbling of Keynosian vehicles grows louder.

I hear the sound of their tires against the rocky ground, smell the exhaust fumes from the trucks.

Closer.

I hear the clanging of their weapons against the heavy metal vehicles they're driving. There are more than twenty, maybe closer to twenty-five Guardsmen, spread out over five hulking vehicles that sound like transports.

I don't dare risk exposing myself in an attempt to get a visual.

Closer.

The voices of the Guardsmen are now audible. The roar of their engines sound so very Northern to me. Possibly another portion of our technology they've co-opted.

The children are frightened, some literally quaking.

God, I pray these children are no longer burdened with the sins of us foolish adults.

We hold our collective breath as they pass, rapidly heading south.

Finally, Giaan chuckles. "Oh Mother... nearly pissed myself."

Chuckles travel over the group as the tension fades.

"Shhhhh! We still need to be quiet," Dhann says, his young eyes blankly staring into the darkness.

"What is it?" I ask.

"One of them reached out... I think he touched me," he answers, his voice on the verge of cracking into a sob. Like a virus, the others appear to contract in fear as heart rates begin to rise.

"Giaan, I'm scared," another child says, clinging to her sleeve.

"I don't hear anything, Dhann."

"He feels me. I know he feels me. I tried to be quiet, tried to close myself away —"

"Did you reach out, boy?" Giaan asks, her eyes fixed on the back of his head.

"I dunno, Giaan," he says, beginning to cry again.

"It's okay, son, it's okay." She rubs his back in small circles. "I ain't brought ya'll this far only to see ya hurt. We all here for a reason. We here for a reason." Her dark eyes, blind without the light, still manage to fall on me as if I were illuminated. "There are no accidents."

For the first time in a very long time, I start to believe in a God. Maybe I *am* here for a reason. Maybe this, all of this, is not some mass of coincidences bumbling together haphazardly.

Maybe, they are why I'm here.

"Damn it," I exclaim. I hear the slow approach of a few Guardsmen, and my heart sinks. A small contingent seems to have splintered off and is heading in this direction. They're driving slow. Obviously searching... no, not searching, homing in.

I don't understand this connection Dhann claims a Guardsmen felt, but it must be there. He wouldn't lie.

"What's wrong?" Jeevan asks. Even her face, once stern and full of self-assurance, has broken into a fearful expression as she holds tight to a child.

She'll die for them. I can see it. But, will I? The Northern soldier in me says no, not for an enemy. But, the true me, the Jocelyn that still exists somewhere deep inside of this body, she says, yes. That Jocelyn, the real Jocelyn, she will die to save these children. That is who I am. And with that realization, something changes in me. It's as if a weight has been removed, a fog lifted. I feel myself breathe deep as I smile inwardly.

To acknowledge to oneself who you are is freedom. I know what I will do, to do anything else would be a prison for my soul.

"There's a group headed this way. Five, maybe six moving slowly in a vehicle. They're searching."

"They're going to find us."

"I don't want to die."

"I want my mommy."

"Don't let them get me."

"Hush!" Giaan says, her voice a harsh whisper. "Jocelyn, I know ya don't know me from nothing, but I need ya to get these here children to safety. They're our future. The future of the Keynosian way of life. My life, it ain't worth even one of these babies. I know ya don't understand that, but ya don't need to. So please, just take as many of them as ya can. Take 'em and run."

"No, Giaan, your baby," Jeevan pleads.

"Hush girl," she replies, her eyes filling with tears. "The Earth Mother will have me and my child if it means the life of these here children. So, if this is my end, it will be an end with great meanin'."

"No," I say, holding my eyes to the floor in the darkness.

Shocked, Giaan draws her head back sharply. "What?"

"No, I'm not going to do what you're asking of me."

The response stuns her. Full and heavy with unspoken sorrow, waves of pain and turmoil seem to wash over her face. "Miss Jocelyn," she starts, her voice begging, "look, I'm pleadin' with you. Get them to —"

"No. No. No. I'm not going to let you sacrifice yourself." Her expression changes as she realizes what I mean. "I won't let you sacrifice yourself or your unborn child."

"You can't defeat five Guardsmen," Giaan chides. "And there ain't no way I can move these children outta here fast enough to outrun them. But you, you can do it. I saw you run, Jocelyn. I saw how strong you are. They ain't gonna catch you." She pushes Surat towards me. "Just carry as many of these babies —"

"Stop it. You hear me?" I order her, my finger pointing to her blind eyes. "Stop it. I'm not going to let you or any of these children die today. I won't, I can't."

I failed to protect Emma. I failed that young girl at the forward base. I failed to protect Oa, my sister. I'm failing now to keep a watchful eye on Patricia. Failed in marriage. Failed at even becoming a mother. But this... this I won't fail. I *will* save these children. I *will* save Jeevan and Giaan. I *will* save the unborn baby my newfound friend is carrying.

340

I'll save them even if it costs me my life.

I pull out my two remaining k-bars and stuff them into my mouth. I'll need every drop of energy I can muster. "Giaan," I call to her, feeling the crumbs bounce on my thighs. "I'll engage them, move them away from this location. Give me an hour to get it done. They should be long gone by then. Do you understand?"

"You're leaving us?" Dhann questions. I feel his little hands clutch my shirt. I pry his fingers loose.

"Sweetheart, you have to go with Giaan, understand?"

"Don't leave me," he begs.

He doesn't understand, or worse, he does and still he fears losing me.

"Dhann, stop," Jeevan responds, groping in the darkness for the boy. Quickly, her hand finds his. "Honor her act, don't make it harder for her." Even blinded, her eyes, one dark as night and the other an amber jewel, settle on me... and she smiles.

I can still feel his fingers on my shirt. "Dhann, you and the others are the future," I say. "Be the brilliant future you were born to be."

Standing, I walk out of our soon-to-be-discovered hiding crevasse to greet the five warriors that move towards me. I don't look back.

My heart races. The idea of taking on five Guardsmen without help, without cover, is suicide. But, maybe, just maybe, I can buy my fellow travelers time to get away. These Guardsmen won't be able to pass up killing me, a ranger, alone. But this prey will not go down easily. This meal will strike back.

Walking out from the dark crevasse slowly, I begin pushing my body. Based on the clank of metal I hear with every step they take, I know they're carrying weapons, most likely dragon rifles. That means I'll need to adjust my sight as well. That also means I may go blind if I push too hard for too long.

Blind equals death.

I reach the edge of the tall slice of stone that's hiding the children and their caretakers and pass into the warm afternoon sun. As I do so, I'm already vibrating, pushing hard, but not so hard that I reach my peak. I can't burn out. Not now. Now with so much at stake.

My blade is already drawn.

I hear the call of my animal instinct, the desire to stay alive. I consider running. I could save myself. The idea causes me to laugh. How ironic. It was not that long ago I worried about living forever, and now facing the possibility of death, I'm imagining a future for myself: a possible partner as well as a lifelong friend waiting for me... if I can survive. I have a future now. I have something to look forward to. But, there is no future for me if I cannot look in the mirror and love what looks back at me.

I can't move forward hating myself.

I will be more than my past and pain today. I am and will be the woman I want to be, even if that costs me my life.

I guess I'm looking in the right direction now, eh Ophelia?

"It's an Undying!" one of the Guardsmen yells. He's not a young man, probably a little older than I am.

His face is nearly covered in growths. Without another word, he lifts the massive weapon of deadly metal towards me. But, as fast as he lifts the barrel of the dragon rifle, I'm upon him. My once-reluctant blade now flashes with long-lost vigor. It takes only a few strikes to end his life.

By the time I look up, the others have already backed far away and spread themselves out. I doubt I'll catch them by surprise. They're ready for me, moving to trap me in streams of burning metal.

I turn and run. I move fast enough to keep them out of reach, but not fast enough to lose them. I don't want to lose them. I want them to follow me deeper south. I need these Guardsmen to chase me and move far away from Giaan, Jeevan, and the kids.

Of course, they follow.

They release the sounds of doom, chasing me with round after round of gunfire. I try to zigzag, give them a harder target, but it's slowly becoming more and more useless. They're getting a bead on me, figuring out my movements, drilling their bullets closer and closer to their target. It won't be long before one hits. I won't survive by simply running, but I doubt we're far enough away to make them forget about the kids.

I have to fight.

Dodging into action, I turn and use my blade to deflect the rounds pouring in my direction, pushing my eyes and arms in spurts. Shit, I can't keep this up. My eyes already burn with fatigue. My four pursuers respond, holding their positions and spreading out as fast as possible. They think they have me. So, in an instant, I change speed by pushing so hard I break something in my right foot.

The gamble pays off. Grabbing my gun from its holster, I fire on the four Guardsmen and zero in on the one closest to me.

She's good. Her hands are already up and ready to fight. Their tactics are sound, splitting up and trying to cut off all means of escape. But they are not fighting some random runner simply looking to evade. The Keynosians in the Midwest would know this. One-on-one, she doesn't have the speed to stop my attacks.

It only takes a moment for my blade to pass cleanly through her eye socket and down through her jaw, cleaving her skull in two.

The top of her head slides down and topples to the rocky ground below as something in my arm pops under the exertion.

Okay, it's three to one now and I have both a broken foot and an arm that refuses to cooperate fully.

They won't allow me to rest. More shots hammer towards me. Each skillfully placed shot is meant to prevent me from running in any direction. The outside two sweep their shots inward, and the center Guardsmen unleashes his barrage directly down the pike.

Again, I charge, pushing everything so hard that my body screams in pain. I have no other option. I'm willing to shatter this body in order to stop them from hurting those kids.

Something else snaps, this time in my left thigh. I drop my gun and slam into the center Guardsmen at full speed. God he's hard. It's like running into a charged mesh-wall. But, all that I need now is time and this is buying me that. Enough time for my blade arm to

343

recover enough for me to give it another push. So, as the center Guardsmen soars away, I push and snatch him out of the air, clutching his ankle with my left hand and using his body as a weapon against the leftmost Guardsmen. I hurl him at his compatriot with all the force and speed I can muster.

The sound of the collision is grotesque. Bones crunching under three hundred pounds of flesh, the sharp exhale of air from compressed lungs, the sudden irrepressible moan of the soon-to-be dead.

I stand over them, utterly exhausted, both arms disabled, a leg completely useless, and creeping darkness begins to invade my vision. In a few moments, I'll be completely blind.

I expect to die. I'm just too damn tired to do anything else.

"Please, don't kill me," I hear from behind. "I have a family. I just want to see my family one last time, before I die."

The sound of heavy metal striking the ground surprises me. I turn to face the final Guardsmen just as my vision fades away.

It's done. I'm now in total darkness. But he doesn't have to know that.

"This war is stupid, you know? Pointless," I say, slouching forward, no longer able to hide the weariness that's filled my body, my heart. I keep my face turned towards him, or where I last heard him speak.

"Pointless... no," he replies. "It's not pointless, just wasteful."

I laugh. "Wasteful... yeah. That's a much better word."

"We all lose in such a conflict. North and South, we've all lost so much."

I push out my hearing and catch the distant sound of seabirds and surf. The ocean can't be far now. But the most interesting sound is the steady and completely calm beat of this man's heart. He's neither afraid nor anxious. It just beats its steady rhythm of life. "I don't have the strength to harm you," I foolishly admit.

"What's that mean? Are you letting me go?"

I probably shouldn't push my luck. Hope has finally paid me a visit. It's good to see her face. "What I mean is, you should go see your family, spend the time you have remaining with them.

"Can you do me a favor?" I ask.

The Guardsmen stands silent for a moment. "Yes."

"I want you to tell your children tales of the Undying that grew too tired of war. Tell them —"

"Her. My daughter's name is Nirmal."

"That's a lovely name. Please tell Nirmal we are not *all* savages. Tell her... tell her we are not all filled with hate. Apologize to her for the foolishness we adults have wrought. We do not see as clearly as those unmarred by the ignorance of false biases."

I only hear the sound of his breathing. Maybe he's shocked?

"Warrior, can you honor me with your name?" he asks, his words almost hesitant.

Does it really matter if a lone Guardsmen knows my name? No, I guess not. "Jocelyn Martinez. I am a teacher."

As my sight returns, I see him beginning his journey to his family. Southwest. I assume he's taking the route Giaan will be traveling. At the pace he's moving, he'll pass them and be long gone if they actually wait an hour. They will. Giaan will make sure of that.

I really hope he finds his family.

Then it hits me. "Oh my god, I did it! I really did —"

"Aaah!" The sudden sound of hard static wakes me, followed by the distinct whispers of gunfire pinging into my ear through the receiver.

"Goddamn it!" I hear a voice call out. It's Patricia's scraggly voice. Is she talking to me?

"We have to get outta here!" she yells. I jump up and quickly look around. Nothing. There must be something wrong on her end. I wipe the sleep from my eyes and assess the situation. I passed out I think. Pushed myself to complete shutdown to stop those Guardsmen. Now that I've recovered, the pain from the damage is replaced by gnawing hunger. Feels like I've lost twenty pounds of muscle to heal.

"I know that, David! But, if they're waiting at the entrance, we're all fucked! This place is coming down around our ears! FOG or not, none of us will survive getting crushed by tons of rock, wood and metal."

I hear the faint sound of another voice. It's male. David perhaps?

"Yeah, well fuck Jacob! Fuck him and the brass that sent us here!" Another pause. "Does it look like I give a damn?"

She's obviously not talking to me, and it sounds like I'm only getting half of the conversation. Maybe something struck the transmitter and it's now permanently switched on? I hear everything she's saying, but it comes and goes at odd intervals.

I turn south. All of those Guardsmen were headed in that direction, to the facility, most likely to deal with my former teammates.

If all of those Guardsmen are waiting for them at the entrance, they'll fill them all with hot metal when they leave, and if they stay inside of that facility, they'll all be crushed to death.

"Yeah, Rawlings is still out. Without a runner, I don't see how we can —"

Strange sounds erupt in the background, like paper being crumpled. No, that's not paper, that must be the falling stone Patricia noted earlier. Suddenly, there is an eerie silence over the comm, then the sound of someone coughing. "LaPaige, what the fuck? Are we going in fuckin' circles?"

Something turns me, pulls me south, then pushes me towards the facility, towards the twenty plus Guardsmen who are waiting to slaughter my teammates.

"We don't have fifteen minutes, man! This place is coming down right now!"

I hear the crack of Suzy-Q.

"What the hell is wrong with me?" I ask myself, running still. I can't save them from twenty or so Guardsmen. I barely survived five! Going there is suicide for me.

I'm not a hero. I should run away. I should save myself.

"I'm on it!" Again, Suzy-Q cracks off rounds, as Patricia breathes hard over her comm.

I can't let Patricia die.

I see the tracks of the Guardsmen's vehicle and start following them.

I'm not a martyr. I'm just a middle-aged woman who's just now finding herself. An adult who's just realized a basic truth: I choose. And, just look at the shape I'm in. I can't help them, not like this. So yes, I should turn away, head for the ocean, make my way to safety. I mean, I did just save those children back there, very nearly died in the process. That should be enough for any person to earn their way into heaven, right? I've done my part... haven't I?

I can smell the fumes and know I'm getting closer. I'm going to reach those Guardsmen soon, and if I try to attack, even if it's just a strafing, I won't have any shelter on this rocky terrain. They'll drop me within seconds.

"LaPaige! Goddamn it! LaPaige, answer me!" Something happened to LaPaige? He was supposed to be their guide. "Someone get LaPaige and let's move. David, watch your six!"

I can smell the Guardsmen now. Their sweat, the woody scent of their skin, it all draws me closer. There, I see them, just over this rise. Quickly, I navigate up and over the terrain with huge leaps.

I can see them in the distance, waiting with Northern guns at the ready to take Northern lives.

Maybe... maybe I can do something to help? What if I keep my energy expenditure low? Then, once I reach them, I could go all out, forcing my body to the point of complete failure again. Maybe, just maybe I can survive a few passes, but I'll have to move faster than I ever have before. I'll have to pray they aren't more interested in me than they are in my teammates, at least for a few moments. All they need is a fighting chance.

This is so stupid! One FOG against twenty or more Guardsmen? It's impossible. I can't save them! I should just run. These Guardsmen don't know I'm even here, they have no idea I'm right behind them. Even if they did know, they could never catch me.

If I ran, no one would be the wiser. No one would ever know. But, what if they did? No... no one would blame me. It's not like I could actually effect any change in this situation. My death wouldn't even matter. Who would blame me if I fled?

I would. I would hate myself for not doing what is in my heart to do. I couldn't live with the person I saw in the mirror. I couldn't live with myself if I left Patricia to die. If I did commit that atrocity, who or what would I become?

I know. I would become the apathy Ophelia spoke about. I will become the Fallen. You cannot hate yourself and find love in the world.

So yes, I could run and no one would know. Maybe in time, I'd even forgive myself for betraying Patricia. But, that's not who I am, is it? That's not who I want to be. I've come this far and I won't take another step backwards. Not now, and never again will I turn from who I am. If I ran away, I'd be running into the dark night of my soul. I would be running away from myself.

"David, the exit isn't far. We just have to make it through this area. Clarence, watch out!" Suzy-Q snaps in the background.

Patricia is still fighting. She's so strong. I expect no less from her. She's being who she is. She's always traveled towards the person she wishes to become. Such bravery deserves happiness. She deserves to live.

I wonder... was it chance or divine guidance that brought me here? No... no, it was neither. I chose this. I've been choosing it all, haven't I? The good and the bad, all have been choices of mine. I chose to see myself as the reason for my parent's divorce, swallowing their animosity into the pit of my stomach. I chose to marry a man that didn't love me for me, covering myself in layer upon layer of self-doubt and personal suppression. I chose to push a good man away because I was too afraid to open my heart again.

But, in these few years of war, I've been choosing Patricia and Ophelia as my sisters, instead of wallowing in self-hate and loneliness. I chose, despite myself, David instead of self-pity and fear. Instead of choosing apathy, I chose to risk everything to save the children of my enemy, and thus found true love. I found myself.

Those choices have brought me here. Those choices have brought me to this now.

So here I am. At the facility, alone, with insurmountable odds in front of me. Piece of cake.

Hiding behind a five-foot-tall boulder, I take inventory of the sprawling building in the distance. Carved into the mountain's side, it's topped with a massive tree, more wide than tall. The tree's canopy extends out like an expansive umbrella of dark leaves, stretching so far I have to wonder if it's one tree or if hundreds make up its berth.

The tree's roots, thick and serpentine, cleave through the stone facade. It's like the roots are carved from the stone instead of cutting into it. Like pillars, the roots branch downward and into the rocky soil, straight as rods and strong as the mountain they're fracturing.

The structure's entrance, tall and triangular, hides behind these straight and heavy wooden pillars of root.

"David, I see the sunlight. No, there! Up there!"

The Keynosian forces have spread out, setting what looks like explosives at key sections of the thick brown pillars of root. They want to bury my old teammates by destroying the tree's roots.

I'm going to die here, aren't I?

"I wish I could see you again, David. I wish we had the opportunity to explore a relationship.

"Patricia, I so want to be there for you, become aunt to your children and a lifelong friend to my sister. I wanted to experience you outside of the hell-scape called war.

"It hurts to know that I won't be able to see you grow old and cranky, happy and fulfilled.

"I wish I could just see you again, Ophelia. I miss you so much.

"Mom, Dad... I hope you're proud of me."

I can hear the Keynosians approaching cautiously.

"God, I know I've never said much to you over the years. In fact, I've not sought your mercy since I was a child who followed my mother to church. But, please, don't let me die in agony.

And if I have to die, don't let my death be in vain. I know I could never tip the scales in my favor, not after all of the things I've done. But, please let this curse of a body, made for war, shaped for death, be useful for something other than its purpose."

I look up and spot a seabird, wings outstretched, drifting on the winds. "Great Mother, use me to grow something like that, okay? Let my body nourish something beautiful that will soar on the winds. I want that. I would love to feel that kind of freedom."

I hear the sound of weapons clicking to ready.

It's time. Yeah, it's time.

"There it is! The exit!" I hear Patricia yell. "We're almost there!"

And so, I run.

To save the ones I love, to save Patricia, I will become Sehkmet, goddess of war. I will become Durga, the invincible. I will become Hine-nui-te-pō, goddess of death. I will become Kali, and bring unto those that stand in my way, hell. I will save you, Patricia.

Immediately, their weapons bark at my back, voices scream for my death, yet it's all immaterial to me now. I'm here for a reason, and my first charge is the removal of those explosives. My friends and loved ones won't stand a chance if they're buried under tons of rock and rumble.

So, I push hard and feel the remaining dregs of my energy reserve dissipate like smoke. I don't have long. My body can't hold up running on fumes, eating away at the last remnants of muscle my bones are holding onto.

The four Keynosians that were coming for me were nearly knocked down in the wake of my speed burst. Good. It'll buy me some time.

I see the first beach ball-sized clump of red putty, jammed against the outer root that stands far to the left of the entrance.

Another push and my muscles feel like they're being torn asunder. I need speed to scale this wall. So, in one motion, I defy gravity and snatch the explosive from the crevice. It's hard like stone, just as heavy as well, but I can't slow down. I can't give them the chance to stop me.

Quickly, they figure out what I'm after and begin shooting to the location I'll be. I won't allow it to matter. My eyes see it all, pushed so hard the bullets appear to move at me like falling snow. I deflect or evade each shot. They cannot touch me.

Something in my hip snaps.

Ignore the pain. Get the next explosive at the top of the stone facade. It's right there, nestled high on the second root pillar above the facility's entrance.

Again, I soar along the thick woody pillar, and with a hard pull the second explosive is mine.

Something explodes in my shoulder.

I'm falling apart. Too much, too fast, and with no fuel, I can't even partially recover.

Still, I can't stop. Patricia needs me as much as I need her to survive.

The third explosive clings to the outer right of the tree's trunk. The final target.

Still more bullets, some black, most not, sing their song of doom. I leap to the explosive, dodging and deflecting as I go, spinning and twirling in midair. I land upside down with my hands tight around the explosive and my feet pressing hard into the pillar-like root above. With a final yank, I pull the bomb free.

I have them all.

As I fall, I see a spray of metal ordnance quickly flying towards me. The landing is hard, but not hard enough to cause my thigh to explode. That was a bullet. The outer portion of my leg is blown off, exposing my femur. The damage causes me to land awkwardly, falling face-first with three clumps of red held tight in my arms like beach balls.

I have no time for the wound, no time for the pain.

Then, another two shots connect. They're black bullets. One sears across my right cheek, the other rips into my right tricep, spinning me about.

I don't release the bombs, but I now understand what Jackson was talking about. These bullets, unlike the others, hurt immediately. It's like my arm and face are completely engulfed in flames.

You can't die, Jocelyn Martinez. You can't quit, not yet. Your friends need you. Your sister is counting on you. Push on, Jocelyn! Push on!

Somehow, I take off, slower than before, heading towards the far end of the mountain. When I reach the edge, I'll toss the bombs as far as I can and pray I don't get swallowed by the blast.

With all of the strength I can muster, I hurl the explosives away. They hit the mountain and break off pieces from the solid granite mountainside.

Good, one goal down, one to go. I have to move fast, so fast that they'll — "ARRGGGHHH!"

Something explodes behind me. The force of the explosion sends me tumbling head over heels towards the entrance of the facility.

My arm doesn't feel right. My arm! The explosion... it took off my left arm! All that remains is strips of cloth and skin, bone and sinew shattered and torn. It leaves nothing but black blood streaming from where my forearm should be.

Oh god... I'm scared. I don't want to die like this. Not like this.

No, you can't fall now, Jocelyn! It's too soon! Go, Jocelyn, push pasts the pain, past the fear. Push past it all and go!

I hurl myself towards them, focusing on what I have to do. I have to get them to ignore the entrance and focus on me.

My eyes start to darken.

Please God, don't let me fail them. Don't let Patricia die because of me.

I explode into the nearest Guardsmen, my blade flashing in white arcs through whomever stands before me. I dare not halt, not even for a moment. Stopping is failure. Stopping is the death. Stopping means I lose my sister. So, just move! Run as hard as possible, strike with all that's within before your flame fades away!

They scream as I move between them. I hear the calls to stop me, to kill me as I cut from person to person, from vehicle to vehicle. I never knew I was this strong, never knew I had this much strength, and with each passing second, each passing millisecond between those seconds, I feel a lightness. I feel as if I'm flying.

A sudden splash of liquid hits my side, my severed arm. It's an acid seed attack. A sudden searing pain erupts in a bright, green flame.

Flames and smoke envelope the remaining light in my eyes. The burning saps away the last vestiges of my once growing strength. I... I can't get up.

"We're out. We made it out!"

Patricia? They made it. "Patricia!" I scream with all that remains within me. "PATRICIA!"

As the flames begin to burn themselves out, I see my arm, skeletal and blackened. I look down and see blood, my blood, forming pools beneath me. I hear a rush of footsteps in my direction, and I look up just as darkness begins to envelop my sight. As the final streams of sunlight graces these broken eyes, I see my executioners.

They are so young.

Mercifully, the world goes dark when they unleash upon my already broken flesh.

I feel the pressure as bullets enter my body and explode. Somehow, it doesn't hurt. I thought it'd hurt more.

"Jocelyn!" Patricia calls, her voice sounding far away. "Jocelyn? JOCELYN?" She's close. I can hear her movements. She's so strong.

I can't move. I can't see. But I hear her breathing, smell her skin. It is my angel. I listen to her kneel on the earth nearby, and it sounds like she's landed in mud. Oh... no, that's my blood watering the ground.

"Oh no, Jos," Patricia cries. "No... please no. Not you."

"Oh my god, Jos," David says, his voice crumbling.

Don't worry, it doesn't hurt. "No... it's alright. It doesn't hurt anymore. It doesn't hurt." I hear my voice and wonder if it's me. I sound distant, like I'm overhearing myself whisper in another room. "It doesn't hurt." They need to know it's alright.

I feel tears on my face, hands slide underneath me, lift my head. I smell you, Patricia. You're so beautiful.

"It's okay... It's okay. It doesn't hurt. I'm... not... suffering," I repeat, wondering if they can even hear me.

"Motherfuckers..." David says, pain in his voice, hate darkening the tone. "We need a med team. Someone call a med team!!"

353

I hear his rustle. "No, don't leave me. Please, don't... don't leave me."

Patricia's lips press into my forehead. "Maybe, maybe we can save you, Jos," she whispers into my ear, clamping her hands on my chest, squeezing as hard as humanly possible. "You have to hold on."

I'm dying.

Just as I've finally learned to no longer be afraid of life, I'm now not afraid to die. I'm not afraid any longer.

I push my hearing and sense of smell as far as I can. I want to take it all in.

Jackson's alive, still smelling as sweet as ever.

Rawlings. I wish I'd gotten to know you more.

Petersen... I can smell his tears. I'm glad you made it.

Marshall, be good. Become the good man you were meant to be, the good man you are.

"David? David?"

"Yes?"

"I'm... sorry."

"Shhhh, no, no, it's okay. Just be still. We'll... we'll have medics here soon, okay?"

"Pat?"

"It's okay, Jos. Don't struggle. We... they can—"

"I love... I love you, my sister... my angel. I love you."

She says something, but I can't make out the words. I just know she's with me. I feel her lips on my face, her hands still clutching my chest as the sound of my heart slows to the wing-beat of the seabird above. Moments of fluttering, then silence as she floats on the winds, followed by more flutters as she rises to capture the next. She's up there, soaring towards the sea now, gliding on air. She sails silently on the soft currents of the noonday breeze. Beautiful.

That makes me happy. That gives me joy. We are free. I'm free. I'm free because I chose freedom and I chose love.

Funny. At the end I chose that which I once feared would entrap me. Love. I now have both, love and freedom. That makes me happy.

Above, the seabird calls to me.
"I want to soar."

.

.

.

And so, I soar.